Eye of Horace

Jones, Addison L., author.
    Eye of Horace : a novel / Addison L. Jones.
    Philadelphia : Blydyn Square Books, 2015.
    ©2015
        pages cm.
    ISBN
    1. Fratricide — Fiction. 2. Revenge — Fiction.
    813.6 — dc23

Published by Blydyn Square Books, Philadelphia
www.BlydynSquareBooks.com

Cover graphic design by Paul Prizer/Paul Prizer Design Group, Inc.
www.PrizerDesign.com

Book interior design by Kim Shinners/EJB Publishing Services,
    www.EJBPublishing.com

EYE OF HORACE

ADDISON L. JONES

Blydyn  Square Books

1

HORACE

| PRESENT DAY |

The stench slapped him in the face as he stepped inside the nursing home. Mothballs, urine, and death—the smell of old age.

Horace took a glance around and let out a relieved sigh when he saw that the lobby was empty. Usually in these places, there seemed to be at least a couple of quivering, drooling vegetables leaning out of wheelchairs, obviously forgotten by their families and apparently invisible even to the staff. *Strange how you can still smell the old farts even when they're not in the room,* he thought as he approached the battered metal desk where guests were supposed to sign in before visiting whichever decrepit specimen they called their own.

The desk was empty, like the lobby. He sighed, irritated that he was going to have to wait around in this stinking room until someone decided to wander in and greet him. *They should really have a bell so visitors don't have to stand here breathing in this miasma for any longer than necessary,* he thought. He tapped his foot on the ancient linoleum, which had probably once been a shade of green but had faded to a nondescript color that now just looked old. He whistled, trying simultaneously to make as loud a noise as possible to attract some attention and to sound nonchalant, like he wasn't getting more and more pissed off the longer he had to wait. The registration nurse must have had some pretty good hearing. She appeared almost instantly from a back room, breezing toward the desk with a gruesome fake smile plastered on her face.

"Mr. Cairo! Glad you could get here so quickly," she said, squeezing her bulging stomachs (she seemed to have several) between the desk and the wall and thrusting her hand toward him.

He made an effort to raise the corners of his lips into what seemed like an approximation of a smile and pumped her hand once. He noticed right away that she was struggling not to stare at the patch over his left eye, and his hand flew up to adjust it, even though it was already lying perfectly straight. Touching the patch was a nervous tic he had developed over the years, and it always seemed to get worse when the person he was with was having trouble ignoring the patch. For some reason, younger women never seemed to be as repulsed by the patch as older women were. In fact, he had discovered (to his immense satisfaction) that there was an entire subculture of women who actually seemed a little turned on by it. Thankfully, the nurse was not part of that group.

"Is there paperwork or something I have to fill out?" he asked.

The nurse's phony broad smile morphed into a smaller, more genuine, sadder smile. She tilted her head sympathetically as she took his arm and led him to a rickety wooden chair beside the metal desk. He hardly noticed as she pushed him into the chair and slid her bulky form into the rolling chair behind the desk. She ruffled through a stack of paper, as if searching for a particular sheet, then gave up and shoved the whole pile toward him.

"Just a signature there at the bottom," she said as she tugged open the desk drawer and ransacked it, apparently looking for a pen.

He produced a fountain pen from his own pocket. "I got it." He leaned over and scribbled his name on the line the nurse had indicated. He pushed the papers back at her and began to rise.

"If that's all . . ."

The nurse leapt up. "No, no! Mr. Cairo! I have several boxes of your mother's belongings for you."

He frowned. "I'm sure it'll be fine if you just toss that stuff. Or give it to her friends in here, if she had any."

"Your mother was a wonderful woman," the nurse said. Although the sentiment struck Horace as false, her tone sounded sincere. "Everyone loved her. We *all* loved her. I'm so very sorry for your loss."

"Yes, well." He capped his pen and slid it back into his pocket.

"Really, Mr. Cairo, you'll want these things. There are all sorts of amazing things. Scrapbooks, photo albums, notebooks, letters. A real treasure trove, believe me."

He sighed, trying to sound tired instead of exasperated. "All right, all right. Give it to me."

"Juan, the orderly, will help you load everything into your car, if you'll bring it around front."

"Jesus, how much stuff is there?"

The nurse gave him a stiff smile. *She's probably religious*, he thought, *and doesn't like it when someone takes the lord's name in vain or some crap like that.*

"There are four or five large plastic cartons, I think. So if you'll just drive around front . . ."

"I'm already double-parked out front. Right in front of the ambulance."

He could tell that she was trying (unsuccessfully) to avoid scowling at him. "Fine, then. Juan will be out shortly. Take care, Mr. Cairo." She shook his hand but broke her grasp much more quickly than she had done earlier. He couldn't help but smile. Sometimes it was just too easy to offend people, and when it happened this fast, it hardly seemed worth the effort.

He stood leaning against the driver's side door of his Lexus SUV and watched as a burly Filipino orderly wheeled out a handcart loaded with multicolored, scratched Rubbermaid containers and stacked them in the back of the car. The nurse had underestimated; there were six cartons, and they all looked heavy. Horace shook his head, disgusted. Once he got home, there would be no orderly to help him unload all this crap. He'd either have to do it himself or wait until the landscapers came tomorrow and offer to pay them to lug it all inside. Maybe he should just drive down to the docks and dump the crap into the water, right out of the back of the car. It was a tempting possibility.

He pressed a hundred-dollar bill into the orderly's hand without a word, climbed into the driver's seat, and skidded away, sending a shower of pebbles raining down over the hood of the parked ambulance.

The turnpike was jammed with late-afternoon traffic and it took him over an hour to get home. By the time he pulled into his driveway, he was itching for a drink. As he climbed out of the car and looked around at his silent neighborhood, the sky was getting dark and he could smell burning leaves on the wind. When he was younger, he had loved early autumn nights like this. It made him think of school—the first couple of months of the school year, when homework still seemed kind of like fun and you knew Christmas was just around the corner. Back then, it had been legal to burn leaves, so that cozy odor had curled around every tree, every house. Burning leaves had been outlawed years ago, decades probably, but someone was ignoring that, and Horace was glad.

He went inside and flipped on the lights in the foyer. The house smelled faintly of lemon and eucalyptus, which meant that the maid had been here today, polishing tables that Horace never touched and vacuuming rooms he hadn't entered since he bought the damn place. He understood that the house, a sprawling and somewhat tacky (in his opinion) Tudor, was too big for him to live in alone as a bachelor. But he was rich, and he assumed that people expected him to have a huge house. Besides, it never failed to impress the women he brought home, especially since he tended to have an affinity for a trashier type of girl—the kind who was unfamiliar with the trappings of wealth that, to him, had long ago grown a bit tiresome. But just a bit. Money never becomes completely tiresome, despite what the rich like to tell normal people.

He tossed his keys onto a small marble-topped table beside the door and made his way through the dim hallway to the kitchen. Not bothering to switch on the overhead lamps, he fixed himself a drink by the light under the stove hood, which the maid must have left on by mistake. He leaned against the massive center island, with its eight burners that he had never yet used, and took a long sip of gin. He hated the way gin tasted—a little like pine needles marinated in motor oil—but it seemed somehow classier than whiskey, so he was trying to force himself to cultivate a preference for it.

He pulled out one of the heavy oak chairs at the table in the corner and slumped down, leaning forward on his elbows and staring out into the darkening gray of the backyard. As he took another sip of gin, he started to think about the boxes in his car. What the hell could be in them? In all the years he had lived with his mother, he had never noticed anything in her room except for the old-fashioned silver-framed portrait of his father that always sat on her bedside table, and maybe a couple of paperback books. That's all. He had never seen—or at least he didn't recall seeing—any photo albums or journals. The more he sat and wondered what was in the boxes, the more he felt compelled to go outside and drag the damn things inside himself. He turned his glass upside down over his mouth, shaking out the last drops of the foul, evergreen-tinged liquor, then slammed the empty glass down on the table. He sighed and shook his head. Now he was going to have to bring in the fucking cartons. Damn curiosity.

It didn't take him as long as he expected to get the cartons into the foyer, lining them up like stout dominos around the circular walls of the room. He picked a light blue carton to start. Rather than exerting himself any further, he pushed it into the living room with his shins, holding a fresh glass of gin high in the air over his head. As soon as he knocked the carton over the lip of the doorway between the marble-floored foyer and the carpeted living room, he sat down on the floor with a self-satisfied *humpf* and yanked the lid off.

The nurse had been right. The carton was filled with neat stacks of photo albums and binders that looked like scrapbooks or maybe diaries. He lifted out one of the albums at random and flipped through it. The pages were covered with crisp-edged, yellowed documents and black-and-white photographs with scalloped edges, the kind they used to take back in the '40s and '50s. He recognized some of the faces as long-dead relatives: his mother's parents and older people—his great-grandparents, maybe—with his mother and his aunt Nora sitting in front of everyone else, bright-faced children with blond bologna curls in their hair. He closed the album and put it on the floor beside the carton, then reached in to pull out the next one.

"Ooooh," he said aloud as he opened a small pink notebook. "Mom's diary. What year is this? 1954? She'd have been—what? Five or six? Oh, yeah, this one'll be juicy." He shook his head and tossed the book aside. The next one was dated just about a decade before he was born. *Now we're in business*, he thought. He took a slug of gin and started to cough. He slapped his chest to clear his throat. Then he set down his glass and started to read.

2

IRIS

| JUNE 24, 1970 |

Oscar asked me to marry him last night. We had barely had a chance to pull off those wretched rented caps and gowns that smelled like B.O. and dry-cleaning solution before he dragged me away from the football stadium and plopped me down on a bench in the quad. It was the same wooden bench—the one with half a slat missing on the seat—where we did it on our first night away at college, four years ago. It seems like forever.

So I said yes. Of course I did. I love Oscar. More than just love him. He's part of me. I can't remember a time when we weren't together. But now that I've had some time to be by myself—I feel like I'm never alone anymore—I'm starting to wonder if it's a mistake to marry him. I mean, I'm twenty-one years old, and these should be the best years of my life, a time to get wild and have fun and experiment and find myself. And I've never slept with anybody but Oscar. Christ, I've barely even *kissed* anybody but Oscar—unless you count the time Oscar's brother, Seth, kissed me while we were all drunk on beers we stole from our parents and playing truth or dare back in junior high. That's pathetic. We're supposed to be in the middle of a sexual revolution. And me? I'm living more conservatively than my parents did back in the olden days.

This morning, when I got up and came downstairs, my mom was in the kitchen frying bacon. I sidled up behind her and, real casual-like, laid my left hand over her shoulder so my engagement ring would be there, sparkling right in her face. She gasped and spun around so fast to hug me, she almost knocked the frying pan to the ground.

I knew she'd be happy. She would have loved it if Oscar and I had gotten married right after high school, instead of waiting to get through college. And Oscar's mom—he said she helped him pick out the ring, so you know she's on board. Mom pulled me over to the kitchen table and made me sit down so she could twist my hand back and forth and admire the diamond twinkling in the sunlight.

"Did you set a date?" Mom asked.

I yanked back my hand and thrust it down in my lap so Mom would stop gawking at the ring.

"Ma, we just got engaged last night," I said, picking absently at a cold piece of toast.

"Yeah, technically, maybe, but you've known this was coming for, what? Eight years?"

I frowned. "That's the thing. I'm not sure we should be getting married."

"What are you talking about? What, do you want a June wedding? I don't know if you want to wait a whole year . . ."

"I'm not talking about the date. I'm saying I'm not sure we should be getting married at all."

Mom chuckled. "Don't be silly. Who else are you going to marry?"

I rolled my eyes. "Nobody, Ma. I mean, maybe we should branch out, see other people for once in our lives. How do I know he's the right one for me if I've never even been to the movies with anybody else?"

"You're being stupid. You and Oscar are meant to be together. Come on. I can't even remember a time when you two weren't in love. Nobody can. From the very first day Marianne and I plopped the two of you down together in the sandbox at the park, you've been a couple."

"Yeah, yeah," I said. "I've heard this story a million times. And I *do* love Oscar. And I *do* think we'll end up together, but I don't see what would be the harm in waiting a while, just to be sure."

Mom tapped my cheek with her palm, and I could tell she was wishing she could put a little force behind it and slap me back into reality as she saw it.

"Silly girl," she said, pushing herself up from the table and heading back to the stove, where bacon grease was spitting wildly, since she'd left it unattended.

I sighed and went back up to my room. I sat down at the little white desk I used to study at when I was in high school. Four years had passed since I had used it, and it seemed smaller now—almost too small for me to fit my knees under it. I flipped open a little photo album and turned the pages slowly, staring at the images of a slightly younger me, in high school, always hanging on Oscar's arm. There's me in my cheerleading outfit, and Oscar in a muddy football uniform. There we are at the prom, me in my lacy white dress and him wearing his dad's old black tux with a white bow-tie. I shook my head. They might as well have married us that night. It's not like anything has changed in the past four years.

I slammed the album shut and held my hand up so I could stare at the ring some more. Maybe I'm wrong. Maybe I *am* being stupid. It's not like there haven't been bumps in the road. Oscar and I broke up a bunch of times in high school—for maybe a day, which, I realize, hardly counts as a breakup. I don't think he ever actually went out with anyone else, but we both did our share of flirting. It drove Oscar crazy when I went out for coffee with Mr. Folger, the English teacher that all my girlfriends—and me, too—had a crush on. And I admit I was furious when Oscar flirted with Beth Swanson, that slut. But does that count as sowing wild oats, or whatever it is they say? I don't know.

The ring is pretty. It's definitely a good thing Oscar brought his mom to help pick it out. I love Oscar to death, but he's got no taste at all. Last weekend, he was wearing a pair of red plaid Bermuda shorts with a rainbow tie-dye T-shirt. Blech. I'd better go with him to pick out his tux, or he'll show up at our wedding in one of those powder-blue ruffly numbers.

Huh. *Our wedding*. I guess there's my answer. I'm going to marry Oscar.

3

HORACE

Horace grinned. It had never even occurred to him that his mother might have hesitated to marry his father. Even though his father had died before Horace was born, his mother had never so much as gone on a date, at least not as far as Horace knew. She had lived like a married woman, but instead of a husband, she had a ghost in her bed. Finding out that his mother had had a tiny bit of doubt about the course her life was taking made her, somehow, a little more believable as a human being in Horace's mind. She was still a phony, still pathetic, but slightly more believable.

The ice cubes clinked against his teeth as he sucked the last of the gin from his drink. He set the glass down on the ground beside him. The liquor was slowly building up, making his brain float in his head like a buoy on a bay, and he wanted another drink, but he had to piss, too, and his legs, stiff from sitting on the floor while reading his mother's diary, were just sore enough to make him not want to get up at all. He reached into the plastic bin and pulled out a packet of photographs that were still in the paper envelope from the developing center. He shook the prints out onto the floor and smiled as he picked one up, pressing his thumb against it and then holding the shiny print up to the light to see his fingerprint captured perfectly as a smudge. *Prints—so quaint,* he thought. *Haven't seen these in years. It's all digital now, and you're lucky to even get a paper printout of your pictures. Seems like they're usually trapped forever in the bowels of the camera itself. Maybe, if they're lucky, they make it onto some computer hard drive, but never into an album. For all the "convenience" of digital imagery, taking the leap from clicking the button and taking thousands of pictures to actually download-ing them and doing something with them seemed to be much too much work for most people.* Including Horace, who didn't even own a camera at all. What was the point?

He crossed his legs, trying to ignore the pressure in his bladder, and stared at the picture in his hand. It was one of a thick stack of photographs from his parents' wedding. These weren't professional photos. Grainy and poorly composed, they were probably taken by some family member with a crappy instant camera. It was strange that he had stumbled upon wedding photographs when he had just finished reading about his mother's decision to marry his father. Or was it? His mother had been organized—more than organized; compulsive, even—so it was quite possible that she had actually taken the time to place the wedding photographs just beneath the diaries covering the years leading up to the wedding. Yup, she had been pathetic.

The phone rang on the table behind him and he felt himself jump. He always wondered what he looked like when he got startled like that. It felt like he was a cartoon character, jumping ten feet into the air and hanging there, motionless, for a few seconds, pausing to look at the camera before falling in a crash of line-drawn squiggles and stars to the ground. The phone rang again, bringing him back to reality, and as he picked it up, he tried to shake himself into sobriety before punching the talk button and saying hello.

"Yeah?" He hated the gravelly sound of his voice, which reminded him that all the years of hard drinking and smoking and whatever else he had done were starting to catch up with him.

"Horace? It's Aunt Nora. How are you?"

He cleared his throat and shifted the phone to rest on his shoulder. "I'm fine, Nora. What's up?"

"Did you go over to the nursing home?"

"Yeah. Yeah, I did. Did you know Mom had a ton of huge boxes full of crap?"

"What kind of crap?"

"Pictures, diaries, every ticket stub from every movie she ever went to."

"That's not crap, sweetheart. That's your mother's legacy."

Horace laughed. "Well, if that's true, it's very sad."

Nora made the familiar "*tsk tsk*" sound that his mother had always made when she was disappointed in him. It made him cringe, even now that his mother was dead.

"What?" he asked. "Am I a bad son because I don't feel like poring through this load of crap? I'm sure it's great stuff, really, but it would take forever to go through it all. And I have things to do, you know."

He could actually hear Nora smile through the phone line. "Of course you do, sweetie," she said.

"What's that supposed to mean?"

"Nothing, dear. Nothing at all. It's just—well, it's not as if you have a job you have to go to, is it? If anyone has the free time to go through your mother's very important papers, it's you."

"Very important papers, my ass."

"Don't you understand? There could be a clue in there. Something to explain it all."

"Explain what? That mom was senile and a hundred years old and in horrible health?"

"Horace." Nora's voice was soft, tired.

"I know. I'm sorry," he said. "You're right. I'm being a bastard."

"It's a terrible thing to lose your mother, no matter how old you are. And you're not as old as you seem to think you are."

He bit his lip to keep a sarcastic chuckle from popping out of his mouth. "Yeah, you're right."

"So, do you need any help with it all?"

Horace tried to fight off a vision of his aunt Nora, with her baggy-skinned spaghetti arms, trying to lift even the lid off one of these plastic tubs. "No. I can handle it. Is there anything you want me to look for, or save for you?"

She was silent for a long moment, long enough to make Horace blow into the receiver, as if the sound of his hollow, gin-laced breath could tell him whether the call had been disconnected.

"Just the wedding pictures. Your parents' wedding. There'll be a big print of the four of us: your mom and dad, me, and your uncle Seth."

This time, the bitter laugh escaped before he had a chance to censor himself. "What in the name of God would you want *that* for?"

"Someday," she whispered, her voice thin and reedy across the gentle static of the phone line. "Someday, you'll understand. You need reminders. Of better times, better people. A better life."

"Whatever you say, Aunt Nora. Good night."

"Good night."

He pushed the off button on the phone with his thumb and let the receiver fall to the ground. Then he bent over the Rubbermaid bin and dug through the stacks of papers and envelopes and photographs until he found the picture his aunt had mentioned. It was the classic wedding party shot: the bride and groom flanked by their maid of honor and best man. In the case of his parents' wedding, the wedding party was made up of their siblings, who, just a couple of years later, would be married themselves. Somewhere, Horace imagined, in Aunt Nora's house, there was a photograph that was the mirror image of this one—with Nora and Seth as the bride and groom and his own parents as the witnesses. He held up the photograph and stared at it, looking for some sign, some ghostly blur that would indicate just how wrong everything would go after his parents got married. But there was nothing. Only four people with broad smiles, fancy clothes, and a hint of red eye begging for a touch of Photoshop. There was no way anyone could have known.

4

IRIS

Oscar's curled up in bed, snoring. You'd think I would have known he was a snorer before tonight, our wedding night. It's not like we never slept together. I'm starting to wonder if everything you love about a person literally disappears the moment you marry him, to be replaced by annoying traits that will eventually lead you to either divorce him or kill him.

It's not really a lot of fun scrawling in my diary while perched on the edge of the cold bathtub in the honeymoon suite, but I can't sleep, so I might as well pass the time productively.

The wedding went well. I guess it did. It was weird, though. Not at all what I expected, or what I dreamed about. I mean, everything went fine. But it was just *fine*. Not spectacular. Not so beautiful it made me cry. Not even something I'd really remember all that well, if it weren't for the fact that people were taking pictures. It's my fault, though. I settled, like I always end up doing.

I wanted a huge, puffy white dress made of tulle and satin, like Cinderella's ball gown, but of course my mom talked me into wearing her dress, which was pretty, but not what I ever imagined I'd wear. It's just not *me*. I am not a long-sleeved lace dress. I'm a cloud of tulle with a satin bodice and spaghetti straps. So I went into the wedding with a chip on my shoulder, I guess. If I couldn't look the way I wanted to look, then it didn't matter what the rest of it was like. And I let the florist talk me out of daisies, even though they're my favorite flower, and take lilies instead, even though I think they look too funereal, too sad and too dignified or something. What's wrong with daisies? They're such happy, cheerful flowers. But they're cheap—and God forbid we didn't spend more than the gross national product of Taiwan on our floral arrangements. But it's my fault. I'm a wimp, and I didn't stand up for myself, as usual.

But that's not the worst of it. The reception made me want to cry. And not in the good way, the way a bride is supposed to tear up at her wedding. I wanted to cry from loneliness.

Maybe we should have gone to the cocktail hour at the reception instead of hiding in that gloomy little bridal room down the dark hallway so no one would see us until we were announced by the band leader and swirled around in our first dance on that huge marble dance floor. I always thought it was tacky for the bride and groom to be seen scarfing down jumbo shrimp during the cocktail hour alongside their guests and then to be "announced" as if they had just arrived, as if no one had noticed them eating like wolves for the past sixty minutes. But hiding in the little room means your guests get trashed before you even show up. By the time you actually get there, everybody's already well into party mode, and you're just too far behind to ever catch up. And being around drunk people when you're sober is just so depressing.

So we did the little waltz that my mom made us go to Arthur Murray to learn, everybody applauded politely, and then we were set loose to mingle with the crowd, and for some reason, they all barely seemed to notice. I can't speak for Oscar, because he was working his parents' side of the room, schmoozing with the guests and making everyone feel like they were special enough to spend a few moments all alone with the groom. I was supposed to do the same with my parents' guests, but it didn't work out the way I pictured. I expected everybody to ooh and ahh at me and hug me and give me envelopes full of money. Most of all, I expected a few of the men—my grandfather and uncles, at the very least—to ask me to dance. But no. Nobody asked me to dance. Hardly anybody even said hello to me. It almost seemed like I was invisible.

When the band struck up with "The Way You Look Tonight," I looked around frantically for Oscar, hoping to show off the foxtrot we'd learned as a complement to our wedding waltz, but he was nowhere to be found. I figured somebody else would grab me up to dance, but instead, they all pushed past me—literally *shoved* me out of the way; I swear I am not exaggerating—to get to the dance floor with their dates on their arms, leaving me alone among tables strewn with soiled napkins and half-empty champagne glasses. I couldn't believe it. Not a single person asked me to dance at all. Not a single person noticed me, despite the bright white dress and the massive net veil hanging off my head.

So I went over to the table where my mother was sitting with our family and I slid into one of the empty seats. Mom was chatting with one of her cousins across the table and didn't seem to realize that I had sat down, so I leaned over and kissed her on the cheek and said, "Thanks for this, Mom. It's a great party."

She made a face at me that was more a scowl than a smile and immediately turned back to her cousin. And that was that. My eyes were prickling with tears and I had to get up and run out of the room to hide in a bathroom stall for a while. It's never good to let people see the bride sobbing. That's how rumors get started. It's bad enough people ignored me; I don't need them thinking I'm knocked up or something. So I just sat there on the edge of the toilet, dabbing at my eyes with toilet paper, just like I'm sitting here now on the edge of the bathtub and snarfling into a tissue. How could this have gone so wrong? I thought people paid attention to the bride just by virtue of her status on that one special day. But apparently not. Apparently, all those brides I've seen before today had some mysterious trait that I lack, something that makes people want to be around them, something that makes them more interesting or more beautiful or just somehow *better* than me. I've never been more depressed in my life. It's a great way to start out a marriage.

And if your wedding night is supposed to be the best sex of your life, I'm really screwed, no pun intended. Yeah, we did it—sort of. We were so tired from being on our feet the whole night. The ball of my foot had turned green from that sixpence or whatever that coin was that my mom gave me for that traditional "sixpence in her shoe" or whatever that's supposed to be. After we got me out of the dress, with the million and a half buttons down the back (real buttons, not just fake ones with a zipper hidden underneath like the modern dresses have), we had just enough energy to do a few pumps missionary-style and then collapse without even attempting to reach orgasm.

"Good enough," Oscar said. Then he pecked a kiss on my cheek and rolled over to go to sleep. Romantic, no?

I can't believe I just wrote all that. I hope Oscar burns these diaries if I die before him. Maybe I should burn them myself once I hit eighty or so, just to be safe. I don't know if I want my grandchildren reading about their nana getting it on with their grampa.

5

HORACE

| PRESENT DAY |

When he read about his mother and father "pumping," Horace couldn't decide whether he wanted to laugh or puke. He chose to get up and pour himself another very large drink.

He slumped down into an armchair and flipped on the flat-screen TV that was mounted on the wall. Not bothering to notice what was on, he tossed the remote on the ground and leaned back with his drink in his fist and his mother's diary on his lap.

She hadn't made it to eighty, though he doubted whether she would have actually burned anything even if she had. If these plastic bins were any indication, his mother had been someone who believed in holding on to things for posterity. He wondered for a brief moment whether she would have wanted him to burn these things rather than reading the private account of his parents' intimate lives, but he decided that she would have preferred to have him get to know her rather than having him protect her memory. He just wasn't sure if he *wanted* to know her. He had avoided getting close to her all his life. Was now—weeks after her death—the time to start? Maybe, but not tonight. He sucked down the last of the gin, set the glass on the end table, and, tucking the diary under his arm, went upstairs to bed.

A light slap on the back of his head woke him in the morning as he dozed with his face mushed down into his pillow. He waved his hand as if he were swatting a fly before he realized that whatever had hit him was obviously much larger than a fly—and it was standing above his bed. A jolt of panic surged through him and he tried to leap up, but his ankles were tangled in the bed sheet and, instead of rising, he slid off the bed and smashed face first on the cold hardwood floor.

A burst of laughter exploded from behind him and he looked up to see his cousin, Andrew, Nora's son.

"A smooth wake-up, if I ever saw one, cuz," Andrew said, squatting down to pat Horace on the head.

"What the fuck are you doing here?"

Andrew flicked his middle finger on the bridge of Horace's nose, then stood up with a broad smile. "Mom said you needed help sorting through some family photos, so she said I should come by and give you a hand."

Horace sniffed. "Of course she did," he said, peeling the sheets off his legs and dragging himself up to sit on the edge of the bed. There was a dry, hard frog in the back of his throat. A wave of nausea washed over him. How many drinks had he had last night? He couldn't remember. All he could remember was reading about his parents "pumping."

"So, where are these photo albums? Am I in any of them?" Andrew asked.

Horace stood up, trying to ignore the flashing stars of dizziness that were bursting around the corners of his peripheral vision, and pushed past Andrew. He opened the drawer of the end table beside his bed, flipping through the random papers, pens, and condoms inside.

"Looking for something?" Andrew asked, waving a roll of Tums in front of Horace's face.

Horace grabbed the half-empty roll and popped two of the chalky disks into his mouth. "I can handle the photos myself, so you can leave. They're not as interesting as Aunt Nora seems to think they are."

"Liar," Andrew said. "You wouldn't be this hung over if they weren't at least a little bit tantalizing. I know you like to take a nip now and then, but you only get drunk alone when something's bothering you. So what did you find? Naked pictures of your mom? Of *my* mom? Good God, that's a bad image. Eww. Gotta get rid of that picture in my head. Naked supermodel. Naked supermodel. Oh, yeah, that'll do."

Horace choked down the last shards of antacid and scraped the residue off his tongue with his front teeth. "Nothing as exciting as naked pictures. Just wedding pictures and crap like that. And like I said, I can handle it."

"Fine, asshole. You don't have to be such a prick about it."

"You broke into my house and *I'm* the one being a prick?"

Andrew produced a key from his pocket. "I have a key, dickhead. You gave it to me yourself."

Horace rubbed his good eye with the heel of his hand, straightened the patch over the other, and grunted. "Whatever. Would you get out now? I have things to do."

Andrew slid the key back into his pocket and leaned his shoulder against the door jamb, smiling. "What's on the playboy's agenda today? Hmm? Brunch with a diplomat? Or just a few tumblers of gin and a call to a discreet prostitute?"

"Get the fuck out."

Andrew waved his hands in surrender. "If my mom calls, be sure to tell her that I offered to help. See ya, fuck face."

Horace leaned over with his elbows on his knees, fighting an eddy of dizziness, and waited until he heard the front door slam as Andrew left. Then he got up, washed his face, taking care not to get the eye patch wet, and pawed through the hamper, looking for something relatively odor-free to put on. He had lied to Andrew; he didn't really have anything to do today besides maybe going through the photos and diaries some more, so it wasn't worth wasting clean clothes.

He went downstairs, picked up the empty gin glass from last night, and took it with him into the kitchen. He moved to put it in the sink, but lifted it to his nose and sniffed. Deciding it was still clean enough to drink from, he set it on the counter and filled it halfway with orange juice. With the glass in hand, he went over to the breakfast nook where the bottle of gin—now almost empty—still sat. He looked around, as if he expected someone to walk in and catch him thinking about taking a drink first thing in the morning, then unscrewed the cap on the gin and poured what was left into the glass of orange juice. He took a long sip, winced, and set the glass down. It wasn't an ideal combination, but gin and juice was the best he could do this morning. The maid wasn't due to come today, so he was on his own, which meant he'd have to figure out what to make himself to eat and drink the whole day. Maybe a little more gin, if he had any in the liquor cabinet, and later a trip down to the liquor store where the manager knew him by name. He wondered vaguely if that was pathetic as he pushed around the bottles in the liquor cabinet, searching for a fresh bottle of gin but settling for vodka, which, he told himself, went better with orange juice anyway.

The phone rang and he looked around wildly for it. Only the base was on the table where it belonged. He must have brought the handset out into the living room with him last night. The juice in his glass sloshed a little onto his hand as he raced into the living room and grabbed the phone off the floor. Before he pressed the talk button, he paused for a second to lick the liquid off his palm.

"Hello?"

"Horace? Is that you? You sound hoarse."

Is that you? Who the hell else would it be? He sighed. "Hi, Aunt Nora. How are you? Didn't we talk last night?"

"Yes, yes, we did talk. I'm just calling to let you know your cousin might be stopping by sometime this weekend to help you out with the photos and everything."

"Yeah, well, Andrew was already here," Horace said, trying hard not to sound as irritated as he was. "I told him I could take care of it on my own. It's not that much stuff, Nora. Really."

She was silent for a long moment. "What's the matter?" he asked.

Her voice was small. "Why do you resist it so much when people try to help you? Especially family. You've never really wanted to be around us, have you?"

He closed his eyes and sank into the armchair. "You have to admit I have good reason not to want to be around certain members of our family, Nora."

She sucked in her breath, as if she had been punched in the gut. "That was low, Horace. Even for you."

He shook his head. "You're right. I'm sorry. Actually, maybe you can help me. I've been going through this stuff and I might have some questions about things."

"Like what?" Her voice was immediately bright and sunny, back to normal. Jesus, it must be nice to be able to get into a good mood so easily.

"Just things about my mom and dad, their relationship, that sort of thing. Maybe we could have lunch or something and talk."

"Oh, sweetheart, I'd love it. What time?"

"Ooooh . . . you want to do it today? I . . . uh, well, I guess I can do that. Sure, why not? Why don't I pick you up around one and we can have lunch at Roberto's?"

"I can't wait, sweetie. See you then."

He clicked off the phone, tossed it to the ground, and chugged the rest of the liquid in his glass. He'd need to work up a little buzz before he saw Nora. Being a little high was the only way to face her persistent cheerfulness without wanting to kill her. She was a pain in the ass, but maybe she would be able to shed some light on his parents and their marriage. Maybe she could help make his mother seem like a real human being.

6

IRIS

Dear Iris,

> *Merry Christmas, Sis! I guess you're my sister now that you're married to my brother. But that doesn't change a thing about the way I feel about you. Like I told you all those years ago, back when we were all still in high school, I love you more than anything, more than myself, more than my brother or the rest of my family. I know that sounds corny, but I'm not a writer like you. I can't turn simple words into everlasting declarations of love. All I can do is tell you that I love you, in spite of the fact that you made such a stupid mistake and married my loser brother. And I know that someday you'll see your mistake and realize that you love me just as much as I love you. Someday, we'll be together. Someday, we'll start our lives and we'll be together forever and you'll be mine until you die.*

> *With all the love in my heart and my loins,*
> *Seth*

DECEMBER 26, 1970

Can you believe the card Seth gave me for Christmas? Holy crap, he's really lost it this time, I think. I didn't show it to Oscar. He and Seth are competitive and hostile enough to each other. He doesn't need to know that Seth has pretty much crossed the line from brother-in-law to stalker. It's creepy, but despite all the clichés and bold declarations, I know he's harmless. The part about me being his until I die is a little off-putting, though, I've got to say. Don't you usually declare your love until *you* die? I don't think reminding your beloved of her mortality is the best way to win her over. But, hey, that's just me.

So it was our first Christmas as a married couple. We spent Christmas Eve at Oscar's mom's house, and my parents came by, too, so we got our family obligations out of the way and were able to spend Christmas Day alone in the new house. Oscar woke me up early and slipped a string of pearls with a tear-shaped diamond dropping down in the center around my throat. I didn't ask how he could afford it. His job at the newspaper doesn't exactly pay a lot, and, although I respect his desire to be a journalist, I know it's not generally the kind of career that makes you rich. So the gift itself surprised me. But not as much as what he did next.

I was still dressed in my red plaid flannel nightgown, which must have looked ridiculous topped off by a diamond and pearl choker, when he pulled me out of bed and dragged me by the hand down the hallway and into the living room. The sun hadn't risen all the way yet, so the corners of the room were still shadowy with the soft pink of the dawn. The Christmas tree was ablaze with winking colored lights. My head was foggy with sleep and I couldn't remember whether we had turned off the tree lights before going to be the night before (I tend to be a little paranoid about the possibility of fire) or whether Oscar had gotten up and plugged the lights back in this morning so I'd have a festive tree to wake up to. I was so busy with this silly internal debate that I hardly noticed when Oscar helped me get settled sitting Indian-style in front of the tree and laid a green-foil-covered package in my lap.

My fingers flew to the necklace around my neck, rubbing the large diamond between my thumb and forefinger. "Oscar, I think you've already given me more than enough. I'm going to be embarrassed when you see the sad little gift I got for you."

"Open it," he said, sitting back on his heels and watching me.

I hate that guilty feeling you get when you're opening a gift that you know is too good for you, or when someone has given you a gift you didn't expect and you know you have to open it and be grateful even though you're dying of humiliation because you forgot to get a gift for them. It's probably stupid to feel that way with your own husband, but that's me. I'm a worrier. So I opened it.

Inside the box, under a layer of bright red tissue paper, there was a manuscript. No, I'm being too vague. It was a set of page proofs—a book that had already been printed out all fancy and ready to go to press. At first, I thought Oscar had somehow gotten hold of an advance copy of a new book by one of my favorite writers, but then I saw the title—*Angst*—and choked on my own saliva. It was the novel I'd been working on since high school and had finally finished this past summer, just before our wedding. Oscar had had a graphic designer spruce up my plain old typewritten pages and make them look like a real book, except without a cover.

"Oscar, this is amazing. I can't thank you enough. It's so cool to see my book like this. I can pretend like it's being published. So much fun!"

Oscar smiled and took my hands in his. "Babe, I don't think you understand. This *is* being published. By us. We're starting our own publishing house—just like you always wanted to do."

"I don't . . . how? I mean, where did you get the money?"

"My parents are lending it to us. It's not so much, really. Besides, you're a brilliant writer and you're going to make us millions."

"Yeah, right," I said, flipping through the pages and marveling at the fact that I had written all of those words going by in a blur. I let go of the pages and set the manuscript down and laid my palm on top of it. I looked at Oscar and my eyes filled with tears. "Thank you. Really. I don't know how to say how much this means to me."

He crawled over and kissed me, and as he was pulling my nightgown over my head and pressing me down on the cold hardwood, I couldn't stop thinking about how ridiculous the whole notion was of starting our own publishing company with one book—mine. It was a fantasy I'd cherished since I was in high school, but it wasn't something I ever thought we could actually do. We're barely out of college, we have no money whatsoever, and, I have to admit, I'm just not a very talented writer. If we really want to start a company and have any hope of being successful, we would need to find other writers, *real* writers, to do the books. Not me. I'm just a girl who was a pretty good English student in school. Knowing how to dazzle a teacher with an essay on Shakespeare or *The Catcher in the Rye* doesn't quite translate to being able to wow the world with real literature.

Oscar loves me, and that gives him a warped sense of my abilities. But I don't have the heart to tell him so. Maybe I'm being cruel or just plain stupid, but I'd rather let him waste the money he borrowed from his folks on my dumb book and let him see the truth for himself, and after that, he'll realize it was a silly pipedream and he'll go back to his job and I'll try to find one of my own, and we'll just be normal people. I wish it could be the way he thinks it'll be, but, as always, I'm the realist in the relationship. Always have been. But he'll see, eventually. And I won't even say I told you so when he does.

7

HORACE

"So what did you want to know about your mom?"

Horace pursed his lips. The waiter had passed by the table three times already without stopping, and Horace was desperate for a drink. He'd only been with Aunt Nora for about six minutes, but it was enough to leave his throat burning for gin. He threw his arm up into the air, snapping his fingers, hoping the rude gesture would at least attract the attention of someone who could tell the waiter to hurry up and attend to the obnoxious customer at table nine.

"Let me just order a drink, Nora," Horace said. "What can I get for you?"

"Just ice water with a little lemon."

The waiter sidled up to the table with a fake smile on his lips. "*So* sorry to keep you waiting. What can I bring you to drink?"

Horace could feel his voice shaking as he ordered his gin and tonic and Nora's water. That wasn't a good sign. It had hardly been three hours since his last sip of alcohol. Getting shaky so soon had to be a bad thing.

He flashed a smile at Nora and started drumming his fingers on the table, trying to avoid eye contact with his aunt while he waited impatiently for the drinks to arrive. Nora shook her head at him and sighed, then looked down at her menu.

"What are you going to get to eat, honey?" she asked.

Horace saw the waiter leaving the bar with their drinks on a little tray and felt his stomach do an excited flip. Wow. He was really going to have to cut back on the drinking.

"What?" he said, realizing that Nora had asked him a question he had not yet answered.

Nora narrowed her eyes and stared at him. "What . . . are . . . you . . . going . . . to . . . eat?"

"I'm not stupid, Nora," he said, letting out an audible sigh of satisfaction as the waiter slid his gin in front of him. "I just zoned out for a second."

Nora pinched the lemon wedge from her drink between her fingertips before dropping it into the cloudy water. "Whatever you say."

Horace took a long drink, trying hard not to look as relieved as he felt. Carefully, he set the glass down on the table, taking note of the amount of liquid in it so he could be sure to drain it as slowly as possible to avoid getting a lecture from his aunt.

"I'm not all that hungry," he said, longing to reach out and take another sip of his drink but fighting the urge. He smiled at Nora.

"Well, I don't believe that for a second. Why don't we get this appetizer sampler? It'll be good for you to get something in your stomach. And what better comfort food than potato skins and buffalo wings?"

"Fine, fine," he said. "You go ahead and order. I'm just going to run to the restroom."

He got up and almost sprinted through the restaurant, the startled faces at the tables a blur. He paused at the little alcove just off the lobby that led to the restrooms, then picked up speed again and pushed his way through the crowd of people waiting for tables to get to the bar.

"Shot of Jack," he said, not even bothering to sit down on a stool. He slid a ten-dollar bill across the bar and waited with a skipping pulse for his drink. The bartender had not even had a chance to pick up the money before Horace had thrown back the shot, dropped the empty glass on the bar, and turned with stiffened shoulders to make his way back through the restaurant.

As he slid back into his chair, his fingers fluttered over his eye patch. It wasn't an irrational compulsion to make sure the ruined eye was well covered. With the patch, he could pull off an attempt to seem mysterious and tormented. Without it, he was just a circus freak best left alone.

"What is going on with you, Horace?" Nora asked.

He dropped his hand from his eye, grasping it with the other hand and shoving them both deep into his lap. He shrugged. "I don't know," he said. He scanned the table—the glasses, the wilted lily in the bud vase, the wrinkled pink packets of artificial sweetener poking out from the small plastic dispenser. "I don't know what's wrong with me."

His hands reached involuntarily for his gin and tonic, but Nora's pale, skeletal fingers grabbed him first. Although her grip was nowhere near strong enough to hold him, the shock of her touch was enough to make him stop moving. She pressed his hands down, flat against the white table-cloth. He looked at her wildly, but felt a tear bursting from his good eye, so he forced himself to look down to avoid seeing the expression of pity and anger on her face.

"Shhhh," she whispered. "It's going to be okay."

He let out an ironic laugh. "Yeah, right. I don't even know what it *is* that isn't okay. How can you say it'll get better if we don't know what we're trying to fix?"

She reached across the table, raised his chin with her forefinger, and gazed at him. "Everything gets better, eventually."

His good eye locked with hers. "Tell that to Mom and Dad."

She flinched, and he had a brief moment of freedom that he used to tear his hands away from hers and throw himself against the back of his chair. Nora was still leaning over the table, but she had crumpled and was crying softly.

Horace ran a hand over his face and through his hair. "Christ. I'm sorry, Nora," he said. He sat up and reached over to pat her hand. She jerked away from him.

"You don't know what you're talking about when you say things about your parents. You have no idea what they went through. Your mom, especially."

"What do you think I am? A retard? Of course I know what happened." He felt a hot stab of hatred spike through his spine. He slapped the patch over his eye. "Have you forgotten about *this?*"

Nora covered her face with her hands. "I can't do this. I have to go." She started to stand. Panicked, Horace groped for her wrist. He caught the pocket of her seersucker jacket, but it was enough to make her stop and look at him, her eyes glistening with tears.

"Wait," he said, pulling out his wallet and tossing a fifty-dollar bill on the table. "I'm coming with you."

She sighed and used the edge of her middle finger to wipe the tears from her eyes, careful not to smudge her eyeliner. "Okay. Let's get out of here, then."

After he helped her climb into the front seat of his SUV, he got in on the driver's side and sat there, not turning the key in the ignition. Now that they were alone, away from the stares of the people in the restaurant, she was actively crying. He hated when people cried in front of him. He never knew what he was supposed to do—rub their shoulders? Start crying himself? Slap them across the face and tell them to snap out of it? There were too many choices, and none ever seemed quite right. So he just sat there and waited until she was done, glancing occasionally at his watch and hoping she'd pull herself together soon so he could get home and pour himself another drink, to replace the one he had had to leave sitting on their abandoned table.

Finally, her sobs subsided into sniffles and she started digging in her purse. Horace frowned.

"Do you need a tissue?" he asked. "I think there's one of those soft packs in the glove compartment."

Nora popped open the glove box and rooted around through the debris of empty Altoids tins, printouts of Mapquest directions to places he'd long since forgotten he'd been, and scraps of Post-it notes with phone numbers he'd managed to score from girls at clubs and then couldn't remember their names well enough to risk calling. It was a true bachelor's glove box. He just hoped Nora wouldn't pull out a used condom.

"This is ridiculous," she said, slamming the glove box closed and wiping her nose on her sleeve with an over-dramatic flourish. "Good enough."

"Look, I'm sorry. Why don't I just take you home and we can do this another day?" He started to turn the key in the ignition but she reached over and stopped him, resting her tiny, brown-spotted, thick-veined hand on his. He wanted to shake her off, as the irrational thought drifted through his mind that her age spots might creep onto his own flesh if she touched him for too long. He turned and flashed her a smile, and she sat back in her seat, pressing her hands together in her lap.

"You wanted to talk, so let's talk," she said. "Frankly, I don't want to go through this whole nightmare again. Let's just do this now and get it over with."

"Aunt Nora . . ."

"You know, you're nothing like your father. You never have been. And you're certainly not at all like your mother. I don't know how two people like them—so kind and smart and, most of all, compassionate—could have produced a son of a bitch like you."

The sound of profanity—however mild—was startling coming from the lips of his old—and old-fashioned—aunt. He almost laughed, but as humorous as his aunt's comment sounded, the sentiment was harsh and, to his surprise, it cut him.

"You're right," he said, feeling bitter and wanting to wound her back. "I *am* a lot more like you and Uncle Seth."

She gasped, and he immediately wished he had kept his mouth shut. Her eyes filled with tears again and she started swiping her hand against the car door, trying to find the handle without looking at it. She finally made contact and a gust of air swept through the car as she slid from the passenger seat to the ground. Horace leaped out of the car and ran around to the other side. He tried to wrap his arms around Nora to hug her, but the gesture—an unfamiliar one to him, at least in a nonsexual context—was too stiff and he missed her. She pushed past him, walking in her wobbly old-lady-ish gait back toward the restaurant.

"Nora, wait! I'm sorry. I didn't mean it."

She ignored him, and he just watched in impotent, guilty silence as she tugged weakly at the restaurant door until someone had enough mercy to push it open for her from inside. As she disappeared into the darkness of the lobby, Horace leaned back against the side of his car.

"That went well," he said. He waited for a few minutes, staring at the door to the restaurant, until he was sure Nora wasn't coming back out. Then he hopped up into the driver's seat and pulled away, enjoying the sound of his tires screeching against the gravel of the parking lot. Maybe she was right. Maybe he really was a son of a bitch.

8

IRIS

| AUGUST 10, 1974 |

We've been so busy lately, I've hardly had a chance to write. I just got back from a trip to LA to meet with the publicity people about the new book we're putting out for the Christmas rush. It's another one of mine. I'm prouder of the fact that I've been able to find time to write at all, with all the success we've had running our publishing house, than I am of the book itself, which, I have to admit, borders on drivel. But then, I've never tried to pretend I'm a great novelist. If anything, I think of myself as a diarist, more Anaïs Nin than Virginia Woolf. Jeez, even making that comparison embarrasses me. I could never hope to equal Anaïs Nin in my life, not to mention Virginia Woolf or even some crappy novelist like the ones who write those awful fat romance paperbacks you see in the supermarket with the half-naked men and the women in flowing gowns on the cover.

Anyway, the publishing is going well. I hate to say I'm surprised, because that makes it sound like I didn't believe in Oscar, didn't believe he could make a success of this thing, and I'd never want to imply that. Oscar's brilliant—always has been, and I love him to death for it. But publishing can be a cutthroat business, even when you have great material to publish, as opposed to my woefully mediocre stuff. So imagine my surprise when the sales of the first novel took off like a rocket and allowed us not only to lease an office and a warehouse but to offer decent-sized advances to some new and very promising writers (people with a lot more talent than I have!). And since then, we've been doing really well. Everybody's amazed. There was even a write-up about Oscar and me in *Publishers Weekly* a few months back. It's just so exciting.

And there's something even more exciting—something I haven't even told Oscar yet. I think I'm pregnant. I'm nine days late, and I have an appointment with the doctor this afternoon. A baby will make everything just perfect. We're leading a charmed life, there's no doubt about it.

AUGUST 15, 1974

I'm so depressed I could die. Not even depressed. I'm pissed off—at my body, at the world, at God or nature or whatever. I guess I don't need to say that the pregnancy test came back negative. Not only that, but my period waited to show up until ten minutes—literally—before the doctor's office called to say I wasn't pregnant. It's like my body decided to hold out for as long as possible, just so I could have my hopes up really, really high. It's only worth dashing hopes that are high enough to make a real crash. The nurse who called wasn't even nice about it. She just said, "Your test was negative." That's it. And she sounded mean and snotty, like I must have been a moron for thinking I could be pregnant. There was no "I'm sorry" or even a suggestion about why my period might have been two weeks late. Nothing but that smug little matter-of-fact statement. I wanted to jump through the phone line and beat her to death.

So now, I'm lying here in bed, sobbing constantly, except whenever Oscar comes in the room. I'm doing my best to keep this from him. He doesn't need to know how close we came to having a family, only to fail miserably. He's wanted a baby for as long as I've known him, I think. He always talks about the future, and how he'll coach our son's little league team and teach our kids to drive a stick shift and carry them around the yard piggyback and take the whole family out for miniature golf and ice cream cones. I don't want him to know that it might not happen. It's hard enough dealing with my own disappointment. I don't want to have to try to cheer up Oscar, too. And I don't want him trying to console me. That'll only make me feel even worse, like my body is defective. And I'll know that's what he's thinking—that he married a barren old hag. It's bad enough thinking that about myself. I couldn't bear to see it in his eyes.

I can't stop crying. This is so silly. How can I be this upset about losing something I never even had? I feel like I've had an actual miscarriage, or like I've lost a baby I already gave birth to. It's that painful. God, I hope it's that painful. If those kinds of tragedies are even worse than this, there's no way I'd ever survive them. Maybe it's better if I never get pregnant at all. I'd never be able to handle any kind of problem, that's pretty obvious.

For now, I think I'm going to curl up in a ball, pull the covers over my head, and wish for death to come along and carry me gently away.

SEPTEMBER 20, 1974

Weird, weird day today. I was in my office at work, and it was lunchtime. Oscar had gone out to meet with some reps from a new distributor we're considering using for our books, so I was just going to have a sandwich at my desk and keep working. I have a million things to get done if I'm going to make my deadline for finishing up writing the next novel. You might be thinking it sounds dumb to be worried about meeting a deadline that I imposed on myself, but hey, I've got to be disciplined now, and this is the only way that seems to work.

So, I'm sitting at my desk, munching on a tuna sandwich, when who strolls in but Seth. Since he gave me that crazy, stalker-sounding card that first Christmas, he's actually been pretty good. He's been acting almost normal, and for Seth, that's saying a lot. Normal isn't exactly his strong suit.

So he came in and flopped down in one of the chairs in front of my desk, stretched his legs out so he was basically lying sideways in the chair, and just sat there, smiling at me and drumming his fingers on his belly.

I chewed as fast as I could and gulped down the bite of sandwich I had in my mouth, then put the rest of the tuna sandwich down on the desk. Worried that I might have tuna bits stuck in my teeth, I swirled a sip of Coke around in my mouth before I smiled at him. I know it's stupid to care how I look in front of Seth, but something about the way he idolizes me makes me want to be worthy of the adoration. It's warped, I know.

So we were sitting there, both of us smiling like morons but not saying a word. It felt almost like we were having a staring contest, except with silence, both of us holding out to see who would break down and speak first. It was me, of course.

"What's up, Seth? It's nice to see you."

He swung his legs around and sat up straight, leaning toward me with a mischievous gleam in his eyes. "Is it?"

"Is it what?"

"Is it nice to see me?"

I swallowed. He's so good at making me uncomfortable. He's supposed to be family, my brother-in-law, but he makes me feel like I'm a go-go dancer and he's a customer with lots of dollar bills.

"It's always nice to see you. You know that," I said, hoping I sounded casual, like family, and not like someone who's interested in sleeping with him. Because I'm not. Really.

"Well, that's good to hear," he said. I hate the way he talks when he and I are alone. He practically purrs.

I just sat there, looking at him but not making eye contact, feeling my insides twitch with a kind of worry I can't quite describe. And he just sat there, too, staring at me with that amused hint of a smile on his lips— the same one he always has on his face, like he knows he's making me so uncomfortable I might run out of the room screaming at any moment. I was tempted to yell out to Carol, my secretary, and pretend I had forgotten some urgent business, just to have an excuse to bring another person into the room so I wouldn't have to be alone with him anymore. Instead, I just sat there, biting my lip and fiddling with a paper clip that was lying on the desk in front of me.

"Do I make you uncomfortable?" he asked suddenly, leaning across the desk toward me. He propped his elbows up on the edge of the desk, folded his hands, and rested his chin on them.

I laughed, trying to sound all casual and breezy, but instead my voice came out shaky and obviously nervous. I tried to cover. "Uncomfortable? Of course not. That's ridiculous. You're my brother. I'm just . . . I'm just a little distracted today. Lots of work. Big meeting this afternoon. You know how it goes."

He leaned back in the chair and crossed his arms over his stomach. "Not really," he said. "Work . . . it's not exactly my thing."

Grateful for a topic I could converse about with some degree of comfort, I seized it. "Have you been thinking about what you're going to do now that you graduated? Or are you thinking about going back to school for your master's or something?"

He sneered. "Hell, no. No more school. That's for damn sure."

"So what do you want to do?"

He grinned. "Whatever it takes to make you happy."

I felt my cheeks flush, and I looked down, grabbing the paper clip and twisting it around with my fingers again. God, I can be pathetic.

"But seriously, Seth," I said, working hard to keep my voice steady. "You must have some plans."

"Oh, yeah. I have plans."

I kept my eyes down, knowing that if I looked up, he'd be staring at me with those intense, lascivious green eyes of his. For just a second, the thought passed through my mind that maybe I *am* kind of attracted to Seth. And having that thought, however briefly, sent a surge through my loins that made me even more embarrassed than I already was. I felt like such an idiot. Seth is nothing more than a kid—barely out of college—and yet I always let him intimidate me like he's some kind of—I don't know what. Even now, hours later, I feel like my brain is full of marbles pinging around and keeping me from making sense of anything.

Finally, mercifully, he stood up and moved toward the door. "Have a good day," he said. I forced myself to look up and smile at him as he left. As soon as I was sure he was gone, I jumped up and slammed the door shut and locked it. My heart was beating so hard, I thought I was going to have a heart attack. The doctors are right. Stress can kill.

9

HORACE

He closed the diary and set it down on the floor, on top of the pile of diaries he'd already been through. His mother had been as anal retentive about recording every day's events as she had been about keeping him clean and safe his whole life—even well past his childhood. A flash of resentment raced through him, which immediately made him feel guilty. Now that he was reading his mother's most intimate thoughts, he seemed to be acquiring a little bit of compassion for her, if not quite respect.

He reached over and grabbed his glass. It was just ice water—not gin. Not even wine tonight. He had decided to conduct an experiment. If he could make it through this evening—after everything that had happened with Aunt Nora today—without a drink, then he was not an alcoholic. Hell, even the lightest drinker would have been aching for a shot of whiskey after that scene at lunch. And what made things even worse was that he knew he would have to either call her or go over to her house tomorrow and apologize. Even if he didn't mean it, which he never did, he hated to say he was sorry. It was just so humiliating. It was like leaning over and kissing someone's grubby feet. In fact, he would rather have kissed a pair of nasty feet with a bad case of fungus than have to say those awful words—"I'm sorry." Nobody deserved to humiliate another person that much, to make someone express regret for doing nothing more than what any normal person would do under the same circumstances. It was a horrible social convention—the kind of senseless tradition that often made him wish he could leave society altogether and go find someplace totally uninhabited to stay, so he would never have to worry about dealing with people and their insane feelings again. The only thing stopping him was that he imagined it would be hard to get booze—or a decent fuck—on an uninhabited island. Not that he'd been getting much of the latter lately, even living right next door to the extremely inhabited island of Manhattan.

He put down the glass and sat there for a long moment, staring into space and trying to decide whether he should just suck it up and go over to Nora's now, or find something else to do to take his mind off everything tonight and deal with Nora tomorrow. He picked up the phone and dialed his cousin Andrew's number. Andrew would be a good barometer for judging the type and extent of apology he would need to prepare for Nora.

"Well, well, well," Andrew said, answering the phone without even a hello. *Fucking caller ID*, Horace thought. *Technology has ruined the world for crank callers*. "If it isn't the asshole who sent my poor mother into a tizzy. She's been crying the whole fucking day, you dick."

"Nice talking to you, too, cuz."

"So what do you want?"

Horace swallowed. "I just wanted to find out how upset she was so I would know how big a flower arrangement I need to order."

Andrew lowered his voice. Horace guessed Nora was close by, within hearing range. "I'd suggest something the size of the wreath they give to the winner of the Kentucky Derby."

"That bad, huh?"

"Maybe worse. I've never seen her like this."

"Shit. I knew I fucked up, but I was hoping maybe she just overreacted and would forget about it after a few hours. Dammit. All right. Well, don't tell her I called. I'll come by tomorrow to see her."

"You might want to stop by Tiffany's or something on your way. She's pissed, but I don't think it's anything that a nice gold watch wouldn't fix."

"And I assume she likes—what?—a men's size large? Something with lots of dials and underwater capability?"

"That sounds like Mom, yeah."

"Good-bye, Andrew."

Horace clicked off the phone and reached with shaking fingers for his drink. As he raised it to his lips, he remembered that it was just water and felt his stomach tighten. He rolled the sip of cool water around in his mouth. It tasted somehow metallic, and maybe a little dusty, if that was even possible.

He slid off the chair and sat down on the floor next to the plastic bins full of his mother's stuff. He had been through everything in the first bin, except for a big pile of envelopes full of photos. Maybe opening them all up and trying to organize them, at least in his own head, would distract him for a while and help dull the throbbing, clenching pull in his stomach that was screaming at him to abandon his experiment and go make himself a drink.

The first envelope contained pictures of his mother and Aunt Nora as very young children. Holding one of the small black-and-white photos up to the light, he stared at the pale round faces framed by blond hair so light it looked white, almost glowing like a halo. *Strange*, he thought, *how alike Nora and Mom looked when they were small, considering how very different they became by the time they were adults.*

He picked up another photo, this one of Nora as a teenager. He laid it alongside a picture of his mother at a similar age. Both photos looked professional—the kind of pictures they make you sit for at school, where a local photographer comes in with a cheesy backdrop of autumn leaves or a too-blue sky. These were black and white, though, so it was hard to tell what was supposed to be in the background. Unfortunately, at least for Nora's sake, the lack of a discernible background drew your eye right to her face—her bumpy, blackhead-speckled, triple-chinned face.

Horace brushed through the photos to find the first one he'd looked at, where Nora and his mother had been around five or six. They were only a year apart; not even a full year. Nora had been born in September and his mom the following August. They had been raised almost as twins. So what the hell had happened to turn Nora into a fat, dumpy house frau with acne while keeping his mother perfectly preserved as a shining blond angel? Sometimes life really fucked people over.

He pulled out another packet of photos and spilled them out on the floor. These were mostly pictures of his parents during their high school years, but in a few, Nora was there, lingering in the background, never up front with everyone else. In fact, you probably wouldn't even have noticed her in most of the pictures if she hadn't been so fat. It was sad, really. But it wasn't like she didn't end up with a decent life. Eventually, she got married and had Andrew. Okay, so maybe her husband, his uncle Seth, had been a bastard, but Horace tended to think that most men were bastards. He should know. He was a bigger bastard than almost anyone he'd ever met.

He thumbed through the photos again, searching for the one of his parents' wedding, where Nora and Seth were standing beside them as maid of honor and best man. Even into her twenties, when the wedding took place, Nora was heavy, pimple-faced, and clearly terrified of the world. The curiosity was rubbing at his spine, begging him to read through the diaries and the letters to find out what had happened to Nora. *Hell*, he thought, *at least it's something to do, other than drinking*. He dug through the stack of diaries and envelopes full of letters and started to read.

10

IRIS
| NOVEMBER 23, 1977 |

I had the best idea yesterday. We were all sitting around the table at Mom's house, filling our faces with Stovetop stuffing and homemade mashed potatoes for Thanksgiving, when I realized that Nora seems to have a little bit of a crush on Seth.

Actually, I first noticed that something was up before dinner, when we were all in the living room. In between bites of cold kielbasa slathered in red horseradish, Nora was sneaking peeks at Seth, who, I have to admit, looked really good in his new navy blue pinstripe suit. Her interest in him made me interested in her, so I pretty much spent the rest of the day stealing glances at her while she stole glances at him.

After dinner, on the way home, I mentioned the whole thing to Oscar. He didn't seem to be quite as excited about it as I was.

"Why shouldn't we try to set them up?" I asked.

"Because Seth's an asshole and Nora's a sweet, shy, schoolmarmish kind of girl. He'll break her heart."

I considered that for a moment, then dismissed it. "But she likes him."

"And he likes *you*."

I felt myself blush. How pathetic, to get embarrassed like that in front of my own husband.

"You know he does, don't you?" Oscar said, shooting me a quick look before turning his eyes back to the road.

I shrugged. "It's just a little crush," I said. I've never told Oscar about some of the things Seth has done and said to me. And this was certainly not the time to bring it up. Better to let him think my interest in getting Seth and Nora together was purely a matchmaking thing, not an effort at self-preservation.

"It's more than a crush," Oscar said. I saw his hands tighten on the steering wheel. I'd never realized how angry Seth's infatuation with me made him.

"What makes you say that?" I asked.

He didn't answer at first. He just sat there and stared forward, as if he really needed every bit of his attention to drive the car. Then he said, "I just know."

We rode along in silence the rest of the way. I stared out the window into the dark, feeling my head reel as the streetlights whizzed past. The tension inside the car was so thick, I felt like I was inside a cocoon, trapped alone on the passenger side, like I could have screamed and Oscar wouldn't have been able to hear me. Only after we had pulled into our own driveway and Oscar turned off the ignition did I make another attempt to talk to him.

"Are you okay?" I asked.

Oscar pulled out the keys and dropped them into his left hand. He started jiggling them, tossing them from one palm to the other. I finally got irritated enough to reach over and take the keys away from him.

"Will you just talk to me, please?"

Oscar sighed. "Seth's in love with you."

I felt the heat rise in my cheeks again. "That's silly," I said, knowing very well that I was lying.

"No. No, it's not. He told me so."

I gulped. "What . . . I mean, what exactly did he say? When?"

"At our wedding. While you were walking down the aisle, he leaned over and told me that someday you'd be coming down the aisle to meet *him*."

I laughed. "Come on," I said. "Obviously, he was just kidding if he really did say that."

"Seth doesn't kid."

"Oscar, come on. You're not really worried about this, are you?"

"You don't know him the way I do. He can be ruthless."

I rolled my eyes. "Sure, he cheats at board games, and I'm sure he would steal a head start in a foot race, but beyond that, he's basically harmless."

Oscar shook his head. "No. He's not."

I know it's a cliché, but when he said that, a chill ran up my spine. Well, I guess that's how something gets to be a cliché—the fact that it's so true.

I wanted to say something, to try to force Oscar to explain what he meant about Seth being ruthless, but the look on Oscar's face scared me. I'd never seen him looking so—I don't know—I guess the best way to describe it is "black." He looked dark and distracted, a little off-kilter and wild—kind of like I imagine Edgar Allan Poe must have looked in the last days before he died in a gutter, all strung out on laudanum or whatever the hell he took. Anyway, I kept my mouth shut and we went inside and went to bed.

I didn't even bother bringing it up this morning when we got up. Oscar looked a little better than he did last night, so I didn't want to set him off again. So instead of talking to Oscar, I called up my mom to see what she thought about trying to get Nora and Seth together.

Mom practically squealed. "That's perfect! Perfect, perfect, perfect! They'd be wonderful together."

"Are you sure? Oscar didn't think it was such as great idea."

"Why not? Maybe Nora is a few years older than Seth, but so what? He's so good-looking."

"That's not really the point."

"Maybe not, but it doesn't hurt."

"Okay. So what do we do?"

"Just leave it to me. I'll call Oscar's mom and set the whole thing up."

"Okay," I said. "And I suppose you'll talk to Nora, to make sure she actually wants to go out with him?"

My mom made a sound like "*Pshaw*," which I didn't realize someone could make in real life, outside of the comics. Then she said, "Of course she wants to go out with him. She hasn't been on a date in years."

"I think you're exaggerating, Mom."

"No, I'm not. It's so sad. But then, she's just so fat . . ."

I frowned. "I hate to mention it, but you're right. I'm a little worried that Seth won't want to go out with her. He can be kind of superficial."

"Don't worry about it. Marianne and I will set it all up. I'll talk to you later, sweetie."

"Bye, Mom."

I hung up the phone and sat there, wondering whether I had done the right thing. Was I really thinking about what was best for Nora, or was I hoping for a convenient way to get Seth to stop obsessing about me? And was Oscar right about Seth? How far would he go to try to get to me? Almost immediately, I regretted the whole thing. But I'm going to be optimistic for once in my life. I'm going to trust that it'll all work out best for everybody in the end.

MARCH 3, 1978

Seth and Nora are engaged! You should have seen how happy Nora looked at dinner tonight when they announced it to us all. She was literally glowing. And even Seth looked relatively happy—happy enough that, at least for now, I'm convinced he's actually in love with Nora and that he isn't just marrying her to get closer to me. God, I'm such a narcissist. Of course this has nothing to do with me. They're in love. They have to be.

JULY 27, 1978

It's late, so I won't write much. I just had to stay up late enough to write a little. Nora and Seth were married today.

I've never seen Nora so happy. And she looked beautiful. She's lost quite a bit of weight over the last few months, since she started going out with Seth. Maybe he's actually a good influence on her. Or maybe she feels like she has to starve herself to be good enough for him. No, no, no. I won't let myself consider those kinds of horrible things.

Anyway, she looked great. Absolutely radiant, just like a bride should be. She let me put some highlights in her hair, so she almost looked blond again, like when we were kids. For some reason, blondes always seem to look thinner than brunettes to me. Maybe that's stupid, but then, I have a lot of stupid ideas, I guess.

She was lucky enough to get to wear her own wedding dress, not a hand-me-down from Mom and Gramma like I had to wear. (Of course, that's mainly because Nora wasn't thin enough to fit in the dreaded "family wedding gown"—she hasn't lost *that* much weight yet.) She picked out something very simple and elegant—plain ivory silk with only a bow and a long row of buttons down the back (fake ones—the lucky girl!), and completely plain in front except for the scoop neck, which showed off her bust nicely. Sometimes I think I'd be willing to put up with being a little bit fat if it would mean I could have some real boobs. I'm not greedy; even a full B cup would be plenty for me. It's just agony not being able to fill out your clothes at all. God, I'm terrible. Poor me, I'm too skinny and I can eat whatever I want without gaining a pound. Everyone should pity me.

So now Nora and Seth are off on their honeymoon, going to Hawaii. I'm still not sure why Nora would have picked a beachy place to go, since I don't think she's put on a bathing suit since she was about fourteen. In general, I've noticed, fat people don't seem to like the beach. Hawaii was probably Seth's choice; in fact, I'm sure it was. He probably wants to sit in a chaise lounge with a frozen drink in his hand and ogle all the half-naked girls, while poor Nora sweats in that terrycloth cover-up she always drapes over herself, to try to make you think she isn't fat or, at least, isn't self-conscious about it. Jeez, I wonder if it's a bad sign that I'm already thinking that Seth is treating her badly. It must be my crazy imagination. I'm supposed to be a writer, after all.

But one thing that happened at the wedding wasn't my imagination. Maybe that's what's got me so nervous. Oscar was dancing with Nora, so I went over to Seth and asked him to dance, figuring it was the nice thing to do, to let him know there were no hard feelings after all the weird things he's done and said in the past. Or, rather, I thought it was all in the past.

We were dancing—kind of a rumba or something, which was impressive. He must've taken lessons or something. So I tried to make small talk.

"I'm really happy for you guys," I said.

"Yeah, I'm sure you are."

"Of course I am. And so is Oscar. Now we're all even more related than we already were!"

I felt his hand press down on my hip as he guided me into a sexy kind of twisting step, and even though I was trying to focus on the dance, I was distracted by the sensation that his hand was gradually slipping downward, brushing over my ass instead of staying put on my hip where it belonged. I tried to talk to cover my discomfort. God, sometimes I'm such a moron.

"You're such a great dancer. Where did you learn to do this?" I asked.

He flashed a toothy smile at me as he pressed me back into a slight dip. "I was born with these moves."

I let out an awkward giggle. "No, seriously. Did you take a class?"

"That's for me to know and you to find out."

"Oh, that's real mature!"

"Hey, you don't need to be mature to be me."

I wrinkled my nose. "What does that mean?"

He stared into my eyes for a long, uncomfortable moment. Then he burst out laughing. "I have no idea," he said.

I laughed. "You're a funny guy, little brother."

His face went sour. "You don't really think of me as a brother, do you?"

"What do you mean? Of course I do. You're my brother-in-law—doubled, now that you're married to my sister."

"I may be married, but I'm definitely not your brother."

I slapped his shoulder lightly, playfully. "You're silly."

He leaned forward and let his lips run along the rim of my ear, then he whispered, "No. I'm not. Believe me."

The music stopped suddenly, or at least it seemed sudden to me. And without another word or even a glance, Seth was gone, across the dance floor, and plastered to Nora's side, like the most devoted groom you've ever seen.

I'm just so confused. I have to assume that he's just kidding around with me, that he's got some kind of strange sense of humor that I just don't get, and that he really does love my sister. Nora's been hurt enough. It couldn't have been easy being fat and ugly and adolescent all at the same time. She deserves to finally be happy.

So why am I so sure this is going to go horribly awry?

11

HORACE
| Present Day |

Horace woke up before dawn and sat up in bed, shocked to find himself in a still-dark but gradually brightening room. Usually, he would be going to bed around this time. He couldn't remember the last time he'd woken up this early, and without even a twinge of a hangover. It was kind of refreshing.

He got up and shaved, showered, and dressed to face what he expected would be a difficult day in gray flannel pants and a lightweight black cashmere sweater. The whole time, he was replaying the diary entries he had read last night in his mind, still in disbelief that, for one thing, Seth had been a big enough dickhead to basically proposition his sister-in-law at his own wedding reception and, for another, that his mother had been so hopelessly naïve. He realized that he shouldn't have been surprised. He had never thought much of his mother and her social skills, but this was worse than anything he could have imagined—although she obviously did have some misgivings about the whole situation. That was probably the biggest surprise. He wondered how long it had taken for his mother to grasp the fact that Seth had only married Nora as a cruel joke. Horace knew he would have to keep reading the diaries to find out. But for today, what he wanted to know was how long it had taken Nora to realize that Seth hadn't married her for love. Maybe he would be able to pry that information out of her when he went over to her house to grovel for forgiveness, which, he did understand, in the sober light of day, he didn't really deserve.

He pulled into Nora's driveway just as Andrew was backing out. Andrew rolled down his window and grinned. "So what did you bring me?"

"Well, I've got some lovely flowers, but I think your mom'll like them better than you will."

"I guess you're right. I'd prefer a nice bottle of scotch. Meet you for a drink later?"

Horace felt a rush of excitement run through his bones and he cringed, realizing it probably wasn't a good thing to be so thrilled about the prospect of having an alcoholic beverage. He stretched his neck from side to side as if contemplating the idea and said, "Maybe. I'll give you a call after I'm done here."

"Sweet. See ya later." Andrew's tires squealed as he pulled out of the driveway and took off down the street.

Horace stared after him in the rearview mirror for a moment, then parked the car and sat there, wishing he didn't have to do this, get out of the car with his stupid bouquet of so-sorry-I-was-a-prick flowers and see Nora. Oh, well. It was probably best just to get it over with. The sooner he faced the familial firing squad, the sooner he could belly up to a bar with Andrew, who tended to become very generous about buying other people drinks once he'd had a few of his own.

He climbed out of the car and grabbed the cellophane-wrapped bouquet. He'd picked tiger lilies—not your ordinary bouquet, but he had a vague memory that Aunt Nora liked lilies, so it was worth a shot. At worst, he'd get credit for bringing flowers; at best, she'd melt when she saw that he had remembered her favorite kind. Either way, he'd be better off than he was now. Couldn't be worse.

He rang the doorbell and stood there waiting on the front porch. He always hated this—it was so awkward standing there, knowing full well that someone inside was on tiptoe, peering at you through the peephole and most likely evaluating how you looked, or even whether you were worth opening the door for. He just hoped he'd get the nod of approval from Nora. Even though he knew she was home—he had to assume that Andrew would have mentioned it if she had gone out—she could very easily not realize he'd seen Andrew and try to pretend she wasn't in.

He was mildly surprised—and majorly nervous—when he heard the scraping sound of the metal lock being twisted open. So she was going to put him to the test. *Better to get it over with*, he reminded himself. *It'll only be worse to put it off.*

She didn't open the door all the way. Instead, she rested the side of her head against the edge of the partly opened door and stared at him with a tired, wistful expression on her face.

"Andrew said you'd be coming by," she said.

Horace sighed. "I told him not to tell you. I wanted to surprise you—with these." He thrust the flowers toward her, but she didn't take them. He stood there with his arm extended, out in limbo, with the orange lilies encased in corny lavender cellophane that had tiny white hearts printed on it. A wave of humiliation ran over him as he realized that the flowers might have been a bad idea.

Or maybe he was wrong. He could see Nora relax as she stared through teary eyes at the bouquet. Her fingers made a small, grasping motion toward the flowers that looked almost involuntary. She pulled her hand back and pressed it against the door. But he could tell he had broken her down. As a single tear splashed down her cheek, she said softly, "I love tiger lilies."

He had to clench his thigh muscles to keep from himself leaping into the air in triumph. Keeping his voice as flat as possible, he said, "I thought you did."

He tried to push the flowers at her, hoping she would give in and accept them. She was clearly torn, but finally, she reached out, pulled the crinkling bouquet toward her, and cradled the flowers in the crook of her elbow, like she was holding an infant.

"Thank you," she said. She took a step backward and drew the door inside with her, making room for him to come into the house.

As he brushed past her he stopped, kissed her on the cheek, and whispered, "I'm so sorry, Aunt Nora. I was a real jerk."

She smiled sadly as she pressed the door closed behind them. "Well, I guess you get that from your father."

Horace, who had already slung himself into one of Aunt Nora's many wooden rocking chairs, looked over at her, startled. "Really? I thought everybody said my dad was the nicest guy."

Nora seemed to freeze for just a moment. Then she laughed and her gaze met his. "Of course he was. I forgot who I was talking to. I tell Andrew all the time that he's acting like his father. I suppose it's normal for me to be a little forgetful now and then, at my age. What do they call that these days? A senior moment?"

Horace forced a laugh. "Yeah, I think that's it. But you're still pretty sharp there, Aunt Nora. You've got a while to go before we'll start making fun of you."

She smiled and sat down, perched on the edge of her faded floral-print sofa, the old-fashioned kind that had dark-stained, highly glossed wood on the armrests and along the back edge. She laid the flowers on the seat beside her and tucked her small hands between her knees, which looked bony even through her pink polyester old-lady slacks.

"So," she said, making eye contact for only a moment before glancing back over at the flowers beside her. "Did you still have something you wanted to ask me?"

Horace frowned. "Do you want me to put those flowers in some water for you?"

She shook her head and brushed the cellophane with her fingertips. "No, no. I'll do that in a bit, after you leave."

"Okay," Horace said, wishing he could get up and leave right now.

Nora smiled at him. "So, tell me. How's it going with your mom's stuff? Finding anything interesting?"

"You could say that," he said, shifting his position so his legs were back on the floor instead of hanging over the arm of the rocking chair. "Mom was obviously a pretty devoted diary keeper."

"Yes, she sure was. I don't think I remember a single night when we were growing up when she didn't scribble in one of those little books for at least a few minutes before she went to bed. Sometimes she'd even sit up with a flashlight, still writing even after Mama told us to get to sleep. She always thought it would be important to be able to remember everything that ever happened to her. Maybe she was right, do you think?"

Horace coughed. "I'm not sure I know what you mean."

"I think you do. You're learning about her, aren't you? I know you never understood her while she was alive. Maybe she made it so you could at least learn to appreciate her after she was gone."

He hated it when Nora was so fucking insightful. "You're right. I guess I am learning a lot about her."

"But you said you had questions about your parents?"

Horace took a deep breath. "Actually, I'm more interested in you."

"Me? I'm about as uninteresting as a person can be."

He laughed and stood up, moving over and sitting beside her on the sofa, careful not to crush the flowers as he draped his arm around her shoulders and gave her a tender squeeze. "That is completely untrue. You come off very interesting, at least according to Mom."

Nora sighed. "Oh, I doubt that. Your mom—she was so full of life, so fascinating. There's no way she could have taken an interest in boring old me."

Horace patted her shoulder. "I'm not going to fight with you about this, but you're wrong, believe me."

Nora seemed to shrink beneath his touch. She whispered, "So what do you want to know about me?"

Horace withdrew his arm and sat mirroring Nora, with his hands tucked in his lap. "Why did you marry Seth?"

She let out a light, airy laugh. "Oh, that's easy. Because he asked me and I knew nobody else ever would."

"Oh, Nora, that's not . . ."

"It *is* true. You don't know. You didn't see . . . you don't know what I looked like . . . what I was like . . ." Her voice was high and shaky, and he was terrified that she was going to start crying again. That's all he needed: a repeat of yesterday's fiasco. He reached over and held her hand.

"It's okay," he said. "I didn't mean to upset you."

She shook her head. "I know you didn't, sweetheart. It's just hard to think back about it and not get upset. I'm sure you feel the same way about certain things."

His fingers moved involuntarily to his eye patch, and he had to force himself to pull them away and touch Nora's hand instead. "You're right," he said. "Sometimes I get really pissed off when I think about things that have happened to me."

They sat there in silence for a long moment. Finally, Horace sucked in a deep breath and blew it out. "Maybe I should go."

Nora shook her head hard. She turned and looked at him through tear-filled eyes, seeming almost surprised to see him still sitting beside her. "Oh, no, you don't have to go. Can I fix you something to eat or anything?"

Horace stood up, still holding her hand. He squeezed her hand between both of his before letting go. "Don't worry about it. I have some things to do and then later I'm meeting Andrew for a drink."

Nora got up and wiped her hands on her hips. "All right. If you have to go. Do me a favor? Don't let Andrew drink too much."

Horace heard a little cackling voice laughing inside him as he said, "Sure. No problem."

He bent down to kiss her on the cheek and headed toward the door. She stopped him in his tracks when she called out, "And don't let *yourself* drink too much, either."

He didn't bother to turn around as he said, "I won't."

"Promise me."

"I promise," he said. He turned his head to look back at her over his shoulder. He forced a small smile. "I promise, Aunt Nora."

He opened the door and was gone.

12

IRIS

| DECEMBER 26, 1978 |

Oscar and I had the whole family over last night for Christmas. I know I was running around a lot, making sure everybody had drinks and hors d'oeuvres and napkins and everything, but I couldn't help but notice how crappy Seth was acting toward Nora. They haven't even been married six months and already he sounds like Ralph Kramden when he's talking to her. And—surprise, surprise—she just sits there and takes it and never opens her mouth to make even a weak protest. How can she be such a wimp? I guess it runs in the family.

I pulled her into the kitchen with me while I was rolling up the individual pieces of lunch meats that I was going to put out on a platter for sandwich fixings. I pretended like I needed help, but really I just wanted a chance to talk to her without everyone else around. It's hard enough to get her to open up and talk without putting her in front of an audience.

I had a piece of bologna in my hand when I finally forced myself to say something. "So, how's married life treating you?"

I cringed when I said it, remembering how much I had hated it when people asked me that during the first few months Oscar and I were married. But at least I felt like I had gotten the ball rolling.

Nora shrugged and reached for a piece of Swiss cheese. I watched out of the corner of my eye as it cracked when she tried to roll it and she tried desperately to shape it into some sort of tube-like object. "It's fine," she said, slapping the piece of cheese down on the platter and reaching for a piece of more supple turkey.

I leaned over to try to peer into her eyes, but she was being diligent about keeping her gaze trained on the table below us. "Are you sure? I thought I sensed—I don't know—a little bit of tension between you and Seth."

She shook her head and said softly, "Maybe it was sexual tension." I thought I heard her laugh a little—an ironic and very sad laugh.

I brushed a finger against her arm, keeping the physical contact brief. I don't know why I hate touching other people so much. I'm just not good at being one of those huggy, touchy-feely people who know how to make other people feel loved and comfortable. But I try, in my own pathetic way.

She stiffened a little and then quickly grabbed another piece of meat, as if she were trying to cover her own revulsion at being touched. I guess that runs in the family, too.

"Are you sure you're okay, Nor?" I asked.

She stopped rolling the turkey for a moment and looked me dead in the eye. "I'm fine."

"Okay, okay," I said. "I just wanted to make sure. You don't seem all that fine, I've got to say."

She heaved a loud sigh. "What is that supposed to mean? How do I seem?"

I stood there for a second, not sure exactly what to say. "Sad. Angry. Timid. Terrified. Take your pick."

"Terrified? Terrified of what?"

"I don't know. Seth?"

She chuckled. "Yes, that's it. I'm afraid of my own husband. A brilliant analysis, Dr. Cairo."

She reached for a piece of bologna, but I grabbed her wrist and stopped her, twisting it just a little bit, just enough to force her to look me in the eye. "What!?" she said.

"It's not all that far-fetched," I said. "I think he can be plenty scary."

Nora pulled her wrist away from my grasp and turned immediately back to the stupid bologna. "You're crazy," she said.

"Am I? I don't think so. Oscar's told me some things . . ."

"Oh, sure. I'd definitely believe one brother's account of how rotten the other brother is. You'll have to come up with something a little better than that."

I took a deep breath. "Okay, then, how about stuff he's said to me?"

Nora went silent. Even her fingers stopped twisting the lunch meat, and her hands hung there, a few inches above the big silver platter, motionless in midair. Then, there was an almost imperceptible sound, like she was deflating, letting out all the tension my comment had created inside her. She began to roll the meat again as she said, "You're lying."

I picked up a piece of roast beef and tore a thin strip of fat off its edge. "You didn't even ask to hear what I have to say. How can you be so sure I'm lying?"

"Because you have *never* wanted me to be happy. You'll stop at nothing to make sure I'm miserable for the rest of my life. God forbid I might end up with something better than what you have. A better husband or a better career or—or—a baby . . ."

I froze. "Are you . . . ?"

Nora glared at me; her eyes were triumphant. "Yes. I'm pregnant."

For a long moment, it felt like time had stopped. I had to shake my head hard to bring myself back to reality. I whispered, "Are you? Are you really?"

Nora's lips spread into a grin that made her look mean. "I am."

I smiled and grabbed her hand, ignoring the cold sliminess of the piece of bologna she was holding. "So am I."

Nora and I stared hard at each other for what seemed like a year. Then she burst into tears and threw her arms around me, sobbing into my shoulder.

"Um . . . are you . . . are you happy or sad here, Nor?" I asked, trying to pull away a little so I could get a look at her face.

Nora let me get as far away as arm's length, but she held tight to my shoulders with both of her hands. "I'm happy," she said. "I'm happy. I was so worried about telling you. I know you've had some problems . . . I was afraid you'd be upset if you found out I got pregnant without even really trying. Are you? Are you mad?"

I reached my hands up to grasp hers, pulling them away from my shoulders and squeezing them. "Of course not. I'm thrilled for you. Besides, the last time . . . I jumped the gun. I shouldn't have assumed I was pregnant so quickly without even getting the test done. This time, I tried not to think about it at all until I was over three weeks late. And then I rushed right out for the test. I'm only six weeks along, but at least this time I know it's for real."

"I'm almost nine weeks," Nora said. "And I haven't even told Seth yet." She turned back to the meat platter.

"Why not?" I asked. "What are you waiting for?"

Nora shrugged, not looking up at me. "I . . . well, I wasn't sure he'd be happy about it."

"I don't understand. What makes you think that?"

She breathed out hard through her nose. "Well, you're not . . . entirely wrong about what you were saying before. He's not . . . he's not always the nicest guy in the world."

I grabbed her elbow. "Has he hit you?"

She waved me away. "No, no, it's not like that. It's not like he's some kind of wife beater. He can just be—I don't know—a little abrasive."

"You know better than to take crap from some guy, Nor," I said. "Mom may be a pain in the ass, but she taught us that much."

She smiled—a little, dreamy smile. "It's easier said than done."

"Nor," I said, still trying to catch her eye. "Is there anything I can do?"

She shook her head. "I'm fine," she said. "And maybe I'm being stupid. Maybe telling him about the baby will be just the thing to make him wake up and realize he ought to be a little nicer to me."

"Hey—go tell him now. Pull him aside, tell him, and then we can announce the news about both of us to everybody. That ought to throw Mom for a loop."

She finally raised her eyes to meet mine. "Okay," she said. "I'll go now."

She put down the piece of bologna she'd been working on, gave my elbow a gentle squeeze, and turned toward the door. She glanced back and smiled. "Thanks, little sister."

"Anytime, big sister."

She breezed through the swinging door, and I caught a glimpse of Seth's face as she moved toward him. His eyes locked with mine and he grinned just before the door swung closed. God, he really is a creepy asshole. I just hope Nora was right, that becoming a father will make him nicer.

I was tucking some sprigs of parsley around the spread of lunch meats when Oscar came into the kitchen, came up behind me, and wrapped his arms around me, resting his palms flat on my belly, as if he expected to be able to feel the baby this early in my pregnancy. He kissed my neck and whispered, "How's my little mother-to-be?"

"Shhh," I said. "Not so loud. I don't want the family hearing about this accidentally." I spun around to face him and kissed him.

"So, what's up with Nora?" he asked, releasing me and reaching for a piece of bologna, which he popped into his mouth like a breath mint. "She looks like she's got a stick up her ass tonight."

He reached out to try to grab a second roll of meat and I slapped his fingers away. "Those are for the buffet. Wait your turn," I said. "And Nora has every right to have a stick up her ass, with that brother of yours for a husband."

His face went so blank, it was eerie. "I was against getting the two of them together from the beginning. Just for the record."

"I don't give a crap about the record. Can't you say something to him? Try to get him to be nicer to her?"

"Seth? Nice? That's hilarious."

"She's pregnant."

"Oh, crap."

"What the hell is that supposed to mean?" I asked.

He shrugged. "I don't know, really. I just don't see Seth as the daddy type, do you?"

I grimaced. "Well, no, but you never know. This could be just what he needs to, you know, grow up and start acting more . . . responsible."

"You mean, start acting less like he's in love with you and more like he's an adult and married to Nora?"

"I wouldn't have used those exact words . . ."

Nora burst in through the door, her face flushed and sweating a little around the fringes.

"What's going on? Are you okay?" I asked. She started sifting through the bottles of liquor on the counter.

"I'm fine," she said, tugging on a big bottle of scotch.

"You're not going to drink that, are you? It can't be good for the baby," I said.

She came over and set the bottle down on the table in front of me, then grinned. "Of course I'm not going to drink it. Seth sent me in to get it. He wants a toast to celebrate."

"So he's happy about the . . . news?" Oscar asked. I almost punched him. But Nora pulled him into a big hug (apparently, she had gotten over her discomfort with being touched) and laughed.

"He's thrilled," she said. "I can hardly believe it myself. He's never happy about anything, is he? But this . . . I'm just so happy."

Oscar gave her shoulders a brotherly squeeze, then picked up the bottle of scotch, dug through the cabinets for some rocks glasses, and said, "Well, I might as well be the one to get this party started."

Before he ducked through the kitchen door, I called to him, "Oscar! Don't say anything to the parents yet. We want it to be a surprise."

"I would never think of ruining your big surprise. But you'd better get your butts out here soon. I can't speak for Seth." He breezed through the door and out of the kitchen.

I grabbed Nora's hand and the meat platter. "Let's go, Mommy."

She beamed at me. "Okay, Mommy."

So we went out and told our parents and they did what you would expect them to do. They hugged and kissed us and demanded to know when our due dates were and started to argue about what we should name these as-yet-unborn grandchildren. And finally, after Nora and I were ready to collapse from answering so many crazy questions, everybody put on their coats and went home.

Then Oscar and I piled the dirty dishes into the sink, ignoring all the soiled napkins, overflowing ashtrays, and chewed-up swizzle sticks, and went to bed, reciting ideas for baby names all the way up the stairs. I was partial to Edward for a boy or Susan for a girl, but Oscar was dead set on Emily for a girl and, for a boy, Horace—God what an awful name.

We play-argued for a little while, then we went to sleep, tucked in each other's arms. Sometime in the middle of the night, I had to pee, so I pried myself out from under Oscar's elbow and sneaked off to the bathroom. And that's when I realized I was bleeding and that, this time, I had really lost something.

13

HORACE

He closed the diary, set it down on his nightstand, and leaned back, closing his eyes. For the first time in his life, he pitied his mother. Although he had known she'd had some reproductive troubles, he had never realized the extent of it—that she had tried and failed and lost and suffered so much, just to give him life. It was a harsh reality to face, now that it occurred to him how badly he had treated her while she had been alive.

He sighed and sat up, checking his watch. If he didn't leave soon, he'd be late to meet Andrew at the bar, and he was already dying for a drink. In fact. . . . He got up, hurried downstairs to the kitchen, and poured himself a shot of vodka—not his favorite drink, but supposedly, it didn't have an odor, so Andrew wouldn't suspect that he'd already taken a nip before coming out for their "official" drink. Not that Andrew would notice—he drank almost as much as Horace. Maybe even more. It was the one thing they had in common, besides being part of the same screwed-up family.

When he walked into the darkened bar, his good eye took longer than usual to adjust to the lack of light, and he felt a rush of panic flow over him as he searched the crowd for his cousin. The bellowing sound of Andrew's voice brought him back from the brink of what he realized was an overreaction that had risen to near-terror. "Yo, cuz! Over here!"

Andrew, whose hand was raised high in the air with a thick glass full of dark brown liquid held tight in his fist, waved at Horace from the depths of a corner booth. He wasn't alone.

Horace stopped beside the table and laid a hand on Andrew's shoulder. "Andrew," he said. "Good to see you. Who are your friends?"

Andrew thrust his overfull glass in the direction of each of the two women who sat beside him in the half-circle of stuffed leather upholstery that made up the booth's seat. "Horace, meet Angela . . ."

"Andrea," the blonde on the left corrected, extending her hand toward Horace.

"Sorry, Angela," Andrew drawled. "And this is—hang on, I've got it—Karen."

The brunette let out a shrill giggle. "It's Corinne, you dope!" She reached out with wiggling fingers to tickle Andrew's chest through his slightly too-tight black T-shirt.

The blonde patted the seat beside her and said to Horace, "Do you want to sit down?"

Horace inclined his head in thanks and slid stiffly into the booth. A waitress appeared as if by magic and he ordered a gin and tonic and another white wine spritzer (*Christ, how '80s*, he thought) for Andrea. As they sat in awkward silence, waiting for their drinks to arrive, they cast sidelong glances at Andrew and Corinne, who were busy licking and playfully slapping one another, like teenagers on a sofa in the basement right after Mom and Dad have gone to bed.

Horace cleared his throat to try to break up the inappropriate display of affection. Andrew and Corinne both spun their heads to stare at him, their hands tangled in each other's clothing. Corinne planted a sloppy kiss on Andrew's cheek and said, "Andy, you didn't tell us your cousin was a pirate!"

Horace felt his cheeks drain pale, and he reached up to fidget with his eye patch. Mercifully, the waitress arrived with the drinks, giving him something to do besides sit and be stared at by the very drunk Corinne.

The girl's stupid comment sobered Andrew up just enough for him to realize that he should apologize. He shushed Corinne and, in what amounted to a stage whisper, said, "He's not a pirate, silly. He—um, well, he had an accident. It's a long story, and not a happy story, so I don't think he'll be telling it tonight."

Andrew flashed an apologetic look at Horace, who lifted his glass in acknowledgment and took a long sip. Andrew immediately turned back to Corinne and her tongue, leaving Horace and Andrea and their drinks to themselves.

Andrea smiled and shrugged. "So, what do you do for a living . . . Horace, is it? That's an unusual name."

"Unusual, yeah. Not a great name to have on the playground, I've got to tell you. It's enough to get your ass kicked every day at recess."

"Is there a story behind it?" Andrea asked, taking a tiny sip of her drink, so small that it almost looked like she was pretending to drink, as if she were a prostitute or a pickpocket trying to keep her wits about her while dealing with a potential client or victim.

"Supposedly, my father was big into Roman poetry, and named me after that Horace, but I don't know for sure."

"What do you mean? Do you think your dad was lying?"

"No," he said. "Nothing like that. It's just that my dad actually died before I was born, so I only ever heard the story from my mom. And she— well, let's just say she had a tendency to romanticize things."

Andrea nodded. "Understood. It's none of my business, anyway."

"I'm sorry. I didn't mean to sound like that. I'm not really trying to be private or anything. I guess—I guess I just don't feel like talking about my parents tonight. I've been too involved with them lately as it is."

Andrea looked at him out of the side of her eye, clearly wanting an explanation but wary of asking.

He felt himself relax a little, disarmed by her simple and honest interest in him. He smiled. "I must sound like a babbling idiot," he said. "Let me explain. My mom died a couple of weeks ago, and I've been going through all her old photo albums and diaries and stuff, so I feel like I've been surrounded by her and my dad over the last few days."

"I'm sorry about your mom," Andrea said.

He wanted to say that it was no big deal, to say he hadn't really been all that close to his mother anyway, but, after having read the last few diaries, he knew that wasn't true—not anymore. So he just said, "Thanks," and turned back to his drink.

From across the table, Horace heard Corinne break into a refrain of "A Pirate's Life for Me." Andrew frantically tried to cover her mouth with his own, then threw a sheepish grin in Horace's direction and called over, "Next round's on me, cuz. In fact, *all* your drinks are on me."

It was the closest Horace had ever heard Andrew come to a genuine apology, so he decided to ignore the drunken girl hanging off his cousin's tongue and try to enjoy the evening for what it was. Besides, Andrea was surprisingly attractive—much more so than Corinne, which made it all the more shocking that Andrew wasn't attempting to engage Andrea in a public sex act instead of her friend.

"Oh, shit," Horace breathed. It all suddenly seemed much too easy. Were they prostitutes? That would be just like Andrew. . . . Horace smiled weakly and took a big gulp of his drink before signaling the waitress to bring him another. Then he turned to Andrea, determined to figure out exactly what was going on here.

"So, what do you do, Andrea?"

She grinned. "You think I'm a hooker, don't you?"

He held up his hands. "It was just a thought. . . . I mean, knowing Andrew . . ."

"I don't know whether I should just be insulted or whether I should get up and throw a drink in your face."

"Is there a third option, I hope?"

She smiled. "In the third option I tell you that I'm a third-grade teacher and we move on as if nothing had happened."

The waitress set another drink before him and he seized it, clinking it gently against Andrea's wine glass. "I'm for option three."

Andrea nodded and said, "You still haven't told me what you do for a living."

"Technically, I have," Horace said.

"How's that?"

"I haven't said anything about what I do because, to be honest, I don't really do anything."

"So you're unemployed?"

Horace shrugged. "I don't know if that's the right term for it. Other than the years I was in the army, I've never really worked."

"Ah, I do love an independently wealthy man," Andrea said in a tone Horace couldn't quite identify. It was either irony or loathing.

"It was my parents who were the wealthy ones, not me," he said, hoping he sounded wistful and that it would convince her that he wasn't a sleazy, lazy playboy (which, in reality, he supposed he was).

"And what did they do? I assume *they* worked, right?" she asked.

He laughed. "Yeah, they worked. At least I know Mom did. She worked her ass off. After my dad died, she built the publishing company they started together into one of the most successful smaller houses in the country. And she did it all on the road."

"On the road? What do you mean?"

Horace felt his back stiffen. "Um . . . well, we moved around a lot."

"Your mom liked to travel, I guess?"

"Something like that. I don't know. I . . . I don't really want to talk about it." He cast a nervous look at her. "Do you mind if we talk about something else? And not pirates, please?"

Andrea glanced over at Corinne and Andrew and laughed. She turned back to Horace and said, "Do you want to get out of here? And I absolutely do *not* mean that the way it sounded."

"I'd love to. Let me just pull my moron of a cousin aside and tell him we're leaving."

Horace reached over and caught hold of Andrew's ear, twisting it until Andrew held up his hands in surrender and said, "Okay, okay, you got me. What?"

"Come with me for a minute, please."

They slid out of the booth and stood in the shadows behind a heavy pillar. "I'm leaving now. I just wanted to make sure you have a way to get home."

"I've got my truck," Andrew said, producing his keys from his pocket and jingling them in front of Horace's face as if he were trying to entertain a baby with a rattle.

Horace grabbed the keys and stuffed them into his own pocket. "No, you don't. And don't let that girl drive anywhere, either." He thrust a wad of money into Andrew's hand. "Take a cab."

"Thanks, Mom. But I think I can handle it." Andrew held his hand out, clearly expecting Horace to turn over the car keys.

"Not gonna happen, my friend."

"Seriously. What are you, my mother?"

"No, but your mother did tell me to watch out and make sure you didn't drink too much. Since I got here too late to do that, I can at least keep you from driving. Now, do I have to go and wrestle Corinne for her keys?"

From behind him, Andrea said, "No. I drove us here."

Horace nodded and turned back to Andrew. He slapped his cousin lightly on the cheek. "Have a good night, buddy."

As he and Andrea moved away, Andrew called out, "Fuck you, Horace! Fuck you."

Without looking back, Horace yelled, "Same to you, cuz. I'll talk to you tomorrow."

14

IRIS

We had Nora's baby shower today. I don't even know if I want to talk about it. I guess I have to. I guess I shouldn't break a twenty-year-old diary-writing streak over a little jealousy.

Okay, so maybe "a little jealousy" is an understatement. A huge understatement. I was so jealous as I helped her open that massive pile of gifts—all those cute little baby things wrapped up in paper with tiny blue and pink footprints on them—that I had to excuse myself to go to the bathroom and wet my face several times. I hope nobody noticed that by the end of the afternoon, my hair was soaked and I had no makeup left on. But then again, who would have been noticing me when Nora was there, with her giant round belly and her rosy cheeks, for everybody to gawk at?

Most of the people at the shower didn't know about my miscarriages. It's not the kind of thing you tell people, not even your friends—maybe only the very closest ones. And I don't really have any of those. I've got friends, sure, but none that I would freely discuss my reproductive woes with. I confine those awful discussions to the immediate family—Nora, Oscar, and my mom. Frankly, I wouldn't even include my mom if I had the choice, but she's so pushy about everything that it's impossible *not* to keep her informed. Besides, if I don't tell her, she's liable to go around talking about me and my weak uterus to random strangers in the line at the grocery store—that is, if she's not doing it already.

So, of course, all the women at the shower—all of them meaning well and trying to be friendly—kept coming up to me and saying things like "Tick tock" or "Is this giving you any ideas?" or "So, when are you and Oscar going to get down to business?" That's my favorite one, I think. No one is interested at all in our *actual* business, but when it comes to fucking each other without any birth control, everybody's on tenterhooks. Jeez, am I bitter. But seriously, no one has ever come running up to me to congratulate me on the success of one of my novels or the way our company has become such a well-respected little publishing house. That's of no interest at all. And that makes it even harder to believe all the crap that the women's libbers try to feed you: that creating something—like books, in my case—is just as worthwhile, if not more so, than creating babies. Nobody ever goes "goo goo ga ga" over a book. I wish they did. Maybe then I wouldn't have to spend half my life sobbing in bathrooms and the other half being prodded by gynecological specialists trying to ascertain what's wrong with me or with Oscar.

So, today, every now and then, Mom would lean over and rub my arm, as if that would help massage away the stab wounds that all her blue-haired friends had been inflicting on me throughout the day with their questions about my reproductive plans. Then again, I guess having them try to prod me into breeding is better than the alternative: having them pity me for being pathetic and barren.

Nora's been great about everything. She's tried throughout her entire pregnancy to talk about other things when she's with me. She never once told me to put my hand on her belly, to feel the baby kicking. She never dragged me out shopping for little outfits or bottles or nipples or whatever the hell else you need to buy when you're expecting (the kinds of things I'll most likely never have to shop for). But in a way, keeping me on the fringes of her pregnancy has made me feel unwanted, like she would prefer to have other people help her think up names or paint the room the baby's going to sleep in. As much as I appreciate her efforts to protect my feelings, in a way, I resent it, because at the heart of it, it's like a slap in the face—it's Nora saying to me, "You're not good enough, and I am." It's like, after all the years growing up, when I got the better grades and the better jobs and the better husband, she's finally found a way to win, and even though I'm sure she doesn't mean to be rubbing it in, the mere fact of her existence and the existence of her huge drum of a belly is a constant reminder that I am a terrible failure, to my family, to my husband, and to myself. Jesus, I'm crying again even now. Maybe I should ask the doctors to remove my tear ducts the next time they're beating the hell out of me. At least that would help solve *one* of my problems.

Oscar tried to make me feel better after I got home. He noticed right away what none of the women at the shower had seen—my haggard face and the fringe of damp hair. He knew what it meant. He's seen it plenty over the past several months.

"What happened?" he asked, wrapping his arms around me as I slouched into my chair at the kitchen table.

"What do you think? What *has* to happen these days?"

"Honey, you have to keep thinking positive. We're going to figure this out and by this time next year, you're going to be having your own baby shower."

"Yeah, right. I can't believe that anymore."

He kneeled in front of me and gripped my shoulders hard. "You need to believe it. If you can't believe it, then I can't, either, and I rely on you."

"Everybody relies on me. It isn't fair. Who am *I* supposed to rely on?"

"You can rely on me, and I can rely on you. That's what marriage is."

I shook my head. "That sounds all nice and everything, but there's a voice in my head that's yelling, 'Crock of shit! Crock of shit!'"

"Nice attitude. That kind of thinking isn't getting you anywhere. Didn't your doctor say it helps to think positive?"

"Jesus, honey, it's hard to keep thinking positive after everything I've been through."

"I've been through it, too, you know," he said, his voice so soft that I knew I had really offended him.

I sighed. "I didn't mean to say you haven't. I'm sorry. I just feel like crap. I don't mean to take it out on you." I pushed away from him and went over to the counter to grab a handful of napkins to dab at my already-swollen eyes.

"I know. And I'm sorry you had to go through that. But I need you to try to have a better attitude. You've got to envision good things happening if you want them to happen. So just keep telling yourself that by this time next year, you'll be coming home from your own baby shower."

I let out a sarcastic laugh. "This time next year, I could be dead. You could be dead. We could be divorced. Anything can happen."

He stared at me for a long moment, his face a blank mask, and then he turned and walked out. Before I could even catch up with him, he had stormed out the front door and was jumping into his car.

"Shit," I whispered. I watched him go, but didn't try to stop him. I knew it wouldn't help. It was better to let him go for a drive and be angry for a while and then come home. By then, he'd have somehow twisted everything around so that he'd be convinced that the fight had been his fault. I don't know how he does it, but he always does. In the end, I'm never wrong—no matter how wrong I actually am.

So I went back into the kitchen, picked up my wad of moist napkins, and walked into my little office, the tiny room that probably was meant to be a mud closet, a place to take off your dirty shoes before coming into the house, but had become my writing room. Even though I have a real office in a fancy executive building, I still like to do a good chunk of my writing in that room. There's something sentimental about going back to the place where it all started, where I used to sit by the light of a couple of candles and dream of being a writer. I always feel like the writing I do there, in that little room by myself, away from the hustle and bustle of the "real" publishing world, is more honest, more heartfelt, and more innocent in some way. I'm always prouder of what I write at the rickety desk in that room than anything I pound out on my brand-new electric typewriter. In that room, I'm a real writer, not the hack I feel like I've become now that I'm a "professional."

I sat down at the desk and started scribbling random thoughts in a notebook, disconnected thoughts that nonetheless had me bawling within just a few seconds. All I could think about was the fact that I had spent the entire day surrounded by family and friends at Nora's shower, and yet I had never felt lonelier in my life. I kept looking around at the faces of the people sitting around that big U-shaped banquet table. There were old friends of the family—my mom's friends, women who had watched us grow up—and then there were our friends, many of them the daughters of my mom's friends—two generations clamped together by mutual experiences and intertwined relationships. And all of them—every last one—has kids. Except me.

And when people have kids, that's all they ever talk about. So I had to sit there, me and my broken uterus, and listen to it all—how this one's son is learning to walk and how that one's daughter is starting preschool. And what I felt wasn't sadness exactly. It was something different. It was the oddest sensation, like everyone else at that party was moving forward, and I was being left behind. And when I think about it now, it's true. I'm in precisely the same place in my life that I was in five years ago, or even ten years ago. I'm with Oscar, I'm living here in the same town where we both grew up, and I'm writing. That's it. No real progress whatsoever. Meanwhile, everybody else is moving fast and furious. And it all comes down to having kids. Without them, life is just living. Sure, you can have good times and you can even have success, but you can't really claim to have *done* something with your life, can you? Maybe that's a terrible thing to say or even to think. I'm sure there are plenty of people out there who do wonderful things, worthwhile things, even if they don't raise a family. There are people like Mother Teresa who serve others and take care of the poor and make life better for people who have no other source of comfort. But those people are the exceptions, the saints among us. When it comes to the ordinary folks like me, having a baby is the only way to make a difference. At least, that's how everybody makes me feel.

15

HORACE

Andrea sat down at the kitchen table and stared out into the blackness beyond the window. Horace yanked open the door to the liquor cabinet and she turned.

"Wow," she said. "You must drink a lot of gin . . . or hardly any, with all those bottles of it."

Horace cringed and started to close the door, then realized he had no reason to hide anything from this woman, who was nothing more than a stranger—a pretty girl who was an excellent prospect for a one-night stand. He pulled out a bottle of gin and reached for a glass.

"You were right with your first guess," he said, lifting his glass in a silent toast and then taking a long sip.

Andrea stood up, came over, and pushed past him, letting her body linger against his just a moment too long. She picked up another glass and poured some gin for herself. She took a sip without flinching at the taste and smiled at him. "Well, at least you don't drink as much as your cousin. I think Andrew was plowed before he even got to the bar."

"I don't doubt it," Horace said. He gestured for her to move past him into the living room, and they settled onto one of the leather couches, the one that faced the dark, cold fireplace.

"Of course," Horace said. "It's debatable whether I drink less than Andrew or not. I think I can hold my own."

Andrea stared at him. "Maybe I shouldn't have let you drive me here. So, tell me. Why do you drink so much?"

"I don't know."

"Sure you do."

"What makes you say that?"

She shrugged and took a sip from her glass. "Everybody knows why they do everything. They just don't like to admit it."

"Is that so? Then can I ask you a question?"

"Why not?"

"Why did you come home with me?"

She laughed. "I don't know."

"Yes, you do."

She looked away, gazing at the fireplace as she took another gulp from her drink. "I thought you were interesting."

"Interesting? That's not one I hear often."

She looked back at him. "What *do* you hear often?"

"Oh, lots of things. Sad. Tortured. Rich. Scary."

"What kind of woman would go home with you if she thought you were scary?"

"You'd be surprised."

Andrea drained the last of her gin and set the glass down on the end table. She shifted toward him and leaned her head against the back of the sofa. "*Are* you scary?"

Horace put his glass down on the floor beside his feet and slid toward her, pressing his palm against the nape of her neck, under her hair, and pulling her to him. "You tell me."

He kissed her hard, not waiting for her lips to soften under his before grasping her around the waist with his other hand and pushing her down on the couch as he stretched out on top of her. He ran the tip of his tongue along her neck, pausing to try to open the delicate pearl-shaped buttons of her blouse, which made him feel as bulky and uncoordinated as a yeti. He let her hair loose and used both hands to tear open her blouse, the buttons popping and flying through the air. She gasped and stared into his eyes with an expression that looked like terror.

"Are you scared now?" he asked.

She narrowed her eyes, then smiled as she reached down and tugged his zipper down, letting his dick burst through the hole in his boxer shorts. She wrapped her fingers around it and squeezed. Now it was his turn to gasp and she laughed.

"You don't scare me at all," she said. She flicked her tongue along the ridge of his front teeth, then bit down hard on his lower lip.

He leaned down, trying to kiss her again, but she laid her palm against his chest and stopped him.

"What?" he asked. "What's wrong?"

"Show it to me," she said.

He glanced down at his penis, still cupped tightly in her hand, and laughed. "I think you've seen it," he said.

"No. Not that. You know what I want to see."

He reached up and touched his eye patch with the tips of his fingers. Something inside him went cold, and he yanked away from her.

"What's the matter?" she asked. "I want to see."

"No, you don't."

"Yes, I do."

"Well, you can't." He shoved her hand away and tugged at his zipper.

She pulled back and leaned against the arm of the sofa. "What's wrong? I didn't mean to upset you."

Horace stood up and ran his fingers over his fly to make sure the zipper was closed. "I'm not upset. I'm just tired."

Andrea frowned. "Shit. I'm sorry. I don't know what the hell I was thinking . . ."

"Come on," Horace said. "I'll drive you home."

She leapt up from the couch and took hold of his hands. "Hey, come on. We can still salvage this evening, can't we? Here. How's this?" She leaned forward and kissed him, letting the tip of her tongue dance along the seam of his pursed lips, seeking a point of entry. He put his hands on her shoulders and backed away from her.

"Maybe some other time," he said.

Her face fell, but she nodded and pushed past him to pick up her purse from where it lay on the floor beside the couch. "Okay," she said. "I can take a hint. Just let me call a cab."

"I'll drive you."

She shook her head. "No, thanks," she said. "I'd rather not ride in a car with someone who hates me so much."

Horace sighed. "I don't hate you . . . ugh. This is ridiculous. Here. Here! Have a good look!"

He tore the eye patch off his face and hurled it to the ground, exposing his sunken, empty eye socket. Andrea gasped, but he couldn't tell whether she was horrified at his disfigurement or just surprised at how quickly he had changed his mind about letting her see it.

Her shoulders heaved once as she sucked in a long, hard breath. Then she visibly relaxed as she came toward him. She held the back of his head with her fingertips and brought his face down toward hers. Then she stood on her toes and brushed her lips across the puckered eyelid.

A shiver ran through him. He felt a hot lump form in the back of his throat and tears spring to his eye. He kept his gaze down, avoiding meeting hers. She laid her palm on his cheek and kissed him on the cheek.

"Thank you," she said.

He laughed. "I've never had anyone thank me for exposing my hideous eye."

"Maybe you've been hanging around with the wrong kind of people," she said.

He smiled and leaned down to press a tentative kiss on her lips. "Maybe you're right."

She kissed him back, using the tips of her manicured fingers to work open the buttons on his shirt and gently pulling him backward. "Where's the bedroom?" she asked.

"Allow me," he said, hefting her up so her legs were wrapped around his waist and carrying her to the stairs. Her hands were sliding beneath the waistband of his pants as he navigated the staircase and made his way to the bedroom to lay her on the bed. She kept her legs wrapped around him as she pushed his shirt down over his shoulders. He shrugged out of it and pressed down against her, nipping her along the neck and pulling down the cups of her bra to expose her breasts. As he took her nipple between his teeth, she let out a soft gasp. Her eyes locked with his and she smiled. Hooking her fingers in his belt loops, she yanked his pants down around his waist, exposing his penis. She reached down and lifted her own skirt, revealing smooth skin not covered by panties.

"Allow me," she whispered, guiding him inside her. As Horace began to rock against her, feeling her tremble beneath him, it occurred to him that this was the first time in his life that sex had felt at all like something you might refer to as "making love." He wondered whether this was what his parents had experienced, if this was why his mother had remained so devoted to his father even decades after his death. Maybe this was what it was all about.

16

IRIS

Nora had her baby today. It's a boy. They named him Andrew. Kind of dull, I think, but then, it's not my kid. Besides, it's better than Horace, which is what Oscar is still determined to name our baby, if we ever get lucky enough to have one. I keep trying to tell him that what sounded good in ancient Rome doesn't necessarily translate into a great name in twentieth-century America. But we've come to an agreement. If we have a girl, I get to name her; if it's a boy, Oscar gets to do the honors. Now I just have to cross my fingers and hope we get a girl. God, I'm being so stupid. I should be crossing my fingers that we get anything at all.

Nora went into labor around ten-thirty last night. Seth, predictably, wasn't home, so she called me and begged me to take her to the hospital. Oscar and I crawled out of bed and threw on jeans and T-shirts and drove over to pick her up. I was really kind of hoping that Seth would have shown up by the time we got there, but of course he hadn't. And worse, Nora didn't even know where the hell he was. Not that she ever does.

She was crying when we walked in, hugging her huge belly and rocking herself back and forth like a little kid or an idiot savant.

"What's the matter? Are you in pain?" I asked. Realizing what a stupid question that was, I followed up with, "I mean, unexpected pain?"

Nora just turned to me with her bleeding eyes, the tip of her nose as round and red as a cherry, and sobbed, "Where *is* he?"

Oscar flashed me a look and handed me the keys to the car. "Here," he said. "You take her over to the hospital. I'll get Seth and we'll be right behind you."

I leaned over and whispered in his ear, "Do you have any idea where he is?"

"Unfortunately, yes."

My teeth clenched, but I threw a smile on my face and turned to Nora. "Come on, sweetie. It's baby time."

I don't think Nora even noticed that Oscar wasn't with us as I bundled her into the passenger seat and took off in the direction of the hospital. Of course, she was crying so hard and moaning about Seth not being there, it's possible she didn't even notice that *I* was there. I didn't bother trying to talk her down or make her feel better. It just didn't seem worth the effort.

By the time we had her registered and settled into her room at the hospital, Mom was there, with Oscar and Seth's mom, and they were pretty much taking over everything. Between the two of them barking out orders at the nurses and force-feeding Nora ice chips, I think Nora actually forgot for a while that Seth was missing. And by the time they were wheeling her into the delivery room, sometime in the middle of the night, Oscar came running down the hallway, announcing to anyone within range of his bouncing voice, "Seth is on the way!"

Nora stopped her annoying childbirth-style breathing and turned to look at Oscar. "Where is he?"

Oscar slid to a stop, his sneakers squeaking on the shiny floor. "He—uh, he had to hit the rest room."

Nora sighed and let herself fall limp against the raised back of the rolling bed. "Thank God. Okay, then, I'm ready to go."

The orderlies wheeled her through the swinging doors to the delivery wing. Then I grabbed Oscar's hand. "Where is he, really?" I asked.

He rolled his eyes. "He wanted a Chunky bar, so he stopped at the gift shop."

"Oh, for God's sake. Did you at least tell him to buy something for Nora and the baby while he's down there?"

Oscar shrugged. "What would be the use?"

The door to the staircase burst open and Seth popped into the hallway, his fist jammed up against his mouth as he gnawed on the corner of his candy bar. He didn't bother to stop chewing as he asked, "So where'd they take her?"

I wanted to rip the fucking Chunky bar out of his hand, but I managed to restrain myself. "Where do you *think*? They went to the delivery room. Get your ass in there."

He stopped as he moved past me to brush a kiss onto my cheek. "On my way, beautiful."

With a last wink in my general direction, he disappeared through the doors and Oscar and I were left alone with our frantic, buzzing mothers to wait for the baby to come.

Finally, sometime around four A.M., Seth came wandering casually out from the delivery room, munching on another goddamn Chunky. He flopped down in one of the ugly orange chairs, across from me and Oscar, and laid one of his legs over the other as he sat there, not saying a word, licking his stupid, chocolate-covered fingers.

We all sat there, dumbfounded, not knowing what the hell to say. Normally, you expect the father of the newborn child to come running out with cigars for everyone, happily declaring whether the baby is a boy or a girl and providing a report on how the new mother is doing. Not Seth. He just sat there, obviously enjoying the fact that we were dying to know whatever it was he already knew.

It was my mom who finally said, "Well?!"

Seth looked up, his face blank, as if he were surprised to notice that there were other people in the room. He pulled himself up to a somewhat straighter sitting position, smiled, and said, "Oh. It's a boy."

The new grandmothers jumped up and started hugging each other as they danced around the waiting room.

"And how's Nora doing?" I asked, careful not to get overexcited like Mom and Mrs. Cairo were doing, just in case. That's the worrier in me; it's always ready to spring to life.

Seth shrugged. "She's fine, I guess. I think she's sleeping."

"Nice," Oscar muttered to me. Louder, he said, "Can we see her? Or the baby?"

Seth sighed like he was annoyed. "What am I, the doctor? I guess you can see her. Do what you want."

Oscar crossed over to Seth in one stride and grabbed him by the collar of his shirt, lifting him all the way up to his tiptoes. "Listen up, little man," he said. "You're going to wipe that smug look off your face and then you're going to go over to that nurse's desk and find out exactly what we can do and who we can see. And I mean now."

He released Seth, who stumbled and fell back into his chair, staring up at Oscar with a look on his face that I can only describe as pure hatred. The two of them were just locked there, glaring at each other, their faces glowing red and tinged with angry sweat. Reluctantly, I decided I had better step in and try to defuse the situation before they came to blows.

I slid past Oscar, using my stiff, extended arm to try to push him back toward the couch we'd been sitting on. I laid my other arm around Seth's shoulders and touched his forehead with my own. Instantly, he went limp and a smile broke across his face.

"Seth, sweetie, come on. Go and find out if we can all go see Nora. And your new son. Okay?"

He looked almost drugged as he grinned at me. He nodded slowly, looking dazed, then turned and walked away to talk to the nurse.

"Nicely done," Oscar said. He was scowling, though, so I wasn't sure if he was actually glad I had stepped in or not.

The grandmothers had stopped dancing and were now watching the rest of us in paralyzed silence. Sometimes it seemed like they were a little bit afraid of the "boys," as they always called Oscar and Seth. Despite all the fights and tension, it never really occurred to me that the two brothers would ever actually hurt one another. It seems odd to me that anybody would believe that. All siblings fight. It comes with the territory.

So, anyway, we got to go into the room and see Nora, who was awake but tired, and beaming brightly, now that she had Seth (and her baby) at her side. We all sat around, passing the baby from one set of arms to the next, and gushing over how beautiful he was. And he is. I admit it. And I can even say that now without bursting into tears. I'm happy for Nora. She deserves to have a gorgeous, healthy baby. I just wish I did, too. *Had* one, I mean, not deserve one. Or maybe I *do* mean I wish I deserved one. . . .

After the nurses finally kicked us out, Mom and Mrs. Cairo drove me home so I could lie down and get some rest. Even though we hadn't really been needed, at least not technically, Oscar and I had stayed up all night at the hospital, so I was exhausted. And everybody's always trying to get me to rest more, as if my ovaries are just tired and that's why I can't get pregnant.

Oscar said he was too wired to sleep, so he said he was going to take Seth out for a celebratory drink. It was only ten in the morning, but I didn't say anything. I figured he wanted to talk to Seth in private, so I didn't want to interfere. Besides, I assumed that if anybody could get through to Seth and get him to stop being such an ass toward Nora, it was Oscar. As much as Seth is always acting like he's trying to come on to me, it's obvious that deep down—maybe *very* deep down—he has a lot of respect for Oscar.

And I was right. When Oscar got home in the late afternoon, looking all bedraggled, with a day's growth of beard and the most stereotypical circles under the eyes I'd ever seen, he seemed pleased with the way his conversation with Seth had gone. He told me he had taken Seth over to this dingy little neighborhood bar, a place called Jack's Tavern. Set into the corner of a really old-looking strip mall, it was kind of a scary place. I'd only ventured in there once, curious about it, because the guys we went to high school with were always talking about going there to play pool since they never got carded. I sat there with my friend Kelly and drank a Bud faster than I'd ever drunk anything before, and then the two of us got out of there even faster, before anyone had a chance to try to talk to us. But I guess the place probably wouldn't seem as scary to Oscar or Seth. Bars are always friendlier places for men than for women, I think.

"I asked him what he was planning to do to support his wife and child," Oscar told me.

"Wow," I said. "What brought that on?"

"You mean, other than the fact that he hasn't worked a day in his life?"

"Well, yeah. Why bring it up now?"

Oscar shrugged and flung himself onto the couch beside me. "I guess I just don't want to be the one who ends up taking care of Seth and his entire family."

I patted his thigh. "Don't be silly. They'd never ask us for money."

He laughed. "That's what *you* think. He's already borrowed money from me a bunch of times."

"Are you kidding? Why wouldn't you tell me something like that? It's my money, too."

"I didn't think it was a big deal. It was only a couple grand. It's not like we can't afford it." He picked up my hand and squeezed it. "Speaking of which, I was thinking, maybe we ought to look into getting a place in the city. It might be a good idea to be closer to the action, so to speak. I mean, come on. How many big-name publishers are located in New Jersey?"

"No way," I said. "I love New York, but I'm not living there. Not gonna happen. You can't ask a Jersey girl to move out of Jersey. That's like—like asking a Canadian not to watch hockey. Or asking someone from West Virginia not to marry their cousin."

"Come on. It would be great. We could get a big apartment with a nice view. And we could walk to the office. No more New Jersey Transit."

Now I was really getting upset. "I *like* New Jersey Transit. I like the way there's always hot air blowing from some vent you can't find, and the way the train always smells like pee and hot pretzels. I wouldn't give up that commute for anything."

Oscar shook his head. "You're crazy."

"Maybe so. But that's something we can talk about some other time. I want to hear what Seth said."

"All right, all right. We can talk about moving another time."

He sat there, looking at his fingernails and deliberately driving me crazy because he knew I was dying to hear what he and Seth had talked about.

"Come on!"

He smiled. "Okay," he said. "This is good, actually. You're gonna like this story."

"Oscar, so help me God, if you ever want to have sex again, you'd better tell me what happened."

"Okay, okay. He actually has a business idea. He's planning to open up a . . . well, like a mini-spa—one of those places with the special beds so people can get a tan any time of year."

"Huh," I said. "And where's he getting the money for that?"

Oscar made what I can only describe as a sheepish face.

"Oh, great. *We're* giving him the money?" I said.

"It's only a few thousand, and besides, you can look at it as buying security for your new godson."

I smiled. "They haven't asked me to be godmother."

"Not yet, but they will. Seth even mentioned it to me. We're the godparents. Then again, who else would they ask? Nora's so shy, she barely has a friend in the world. And Seth? Well, he's just an asshole."

"True enough," I said.

"I think this is a good thing for Seth. I mean, think about what kind of people go to a place like that. Mostly young, attractive women, I would guess. So he'll enjoy himself and make some money at the same time. It's really a perfect setup."

"Not for Nora," I said.

"Well, let's try not to think about that aspect of it. He's already trying to find a location. He wants to get the place open by Christmas."

"Ambition. It looks strange on Seth."

"Let's just be happy he's finally getting a job. Now, how about that sex?"

Sometimes Oscar can be a real pain in the ass.

17

HORACE

| P R E S E N T   D A Y |

The telephone rang and Horace moaned. Not opening his eyes, he slammed his hand along the edge of the nightstand, trying to find the phone. He finally grabbed hold of it and put it to his ear. Before he could even say hello, the voice on the other end hollered, "You asshole!"

Horace sighed. "Good morning, Andrew."

"Good morning, my ass. I had to spend the night at that chick's house. The whole fucking night, and it's all because you wouldn't give me my god-damn keys."

"It seems like you made it home all right, though, huh?"

"Not even. I had to spend the night at that skank's place—that Karen."

"Corinne."

"What?"

"Her name was Corinne."

Andrew made a loud huffing sound. "Karen, Corinne. One name is the same as another when a chick is a lousy lay."

Horace dragged himself up to a sitting position and rubbed his palm over his face, realizing he wasn't wearing his eye patch and taking a quick scan of the bedroom to try to find it. He suddenly remembered that he had left it downstairs, on the floor, where he had flung it last night. And then he realized that his eye patch wasn't the only thing not with him. Andrea was gone, too.

"Andrew, what do you want?"

"I want my fucking keys, man."

"Of course you do. All right. I have to shower, but I'll come by as soon as I'm up and about."

"I'm not home, you retard," Andrew said. "I'm still at Karen's. Fuck the shower. You have to come and get me *now*."

"You're still there? I thought you said she was a lousy . . . never mind. What did you stay there for?"

"Because you took my fucking keys."

"Yeah, I did, and I gave you cab money, too. Why didn't you use that to get home?"

"Uggh!" Andrew cried. "Because I needed it to pay Karen!"

"Pay her for what?"

"Good God, man, what do you think?"

"Wait, wait, wait. Karen's a hooker? . . . I mean, Corinne?"

"Well, duh."

Horace felt his throat close up. He managed to choke out, "But Andrea's not. . . . Is she?"

"Did you have a lobectomy or something?"

"You mean lobotomy. And no. Andrea told me she was a teacher."

"Yeah, well, I told Karen I was an astronaut. That don't make it true, buddy."

Horace got out of bed, feeling his heart flutter with panic. It wasn't like he hadn't slept with prostitutes before, but if Andrea had been a hooker, then everything that had happened last night had been an illusion. No, not an illusion—a betrayal.

He sucked in a long breath and let it out through clenched teeth. "Okay, Andrew. Just give me the address and I'll leave right now."

He scrawled the address on a scrap of paper he found on the nightstand, then pulled on a pair of shorts. Trying to ignore the screeching alarm of panic that was going off in his brain, he trotted down the stairs and went to the living room to search for his eye patch. His cheeks flushed with shame at the mere thought that he had bared his eye, bared his *soul*, to a prostitute. He had never felt so stupid.

As he adjusted the patch over his eye, he heard a rattling sound coming from the kitchen. Too angry to be afraid, he poked his head around the corner and realized that he was not the least bit surprised to see Andrea there, standing at the stove wearing her wrinkled, buttonless blouse from the night before and a pair of his sweatpants, which were bulged up around her ankles, almost entirely covering her bare feet.

She turned when she heard him come in, a spatula in her hand. "Good morning! I'm making you breakfast. Did you know you only had two eggs?"

Horace coughed. He was so confused and uncomfortable, he hardly knew what to do. "I thought you had left."

She smiled before she turned back to the pan on the stove in which she was frying the two sad, lonely eggs. "Not my style, sweetheart."

"Umm. Uh. So, uh, what do I owe you?"

"For breakfast? Nothing. It's your stuff. Don't be silly."

Horace slid into a chair at the table and fiddled with a hangnail on one of his thumbs. "No, I mean, um, you know, for last night."

She put the spatula down beside the stove and turned slowly to face him. "What the hell are you talking about?"

He looked up, saw that she was staring at him with steely eyes, and looked back down at his fingers. "I mean, I appreciate breakfast and every-thing, but I want to settle up."

Without turning around, she switched off the stove with her fingers, then crossed her arms over her chest. Her words were clipped and precise. "Do you still think I'm a prostitute?"

"Well, you know, Andrew said . . ."

"Oh, *Andrew* said. Well. That makes all the difference. He's obviously very wise."

Horace felt something break open in his chest and suddenly he felt light and airy, no longer crushed beneath the weight of the humiliation of thinking he had fallen in love with a hooker. "So, you're . . . you're not a . . . well, you know?"

Her eyes narrowed. "No. I am not. And if I recall correctly, I told you last night that I was a teacher. I just took the day off today. Why would you even consider listening to Andrew about something like that when I already told you the truth?"

Horace bit his lip. "Well, he's my cousin. And he said that Corinne . . ."

She laughed. It sounded hard and bitter. "Corinne is a legal secretary."

Horace burst out laughing. "You've got to be shitting me. Why does Andrew think she's a hooker?"

"Maybe because he's a moron?"

Horace shook his head. "God, Andrea. I'm so sorry. I don't know what I was thinking."

She stared down at the floor. "Well."

He got up and went over to her, trying to decide whether he should put his arms around her or not. A tingle of fear inside him told him that she would shun him if he tried.

"Andrea, really. I'm so sorry. I don't even know what to say."

She threw up her hands. "Neither do I. But I guess it's time for me to leave."

She started to brush past him, but he moved to stop her. "Come on, you don't have to leave."

"I think it's best. I'm so angry right now. You don't want me here, trust me."

"Please, don't go."

"I have to," she said.

"Okay, okay, then let me drive you home. I have to go over and bring Andrew his keys, so I have to go out anyway."

"I'd rather call a cab, to tell you the truth. Dammit. I knew I should have driven myself here last night."

"But—I want to talk to you. I need to apologize . . ."

"Look, if you have even the remotest thought of seeing me again, you'd be better off letting me call the cab. Maybe if I cool off I'll be willing to consider seeing you another time. But trust me. If I let you drive me home, you'll have blown it by the time you pull out of your own driveway."

Horace sighed. "All right, if that's what you think." He dug into his pocket and pulled out his wallet. "At least let me give you money for the cab."

"Great. Why don't you leave it on the nightstand and I'll take it on my way out?"

"Oh, God, I didn't mean it like that. Christ, I really am fucking this up."

She smiled and her face seemed to soften. "That's the understatement of the year." She shook her head and moved over to him, laying her palms against his shirt. "I like you better when you're scared."

He heard his voice shake as he said softly, "I was never so scared in my life as when I thought you were a hooker . . . I mean, when I thought, you know, that I'd never see you again."

She leaned over and kissed him. "Honesty. That's a start. Now, why don't I get dressed and call that cab so you can get out of here?"

"Leave your number, okay? I'll call you later today."

"Sure, okay. Now go."

She patted him on the chest and turned to hurry up the stairs and get dressed. He stood there in the kitchen, staring blindly at the half-cooked eggs on the stove, and wondering whether the fact that he wanted to run up the stairs and pin her down on the bed before she could get out of his sweatpants made him a pervert. He tugged off a piece of egg white and nibbled at it while he strained to listen to Andrea moving around upstairs. When she came down, she had her jacket zipped tightly over her gaping blouse, apparently trying to hide her semi-nakedness well enough to face a cab driver.

"I called a cab," she said. "Go get Andrew. I'll wait outside on the porch, if you want."

He smiled. "What, do you think I think you're going to rob me? You can stay in the house."

"Nope, I'll be outside. We're not quite there yet."

"Where?"

"At the point where I feel comfortable sitting around in your house when you're not here. Hell, I don't really feel all that comfortable in your house when you *are* here. So go see Andrew. And call me later." She kissed him and popped out the front door.

He picked up his keys off the table in the foyer where he had tossed them the night before and followed her outside, pulling the door closed behind him. "You're a strange girl, do you know that?"

He leaned down and kissed her, quickly and tentatively. She smacked her lips. "Yup. I know it," she said. She sat down on the step, looking beautiful with her disheveled hair, her wrinkled and ruined silk blouse, her black blazer, and her slim black skirt that was too dark against her pale, bare legs. She gave him a little wave as he climbed into his car.

As he pulled the door closed behind him, he thought he heard her humming. There was definitely something about her. But he would think about that another time. For now, he had to deal with Andrew.

When he finally pulled up in front of the townhouse complex where Corinne apparently lived, Andrew was lounging against the hood of a little black Audi. He smiled and spread his arms wide as Horace cruised to a stop.

"My cousin is a stand-up guy," Andrew said, hopping into the car. "Saving me from the embarrassment of having breakfast with a prostitute."

Horace took a deep breath as he thought about whether to bother explaining to Andrew that he was wrong about Corinne and that he had just paid to have sex with a legal secretary. It seemed almost poetic enough to be worth the effort, but he decided to keep his mouth shut. Andrew would never believe it anyway.

"So, cuz, let me take you out for a drink as a thank-you."

Horace glanced at his watch. "It's eleven in the morning. Besides, shouldn't you be at work?"

Andrew grinned. "Nope. Not me. I quit."

"You quit your job? When?"

"Oh, well, I didn't actually go in and *say* I was quitting. I figured they'd just figure it out once I didn't show up for a few days."

"Tell me again, what was the job this time?"

"Market research."

"Ah," Horace said. "Telemarketing. An honorable profession."

Andrew turned to look out the window. "Look who's talking."

"You forget," Horace said. "I'm the family screw-up. The good-for-nothing. The black sheep. You—you're supposed to be the *good* kid."

Andrew shrugged. "Your way seems like a lot more fun."

"You'd think so, wouldn't you?"

He noticed Andrew's puzzled expression out of the corner of his eye, but chose to remain quiet and just wait Andrew out. It never took long for Andrew to jump in and fill a silence—whether it was an uncomfortable silence or not.

"So, how about that drink? We have to go to the bar anyway, since that's where I left my car."

Horace shook his head. "I promised your mom I wouldn't let you drink so much."

"You? *You* promised? Who the hell are you to say I drink too much?"

"Look," Horace said. "I don't give a shit how much you drink, but I don't want a drink, so I'll just drop you off at your car and we'll leave it at that."

Andrew laughed. "I'll *bet* you don't want a drink."

"What's that supposed to mean?" Horace asked, even though he already knew the answer.

"You're the biggest drunk I know, that's what it means."

"Yeah, well, at least I didn't pay a girl who is *not* a hooker for sex."

Andrew wrinkled his brow. "That Karen was definitely a hooker. She took the money, didn't she?"

"That doesn't mean she's a hooker. I'd bet most women think they deserve to be paid after spending the night with you. I don't even have to have sex with you to feel like I deserve some cash for keeping your sorry ass company."

"Pull over. I'll get out here."

Horace chuckled. "Oooh, what a martyr. The freaking bar is fifty yards ahead. Please, *please*, let me drive you the whole way."

"Just pull over, asshole."

"Fine." Horace slammed on the brakes and smiled at the screeching sound the tires made. "I'll see you when I see you."

"That won't be anytime soon, I promise you that." Andrew slid out of the car and slammed the door shut behind him.

Horace fought off a grin as he sat at the side of the road watching Andrew plod along, pouting, toward the bar. Horace let the car idle, cruising along right beside his cousin. He couldn't stop himself from rolling down the window and making matters worse.

"This ought to qualify as your exercise for the day, Andrew," he called.

Andrew flipped him off without turning around.

"Okay, then," Horace said. "It's been great talking to you, cuz. And make sure you tell your mom that I made sure you didn't drive home drunk."

"Fuck you," Andrew muttered.

Horace bit his lip and gunned the engine, wishing as he sped away that there had been some gravel the car could have kicked up to smack Andrew in the face.

18

IRIS

| DECEMBER 26, 1979 |

The Newark Star-Ledger
December 26, 1979
Publishing CEO Goes Missing

> *Oscar Cairo, CEO of the independent publishing house Cairo Books, was reported missing on Christmas morning by his wife and business partner, Iris Cairo. The last person believed to have seen Cairo was his brother, Seth, who said Cairo attended the December 24 opening of Seth Cairo's new salon, Cairo Tans, a tanning and spa facility. The Cairo family is offering a $100,000 reward for information leading to the safe return of Oscar Cairo.*

I can't believe I'm writing this. I can't believe any of this can really be happening. On Christmas Eve, in the afternoon, we all went over to Seth's new tanning salon. Seth was having a big grand opening slash Christmas bash, and the whole family showed up to support him. We all felt like we had to be there, considering that this is pretty much Seth's first job ever.

Oh, God, what the hell am I doing, babbling on about Seth and his stupid party? Oscar's gone. Just gone. He kissed me good-bye as I was leaving the party at the tanning salon and said he'd be right behind me. And that was the last I heard from him. No phone call, no anything. How can this be happening? Christ, I don't even know if he's all right. Did he leave me? Did he just randomly decide he doesn't want to be with me anymore? On Christmas FUCKING Eve? Is he hurt? I called every hospital within a 300-mile radius, and no one has seen him. Nobody even has a John Doe waiting to be claimed by his family. I even checked with the morgues and funeral homes, and nothing. At this point, I'm so crazed, I'd almost rather have someone show up with a body, just so I don't have to wonder anymore.

Did I really just say that? My God, I'm losing my mind. And it doesn't help that both of our moms have been here the whole time, driving me even crazier than I already am. And Nora is here, with little Andrew wailing constantly. Yeah, a colicky baby is the perfect addition to my nightmare.

And Seth. He's here, too, and he's hardly bothering to try to hide the fact that he's almost pleased that we don't know where Oscar is. He keeps coming over and trying to hug me, but it's not a brotherly hug and I'm not stupid. We don't even know where Oscar is and he's trying to move in on me. I always knew there was something a little off about him, but I never thought he'd be this tacky. Is tacky even the right word? It's more than tacky. It's sick. Inhumane. Cruel. Despicable.

The police have been here, too, drinking my coffee and eating my Christmas cookies—the ones that I never got to set out for my guests, because there were no guests, other than the family and the cops. I'm surrounded by people on all sides, loud people, people who are on the phone or on radios or wandering around with those walkie-talkie things, and I've never been so lonely. Oscar should be here with me, laughing at it all. He'd crack up at the fat sergeant who seems to be running the show. This guy has a white mustache—but it's not a mustache; it's powdered sugar. He just eats those miniature white powdered donuts all day (what a stereotype!), and he never notices that he's got the sugar all over his face. And no one tells him, because they're all laughing about it behind his back. They're actually laughing in my house, while they're supposed to be trying to find my husband.

Oh my God, what if he's dead? I shouldn't even think about that. But I can't help it. It's out there. Especially now that it's been two whole days. Oscar has never been able to stay away from me for two hours, much less two days. I know there is something horribly wrong if he hasn't even tried to contact me. So then I start thinking he's dead. Lying in a ditch somewhere or, God help me, weighted down in the Passaic River, the accidental victim of a misplaced mob hit.

Or maybe he left me. I would never have thought it was possible, but then, I never thought any of this was possible. Is it crazy of me to be hoping that he just doesn't love me anymore? That he's out there somewhere, shacking up with some other woman, blissfully ignoring the fact that he has a wife back home who is in agony trying to find out where he is? If it's just another woman, I can handle that. I'll tell him it's no big deal. I'll take him back, no questions asked. Or if he doesn't want to give her up, we'll move out to Utah and become Mormons and he can have us both. He can have anything he wants if he'll just come home to me.

I wish everybody would go away and leave me here, alone with my tortured thoughts and the swarming police. They mean well, but having them here is making me think these terrible thoughts. I can't stay positive when I've got these people all around me. Please, God, if anybody has to die, let it be one of them, and let Oscar be alive. Is that a horrible thing to think? Oh Lord, I can't even think straight anymore. I've been awake for—what is it now?—three days straight? Eventually, I'm hoping I'll pass out and sleep for a long, long time, and when I wake up, this will all have been just a nightmare, something I can laugh about with Oscar while we get ready to have everybody over for Christmas.

DECEMBER 28, 1979

The police say Oscar's dead. They say they found some blood that matches his type in the alley behind Seth's tanning salon, where a lot of us parked when we went to the grand opening party. I asked them if it was so much blood that he couldn't have survived whatever wound he had, and they hedged. The fat sergeant with the powdered-sugar mustache looked down and gave me a line of babble about how it's difficult to predict how much blood someone can lose and still live. That just means Oscar could still be alive, out there, somewhere. Maybe he's got amnesia. Or maybe he's been kidnapped and someone is holding him until they can decide how much ransom to ask for. I know he's still out there. I know I would feel it, deep inside of me, if he were dead. So I refuse to give up hope.

I can't convince anybody else to keep hoping along with me, though. Oscar's mom is arranging a funeral service, even though there's no body and no proof that Oscar's really gone. And my mom keeps sitting down next to me and letting out these melodramatic sighs. She's trying to get me to break down, to start sobbing, and accept that my husband is dead. I won't do it. Not until somebody can show me some incontrovertible evidence that he's gone. I won't believe it. Not ever.

DECEMBER 30, 1979

Nora showed up at my doorstep early this morning. It was barely dawn and she was still in her big old flannel pajamas, with Andrew mewling and pawing at her covered breast with his tiny fists.

"What's the matter?" I asked. I was rubbing at my eyes, wincing when the dried-up gravel that had crusted around the corners scraped against my skin.

Nora came inside without saying a word. She sat down on the couch with Andrew squirming on her lap and just stared at the floor.

"Nora? What's going on?"

"Seth's gone."

A cold shock ran through me. I felt the same heavy dread that I had felt a few days earlier when I first realized that Oscar wasn't home on time and that something was wrong. "What do you mean?" I asked, enunciating each word slowly and clearly, like she was a two-year-old.

"He's gone. I woke up this morning and he wasn't in the bed."

I shook my head and sat down beside her. "He probably just went to the salon. Did you call him?"

"You don't understand. He left a note."

Andrew started wailing and Nora didn't seem to notice, so I picked him up and tried bouncing him on my lap. I turned back to Nora. "What did the note say?"

She slid her hand down her side, as if she had a pocket, but she didn't and she looked up, staring, confused, at her empty hand. I grabbed her hand and held it tight. "What did the note say?" I repeated.

"I don't . . . I don't have it," she muttered.

"I know, but you read it, didn't you? What did it say?"

"He said he was leaving me."

"That's it? No explanation? Just that he's leaving?"

Nora shrugged. She looked like she had just witnessed a murder, and I guess, in a way, she had—the murder of her marriage to Seth.

"Where is the note?" I asked.

"In the car, I guess," she said. She was slowly starting to come around and make more sense. "Go get it. There's a note for you, too."

"What do you mean? A note from who?"

"From Seth."

"For *me*? Are you sure?"

She sighed. "I'm not stupid. I know. I know that he always wanted you, and not me."

"Nora, don't be silly . . ."

She put up a hand to stop me. "Don't even bother. Just go get the notes."

I ran out to her car and found two envelopes on the front passenger seat, one torn open and the other still sealed. And the sealed one did indeed have my name written on it.

I brought the envelopes back into the house and sat down on the couch. I handed Nora the opened envelope. She pulled the folded note out, shook it open, and read it to me:

Dear Nora, I know this will be painful to you, but I have no choice. I'm leaving. I have to. You know we haven't been happy, and it's better for both of us, in the long run, if I leave now. Please give the other envelope to your sister. Seth

She handed the note to me. I scanned it quickly to make sure there was nothing she had left out.

"I can't believe he would just leave," I said. There was a heavy awkwardness in my chest; I was dying to tear open the envelope Seth had left for me, but I realized it was more important to soothe Nora first. I wondered if I should put my arm around her or something. I'm just not good at being there for people.

"I shouldn't be surprised," she said, taking the note back from me and crushing it in her palm. "He never wanted to be with me."

I tried patting her arm. "That's not true."

She made a *tssk* sound, the same one our own mother always makes. Maybe having a baby makes you start doing that, dismissing everybody else. "Of course it's true. I knew it when he asked me to marry him, I knew it on our wedding day, and I knew it when he barely showed up when I was having the baby. I'm not as stupid as everybody thinks."

"Nobody thinks you're stupid. It's not you. It's him. He's always been like this."

"Yeah, in love with you."

"Don't . . ."

"No, *you* don't. Why would he leave you a note, too, if he wasn't in love with you? Don't patronize me. I can handle the fact that my husband never gave a shit about me, but I can't handle the fact that my sister thinks I'm too stupid to realize it."

I slumped against the back of the couch. "I'm sorry, Nor. Really I am."

"It's not your fault. And it's not like I didn't know what I was getting into. I did this to myself."

I turned the unopened envelope over in my hands. "Should I open this?" I asked.

"Yeah, go ahead. I'm curious, actually."

So I tore open the envelope and pulled out the note. I can't even describe what I was feeling as I read it. All I can do is paste the note here, so you can see exactly what it says.

Dear Iris,

By the time you read this, you'll already have heard from your sister that I've left. And I have, but I need you to know that I'll always be there for you. Everything I've ever done has been for you. And it's especially true now.

It's only because I love you so much that I'm going to tell you this. I know that deep down you love me, too, and I know I can count on you to keep this to yourself until you're ready to come to me. So here goes.

The police are right. Oscar is dead. I know because I'm the one who killed him. Even though I know you love me, you're such a sweet person that I know you did have feelings for Oscar, so I know you'd want to know that he didn't suffer. I wouldn't mind going the same way myself when the time comes. It was brilliant, if I do say so myself.

I used the new sensory deprivation tank thing—the one I showed you all when you came to the salon for the party. After everybody left, I asked Oscar to try it out for me, so I could practice working with all the dials and switches. Oscar, noble as ever, agreed right away and climbed on in. And once he got settled, I turned on the switches, but instead of pumping in oxygen like you're supposed to, I pumped in carbon monoxide. He never made a peep. He just went to sleep. I know it's important to you to know that.

Once he was gone, I took his body and hid it away, just so the cops wouldn't find it while they were interviewing us all. But now I have to go hide it somewhere permanently—someplace the cops will never find it—so they can't ever charge me with murder.

That's where I've gone. And that's why I had to leave Nora and the kid behind. Tell Nora she should go ahead and file divorce papers. She can say I abandoned her, which I guess I have. It doesn't matter what she tells them. She just has to get it done, so I'm free when the time comes and you and I can be together, finally, after all these years.

It occurred to me that you might be thinking you'll just give the police this letter and they'll know what happened to Oscar. You're a good girl, so it might occur to you, briefly, that turning me in would be the right thing to do. But you'll come around eventually. I know you will. You and I belong together. I did all of this for you, to free you from the slavery of your marriage to my brother, who was never good enough for you. He wouldn't even have been good enough for Nora. Maybe that's what should have happened. Maybe the two of them should have gotten married and let us live in love, the way we're destined to do. It doesn't matter now, though, because I've fixed everything for us.

By the way, don't even bother giving this letter to the police. There are no fingerprints on it, no way at all to link it to me. Plus, it was typed on your very own typewriter, so everyone will just think you've lost your mind with your grief over losing Oscar. Or maybe they'll even think you killed him.

In case you're wondering about the blood the cops found in the alley, it wasn't Oscar's. It was mine. We're the same blood type. I spill my blood out of devotion—my never-ending devotion—to you.

So I'll go away for now. But I'll be back, when the time is right, when it's safe, and then I'll come for you and we'll be together, forever, the way we were meant to be.

You can tell Nora that the lease on the tanning salon is paid up through June, so she can go ahead and run the place herself if she wants. Maybe she'll make a little money. Who knows?

Until our day comes, my love, remember that I am always there—in your heart. Just listen and you'll hear my voice inside you. And soon I'll have something else inside you, too. Get it?

All my love, as always, Seth

I don't remember folding the note or putting it down or handing it to Nora. All I remember is that one minute I was reading and the next thing I knew I was waking up on the floor and Nora was fanning my face with her hand.

By the time I came to, Nora had already read the note—which made me wonder how long she let me lie there, unconscious, before trying to wake me up. Probably not worth thinking about. Being resentful of my own sister is something I don't need in my life, especially not now—now that my husband is dead and I'm alone, all alone for the rest of my life, which I keep catching myself hoping will be a very short one.

What am I going to do without Oscar? I've never been alone, not for longer than a day or two since middle school. He's been with me through everything, even when I wished he wasn't. God, I hate myself for ever wishing he wasn't with me. How stupid I was not to realize how horrible life would be without him. I'd give anything to have him back. Or to be dead with him. How am I going to survive like this? I won't. I won't be able to do it. Maybe I should wait a few days, until everything settles down, and kill myself. What else have I got to live for?

19

HORACE

| PRESENT DAY |

He slapped the diary closed and reached for the bottle of gin. He had held off having a drink, trying to see how long he could wait before giving in to the persistent little voice in his head. But reading the excruciating details of his father's death was more than any person should have to handle sober, right? He smiled at the burn of the gin in his throat and leaned back in his chair.

He had never thought about his mother much as a human being, had never wondered how she had felt when his father died. She had always been a simple, competent, robot-like woman whose constant cheeriness had been the bane of his childhood existence. A cheerful person may be pleasant to be around in general, but when you're in fifth grade and trying to look tough in front of your friends, having Mommy muss your hair and kiss you and twist the crotch of your pants around to make sure you have enough "room" makes you wish you could die rather than be around her.

He held up the glass of gin and stared at the liquid, noting how it looked almost cloudy when he held it up to the light. So beautiful.

Maybe he should call Andrea. Another night like last night would go a long way toward curing this ache he'd inflicted on himself by reading about his maniacal uncle killing his father. It was crazy stuff. And embarrassing, too—he couldn't believe his mother had actually cut out the newspaper article announcing his father's disappearance and pasted it into her diary, like it was a ticket stub or a wedding invitation. Funny how different he was from her. She had literally saved everything from her entire life, whereas he would prefer to go through life trying to ignore his emotions as much as he could and not remembering the past at all. The past was dangerous—as dangerous as letting Andrew drive you home after a night at the bar. Better to let things lie, and not stir up memories that were best left undisturbed.

He put the drink down and reached for the phone. Despite his intention to call Andrea, he found himself dialing Aunt Nora's number instead.

"Horace? Is something wrong?" He had forgotten she had caller ID. Damn.

"No, everything's fine."

"Okay. Good. So, how are you?"

He smiled. "You mean, 'What the hell do you want? You're disturbing me while I'm watching *Jeopardy*.'"

"*Wheel of Fortune*, actually."

"It's nothing. I'll talk to you tomorrow."

"Sweetheart, it's okay. Pat and Vanna will be there when we're done. Say whatever you have to say."

"Okay." He swallowed. "Why did my mother have me?"

"Horace, my God, what the hell do you mean?"

"I'm reading Mom's old crap, and it's depressing. She saved everything. She even had a newspaper article about Dad's disappearance taped right onto a page. It's crazy."

Nora was quiet for a moment. "Your mom was . . . well, detail oriented."

"I get it. I'm just one of the 'details' she was determined to keep straight."

"Horace, you have no idea what your father's death did to your mother."

He cackled. "Are you kidding? I have a better idea than anybody."

"You think so, but there's a lot you can't possibly understand."

"Why? Because I wasn't there?"

"No," Nora said. "Because you're not a woman."

"What's that supposed to mean?"

"We shouldn't be talking about this over the phone."

"Why not?" he asked. "Do you think the phone's bugged?"

"Don't be a pain in the ass. I just mean, I think it would be better if I explained some things to you in person."

"What's to explain? My mother got pregnant, my father died, I was born, the end."

"No," she said softly. "That's not the end. That's not even the beginning."

Horace had to strain to hear her. "Nora? What's wrong? Can't you talk a little louder?"

"Yeah, yeah," she said. "I'm sorry. I'll speak up." But instead of actually speaking, she fell silent.

"Aunt Nora? Are you okay?"

"I'm fine. It's just . . . well, I promised your mother I'd never tell you this."

"Tell me what?" he asked.

"I guess when someone is dead, all bets are off, right?"

"Will you just tell me already?"

Nora let out a long sigh. "All right. Here goes. Your mother wasn't pregnant when your father died."

Horace laughed. "Yeah, right. Then, what? Am I the product of another virgin birth?"

"Not exactly."

Horace felt something tighten in his chest. "Are you saying that my mom cheated on my father?"

"No! Not that. Your mother would have died before she'd even consider being unfaithful to your father. Huh. If you think about it, she did."

"Did what?"

"Die before being unfaithful to your father."

Horace smiled. It was true. His mother had never so much as dated another man, at least not to his knowledge. She had indeed gone to her grave without ever betraying even the memory of her husband. "Yeah," he said. "I guess you're right."

Neither one of them said anything for what seemed like a long time. Horace started to panic, thinking maybe his phone had dropped the call. "Nora? Are you still there?"

"Yeah, I'm still here."

"So are you going to tell me?"

"Yes. Okay. So, I told you your mother wasn't pregnant when your dad died, and that's true."

"So my dad wasn't my dad?"

"No, that's not what I mean," she said. "You've been reading your mom's papers, right? It must say something in there about how much trouble she was having getting pregnant, doesn't it?"

"Yeah. There's tons of stuff about all kinds of doctors and specialists. It's kind of sad, really."

"You ought to be flattered," Nora said. "Your mom went through all that for you."

"Through what? What did she do?"

"She conceived you through artificial insemination—or, no, it was in vitro fertilization."

Horace exhaled hard. "Oh. Well, that's nothing. Everybody does that nowadays."

"Well, they didn't, at least not much, back then."

"Okay. I get that, but still, it doesn't seem like that big a deal. Unless— are you saying she used donor sperm and that my dad really wasn't my biological father?"

"No, no," Nora said. "There—there was sperm from your father that had been saved from all the tests the two of them went through. They used that, and they were lucky enough to get Iris pregnant on the first try."

"So I wasn't born premature, then?"

"No. That was just what your mother told you so you'd never realize everything wasn't exactly . . . normal or whatever . . . about your birth. She thought it would be easier for you this way. But look at the dates in the diary. Do the math. See for yourself."

"I don't know. I just don't see why it's such a big deal. All this drama. It's just like Mom, though."

"No," Nora said. "Your mother never liked drama. It just seemed to . . . follow her, somehow."

"That's an understatement, I think."

"Hmmm."

"Is there anything else I should know, Aunt Nora?"

There was such a long silence that, again, Horace thought the phone had gone dead. "Nora?"

"No, nothing."

20

IRIS
|JANUARY 1, 1980 |

Seth was right about the police. When I gave them the note, they acted all serious and passed it along from one cop to the next. But after I'd been sitting there all afternoon, waiting to find out what they were going to do, how they were going to go after Seth, a young cop—one I'd never seen before, who looked sweaty and terrified, like it was his first day out of the academy and he was being forced to deal with the hysterical widow so all the other cops could make fun of him—came over and sat next to me on the police station's ugly old wooden chairs and told me there was nothing they could do.

Nothing they can do. Seriously? They know that my husband was murdered—MURDERED!—by his own brother, and there's nothing they can do. Isn't there anything, anything at all, they can do? Isn't there some kind of APB or BOLO or other acronym they can put out? Can't they slap Seth's picture on the news and ask for tips? *Somebody* must have seen him. Seth can't last five minutes without human contact. I'm sure in the day and a half since he's been gone he's already slept with at least one prostitute and thrown back some vodka shooters with the locals at a seedy bar somewhere. Seth is a social creature. Maybe all murderers are, at heart.

So this young cop, who looked like his neck was being squeezed by his collar even though he was actually on the skinny side, says, "Basically, ma'am, if there's no body, there's no murder."

That pushed me over the edge. "You have a signed confession! Isn't that at least grounds for a . . . a . . . a search warrant or something?"

I must have been yelling pretty loud, because the older, fatter cop—the one with the powdered-sugar mustache—hurried over and said, "Mrs. Cairo, is something wrong?"

I laughed so hard I almost peed myself. "Is something wrong? Are you fucking stupid? My husband is dead. My brother-in-law killed him. I gave you a written confession, and yet you refuse to so much as take a casual look around to see if you can find the killer. I feel like I'm in an episode of *The Twilight Zone.* This is insane."

The fat cop bristled and narrowed his eyes. "I assure you, Mrs. Cairo, we are doing everything we can."

"And I assure you, officer, that you are not doing a goddamn thing. But it doesn't matter," I said, leaping up and throwing my purse strap over my shoulder. "I'll find Seth myself."

I started to march away. The young cop called after me, his voice so tense it almost cracked. "But, ma'am, he could be dangerous."

I stopped and looked back at him. "Do you think so? Then why don't *you* try to find him?"

The young cop blushed and looked down. I stood there just long enough to watch the fat cop slap the young cop on the shoulder and say, "Let's get back to work."

I turned and ran out of the building. I sat sobbing behind the wheel of my car for a while, ignoring the people who slowed down as they walked by so they could gawk at the crying woman for a moment. Rubberneckers. My head was swimming—a cliché, I know, but that's really the only way to describe the mixture of confusion, grief, and indignation I was feeling as I sat there. And then I realized that what I had told the cops—that I was going to find Seth myself—wasn't just exaggeration or bravado. It was something I was going to have to do.

JANUARY 30, 1980

It's my first official night on the quest for Seth. I left home this afternoon, with my mother and Oscar's mom standing in the driveway wringing their hands and begging me not to go, to let the police take care of everything.

"But they're *not* taking care of it," I said, as I shoved the last of my suitcases into the trunk and checked to see if it would close.

"Sweetheart, you have to give it time," my mother said. "Everything will get better in time."

I slammed the trunk shut. "Tell that to Oscar."

Mom flinched a little and shot a look at Mrs. Cairo. I pushed past the two of them and pulled the driver's side door open. I hurled my purse over the console onto the passenger seat, then turned to offer my mother a hug.

She embraced me, but didn't stop with the begging. "Iris, you don't know what you're doing. Leave this to the cops."

"Mom, I'm not going to go through this argument again. Just give me a kiss and I'll call you from the road."

She kissed me on the cheek, then snarfled into a wrinkled tissue. Mrs. Cairo hugged me and said, "I may not agree with what you're doing, but Oscar would have been proud of you."

I sucked back a sob before it could get out and make me sound as weak as I was feeling, despite my attempt to seem all strong and determined. "I hope so," I whispered. I kissed her and slid into the car. "I'll call you soon."

They waved until I was out of sight, and then (I imagined), they used their keys to go into my house and make themselves some coffee rather than going out and paying for it. They thought I was just going blindly out into the world, hoping I would run into Seth somewhere and somehow convince him to turn himself in to the police. But I have a roadmap that they don't know about.

A few days after I decided I would have to find Seth—and, more importantly, Oscar's body—on my own, I went to Nora's house and barraged her with questions. She was crying and gulping for air by the time we were done talking, but I was able to get something from her that gave me a detailed agenda for where Seth must have gone: his little black book. Or, rather, his little green book—his address book from before he married Nora (although, from some of the notations I've seen since I've been going through the book, some of the numbers are actually from *after* he married Nora, but there was no need to let her know that; she's been through enough). I left Nora's house, knowing that all I had to do to find Seth was go from one bimbo's house to the next. Eventually, I'll catch up with him.

As I was leaving Nora's yesterday, after saying good-bye, I stopped and said, "Nor, if he calls or contacts you in any way, tell him I said yes."

"Yes what?"

"Yes, I'll marry him."

She choked on a sob and covered her face with her hands. She spun around in place for a moment, like she was drunk, then sank down onto the sofa. "Christ, Iris, don't I mean anything to you at all?"

I went over and sat down next to her. "Honey, I would never do that to you, of course not. But I need Seth to think I would."

"Why?"

"Because then he'll come to me, instead of making me find him."

Nora sighed and patted me on the knee. "You always were smarter than me."

There was a nerdy little voice inside of me that wanted to correct her grammar—"smarter than I"—but I squelched it. Instead, I just said, "It has nothing to do with being smart. Seth is crazy, and if I'm the target of his insanity, it only makes sense that he'll forget about the danger if he thinks I'm returning his feelings."

Nora wiped her face with the back of her hand. "You're right. And I hope he calls, so you don't have to wander all by yourself for too long. Are you sure you don't want me to come with you?"

"And who would take care of Andrew? Come on, Nor. I'm a big girl. I'll be fine."

"Then get out of here, and go get him."

She stood up and offered me both of her hands, tugging me up and pulling me into a hug. "I love you, little sister."

"I love you, too. And I'm sorry about all of this."

She pulled away and wiped her face again. "It's not your fault. I made my own bed, and now I have to lie in it."

So now, I'm holed up in a motel in some nowhere town in western Pennsylvania, scribbling in my journal and drinking some very bad wine that I bought from a crappy little store across the street from the truck stop where I ate dinner. The place I'm staying is one of those motels that's only two stories and has doors on the outside. Oscar always hated these places. Something about the doors on the outside freaked him out. I don't know why. Personally, it seems safer to me to be able to go right from your room to the outside world, in case there's a fire or something. But maybe that also means it's easier for the outside world to get to *you*. Oscar knew more about that than I do.

So I've got Seth's address book and it's just loaded with names, which is intimidating, since it means there's a lot of ground to cover for one person traveling alone. But, thanks to Oscar's vision for our publishing company, I have plenty of money and I can get along fine without working for a while—a long while.

Tomorrow, I'm heading to a small town outside Pittsburgh to see someone named Mandy Merrick. That's all I know about her—her name and her phone number, which helped me find her address. Beyond that, she's a mystery, just like all the other women whose names appear in Seth's book. It's strange that Seth even knew people out here, or anywhere, really, other than close to home. I mean, sure, he went to college, but that was relatively local, and he never worked a job where he would have had to travel. He never really worked a job at all. The only traveling I ever knew Seth to do was one cross-country trip he took with a buddy of his over the summer after he graduated from college. It's hard to believe he met—and slept with—so many women on that trip alone, but I can't figure out any other explanation for the names in this book.

So tomorrow I'll meet Mandy and see if she can help put me on Seth's trail.

JANUARY 31, 1980

Well, that was a waste of time. Mandy Merrick is such a ditz, she barely even remembered Seth. I guess I shouldn't be as surprised as I am. A one-night stand with someone who's passing through your town is hardly something most girls would detail in their scrapbooks.

I met Mandy at the coffee shop where she works as a waitress. Another big surprise—Seth likes to pick up dumb blond waitresses at hole-in-the-wall dives. (I don't know why I always go along with the stereotype and assume that blondes are dumb, considering I'm blond myself, but in Mandy's case, the shoe fits.)

I sat down at the counter and waited (an inordinately long time) for Mandy to stop chatting with a flannel-shirt-wearing, bearded redneck at the other end of the counter and come down to take my order. When she finally sidled up to me, pad in hand, she said, "Whatcha want?"

I thrust my hand out and said, "Miss Merrick? I'm Iris Cairo. We spoke on the phone."

She cracked her bubblegum and peered at me through narrowed eyes. "Who?"

"Iris Cairo. Remember? I called to set up a meeting so we could talk about a man you might have met a few years back—Seth Cairo?"

"Oh, yeah, I remember you. Ivy Castro."

"Iris Cairo." This woman was a walking blonde joke.

"Sure, whatever. So what can I do ya for?"

"I'm looking for Seth Cairo. He's—um—he's missing, and we're all very worried about him. Your name was in his address book, so I thought you might have been in touch with him recently."

She frowned and tucked her pencil behind her ear. For a moment, I caught myself thinking about how easy it was for most people to tuck things neatly behind their ears. Whenever I try to do it, the damn thing slips right out. I guess maybe I have narrow ears or something. God, I think about some really pointless things.

"You got a pitcher or something?"

I stared at her for a second, trying to figure out why she would want me to give her a pitcher. Then I realized that she meant *picture*.

"A picture. Yes. I do have one. Here." I pulled the photo of Seth I had brought with me out of my purse and handed it to her. It was a three-quarter portrait of him taken in the lobby of the church right after he and Nora were married. It occurred to me that maybe I should have brought a more casual photo with me, one where he wasn't wearing a tuxedo, in case some of these women had photographic memories, and would more easily remember him wearing the T-shirts and jeans he usually wore.

Mandy held the photo so close to her face that she looked absurd and studied it. Then, abruptly, she handed it back to me and said, "Nope, don't know 'im."

I resisted the urge to shove the picture back under her nose. Instead, I just said, "Are you sure? If you never met him, why would he have your number in his address book?"

"I dunno. Maybe he got it from somebody else."

"Like who?"

"Hey, I ain't no detective."

I bit my tongue. "Well, neither am I, but it's really important that I track Seth down. Are you sure you don't remember him? It would have been a few years ago. During the summer. He was passing through with a friend of his?"

She took the photo back and looked at it again. "I dunno. Maybe he looks a little familiar. But I meet a lotta people, ya know?"

She laid the photo down on the counter and said, "So, what can I getcha?"

I sighed, realizing the conversation was over. "Coffee, please."

So tonight I'm in another hotel—this one a decent-enough Hyatt with the doors on the inside. And with the exception of the captivating Mandy Merrick, I pretty much haven't talked to another human being for days. I'm starting to get lonely. Not just "Oh, I'm by myself, maybe I'll watch a little TV" lonely, but the crushing, oppressive, can't-think-of-anything-else kind of lonely. I could call someone—my mother or Nora or a friend—but I feel like that would just make me feel worse. It would remind me that I'm on my own in this, that no one else thinks I should be doing this, and nobody supports me in the least. I'd rather not be reminded that I'd feel all alone even if I were with other people.

So I'll sit here on this too-hard bed with the scratchy, cold bedspread and try to read a book, while the TV glows silently in the background, turned down as low as it'll go. It keeps me company. It's my only chance to have a "human" voice around that's actually friendly. But I can't read. All I can do is think about Oscar and wonder what we'd be doing tonight if he were still alive, still with me. And then I start crying all over again. You'd think I'd be getting used to the idea of never seeing my husband again. But every night I go to sleep and when I wake up in the morning, it hits me all over again. It's like I have no memory. All it takes is an eight-hour span of sleep to make me forget everything. It's torture.

Tomorrow I'll get back on the road. The next person I have to see is in Ohio, someone named Kate Cameron. Let's hope she's at least slightly more intelligent than my new friend Mandy.

21

HORACE

| PRESENT DAY |

He was invited to a party. It was one of those swank, upper-crusty parties where the old guard of the book industry mingled with the hip, fresh, up-and-coming writers. It was always amusing to Horace to watch the two sides mingle—the graying, wrinkly publishers and high-powered editors trying to impress the long-haired, stubble-faced, bohemian-looking writers who were more interested in sucking down drinks than talking about literature. Sometimes you had to wonder how the writers were able to produce anything publishable at all, when you considered how drunk they usually were and how intensely uninterested they seemed in books. His mother had always told him that things were different in the old days. The writers were still drunks, but they actually cared about words and voice and narrative and all that crap that put Horace to sleep whenever he thought about it. Today's writers were mostly so-called memoirists, who won brief glimpses of fame by publishing gory exposés of their often-imaginary pasts. They were tabloid writers, not authors in the traditional sense, Iris had always said. Horace didn't care. It was just a party to him. As long as the booze kept flowing, he was happy to put in his appearance.

It was stupid, really, that people kept inviting him, considering he hadn't actually worked a day at Cairo Books in his life. His entire interest in the literary world consisted of watching the amount of money in his bank account grow. He didn't have to work at the publishing house, and it was probably best that he didn't. He couldn't remember the last book he had read all the way through—other than his mother's diaries.

He had hardly crossed the threshold into the penthouse apartment of the old crone who was hosting the party before he was accosted by a shrill voice. "Horace! So good to see you!"

He turned to face the ancient hostess, who was draped in long strands of pearls and pale pink silk that made her look like a corpse that had escaped its coffin to take a little walk. "Gloria," he said, leaning down to kiss her cheek. "Thanks for inviting me."

She grabbed his hand and squeezed it tight. "I just wanted to make sure you knew how sorry we all were to hear about your mother. She was a wonderful woman, truly an original."

"Thank you." His stomach began to churn as it occurred to him that he had been invited here specifically because people were interested in learning the nitty-gritty details of his mother's death. And that was something he preferred not to talk about.

Gloria took him by the elbow and steered him into the depths of the apartment. From every side, people stopped in the middle of their conversations to gawk at him. Usually, in public places, when people stared at him, he assumed it was because of the eye patch. But here, where everybody knew virtually everything about his family history, he knew it was for other reasons.

"Horace, you know Evelyn, from Dearbourne Publishing, don't you?" Gloria said, nudging him in the direction of a late-middle-age woman with hair dyed the color of Dr. Pepper. She put out her hand and he shook it, then he shoved his right hand into his pocket to try to avoid having to meet anybody new.

"Yes, I think we've met, way back when," he said. "How are you?"

Evelyn cast a wink at Gloria, and Horace could tell she thought he hadn't seen it. Gloria patted him on the arm and said, "I've got to go make the rounds. Have a good time, you two."

Great, he thought. *Stuck talking to the matronly hag with the burgundy hair.*

Evelyn tilted her head to the side, that classic gesture of feminine sympathy. "I heard about your mother. I'm so sorry."

"Thank you. Well, she lived a good life."

Evelyn's eyes narrowed as she studied him, clearly trying to determine whether he was kidding or not. "Yes," she said. "I guess she did."

A black-tuxedoed waitress slid by carrying a forest of champagne flutes on a silver tray. Horace timed his grab carefully and took one without spilling a drop as she hurried past. The waitress was long gone when Horace realized that Evelyn didn't have a drink, and that he was going to have to sacrifice his own for the sake of propriety. He handed her the champagne and she grinned.

"Why, thank you," she said. "What a nice young man you've turned out to be."

Horace shrugged. "Do I still qualify as a 'young man'?"

She licked her lips and touched his forearm with her ropy-veined hand. "You do to me."

He forced a smile. "Thank you." He looked around, desperate to find something, anything, that would qualify as an excuse to leave Evelyn and head for the bar. As it turned out, the excuse found him.

From over his shoulder, he heard, "How ya doin', cuz?"

Horace swung around to see Andrew standing there holding two well-filled rocks glasses with brown liquid in them. He shoved one into Horace's hand. "This round's on me, buddy," Andrew said.

Evelyn's head was bouncing back and forth between Horace and Andrew, and she had a look of alarm on her face, as if she had only just now realized that Horace had no intention of sleeping with her. For his part, Horace couldn't decide whether to introduce his cousin to her. Finally, he sighed and elbowed Andrew in the ribs.

"Evelyn, have you met my cousin, Andrew?"

She extended a stiff hand, obviously miffed at the unwanted interruption. Andrew took her hand in his own, but instead of just giving it a polite shake, he raised it to his lips and brushed a kiss across her fingers. "My pleasure," he said.

Evelyn flushed red, but Horace could tell she was pleased, not angry. When Andrew finally released her hand, she fanned her neck with her fingers before taking a long gulp of her champagne. Maybe Andrew wasn't entirely useless, after all.

"And what's this you've brought me, Andrew?" Horace asked, raising the glass of booze to his nose for a sniff.

"Your favorite. Bourbon."

"Since when is bourbon my favorite?"

"You're right. You don't have a favorite. You'll pretty much drink anything."

"I think you're talking about yourself."

Andrew sneered, but quickly wiped his face blank and turned his attention back to Evelyn. "And how do you know my dear cousin, miss?"

Evelyn's words came out all breathy. "His mother's publishing house was one of my main rivals. I'm president of Dearbourne Publishing."

Andrew bowed his head. "That's very impressive. And what type of things do you publish?"

As Evelyn started to rattle off a list of literary genres, Horace took the opportunity to peel away from her and Andrew. He waited for a moment to make sure they hadn't noticed his departure, then bolted for an empty couch in the back corner of the room. From here, Horace had a great view of his cousin putting the moves on Evelyn. *Andrew*, he thought, *will fuck anything that breathes*. On the up side, at least this time Andrew could be pretty sure that this woman wasn't a hooker.

But what the hell was he doing there? Andrew had probably never read a book, much less worked on one, so it seemed odd he would show up at a publishing party. He had to have been sent here by someone— either someone who hated Horace and wanted to rattle him or someone who loved him (like Aunt Nora) and wanted to protect him. But from what?

And then he saw exactly what Andrew had been sent to distract him from: Richard Riley. A popular writer, Riley wasn't known just for his novels. His most successful book had been his best-selling biography of Horace's very own uncle Seth.

The moment Horace noticed Riley sashaying away from the bar and surveying the room, he threw up his hand, trying to hide his face behind the brown liquor of his drink. The glass wasn't tall enough. Riley quickly picked him out and headed over.

"Cairo," Riley said, his voice booming. "Great to see you." He thrust his hand at Horace, who stared at it for a long moment before breaking down and deciding it was easier just to shake the man's hand than to start a fistfight here in Gloria's penthouse.

"Riley."

Riley flopped down beside Horace on the sofa, too close, and Horace scooted over as much as he could until he was almost hugging the couch's arm.

"So sorry to hear about your mom, man," Riley said. He took a swig out of his glass. Even from a foot away, Horace could smell that Riley was drinking gin and he felt a visceral clench in his bowels. Trying to fight the urge to run to the bar and get a gin for himself, he sucked down a long sip of his bourbon.

"Thanks," Horace said.

"Terrible way to go," Riley said.

"Yes. Sure."

"Heard from your uncle lately?"

"Thankfully, no."

"I saw him a couple of weeks ago. He's looking well these days. He asked about you, of course. And your mom."

"Whatever. Look, I've gotta . . ."

"Nice guy, really, your uncle. It's a shame, everything that went down with him and you and your mom."

"He killed my father."

"Allegedly."

"I don't want to talk about this now. If you'll excuse me . . ."

Horace tried to get up, but Riley laid a heavy hand on his arm and he fell back onto the sofa. "What do you want, Riley?"

"Nothing. Just being friendly."

"Well, I don't need any more friends."

"Don't be a jackass, Cairo. You really ought to be nicer to me."

"Why's that?"

Riley smiled and raised his glass to his lips. Before taking a sip, he said, "I'm writing a biography of your mother."

Horace leapt up, sloshing a bit of bourbon onto his sleeve. "See you around, Riley."

Riley stood up and leaned close to Horace's ear. "I would think you'd want to talk to me. Get your side of the story in, you know?"

"My side of the story is the true side. There's no other way to look at it. Besides, you don't seem to need me to tell you the facts. You found plenty of crap to fill up your last book. I'm sure you'll do the same this time around."

"Hey, I'm an award-winning biographer."

Horace smirked. "The only award you'll ever win is a Darwin award, if you're lucky."

"That's what you think."

"See you around."

He turned to walk away, but Riley stopped him by saying, "So I take it you won't be granting me an interview?"

"Fuck you, Riley."

Horace moved toward the bar, pouring the rest of the bourbon down his throat as he walked. By the time he got there, he had an empty glass and a raging headache, brought on by his conversation with Riley. He slapped his glass down and ordered a gin. He watched with too-eager anticipation as the bartender pulled out a fresh glass and poured in a few fingers' worth of the clear liquid. As soon as he had the drink in his hand, he brought it to his lips, pausing only to lay a few crumpled dollar bills on the bar as a tip.

"You okay, cuz?"

Andrew had appeared, without Evelyn on his arm, out of nowhere. *Strange*, Horace thought, *how someone as loud, boisterous, and crude as Andrew can move around so stealthily.*

Horace turned to face Andrew, leaning his back against the edge of the bar. There was plenty of room. At a private party like this, only the true alcoholics hovered around the bar the whole time. Normal people took their drinks and mingled, only returning to the bar when absolutely necessary.

"What are you doing here?" Horace asked, fighting the urge to take another sip of his drink. As the words left his mouth, he made a deal with himself that he would wait until after Andrew had answered before taking another drink.

Andrew smiled, a slow and lazy smile. Horace started to count in his head: one Mississippi, two Mississippi. Still Andrew didn't speak. For a moment, it occurred to Horace that Andrew must have read his mind and was holding out on answering for as long as he could, just to torture Horace. The logical part of his brain rejected the notion, but the rest of him began to pulse as he waited for the opportunity to taste his gin.

"Mom asked me to come." Finally. Horace didn't even bother to hide the shaking of his hand as he rushed to raise the glass to his lips. He took an extra-long sip, then lowered his glass and smiled at Andrew.

"Of course she did," he said. "But how'd you even get in?"

"I told the old chick at the door that I'm your assistant and I had an urgent message for you."

"Brilliant." Horace took another sip of gin, draining the glass and motioning to the bartender to pour him another. "I take it you're not pissed at me anymore?"

Andrew shrugged. "I don't hold grudges. So, you want me to kick that dude's ass?"

"Who, Riley?" Horace asked, gratefully accepting his fresh drink.

"I don't know his name," Andrew said. "That dude you were just talking to."

"That's Riley. Richard Riley. He's the one who wrote that book about your dad."

"I loved that book."

"Of course you did."

Andrew held up his hands. "No, no," he said. "I mean it. It was probably the only book I've read all the way through since college."

"Too bad it was fiction."

"What?"

"Fiction. Made up. Not true."

Andrew shrugged. "Tomato, tomahto."

Horace finished his second gin and set the glass down on the bar. "Well, thanks for coming, Andrew, but I think I'm going to get out of here."

"How come? It's awesome here. Fucking great spread. Not to mention the free drinks."

"The free drinks are exactly why we should hit the road. We're both drinking too much these days."

"Speak for yourself, cuz. Drinking makes me charming."

"That's debatable. Anyway, I'm out of here. Talk to you tomorrow."

Andrew punched him on the shoulder. "Have a good night. I'm gonna hang out a while longer. I think that Evelyn lady likes me."

Horace grimaced. "I'm not at all surprised that she does," he said. "Just do me a favor—don't drive home if you have more than two of those bourbons. Or any other drink, for that matter. Your mom'll kill me."

"Yeah, yeah. Just go, ya old fogey."

Horace patted Andrew's shoulder in good-bye and weaved his way through the crowd, shaking hands and thanking the hostess as he went. After a few torturous minutes, he was out the door, free and clear. He let out a long sigh and leaned back against the wall of the empty hallway. He pulled out his cell phone and dialed.

"Andrea? Hey, it's Horace. Want to get together?"

22

IRIS

I'm starting to feel like an investigative journalist. That, or Jack Kerouac. Being on the road really sucks.

I met Kate Cameron this afternoon at her office. She's a secretary at a company that sells pork or bacon or something. (Well, I guess bacon *is* pork, but you get my point.) Other than the fact that she had frosted blond hair and a plunging décolletage, I would never have taken her for one of Seth's girls. She actually has a brain. But even so, she didn't really tell me anything that could help me.

I walked into her office—well, it's more of a cubicle, but people always refer to them as "offices," I guess to delude themselves into thinking that they have some privacy, or maybe some clout. She shook my hand and told me to sit down in the metal-backed chair that was squeezed in so tight my knees were rubbing up against the front of her desk, catching on my nylons every time I breathed. A cubicle doesn't leave a lot of leg room for visitors, I guess. I'm lucky I've never had to work in one.

Kate was smiling. She obviously had no idea why I was there to see her. "So, Mrs. . . . uh . . ."

"Cairo. Call me Iris, please."

"Sure, great. Iris. What can I do for you?"

I took a deep breath and dove in. "Well, I'm hoping you can help me track down my brother-in-law, who's missing." I reached into my bag and pulled out the photo of Seth, passing it to her over the desk.

She studied it for a moment and her smile faded. She sighed and put the picture down on the desk, but she kept looking at it. She didn't say anything, though, so I wasn't sure whether she remembered him or not. Finally, I broke in. "Do you know him?"

She gave me a wistful smile and the briefest eye contact before she glanced back down at the photo. She touched the corner of the picture with the tip of her fingernail. "Yeah, I know him. Or, at least, I knew him."

"When was the last time you saw him?"

She shook her head. "Practically the same minute as the first time I saw him."

"I'm sorry. What do you mean?"

"I mean, I met him in a bar maybe three, four years ago. He spent the night at my place, made me a gorgeous breakfast the next morning, and told me he thought he was falling in love with me. We . . . well, you know . . . again that morning, and then I hopped in the shower. He said he wanted me to show him my town, because he was ready to move here. But when I got out of the shower, he was gone."

"Wow."

"It's my fault, really," Kate said. "I'm not normally a stupid person. But I guess I'm a romantic. And Steve was definitely romantic."

"Um—his name's Seth."

She wrinkled her nose. "Huh. He told me his name was Steve."

"Are you sure? It's been a while, maybe you just forgot."

"No, I'm sure," she said. "I remember, because he said his name was Steven Lewis, and that made me think of Robert Louis Stevenson."

"That's so strange," I said. "Why would he make up a fake name?"

"I don't know. Maybe he didn't want to risk having me track him down. If he does this sort of thing a lot, I wouldn't be surprised if there have been a few women out there who didn't take it well."

"I'm counting on it."

We shook hands and I drove back to the motel. I was gearing up for another night alone in a smelly room with bad TV reception when I noticed that the message light on the phone by the bed was flashing. Nora's the only person I've contacted at all since I've been on the road, so I knew the message had to be from her. I could barely dial the front desk fast enough. The message was just "Call me"—no name or number, so it had to be Nora. I dialed her house and waited for her to pick up.

But she wasn't the one who answered the phone. When I heard the voice at the other end of the line, I thought I was losing my mind.

"Seth? Is that you?"

"I was afraid you had forgotten about me," he said.

"What are you doing there? Is Nora okay?"

"I assume she's okay. I haven't seen her. She's away for the weekend."

"She didn't tell me anything about that."

"She didn't know."

I felt a cold shock pass through me. "Please tell me you didn't do anything stupid."

"Define stupid," he said.

"Seth, goddammit! What did you do to Nora?"

He burst out laughing. "Nothing. I just sent her a coupon for a free stay in Atlantic City, so she went away with my mother for a few days."

"Where's the baby? Why are you there? What the hell is going on?"

"I could ask you the same question," he said. "Where are you?"

"I don't think I want to answer that," I said. I felt like I was on a merry-go-round moving at warp speed. I was seeing visions of Seth and Oscar and blood and teeny tiny dead babies.

"Oh, come on, now," Seth said. "I thought you'd want to talk to me."

I held the phone against my shoulder and pressed my fingertips against my eyelids, trying to will away the awful pictures in my head while trying to figure out what to say to Seth. If I could play him right, I would be able to cut this crazy trip short. I just had to find a way to convince him that I *did* want to be with him. It was the only way he'd come back voluntarily. Although, I thought, he's already back. *I'm* the one who's away now. If I could just get the police to go over to Nora's, they could catch him . . .

"Yo, Iris?"

I took a deep breath and pulled my hand away from my eyes, trying to ignore the blinking spots left behind by the pressure of my fingers. "Sorry," I said, fighting to keep my voice steady. "It's just so strange to hear your voice after all this time."

"Good strange, though, right?"

I pushed an airy laugh out of my throat and tried to resist my gag reflex. "Yeah. Good strange. I have to admit it."

"So, when am I gonna see you?"

"Well, that's up to you," I said. Christ, it was hard to talk to him and sound flirtatious without screaming obscenities or puking all over myself.

"Tell me where you are and I'll come to you," he said.

"If Nora's away for a few days, why don't I just fly home and meet you there? We would have both of our houses all to ourselves, and we could have a real heart-to-heart talk."

He was quiet for a long time. Then he said, "No. Can't do it. I can't risk staying here."

"What do you mean?"

"How do I know you haven't already called the police and told them where to find me?"

Damn.

I faked a chuckle. "And how exactly would I have done that? I've been on the phone with you this whole time. What, do you think I'm contacting the cops telepathically?"

He laughed. "I guess you're right about that," he said. "But still. I can't risk the chance that you'll call the police as soon as you hang up with me. I'll come to you."

I held my breath for a moment, then released it as quietly as I could. "Okay."

"Great, so where are you?"

Before I could think up a good lie, someplace neutral where I could meet him safely, I blurted out the actual city.

"You haven't talked to Kate, have you?"

"You actually remember Kate?"

"Sure," he said. "I remember everything."

"Yeah, me too," I said, too softly for him to hear.

"Iris? Did you say something?"

"Sorry," I said. "No. I . . . um . . . just had a hiccup."

"Okay. I'll be there the day after tomorrow. Where are you staying?"

This time, I thought before speaking, and I gave him the name of another hotel, a couple of miles away. I figured it would be safer not to let him know where I was really staying.

"I'll be there," he said. "What room?"

"Just meet me in the bar," I said. "We'll have a drink."

"Good idea, loosen ourselves up a little. Okay, then. I'll see you in two days. I love you."

"Yeah," I said. "I . . . uh, I love you, too."

That part really hurt. I spent the next half hour retching in the toilet and begging Oscar's forgiveness. Then I stretched out on the bed and sobbed.

23

HORACE

| PRESENT DAY |

"Can I get you a drink?" Horace asked.

"Just water," Andrea said.

"Really? Are you sure? I have plenty of other stuff here. Wine, beer, assorted liquor."

"Just water," she said. "And I think you should have the same."

Horace flinched. "What's that supposed to mean?"

"Are you an alcoholic?" Andrea asked. She settled onto one of the stools at the center island of the kitchen and stared at him hard, without blinking (or, at least, without blinking enough for him to see).

He put down the bottle of merlot he had been waving at her, trying to convince her to take a drink, and leaned against the sink, wondering for a second whether the edge of the sink was wet and whether his pants were getting damp.

"I don't know," he said.

She smiled. "I'll take that as a yes."

He turned around and opened up the cabinet, digging around for a glass. He thrust the empty glass under the faucet and waited until it was full of water before slamming the faucet off with his wrist. He walked over and slapped the glass down in front of Andrea, ignoring the mess he made when the water sloshed over the sides and pooled on the wood surface of the table. Then he turned and went back to the sink and leaned against it, as if he had never moved.

"Thank you," Andrea said, picking up the glass and watching the stray drops of water rush down the sides and plop down onto the table. She took a sip and set the glass neatly back down into the puddle.

"Look," Horace said. "I'm . . . uh . . . I mean, I don't . . . ."

111

"Ah, eloquence."

"If I had realized you were such a bitch, I would never have taken you out."

"You didn't take me out," she said, running her finger through the puddle and dragging the water along. "You took me home, fucked me, and sent me on my way."

"Bullshit."

"Which part did I leave out?"

His hand was shaking as he raised his fingers to his eye patch. "I don't want to talk about it. Why don't you just go?"

She stood up and came over to him. He squirmed as she wrapped her arms around his waist and leaned in to kiss his neck. "You're touchier than I remembered," she said. "And cuter, too."

"So glad I amuse you," he said. He grabbed her elbows and tried to push her away from him, but the effort was half-hearted.

"Come on," she said, pressing her hips against his. "You know you like me."

"I thought I did, but . . ."

"You do. You're just pissed because I called you on your drinking problem."

"What are you, a shrink? I've seen plenty of shrinks, and I don't need to be analyzed by you."

"I think you do need to be analyzed, by somebody, whether it's me or not. It's not just drinking. Your behavior in general is self-destructive."

This time, he used a little force when he pushed her and he managed to break away from her grasp and move over to the center island, leaving her stranded alone at the sink.

"I don't think you know me well enough to say what my behavior is like."

"You drink like a wino, and the other night, you fucked me—a total stranger—without bothering to put on a condom. Self-destructive."

He smiled. "And what about you? As I recall, you threw back a few drinks yourself, and, as for the condom issue, well, it takes two to gonorrhea."

"Really? How many does it take to chlamydia?"

He laughed in spite of himself, and he could feel the air in the room relax, the tension between the two of them melting away. She came over and sat on the edge of the island, right in the puddle, and he sat down on a stool, pulling her between his legs and patting her on the ass.

"You'd better watch out, or I'm going to fall in love with you," he said.

"That's the plan."

They skipped drinks of any kind and went to bed. In the morning, she woke him by running her fingernails over the bare skin of his chest and pinching his nipples gently.

"Good morning," he mumbled, grabbing her hand and kissing it without opening his eye.

"So why did you call me last night?" she asked.

"I wanted to see you." He opened his eye and pulled himself up a little, so he was looking down at her as she lay there with her head on his chest.

"Yeah, but there was a bigger reason than that."

"How do you know?"

"I just do."

He frowned. "I was at a party."

"Yeah? And?"

"And that's it. The party was boring, so I left and called you."

"Aaannnh!" she said, her voice sounding like the buzzer that goes off on a game show when you get the question wrong. "Try again, please."

"Okay, it was boring and I ran into my cousin there, so I was annoyed."

She squinted and gazed up at him, clearly analyzing something about him. It made him uncomfortable. "Nope. That's not it, either."

"You're good," he said. "You're right. It wasn't Andrew that pissed me off. It was this asshole, Richard Riley."

"The writer?"

"You know him?"

"Not personally," she said. "But I've read some of his stuff."

Horace stiffened. Was he in bed with a Riley fan? He thought he might throw up.

"He stinks," she said.

He exhaled hard in relief. "Thank God you said that."

"I take it you don't like him very much."

"Not at all. He wrote a book about my uncle, and now he says he's writing one about my mother."

She stared at him with a screwed-up expression on her face. "What do you mean? Who the hell *are* you?"

"Horace Cairo. My mom was Iris Cairo, from Cairo Books, and my uncle . . ."

"Seth Cairo is your uncle?"

"Do you . . . know him?"

"No, no, just what I've read in the news. Jesus."

"I thought you knew," he said.

Her eyes widened. "Oh, my God. You thought I went home with you because you're famous. Or infamous. Or whatever you are."

He shrugged. "Most women do."

"My God, you poor thing. No wonder you're so fucked up."

"Thanks."

"You know what I mean."

"Yeah. I do." He stretched his neck to kiss her, but she only let him peck her on the lips before covering her mouth with her palm.

"Morning breath," she said. "I'd better go rinse out or you'll be running for cover."

"The hell I will." He grabbed the back of her head and pulled her to him, crushing his mouth against hers and thrusting his tongue between her lips. He felt her tense for a moment, but only a short moment, before she let her lips go soft and move in response to his. He cupped his hand around one of her breasts and tweaked her nipple between his fingers, just as she had been doing to him to wake him up. She moaned.

"Like that, do you?" he said. She smiled and lapped at his lips with her tongue. "Then you're going to love this."

24

IRIS

I got to the hotel bar half an hour earlier than the time I was supposed to meet Seth. I picked a small round booth tucked into a dark corner, with one of those red glass candleholders wrapped in white plastic netting on the table. The booth may have been dank and not so luxurious, but it gave me an excellent view of both the entrance to the bar and the bartender, whom I was planning to make my co-conspirator.

I waited for the bartender to come over and take my order. He was a young blond kid of medium height and build, athletic-looking, the kind of boy who probably played baseball or maybe tennis in high school—not football; he was too small for that—and was now bartending to pay his way through college at the state school a few miles outside of town. He looked dull enough not to be suspicious of the people he was serving, but at the same time bright enough and serious enough to be willing to help out a desperate woman, especially one with money.

"What can I getcha, ma'am?" he asked, draping a stained white bar towel over his forearm.

I slid a hundred-dollar bill across the sticky surface of the table toward him. "I'd like a martini, and a favor."

He frowned for a second, then brightened, obviously assuming I was joking, or was just going to ask for an extra olive in my drink. I almost felt sorry for him.

"Yes, ma'am. What can I do you for?"

I glanced at my watch. "In about twenty minutes, a man is going to come here to meet me."

He blushed a little and couldn't make eye contact.

"No, no, it's nothing dirty," I said, doubting my former assessment that he was smart enough to be able to help me. "Just listen."

He nodded, but still kept his eyes trained down on the table, staring at the hundred-dollar bill as if he had never seen so much money before.

"Okay," I said. "Well, this man is a criminal. And I'm going to try to get him to turn himself in to the police. But I have to talk to him first. Understand?"

His face drained pale. They probably don't see much crime around these parts, I figured, other than good ole boys making moonshine. To put the kid at ease, I lied a little.

"Don't worry," I said. "He's not violent or anything. It's just a minor crime. But I need you to do something for me."

He let out a relieved sigh and nodded. "Anything, ma'am."

"Okay. I'll be talking to him, and while I do, I need you to just keep an eye on this table. And when you see me do this . . ." I pulled my hair back into a ponytail with both hands, fluffing the hair and then letting it go, so it flowed wildly around my shoulders. "When you see that, I need you to call the police and tell them to get here right away, because there's a criminal at large who needs to be arrested. Can you do that?"

He stared at me for a long moment, his lips quivering, as if he were repeating my directions silently to himself to make sure he would remember them. "Yeah," he finally said. "I can do that."

I smiled and shoved the hundred-dollar bill toward him. "Great," I said. "And when the cops take him away, there will be two more of these for you."

A goofy grin broke out over his face. "Thank you, ma'am. Thank you. I won't let you down."

He was just standing there, smiling at me. "Can you go get my martini now?" I had to ask. He blushed again and bowed in apology, before turning and fleeing to the safety of the bar.

I sucked down the first martini almost before the poor kid had a chance to get back to the bar again after bringing it to me, and I quickly raised my finger to order a second. I wanted to be relaxed, as relaxed as possible under the circumstances, by the time Seth got here. As I took a sip from the second glass, I reminded myself that I needed to be relaxed, not drunk. Definitely not drunk. So I tugged the olive off its little plastic sword, sucked on it for a minute, and chewed it up, but kept the martini itself at arm's length as I stared at the door, my heart fluttering, watching for Seth.

He strode in exactly as the minute hand on my watch moved across the twelve, marking the precise hour of six. His eyes found me immediately and he grinned. In spite of myself, I felt a stirring in my loins. He looked good. Great, actually. And he looked so much like Oscar. That's what it was. I have to try to make myself believe that. I wouldn't be able to handle it if I thought I was attracted to the man who murdered the love of my life.

He slid into the booth beside me and kissed my cheek as he reached over and took my hand in his, just a little too tightly. I felt a panic rush through me, an irrational fear that, because he was holding my hand, I would never be able to get away from him.

"You look terrific, Iris," he said, squeezing my hand. "Like always."

"Thanks," I said, tugging my hand free and using it to grab my drink. I flashed him an apologetic smile, as if I couldn't have used my other hand to pick up the martini. Anything to break his grasp, I figured.

"You're tan," I said, taking a long sip of the cool gin. "Have you been in Florida or Hawaii or something?"

He laughed. "You forget. I own a tanning salon."

I squinted at him. "But you've been . . . away."

"That I have. But once you're in the biz, you can pretty much find places to get a tan when you want to. Professional courtesy."

"Ah, I see."

He just kept looking at me with that easy smile on his face. I could feel my spine starting to crawl in discomfort. I sucked down another long sip from my drink, almost emptying it. I glanced over at the bar and raised my finger. The nervous bartender was already staring hard at our table, clearly waiting in uneasy anticipation for my signal. My request for another drink sent him into a tizzy. He tossed his bar towel over his shoulder and came running over, scooping up my empty glass and then addressing Seth, stuttering so hard he would have been incomprehensible if we had been in any setting other than a bar.

"W-whatttt can I . . . uh, sir . . . um, s-something to . . . uh, drank? I mean, drunk? I mean, drink?"

Seth spat out a burst of laughter and patted the poor guy on the arm. "Relax, kid. It ain't that complicated. I'll have what she's having."

As he turned back toward the bar, the boy flashed me a terrified look. I pursed my lips and widened my eyes, trying to will him to relax. He practically scurried to the bar, where he clanked around in the sink and knocked a couple of liquor bottles together so hard, it sounded like they nearly shattered.

Seth smiled. "That is one messed up kid," he said. He draped his arm over the back of the booth, not quite touching my shoulders, but obviously demonstrating his intent to keep me close.

I forced a laugh. "Yeah, you'd think it wouldn't be such a trauma to mix a couple of martinis, right?"

"Since when do you drink martinis, anyway? Wasn't that Oscar's drink?"

I shrugged. "I guess. But I felt like having one. I guess I'm a little nervous."

"Because of *moi*? That's silly."

"Well . . ."

He let his arm slide down to rest on my shoulders and leaned over to brush his lips against the side of my neck, just under my ear. "Nothing to be nervous about, sweetheart. This is meant to be."

Mercifully, the bartender arrived just then with our martini glasses, which were sitting in a pool of spilled gin on his little tray. He was shaking so hard as he set the glasses down on the table, I was surprised he managed to keep any of the liquid inside the glasses at all.

"Anything else?" he asked, his voice cracking.

Seth pulled a ten-dollar bill out of his wallet and pressed it into the boy's palm. "Relax, kid. You've got a long night and a lotta drunks ahead of you."

The bartender made a grimace that passed as a smile, crumpled the bill into his fist, and ran back to the bar without glancing back. Christ, I thought. I hope he's going to be able to dial the phone when the time comes to call the police. For a second I wondered if I should have asked one of the drunken businessmen huddled at the bar to help me instead of this poor terrified kid.

"So," Seth said, taking a quick sip of his drink. "How have you been?"

I sighed. "Fine, I guess. How about you? Where have you been hiding out?"

"Hiding out?"

"You know what I mean. Nobody knows where you've been."

"And you know why."

"Well . . ."

"You say that a lot, you know."

"Do I?"

"Well . . ." He smiled.

I reached for my drink. I was going to be plastered if I kept sucking down these martinis, but it was easier to drink than try to find the right things to say to Seth.

"So have you come to a decision?" he asked.

"About what?"

"About whether you're going to turn me in or not."

I felt the flash of panic before I could stop it and I wondered if it had showed on my face.

"Why . . . why would you think that?" I asked, grabbing at my drink and feeling it slosh over the edge of the glass and wet my hand.

"Because you arranged something with that poor stuttering kid who's bartending, and I need to know how long I've got before I have to get the hell out of here."

Fuck, I thought. He must have gotten here earlier than I realized and watched me the whole time while I talked to the bartender and got myself ready to see him. It had never occurred to me that Seth would be so smart.

He touched my hand, which was still damp and a little bit sticky from where I had spilled the martini on myself. "Don't worry," he said. "I'm not going to hurt you."

I looked at him sideways. I had never been so scared. It was as if we were alone together in some desolate canyon, where no one would hear me scream, and not here in a semi-crowded bar in an upscale hotel, where I was surrounded by businessmen and even a concierge. It was like Seth and I were alone in the world. I tried to swallow and realized my mouth was too dry to do it.

I felt tears well up in my eyes and groped blindly for my drink. I finally managed to grasp the glass by its stem but when I got it up to my mouth, I realized it was empty. My head started to spin, and I couldn't tell whether I was getting drunk or whether the fear had simply taken over, leaving me without the ability to engage in rational thought.

Seth took the glass out of my hand, stood up, and went over to the bar with it. Trying to get some spit to squirt out of my salivary glands, I watched him as he ordered us two more drinks and stood there while the nervous bartender made them.

Seth came back over and set the glasses down on the table. He slid into the booth and casually took a sip from his drink. As he put the glass back down, he asked, "So did you do it yet?"

"Do what?"

"Call the police. Or have the bartender do it."

I sighed and cupped my hands around the stem of my glass. "No," I said softly. "I didn't."

"Mind if I ask why?" he said, leaning down a little to try to catch my eye.

I stared straight down, watching the dim yellow light from the sconces on the walls reflect and twist in the cold liquor in my glass.

"I don't know," I said.

"Mind if I make a guess?"

"Would it stop you if I said I *did* mind?"

"No," he said. I could tell that he was smiling without even looking at his face. "I guess it wouldn't. So here goes. You still have feelings for me."

I looked up and turned toward him. "Still?"

"Yes, still. You've never wanted to admit it, but there's always been something between us."

I shook my head. "Only on your side, Seth."

"You can deny it all you want. I know the truth. And so do you." He reached for his drink and stared at the bartender for a long moment, probably watching to see how jumpy he could make the poor kid.

"Even Oscar knew it," he finally said.

"Bullshit!"

Seth shrugged. "Hey, I know what I know, and that's what I know."

"I'm leaving," I said. "I don't know what I thought I was going to accomplish by coming here. You'll never change."

"Come on, Iris," he said. "You wouldn't want me to change."

"You think so? Fine. Then be yourself. You've always been honest—to a fault, really. So tell me the truth. Where is Oscar's body?"

He laughed. "That is the one thing I can't tell you."

"It was worth a shot," I said. I grabbed my purse and started to slide out of the booth, away from him. He put out his hand and took hold of my wrist, holding it tight. I stopped moving and turned back to him.

"Let go of me," I said, trying to sound firm, but there was a tremor in my voice.

"Don't go," he said.

"Why should I stay? It's sick. Think about it. I'm sitting here having drinks with the man who killed my husband."

"Why not say that a little louder?" he said.

"Fuck you, Seth. You're lucky I didn't call the police. Now let me go."

He released my hand too suddenly and I almost fell over. "Good-bye, Iris. I'll see you soon."

I got up, keeping my eyes on him the whole time as I stepped around the table and moved toward the door, like I thought he might jump me from behind if I turned my back to him for even a second. He was still sitting there, holding his martini between his hands, when I turned and ran for the parking lot.

25

HORACE

As she was leaving, pulling on her clothes as he lay in the bed watching, Andrea made him promise not to drink today. He glanced at his watch. It was not even eleven A.M. yet.

"Sure, whatever," he said.

She came over to the bed, leaned down to kiss him with her blouse hanging unbuttoned in his face, and said, "I mean the whole day—and that includes tonight, too."

He reached his hand inside her blouse and cupped her breast with his hand.

"You didn't say anything about the night," he said.

"Well, I'm saying it now."

He pulled his hand away and sat up straight, pressing his back hard against the cold headboard. "Seriously," he said. "I don't think I have a problem, at least not as bad as you seem to think I do. I can handle myself."

"Yeah, sure you can," she said, sliding the last of her buttons through the loop. "But later on, when the little voice in your head starts arguing that you should have just one little drink, you'll be wishing you had admitted it was a problem to me now."

"Little voice?"

"Hey, I quit smoking three years ago. I am very familiar with the little voice that tries to talk you into doing something you're not supposed to do, especially something you've promised yourself you wouldn't do. It's a powerful thing, for being such a little voice. And, Horace," she said. "I know you've got one."

He tucked the sheet around his thighs and avoided looking up at her. "I don't know what you're talking about," he said.

She smiled. "Sure, you don't. I'll talk to you later."

He watched her blow him a kiss on her way out of the bedroom, and listened as she skipped down the stairs (at least, that was how it sounded) and out through the front door.

"Fuck," he whispered. "There's no way I'm making it to five o'clock, much less through the whole night, without a drink."

He sighed and felt his lips twist into a sneer. He hated being proven wrong, and he especially hated knowing he was wrong all along, like he had been just now, talking to Andrea. He knew he was a drunk, and he preferred not to think about it. Stories about drunks were boring, even when you *were* one, so he liked to pretend he was tortured in other, more interesting ways. Maybe he was, but he was still also a drunk at the heart of it, and that pissed him off.

He got up, ignoring the sticky feel of his bare, post-coital crotch, and pulled on the same pair of boxer shorts he had been wearing last night. He was already in a bad mood, which made him decide that he wasn't going to bother showering before beginning his day, so he might as well keep on the same clothes from yesterday, too. How much worse could the stink be?

Still wearing just the boxers, he sat back down on the edge of the bed and tugged open the drawer in the bedside table. Inside was the latest in the long line of his mother's diaries that he had been reading. He'd been through four or five volumes, and he hadn't even been born yet. His mother had certainly been prolific. And that was exactly why Richard Riley was planning to write a biography about her. Besides the fact that her entire adult life was one enormous fucked-up mess, she was still a brilliant writer who had published over forty books in her life, which was a relatively short life by today's standards. But just because she had been a great writer and had led a screwed-up existence that rivaled the stories she spun in her novels didn't give someone like Riley—an opportunistic prick—the right to invade her personal world, especially now that she was dead and couldn't defend herself.

That was the real problem, Horace realized. He was the one who was left to defend her memory, and he didn't have the energy or the ability (he was certain) to do it. But there was nobody else—except maybe Aunt Nora or, God forbid, Andrew—and he knew it was his responsibility. That's why he knew he had to find Richard Riley, talk to him, and, if necessary, beat the living shit out of him.

He was able to arrange a meeting, using Clara Bergen, his mother's former secretary at the publishing house, as a go-between. According to

Clara, Riley had sounded excited at the prospect of meeting Horace for a drink. He must have been thinking that Horace was coming around to the idea of Riley's writing about his mother, and that Horace wanted to be a part of the process, to make sure he got in his side of the story.

Riley was way off base.

Horace got to the bar a few minutes early and asked for a booth in the back, from which he could watch the door and know the precise moment when Riley walked in, all puffed up and self-important and gloating over the fact that Horace had backed down and chosen to take part in the writing process instead of waiting for the finished book to come out and then trying to sue. At least, that's what Horace imagined Riley would be thinking.

A nondescript brunette cocktail waitress appeared almost instantly after Horace sat down, with one of those little notebooks and a pen in her hand. *How hard is it to remember one person's drink order without writing it down?* Horace wondered.

"What can I get you?" she asked, her pen poised above the pad, ready to go.

Horace looked past her at the long line of bottles lined up on the mirrored wall behind the dark mahogany bar, the light of a few tiny spotlights glinting off their surfaces and casting colorful shadows on the opposite wall. Just the sight of those green, brown, and clear bottles made something twist with longing inside Horace's stomach, but he remembered his promise to Andrea this morning, that he would go without drinking for the entire day. With a little burst of laughter, he had an epiphany: The only reason he had chosen today to meet with Riley was to give himself a semi-legitimate excuse for having a drink. He really had become pathetic.

He felt his shoulders clench as he spoke, but tried to shrug off the heavy sensation that Andrea was hanging over him, judging him and finding him unworthy: "Gin and tonic, twist of lime."

The waitress scribbled down all six words, mouthing them silently to herself before she turned and scurried toward the bar.

Horace looked around, confirming that Riley (and, for that matter, Andrea) wasn't here. Other than a few slouched-over old drunks perched on stools at the bar, Horace was alone. He glanced at his watch. He still had a few minutes before Riley was due to show up, and he pictured Riley as the type of person who swept into an appointment a few minutes late on purpose, just to make sure the person he was meeting was impressed by the fact that he was important enough to have other things to do—things that were more worthwhile than the current appointment.

Horace reached inside the briefcase he had brought with him and pulled out the volume of his mother's diary that he was currently reading. He propped it open with his thumb and began to read, pausing only to cast a brief smile at the waitress when she returned with his drink balanced precariously on a tray. Absorbed in his mother's world, he didn't notice when Riley walked in and made his way to the table.

"Good book?" Riley asked, leaning over the table and pressing his palms down on its edge so he could peer at Horace in the semi-darkness.

Horace tried to fight the startled feeling that seized him at the sound of Riley's booming voice. Keeping his own voice level and strong, he said, as he shoved the diary back into his briefcase, "Nothing you'd be interested in. After all, you didn't write it."

Riley smiled broadly and slid into the booth beside Horace. "Ah, so true. I do prefer good literature, and the best way to tell if something is good is to find out whether I've written it or not."

The over-eager waitress returned with her pad and pen and nervously took Riley's order—a double bourbon on the rocks. She was still writing as she turned away to head toward the bar and get his drink.

Riley laughed. "Now *she* would make a great character in a book."

Horace took a sip from his drink. "I thought you only wrote nonfiction these days."

Riley shrugged and spread his arms across the back of the booth. "There's a fine line between fiction and nonfiction."

"Especially when *you're* writing it," Horace said.

Riley let his right arm slide down to clap Horace on the back. "Sounds like someone's a little bitter."

"You'd be bitter, too, if someone was spending the bulk of his career spreading lies about your family."

"What makes you think I don't know what that feels like?" Riley asked, a mask of seriousness on his face.

"I don't think you even have feelings, Riley," Horace replied.

The waitress came back, balancing the tray with Riley's bourbon on it carefully between both of her hands. She set the drink down on the table, then turned and fled, as if she were afraid she would be asked to fetch another drink and realized she hadn't brought her pad and pen with her.

Riley took a short sip of bourbon and winced as he set the drink back down on the table. "I only order this shit because I hate the way it tastes."

Horace shook his head. "That makes a lot of fucking sense."

"It does if you don't want to get drunk," Riley said. "And as someone who makes his living observing the actions of other people, it's a good idea for me to stay sharp."

"I don't think you'll ever be sharp, no matter how little alcohol you drink."

Riley just smiled and leaned back into the squeaky leather of the booth. "So what did you really want to talk to me about, Cairo?"

"You know what I want to talk about."

"Ah, yes. The book. I really think this one is my masterpiece."

"What do you mean? Have you already written it?" Horace asked.

Riley shrugged. "Not all of it, no. But I'm close enough to finishing that I know how good it is."

"What kind of standard are you using to judge it? Because I've got to tell you, everything else you've ever written is crap."

Riley smiled. "You wouldn't be saying that if you were a thirty-nine-year-old housewife hoping to get a cheap thrill by reading about the glitterati."

Horace laughed. "My family hardly qualifies as glitterati."

Riley held out his hands. "I don't know about that. Think about it. Your parents were fabulously rich entrepreneurs, and your uncle, despite the fact that he's a felon, is an interesting character—the kind of guy a horny housewife would love to think about while she sticks her finger in her twat."

"This conversation has taken a pleasant turn."

Riley used his knuckle to push Horace's drink closer to him. "Come on, buddy," he said. "All you need is a little drink to loosen you up."

Horace backhanded the glass, sending it shooting across the table and off the edge. It landed with a room-stopping shatter on the floor. The tense waitress glanced up from her post at the end of the bar with a look of stricken horror on her face. She grabbed a towel from a small rack tacked to the edge of the bar and ran over with her feet too close together, like a wind-up toy. She didn't even peek up at Horace and Riley as she wiped up the spilled gin and slowly collected the tiny pieces of broken glass, placing them into the towel, which she had laid over her palm.

"You'd better bring him another, sweetheart," Riley said, leaning out of the booth far enough to poke the girl in the ribs. She leapt up, startled, and almost dropped the towel full of glass.

She looked from Riley to Horace and back. "Another gin and tonic?"

Riley laid his wallet on the table and opened it, tugging out a fifty-dollar bill. "Yes, another gin and tonic. And this one's on me."

Before the girl could take the bill, Horace swiped it out of Riley's hand and slapped it back down on the table. "I'll just have an ice water," he said, staring hard, defiant, into Riley's eyes.

"Yes, sir, ice water. Coming right up." The girl ran back to the bar, where an older, male bartender was standing with his arms folded over his barrel chest and an annoyed look on his face. Horace watched as the man apparently chewed the waitress out for breaking the glass. For a moment, he thought about getting up and going over to defend the girl, to tell the man that he was the one who had broken the glass, but when he saw that Riley was still smiling at him, amused at his behavior, he decided that dealing with the asshole writer was a bigger priority.

"So what is this?" Riley asked, twirling his bourbon glass around and around with his forefingers. "Going clean and sober, are we?"

"It's none of your goddamn business, Riley."

"Then why did you ask me to meet you here? Obviously, something is my business."

The waitress returned with a tall glass of water that had a sickly looking slice of lemon wedged down among the tightly packed chunks of ice. She set it down and fled before either of her customers could ask her for something else.

Horace stared at the glass, imagining that it was full of gin, and realized that this was going to be a defining moment in his life. If he could get through the next ten minutes or so without taking a drink, he would never have to drink again.

"Go ahead, Cairo," Riley said with a smirk on his face. "Take a sip. You'll love it. So clean and refreshing."

Horace grabbed the glass and sucked down a few gulps of the water, which tasted faintly of dish soap. Trying to keep his hands from trembling, he put the glass back down on the table and pressed his palms together.

"Okay," Horace said. "Let's get this over with."

Riley had a Cheshire cat smile on his face. He was loving every minute of this bizarre meeting.

"If you publish this so-called biography without my authorization or approval, I'll sue you and your publisher for all you're worth, and after that, you'll be lucky if you can get work writing term papers for high school kids."

Riley sat back and crossed one of his legs over the opposite knee. "You forget, my friend, that your mother was a public figure. I don't need your permission to write about her. Or you, for that matter."

"Maybe so," Horace said. "But if what you write is inaccurate, that'll be libel. And your career will be over. I promise you that."

Riley stopped smiling, uncrossed his legs, and leaned over, close to Horace. "Don't you think your mother's story is worth telling?"

Horace sat there for a second, staring into Riley's eyes, which glowed with what Horace could only describe as evil. "I do," he said. "But you're not the one she would have wanted to tell it."

"Oh? Then who would be the right person?"

Horace took a deep breath and let it out slowly through his pursed lips. "Me."

"You?" Riley said. "You're going to write a book about your mother? Come on. I know you're blind in one eye, but even you can see that wouldn't be an intelligent idea."

"Fuck you, Riley," Horace said, his fingers reaching up to brush against his eye patch.

"Seriously, though," Riley said. "Why don't you leave the writing to professionals?"

"Like you?"

"Yeah," Riley said. "I'm one of the best. Probably *the* best."

"If we're talking about tabloids and sensationalism, then you're probably right."

Riley sneered. "I'm a biographer."

"You're a paparazzo."

Riley moved to stand up, but stopped and turned back to Horace. "Cairo, really, I'm trying to be helpful here. Trust me. People want to read sensational shit—and I know how to get that angle on things. Even without your help, I'll be able to capture your mother's innermost thoughts, her personality."

Horace smiled. "Yeah? Well, so will I. I'm not going to write the book. I'm going to publish her diaries."

"Diaries?"

Horace nodded. "There are dozens of them. Mom was about as prolific a diarist as Anaïs Nin. So top that, Mr. Biographer."

Horace slid out of the booth and started to walk away, then realized that he had almost forgotten his briefcase, which was full of his mother's papers and the current volume of her journal. He ran back to the booth and grabbed the case just as Riley was leaning over to reach for it.

"Nice try," Horace said. "But this is mine. And so is my mother's story. Have a nice day, Riley."

26

IRIS

| FEBRUARY 9, 1980 |

I only stopped back at the hotel long enough to grab my things and pay the bill. Then I jumped into the car and drove west toward the purple sunset, not bothering to pay attention to what road I was on or what towns I was passing. I just needed to put as much distance between me and Seth as I could as fast as possible.

Even after the sun had gone down and I had to pull the button that turns on the headlights, I just kept driving, ignoring the bright white letters and the big green signs that declared what city each exit on the highway would take me to. I no longer remembered where I was supposed to be going or even why I was driving down some strange, dark road in an unfamiliar state in the middle of the night. All I could do was replay my conversation with Seth over and over in my head.

Sometime just before dawn I noticed that the gas gauge was nearly on empty and pulled into a gas station—the old-fashioned kind with only a single pump and a rundown building outfitted with several bays for car repair, all of which stood empty and reminded me of the eye sockets in a skull. I tensed my shoulders against the shiver that ran through me and dug through my purse for my wallet as the old man who apparently owned the station came over to wait on me.

"Fill 'er up?" he asked, with a bulge of chewing tobacco puffing out his lower lip.

"Yes, please," I said, handing him a fifty-dollar bill. "And keep the change. I'm in a hurry."

The man grinned and tugged at the edges of the crisp bill, making it snap. "Thankee, miss."

I rolled up my window and laid my head on my arms over the steering wheel, closing my eyes and letting the desire to sleep take me, if only for a moment, while the old man filled the gas tank. I was going to have to stop at the next motel I saw. I knew I was too tired to drive any farther tonight, and besides, I was supposed to be following a plan. And now that I had seen Seth and messed up any chance of getting him arrested, my only hope was to figure out where Seth had hidden Oscar's body. I'd been driving so long and so aimlessly that I was probably a whole day off course. But at least I was safe. And Seth was miles behind me, with no idea of where I had gone.

The old man tapped the trunk of the car to let me know he was finished pumping the gas.

"Excuse me, sir," I called out the window. "But is there a motel or hotel nearby?"

The man spat a bullet of tobacco juice out the side of his mouth. His blackened, grimy hand scratched at his head, as if he were confused, but his voice was sure and steady when he answered.

"'Bout a mile and a half down that a-way, you take a right when you seen an old red barn, half burnt out. Then you go a bit, mile or two, and you'll see Pine Ridge Motel. They always got a vacancy."

"Thank you," I said as I started the engine.

"Good luck to you, miss," the old man said, his weathered face suddenly a mask of compassion that startled me.

I shuddered. Now I'm starting to imagine things, I thought. I'd better find this motel and get some sleep.

The old man's directions were so accurate, it was almost eerie. As I turned the corner by the half-burned barn, the morning sun peeked up over the low mountains in the distance. It was an odd time to be checking into a hotel, but maybe that was a good thing. If Seth was following me, he would probably have expected me to stop last night at one of the many roadside motels I'd passed during my blind, terrified drive. He would never come this far and expect to find me. That gave me time—at least half a day—to get some rest and keep ahead of him.

I checked into the motel under the name Charlotte Brontë (which didn't even make the clerk blink) and fell into a deep sleep almost the exact moment my body hit the stiff bed with its cool, shiny bedspread, which I didn't even bother to climb under.

When I woke up, the small clock with the scratched face on the nightstand read 10:35, but the room-darkening curtains were drawn and I couldn't tell whether it was morning or night.

I rolled over and off the bed and went to the window. Although the sky was gray and the sun hazy, it was clearly daytime. That meant I had slept maybe four hours or so. It would have to be enough. I wanted to get back on the road as soon as possible. On the road, always moving, I'm safe. The longer I stay in one place, the easier it will be for Seth to find me. It's weird how things have turned. First, it was me looking for him, and now it's him hunting me down. At least, I assume he is. It feels like he is.

I went back to the bed and opened my purse, taking out the little green address book I'm using to track down Seth's women.

The next name I had marked was Shondra Cantwell, in Perrysburg, Ohio. I figured if I washed up and changed my clothes right away, I'd be able to head toward Shondra's today, but first I had to figure out where the hell I was—whether I was still somewhere in the backwoods of Pennsylvania, or whether I had crossed into Ohio at some point during my feverish drive through the night.

I picked up the phone and dialed the front desk. A man with a nasal voice answered, sounding harried and put out, which seemed odd for someone working at a motel that likely saw no more than a hundred or two visitors in a year.

"Hi," I said. "I was hoping you could tell me what town this is."

The nasal man coughed. "What do you mean?"

"What town are we in?"

After letting out an angry-sounding sigh, the man said, "Parkertown."

I bit my lip, reluctant to sound any more foolish than I already did. "Yes, okay, and what state is that in?"

"You've got to be kidding," the man said. "What is this, some kind of joke?"

"Just tell me—what state is this, Pennsylvania or Ohio?"

"Ohio. I'm hanging up now."

The line went dead and I let the receiver fall back into the phone base. Crap, I thought. I still had to find out whether I was anywhere near Perrysburg. I decided to just check out and find my way back to the gas station where the old man had given me directions to the motel. He'd be able—and willing, I figured—to help me.

Showered and dressed in a loose-fitting floral sundress (which was all wrong for the winter weather, but then, I had packed for this trip too fast and in too much of a rage), I took a last look around the room to make sure I wasn't forgetting anything. I slung my suitcase strap and my purse over my shoulder and went to the car, grateful that I paid for the room in full last night (or, rather, this morning) so I didn't have to face the disdainful, nasal desk clerk to check out.

Skittering gravel as I drove away, I tried to remember the route—simple as it was—back to the gas station. I could only hope that the same old man would still be there.

There were no other cars at the gas station when I pulled up beside the pump. The door to the little station house opened and the same old man stepped out. I almost cried out in joy.

"Miss," the man said by way of greeting. "Sumpin' I can help ya with?"

"I hope so," I said, pulling out the paper with Shondra's address on it. "Can you tell me how to get to this town? Perrysburg?"

"You ain't got too far to go," he said. "Just 'bout fifty miles." He guided me with his vibrant, landmark-sprinkled directions to the appropriate interstate and told me exactly which exit I would have to take.

I reached for my purse, intending to pull out some cash for a tip, but the old man's gentle touch on my forearm stopped me. I turned to meet his gaze.

"Is there sumpin' I can do for ya, miss? Ya seem—I dunno—lost."

I sighed and had to blink back tears. This stranger seemed to be more tuned in to my desperation and misery than even my family had been when I told them I was setting off on this foolish journey.

"I don't think so," I said. I shrugged. "But you know what? Here," I said, handing him the picture of Seth I've been carrying around in my purse. "I know it's a longshot, but maybe you've seen this guy passing through?"

The man studied the picture with a frown of concentration on his face. Then he handed back the picture. It had been stupid even to ask, I thought, shoving the photo back into my purse.

"Yeah, I seen 'im," the old man said.

I whipped around to face him. "You have?"

"Yup. Maybe a month or two back, I'd reckon."

"Oh my God, you have no idea how much this helps me. Do you remember where he was headed? Did he say?"

The old man scratched his head and readjusted the rim of the black-smudged cap he was wearing. "Yup, he did."

"Where? Where was he going?"

"Same place as you, miss. Perrysburg."

I squeezed my eyes closed to hold the tears back. If Seth had come this far, he had certainly gone to see Shondra, and it was possible—very possible—that he had concealed Oscar's body somewhere nearby.

"Thank you," I said. "Thanks so much. Is there anything else you can remember about him?"

"Yup, yup, I can. Only 'cuz it was such an odd thing."

"What's that?"

"He bought a tarp and a garden shovel off me."

"You sell that kind of equipment?" I asked, my eyes surveying the ramshackle station.

"Not usually, no. But he asked if I had 'em, and when I said yup, he give me five hundred dollars cash for 'em."

Jesus, I thought. Seth had bought the very tools he needed to bury my dead husband's body right here at this gas station.

I thanked the old man and pressed a hundred-dollar bill into his hand. He tried to protest, but I said, "You've helped me so much. You may even have saved my life. So thank you."

Not pausing to watch him take in my words, I hopped into the car and pulled back out onto the open road. In about an hour, I would be in Perrysburg, and I'd be able to meet Shondra Cantwell, who might just help me solve the mystery of where Oscar's body is hidden.

27

HORACE

"So she's your mother's sister?" Andrea asked, staring out the window on the passenger side of the car at the gray New York buildings swishing by on a gray New York morning.

"Nora, yeah," Horace said. "They were only a year apart, but they were so different. Mom was always so—I don't know—in motion. She wasn't outgoing, necessarily; that's not why she seemed larger than life. She was just kind of quietly confident in herself. Does that make any sense?"

Andrea smiled and nibbled at a hangnail on her pinkie. "Yeah," she said. "It does. When I really stop and consider my life, I wish I could be that way. I wish I were the kind of person with energy bubbling out of them, always doing something or making something."

"That was Mom," Horace said. He leaned forward to stare up at the red light, drumming his thumbs on the steering wheel as he waited for it to change. When it did, he slammed his foot on the gas, but had to stomp on the brakes because the cab in front of him had hardly inched forward.

"And Nora? What's she like?" Andrea said, trying to distract him from the irritating congestion of the traffic.

"Nora? Well, she's different now from the way she was when I was a kid, but she's still nothing like Mom. She's always been so, like, mousy. You know what I mean? Timid and scrunched up, like she's afraid of the world. She's better now, I guess. But still. She lets Andrew walk all over her. She lets everyone walk all over her. Except me. For some reason, she stands up to me."

The traffic started to move and Horace could see the green light over the entrance to the Holland Tunnel. Another fifteen minutes, maybe, and they'd be out of the stinking city and back in Jersey. He laughed inside, thinking how funny it was that all his life he'd been ashamed of being from New Jersey and had counted the days until he could get his own apartment in Manhattan, and now that he could afford any apartment—even an amazing penthouse with a view—he would rather settle himself in a semi-quiet New Jersey suburb, where he could watch slim, tanned soccer moms cruise down the streets in their oversized luxury SUVs.

"So why are we going out to see her?" Andrea asked.

"What?" Horace realized that he had distracted himself thinking about his neighborhood and had forgotten all about Andrea sitting there beside him, craning her neck to see over the cars ahead of them.

"Sorry," he said. "Traffic. What were you saying?"

"Why are we going to see your aunt Nora?"

"I don't know, really," he said, hitting the gas with an almost gleeful surge of energy as the car passed through the mouth of the tunnel and into the strange, eerie non-darkness, lit by flickering fluorescent bulbs.

"I guess I kind of want to get her permission to do the book of Mom's diaries," he said. "Not that I need it. Mom left all that stuff to me. But it would be easier if Nora approved."

"That makes sense," Andrea said, turning to stare out the window at the blur of the tunnel wall.

He reached over to touch her hand with just the tips of his fingers. "And I want her to meet you," he said.

She turned to smile at him. "My, oh my," she said. "Sounds like someone's getting pretty serious here. Introducing me to your family. We must have been together—what?—two weeks now?"

"Don't be a pain in the ass," he said. "You know perfectly well how long we've been together."

She tapped her forefinger against her cheek, as if she were deep in thought. "I'm not sure," she said. "Do we count from the night we met and fucked for the first time, or from the first time we actually went out on a date as two sober, consenting adults?"

He grinned and rubbed his palm along the inside of her thigh, which was bare for a few inches above her knee, before her skirt's hem fell over her lap. "I say we go with the first one," he said.

She smiled and put her own hand over his, pushing it up and under the flap of her skirt until his fingers were grazing the edges of her panties and slipping beneath them.

"I would tend to agree," she said, spreading her legs just enough for Horace's hand to open between them. She laid her head back and closed her eyes, biting her lip rhythmically as he fingered her. Horace tried to concentrate on the road as they burst out of the tunnel and into the bright, sunlit world, but he had to take his eyes off the highway long enough to watch her shudder just a little as she came. When he took his hand away and put it firmly on the steering wheel, she opened her eyes.

"Now that was something to remember," she said.

They drove the rest of the way in silence. Every now and then Horace raised his fingers to his nose to sniff in her essence. He would have stuffed his fingers in his mouth and licked her scent off them if she hadn't been sitting there right beside him, watching his every move with that sly, sexy smile twitching at her lips.

When he pulled into the driveway, he noticed that Andrew's car wasn't parked there. "Thank God, Andrew's not home," he said. "I think you've already been around him enough to last a lifetime."

Andrea shrugged. "I don't think he's as bad as you make him out to be."

"He's an abrasive drunk," Horace said.

Andrea flashed him a smile but quickly clamped her mouth shut.

"I know, I know, I'm a drunk, too," he said. "Let's not talk about that right now."

She put up her hands in surrender. "It's fine. Let's go in."

Nora opened the door before Horace could touch the bell.

"Get in here, kid," she said, holding open the screen door with her elbow and pulling him in by grasping him around the neck.

Horace leaned in to kiss her on the cheek, then ducked under her arm and into the living room to make way for Andrea to follow him inside.

"And this must be the famous Andrea," Nora said, extending her hand for Andrea to shake.

"It's so nice to meet you," Andrea said.

"Likewise. My nephew really likes you, you know."

"Aunt Nora!" Horace said, feeling himself blush like a schoolgirl.

"What?"

Andrea smiled. "I don't think you're supposed to tell me he likes me. It's supposed to be a big secret."

Nora waved her hand in dismissal. "What nonsense. In my day, we told each other right straight out whether we liked each other or not. We didn't play all these games."

"Sure, whatever you say, Aunt Nora," Horace said. "You forget that I've been reading Mom's diaries. Even if *you* never played games, Mom sure as hell did."

Nora ushered them over to the couch. "Well, your mother . . . she was something else."

"What was she?"

Nora shook her head. "There's no word to describe her. She was just—Iris." There was a long silence as Nora sat staring at her palms with an expression on her face that made her look like she had never noticed her own hands before.

"Aunt Nora? You okay?" Horace asked.

She looked up at him and smiled. "Of course. Now, what can I get you kids to drink? Wine? Beer?"

Horace looked over at Andrea, but she kept her eyes down on her lap, obviously waiting to see whether he would choose to have a drink or not.

"Just water for me," he said. Andrea looked up, her eyes wide with surprise.

"Same for me," she said. "Can I help you?"

Nora waved her off. "I'll be back in a flash."

As soon as Nora had left the room, Andrea reached over and took Horace's hand in hers. "I'm proud of you," she said.

"Hey, just trying to do the right thing. You know I'm a Boy Scout these days."

They sat in comfortable silence, listening to Nora clanging around in the kitchen. Her banging and the loud rush of the faucet almost masked the sound of Andrew's car screeching to a halt in the driveway, but not quite.

"Fuck," Horace said, pulling his hand away from Andrea's and getting up so he would be standing and ready to face Andrew when he walked through the door.

Andrew burst in with his characteristic grin on his face and his keys jingling between his fingers.

"What a surprise!" he said. "My favorite cousin and his little girl-friend. How have you been, Angela?"

Andrea got up from the couch to shake Andrew's hand. "It's Andrea," she said.

"Jesus, Andrew," Horace said. "You've met her like four times now and you still can't remember her name. What are you, retarded?"

"Don't use that word," Nora said as she breezed into the room with a glinting silver tray in her hands, the kind people get as wedding gifts and then never use even once. She set the tray, which held a pitcher of water and three glasses, on the coffee table, then moved over to shut the front door, which Andrew had left wide open.

"Hey, Mom," Andrew said, pushing past her to get a better view of the tray on the coffee table. "What the hell is this we're drinking? Vodka straight up? I didn't know you were such a wild woman, Ma."

"It's water, sweetheart," Nora said, bending over to fill the three glasses. "If you want something else, go and get it for yourself in the kitchen."

Horace grabbed Andrea by the hand and pulled her over to the couch, where they sat back down and accepted the glasses of water that Nora handed them.

Andrew watched them sip from their glasses with a look of amusement on his face. "Ugh," he said. "Water. I can't drink that crap, at least not without a splash of scotch." He laughed but no one else joined in.

"So what are you doing here, cuz?" Andrew asked, perching beside his mother on the edge of the loveseat.

"I wanted Aunt Nora to meet Andrea," Horace said. "And I had something else to discuss, but I think maybe we'll save that for another time."

"Not because of me, I hope?" Andrew asked.

"Well, actually . . ."

Nora broke in. "Andrew, why don't you go on up to your room? Obviously, your cousin has something private to talk to me about."

"I don't get it," he said. "What the hell could he possibly have to say that I can't hear? I'm his fucking cousin. We're as good as freaking brothers."

Horace sighed. "It's fine," he said. "It doesn't matter if Andrew hears this. It's not that important."

"I'm disappointed already," Andrew said with a smile.

Horace ignored him and looked to Andrea, who nodded in support. Taking a deep breath, he said, "Well, it's pretty simple, really. I want to publish Mom's diaries and I was hoping to, I don't know, get your blessing, I guess."

Nora wrinkled her brow. "I guess you never got the same letter from her that I got, a few weeks before she died."

"A letter? No. What did it say?"

"That she wanted you to edit and publish her diaries."

Horace let out his breath in relief. "Huh. Weird. That's great. I'm so glad. I was really afraid you would be against the idea."

Andrew piped in at that point. "And will Mom be getting a cut of the profits from this little enterprise?"

"Andrew, shut up," Nora said.

Horace shrugged. "I thought maybe we could give the profits to one of Mom's old charities, like the SPCA or something."

Andrew stood up. "I don't think so, cuz," he said. "I think we ought to split the profits between your side of the family and ours."

"We're the same side of the family, dumbass," Horace said.

"Then that's even better. More money for us."

Nora patted Andrew on the arm. "It's Horace's mother and Horace's project. We'll do whatever he wants to do."

"And what about Riley?" Andrew asked.

Horace froze. "What about him?"

"Are you going to give him an interview?"

"Of course not," Horace said, almost spitting the words through his teeth.

"Well, I am," Andrew said.

"You have got to be kidding," Horace said. "You're going to help that son of a . . ."

"Why shouldn't I?"

"Because he's a parasite and a liar and he has done his best to wring every drop of money he can out of this family."

"Yeah," Andrew said. "I kind of like him."

Horace took Andrea's hand and leapt up from the couch. Pausing to lean down and kiss Nora on the cheek, he started for the door.

"We're out of here."

Nora slapped Andrew on the shoulder. "Now look what you've done. Can't you be a good person every once in a while?"

Andrew crossed his arms over his chest. "I don't see what the big deal is," he said.

"That's exactly the fucking point," Horace said. "Sorry, Aunt Nora, but we have to go."

There were tears in her eyes as she nodded. "I'll call you tomorrow, honey," she said.

"Nice to see you as always, Andrew," Horace said. He pushed Andrea through the doorway before him and let the heavy oak door slam shut behind them.

28

IRIS

| FEBRUARY 10, 1980 |

Finding Perrysburg was easy with the old man's directions. I passed a sign that welcomed me to town at 12:30. Now I just had to find a hotel and give Shondra Cantwell a call.

I didn't stop at the first hotel I passed, an upscale-looking Hilton. Instead, I continued on and took a room at a somewhat dilapidated Red Roof Inn. I knew Seth would expect me to opt for luxury, just because I could afford it, just because that was what *he* would do. But I didn't care how nice the paintings on the walls were or whether the drapes were fraying at the edges from being opened and closed too many times. Now that Oscar is gone, I feel like it doesn't matter where I am. One place is as good as any other.

I settled into the room and pulled back the curtains to check out the view. Mostly, the surrounding area seemed to be farmland, with houses dotting the landscape here and there. I wondered how Seth would have even met a woman from a town like this. He wasn't exactly the type to go out cruising for farmers' daughters. But then again, a woman was just a woman to Seth, I figured. A cunt is a cunt. (God, I hate that word.)

I went back to the bed and sat down beside the phone, pulling out the green address book. As I did, the picture of Seth slipped out and fell into my lap. I picked it up and stared at it hard.

If you just looked at his picture, you'd probably never guess that he was a murderer or even just a stalker. He's too good-looking. You'd think he was a former football or tennis player, someone who had cruised through college taking simple business courses and then went into the family business, selling whatever widgets or doodads his family had been making for generations. How wonderful life would have been if that were indeed Seth's story, instead of the Shakespearean tragedy his life (and my own) really is.

I shoved the picture back into my purse and picked up the phone. It rang seven times and I was about to hang up when a woman answered, panting. "Hello?"

"Uh—yes, hi. I'm looking for Shondra Cantwell, please."

"Speaking."

I felt a surge of gratitude run through me. "Is this a bad time?" I asked. "You sound out of breath."

"No, no," Shondra said. "I was just outside in the greenhouse watering the plants and I had to run to get the phone. How can I help you?"

"Well, this is going to sound like a strange thing to ask, but I'd like to meet you."

"Who are you? Did you say?"

I winced. "I'm sorry, no, I didn't. My name is Iris Cairo. The reason I need to see you has to do with—"

"Seth. Seth Cairo. Right?"

"How did you know that?" I asked.

"Not all that many Cairos running around, are there?"

"I guess you're right about that."

"So when do you want to come by?"

"Whenever is convenient for you," I said. "I don't want to put you out at all."

"Do you know where I live?" Shondra said. Her voice was lower and her breathing more even now.

"I have your address, yes," I said.

"Then come on over whenever you want. I'll be here all day."

The phone line went dead, and I pictured Shondra (who, at this point, I envisioned only as a shapely female body with no face or even hair) trotting back out to her greenhouse and picking up a long hose that was leaking around the nozzle.

It was time to get out of here.

I hopped into my car, feeling almost happy for the first time in longer than I can remember. For the first time since I had left on this trip, I felt like I was close to finding something—like maybe I was finally close to uncovering the truth and bringing Seth to justice.

Shondra's place wasn't hard to find. Even though none of the little Cape Cod houses on the street were numbered, hers was the only one with a greenhouse beside it that almost dwarfed the house itself. I wondered what the hell Shondra was growing out here that needed to be tended even at this time of year, at the tail end of a bad winter. Somehow, I doubted it was watermelons or green beans.

I parked the car behind an old red pickup truck and turned off the ignition. A shiver of fear ran up my spine when I thought about the fact that Oscar's body could be buried somewhere around here, maybe even close enough for me to touch. It was time to find out.

I started up the walk, glancing over at the absurdly large greenhouse as I went. That's when I noticed a big mound of dry dirt, piled up beside the greenhouse, like something had recently been buried there. It looked like a grave. I gagged and had to stop walking. My breathing had stopped and I clutched at my throat, as if I were choking. It's good, I was yelling inside my head, trying to rationalize, to bring my emotions—and my body—under control. It's good if this is the place. If this is the right place, then this is all over. I sucked in a huge breath of air in a ragged gasp. Then my brain, the feeling part, whispered a reply to the rational part: It's not over. This has only just begun.

I sighed and kept walking up to the front door. I rang the doorbell, straining my ears to make sure the rusty-looking thing was actually making a sound inside the house. The door opened almost immediately, as if Shondra had been sitting right beside it, waiting for me to get there. That made me feel suddenly self-conscious, when I realized it was possible—even likely—that Shondra had been watching me from behind the door the whole time since I had pulled into the driveway. It made me feel naked. And—maybe this is weird—fat.

"Iris?" Shondra asked, holding the door open so I could step inside.

"Yes," I said, holding out my hand for Shondra to shake. Shondra wiped some invisible dirt off her hand onto her jeans before shaking my hand. "Thanks for meeting me."

Shondra escorted me over to a couch that had a small hole in one of its cushions, through which a tuft of foam was peeking out. "Please, sit down," Shondra said. "Can I get you something to drink or anything?"

"No, no, thank you. I'm fine. I don't want to take up too much of your time."

Shondra sat down in an armchair next to the couch and leaned her head on her forearm, staring at me intensely. We sat for a long and awkward moment in silence before I realized that Shondra wasn't going to be the one to start the conversation. I was going to have to handle that myself.

"So," I said. "You know Seth."

She smiled. "In the biblical sense, yeah, but not much beyond that. Actually, not at all beyond that."

I laughed in spite of myself. I liked Shondra already. I found myself wishing we were meeting under different circumstances. She could have been my friend, and God knows, I could use one—one who isn't related to me and doesn't have a stake in the tragedies of my life.

"So how did you . . . um . . . meet him?" I asked.

She leaned back and folded her arms behind her head, looking easy and casual—the way I always wish I could look. I tend to think I look like a herky-jerky robot, all stiff and awkward, most of the time.

"Exactly the way you'd expect—in a bar," she said. "It was only recently, maybe a month or two. I stopped in this little hole in the wall place that's got cheap drinks and great chicken wings, just planning to grab a bite before going home and going to bed. Seth came up and sat next to me at the bar."

"What did you talk about? I mean, what did he say to, you know, get your interest?"

"You mean, what kind of line did he use to pick me up, right?" She grinned as she stretched her arms out in front of her.

I smiled back. "Yes, that's exactly what I mean. So, what did he say?"

Her smile faded and her eyes drifted down to the floor, staring at nothing, so far as I could tell.

"That's the thing," she said, her voice suddenly soft and somehow vulnerable-sounding, if that makes any sense. "I don't remember."

"What do you mean? You remember his name and what you ate—how can you not remember what he talked about?"

She shook her head, glanced at me, then looked down at the floor again.

"I don't know," she said. "I didn't think I was drunk. I only had two scotches, which isn't a lot for me, sad to say."

I broke in. "Do you think he drugged you?"

She shrugged. "I couldn't say for sure, but yeah, it's a possibility. I can't remember that. Really, all I remember is the way he looked and that smile of his. At the time, I kept thinking it was a movie star smile. But now . . ."

I frowned. "But now?"

"Now I think it was the same kind of smile I imagine the devil would have."

A tingle ran down my spine. Yes, another cliché, but I'm trying to be accurate here, and a tingle is precisely what I felt.

There was a long moment of silence as I tried to figure out what I should say next, what I could ask her without upsetting her or making her relive something she clearly didn't want to remember.

"Okay," I said. "I understand that you don't have a clear memory of what happened . . ."

"I don't have *any* memory of what happened," she snapped.

I felt myself suck in a breath. After a moment, I forced myself to let it out and then I continued. "But . . . well, obviously, you remember sleeping with him."

She kind of shrunk in on herself, wrapping her arms around her torso. "Not exactly," she said. "I only know I had sex with him because there was a used rubber on the floor the next morning."

"My God."

Shondra smiled weakly. "It's not so bad," she said. "At least he used something. Could have been worse. I could be telling you this story with my crotch all aflame from herpes. Small blessings, right?"

I smiled and shook my head. "You're braver than I am."

"I'm not brave," she said. "I'm stupid. But I guess I'm lucky."

Luckier than you realize, I thought. Not everybody survives an encounter with Seth.

Thinking about Oscar's murder reminded me about the mound of dirt outside. It was time to bring it up.

"Um—I'm sorry if this seems nosy, but—can I ask what that mound of dirt is, next to your greenhouse?"

Shondra made a face, like she thought I was crazy—which, I understood, was a reasonable assumption.

"Why do you want to know?" she asked.

I closed my eyes. Somehow, I had thought I'd be able to get through this trip without actually having to tell anybody about Oscar being murdered. I realized suddenly how stupid that had been.

I opened my eyes. "Well, that's kind of the whole reason I'm here. See, back in December, Seth killed his brother—my husband, Oscar. And I think he buried the body somewhere near here."

The look on Shondra's face was a painful combination of horror and sympathy. I looked away, as my eyes filled with tears.

"Good God . . ." she whispered.

I glanced back up at her and two hot tears slid down my cheeks and splashed on the front of my blouse. I smiled just a little. "So, you see, that's why I ask."

Shondra stood up and paced a circle in front of me. "Jesus. I wish I could tell you I didn't know what's buried there, so maybe you'd have a chance of finding what you're looking for. But I can't—there isn't actually anything buried there. It's just what's left over after I had a pile of dirt delivered last fall, for my garden. You know. That's all."

She sank back into her chair and shook her head. "I can't even begin to know what you must be going through. I knew Seth was a bastard. But a murderer? That never even crossed my mind."

"Of course not," I said. "Why would it? I knew him as well as anybody, and I would never have thought he could . . . well, I just never thought."

I got up and wiped my face with the heel of my hand. I held out the other hand—the one that wasn't wet with my tears—to shake Shondra's hand. She took my hand in both of hers.

"I'm so, so sorry. I—I don't know what to say to you." She dropped my hand and spun around, pulling a small notepad and a pen out of a drawer in the end table. She scribbled something on a sheet of paper, then thrust it into my hands.

"Obviously, you already have my contact information," she said. "You found me, after all. But here it is again. If you ever need anything—and I mean anything—don't hesitate to get in touch."

I closed my eyes and bowed my head in thanks. I smiled and shook her hand once more, then turned toward the door. Before stepping outside, I realized I had one more question I wanted to ask her.

"So," I said. "What is it you're growing out there, this time of year? I mean, well, if you don't mind me asking."

Shondra chuckled. "You think I'm growing pot, don't you?"

I grinned. "Well . . ." We both laughed. "So what are you growing?"

She flashed a wicked smile and put one hand up to the side of her mouth, like she was about to tell me a secret. In an exaggerated stage whisper, she said, "Poinsettias."

29

HORACE

| Present Day |

"It's like watching children on a playground," Andrea said.

Horace ignored her. Or, rather, he pretended to ignore her. Inside he was frothing at the mouth.

"Oh, of course," she said. "Pretend you're ignoring me. You can't keep that up too long. You're already close to the edge. I can tell. How long will it take before you lash out? One . . . two . . . three . . ."

"All right, enough. You win."

"Three seconds? Wow. I would have guessed four or five at least." She leaned over and brushed her lips against the rough stubble at the edge of his jawbone. "But, then, you aren't very patient about anything, are you?"

"Not now, okay?"

She sat back in her seat and stared through the windshield at the darkness of the road rushing toward them. "Seriously," she said. "What is it about your cousin Andrew that pisses you off so much?"

Horace spat out a burst of laughter. "Are you kidding?"

"I mean, I know he's a pain in the ass," she said.

"Well?"

"That's not it."

"How the hell do you know what 'it' is?"

She smiled at him, sideways, knowing he would only see her in his peripheral vision anyway, and that it always made him laugh when she kept her eyes on the road, as if she were the one driving. "I think I know a lot more about you than you realize," she said.

"Oh, yeah? Like what?"

She kept her eyes trained on the road in front of them. "Like right now, you're wondering if I'll be able to stare straight ahead longer than you will. You're thinking that I might be a more alert backseat driver than you are a regular driver."

He slammed on the brakes and looped the car over to the side of the road. "You're unbelievable."

"What? You're mad?"

"No, I'm not mad. You were right. That's exactly what I was thinking. How did you know that?"

She took his hand and fluttered her thumb over his palm. "I don't know. I just . . . know."

"Marry me."

"You want to marry me because I can read your mind?"

"I want to marry you because I love you."

"I love you, too."

"That's not an answer," he said.

She grinned. "Oh, it's not? Can you repeat the question?"

He reached his hand behind her head and seized her by the hair. He pulled her mouth to his. When he finally let her go, she was still smiling, her eyes wet with tears.

"Is that a yes?" he asked.

"Yes," she said. "Of course it's a yes."

The next morning, Horace propped himself up on his elbow and traced the line of her body, wrapped tight in the sheet, with his finger.

"So, when do you want to have this wedding?" he asked.

She smiled. "I don't need a big wedding."

"I thought every little girl dreamed of her big white wedding."

"I'm not a little girl anymore. Besides, we have bigger things to deal with right now."

"Like what?" he said.

"Like getting your mom's diaries ready to be published."

He laid his palm flat against her hip. "You'd help me with that?"

"Hey, I'm a teacher. I know a little bit about writing. But you should probably just have one of the editors at your mom's company do it."

Horace shook his head. "I need to do this myself. It's important. I feel like I owe it to . . . I don't know."

"To your mother?"

He shrugged. "Maybe. Or maybe to myself. I think I need to get through all those diaries, all that stuff, to learn something about my parents, about my life. I don't know—I feel like there's something I need to find out."

"Ooh," Andrea said, shivering. "That sent a tingle through me. No idea why, but you gave me the creeps a little there. Like you have some tragic secret that's going to turn the world upside down."

He leaned down and kissed her. "Maybe I do."

30

IRIS

I checked into a crappy motel after leaving Shondra's. Even though the tub is lined with rust stains—God, I hope those are just rust stains—I filled it up and slid in, hoping the steaming water would help me forget that I was being crushed by disappointment. I know I shouldn't have gotten my hopes up when I went to Shondra's place, but after the old man at the gas station told me Seth had been there and bought a shovel and tarp, it seemed like a natural assumption that he'd buried Oscar here. So where the hell did he go? There's only one name from the address book that belongs to anybody even remotely near here—and she's in Indiana. I guess I have some more driving ahead of me.

NOVEMBER 10, 1980

It's been a long time since I've written. Months. I feel bad about that, but after the letdown with Shondra, I rushed out to Indiana, figuring I'd have to get lucky with the next woman. But I didn't. She wasn't the one. She was just a girl Seth met once on a trip to Florida in high school who had moved to Indiana after college. She barely even remembered him. It made me so mad, I couldn't write that night. And I couldn't make myself write any night after that. It was getting too hard to face my own thoughts every single day. It was hard enough having to be alive without Oscar. Having to be alone with just myself and my sadness was too much. It was easier just to crash on the bed every night and watch TV and not let myself think.

After Indiana, I moved on to Kansas and Oklahoma and Texas. And nothing. Every place I tried was nothing but a dead end.

It's been so long, and I've tried so hard not to think about anything, but that's not the problem. I've been running after Oscar and running after Seth, but really, I've been running away from myself, and it's time to come back. So here I am.

Today I have to find a woman named Jennifer Monroe. It sounds like such a simple, all-American kind of name. I picture Jennifer as a cheer-leader with ash blond hair tied up in pigtails with those white woolly rib-bons hanging down. If she's anything like that at all, this visit should go okay. Of course, you never know what you're getting into with one of Seth's girls. She could be a real moron like that waitress or an amazing woman who ended up a victim like poor Shondra. Or she could be like me.

* * *

God, what a day I've had. I'm curled up in a smelly hotel chair, pressed up against the radiator, trying to keep warm. When I checked in, this room was so cold, you'd think nobody had stayed here in years. Maybe they haven't. This town seems to be a real dump.

But there's good news, I think. I'm pretty sure Jennifer is the one.

I got to the house a little before noon. Jennifer lives on a farm—or, at least, it used to be a farm. Now it seems to be just a vast spread of overgrown weeds with a crummy double-wide trailer home sitting in the center, with the ragged remains of a white picket fence tacked up around the perimeter. The place made me think of those lonesome towns in areas like rural West Virginia, where the people used to be coal miners until the mines ran out, and now they're subsisting on a diet of squirrel and assorted critter. But we're in Texas, where I imagined everything would be big and impressive, shiny and massive, like a cattle ranch run by an oversized man in an oversized hat with an oversized buckle on the belt around his over-sized belly. This isn't the Texas I pictured in my mind. Except for the size of the oppressive desperation, there's nothing big about Jennifer Monroe's life at all.

With all the other women I've seen, at least since Shondra, I pretty much came right out and said what I was looking for as soon as I got there. I told my sad tale and they listened with interest but distance, because they knew they couldn't help me. But as soon as I pulled up in front of Jennifer's trailer, with my tires kicking up dust all around the car, I knew something was different here and I was going to have to take a different approach. Maybe it's a longshot, but I think this is the right place. I noticed something as soon as I stepped out of the car: a shovel resting against the shell of a shed or maybe what was once an outhouse. Yes, I realize that pretty much everybody owns a shovel. But it's like this one had a cosmic power, like it was calling out to me, almost taunting me, saying, "I know where your husband is. . . ." Is that stupid? I don't know. But I decided I was going to ease into the story when I met Jennifer.

It was when she answered my knock at the door that I actually decided what I was going to do. You see, Jennifer had a baby in her arms. And the moment I looked at its face, I knew it was Seth's child.

Jennifer had only a hint of a Texas drawl, which surprised me. For some reason, the run-down farm and the trailer made me expect a real redneck kind of girl—the kind with cut-off shorts and a red gingham shirt tied at the waist. But she sounded almost . . . smart. God, that sounds terrible, like I think people from the South can't be intelligent, but I hope you know what I mean.

"Can I help you?" she asked, shifting her weight under the baby she held over her shoulder.

I had to think fast. "Hi," I said. "My name is Iris. Iris . . . Harrison." (I threw in my mom's maiden name, since that was the only last name that came to me.)

"Yes?"

"Um, well . . . I've been hired by someone who cares about you."

She screwed up her face. "Hired to do what?"

I smiled. "To help you with the baby."

Jennifer glanced down at the child, then looked back up at me. "Who hired you?"

I broke eye contact and looked down at my feet. "I'm not supposed to say."

"Well, I can't just let some stranger into my house . . ." She looked back inside the trailer, as if she suddenly realized that calling it a "house" was a bit of an overstatement.

"I can't tell you who sent me, but I can tell you it's someone you know well." I don't know what I was hoping she'd think. Part of me wanted her to mention Seth, but I was afraid that if she did, I'd end up pouring out my whole story and blowing the deal. I was determined to get into that trailer and into that woman's life, if only to meet that baby, who was half country girl and half pure evil.

"It was my granddaddy, wasn't it? He won't come see me or the baby, but he feels guilty now," Jennifer said.

I felt my face brighten. "I can't say, but . . ." I nodded vigorously.

Jennifer smiled. "I knew it," she said. "That man always did love a baby, whether he thinks it's a bastard or not."

I shrugged. "I don't know anything about the circumstances . . ."

Jennifer stepped aside and motioned me into the trailer. "Sit down," she said.

I sat in a small armchair and she sat down on a squashed-looking brown plaid couch, laying the baby over her shoulder.

"This here," she said, nodding at the baby, "is Seth."

I shuddered, but tried to cover with a smile in the baby's direction, even though his head was turned away from me and he couldn't have seen it, even if he had been awake.

"He's named after his daddy," Jennifer said. She smiled sadly. "Which is probably stupid, 'cause I ain't seen his daddy since the weekend this little guy got started."

I tilted my head, hoping to look sympathetic. "I'm sorry to hear that. Is he . . . dead?"

Jennifer laughed. "Hell, no. Least, I don't think so. Guess anything's possible. He's just a rat bastard who got me knocked up and ran off without another word. He doesn't even know I had his baby."

I swallowed hard. "And you can't get in touch with him?"

She shook her head. "Nah. I never got his phone number. And he wasn't from around these parts anyhow. He's from up north. You sound like you're from up north. Are ya?"

"Yeah. Yeah, I'm originally from New York." Okay, so that was a little bit of a lie, but I'm thinking New York and New Jersey are all just one big blur to a girl from a cruddy old farm in Nowhere, Texas.

"Huh. And you're all the way down here now."

"Needed a change of scenery."

She stretched her neck up to glance out the front window. "We ain't got much in the way of scenery here," she joked.

I smiled. "How long have you lived here?"

"Farm's been in the family four generations, but it ain't been worked since my daddy passed on, ten, twelve years ago. My mama got married again when I was around sixteen and moved up to Dallas with the new man. I stayed here, and my granddaddy took care of me. Until I started running around with a boy he didn't like. Then he up and took off, back to his own place. I was eighteen, and I been living here ever since."

"I don't mean to be nosy, but do you . . . work? I mean, how are you supporting yourself and little . . . Seth?" I almost choked on the name.

"I was waitressing at a joint in town till the baby came, but since then, it's been just me and the baby and the tumbleweeds. Lucky thing God makes it so a mama can feed her baby for free, you know?"

I sighed. God, this girl was pathetic—and I don't mean that as an insult. I mean the pathos you felt in her presence was just overwhelming.

"Well, I'm here now, and I'm here to help in any way I can," I said.

She smiled. "I can't believe Granddaddy did this. Maybe I should call him . . ."

My heart jumped. "I wouldn't," I said, trying not to sound panicked. "I wasn't supposed to tell you he sent me, and I don't want to get in trouble. I need the job. You know how it is."

"Sure, right. Forgot about that part." She moved the baby to her other shoulder and it whimpered in its sleep. Her face brightened. "My God, I just thought of it—if you can be here with the baby a few hours a day, I could go back to waitressing and make a little money. That would be a godsend. Oh, Granddaddy knew what he was doing!"

I grinned. "Yeah. He sure did."

31

HORACE

| PRESENT DAY |

Horace was settling down into his leather recliner, with one of his mother's journals in his right hand and a bottle of water in his left—water, because what he really wanted was gin. The phone rang. Horace scowled at it. Even though he had Monday night football blaring on the plasma TV in front of him, he had otherwise been hoping for peace and quiet while he read. He reached for the phone.

"Yeah?"

"Hey, cuz."

Horace let out a sigh. "What do you want, Andrew? I've had about enough of you over the last few days."

"I know, I know, but this is important.

"Unless it's an apology for what you said about helping Richard Riley with his sleazy book, I don't really want to hear it."

There was a long pause. "Well, there's that."

Horace closed his eyes, exhausted. "There's what?"

"The—the apology."

"Holy shit on a shingle. Am I hearing things or did Andrew Cairo actually just admit that he was wrong for the first time in his life?"

"Hey, man, don't make it harder than it already is," Andrew said. "I hate saying sorry."

"And you wouldn't be doing it now if your mom wasn't making you, right?"

"No, cuz, I swear. Mom has no idea about this. She hasn't talked to me since the other day when we saw you and Angela."

"Andrea."

"What?"

"Andrea. That's her name."

"Huh. Are you sure?"

"I think I know the name of the woman I'm going to marry."

"No way! You didn't really propose to the bitch, did you?"

"Don't call her a bitch. You sound like a fifteen-year-old," Horace said.

"You didn't answer the question. Did you really fucking propose?"

"Yeah. I did. And I'm really happy about it, so unless you have something not asshole-ish to say, just keep your mouth shut."

"Fuck no," Andrew said. "I'm happy for you."

Horace felt his eyebrows go up. "Seriously?"

"Hell, yeah. I'm the best man, right?"

Horace frowned. He would have loved to say no, but who the hell else was there?

"Yeah, I guess you are."

"Fuck yeah! Bachelor party!"

"That explains it," Horace said. "You're less excited about my marriage than about the prospect of going to a titty bar."

"Damn straight. Aren't you?"

Horace laughed. "Sometimes it's harder than it should be to hate you."

"You know I'm just kidding, man. It's great you're getting married. Maybe I'll get bored enough to do it myself someday."

"So what was the other reason you called? I got the impression you didn't really call to apologize."

"Okay," Andrew said. "But just remember that you've really been liking me up till now."

"This can't be good."

"You might not think so, no," Andrew said. "But you've got to look at the big picture."

"Okay, tell me."

"I have a meeting with Riley tomorrow night, and I think you should come with me."

"Are you out of your freaking mind?"

"No, man, no. Check it out. I'm gonna tell Riley I can't give him the interview he wanted."

"And why is that?"

"Because I'm going to help you instead."

"You're on a real nice-guy kick today, aren't you?"

"I don't know, man. I've just been thinking. And family—it's important, you know?"

"Yeah," Horace said. "I know. So why do you need me to be with you for this Riley meeting?"

"I just thought it would be easier if I had a wing man. Moral support, whatever. I'm afraid he'll wait till I'm drunk and take advantage of the situation."

Horace chuckled. "Now, that would be getting a taste of your own medicine."

"What do you mean?"

"Never mind. Where are you meeting him and what time?"

"I'll pick you up around seven tomorrow night. You're doing me a favor, so you deserve to have your very own designated driver."

Horace felt his stomach clench with a craving for gin. He swallowed hard.

"That's okay," he said softly. "I'll drive. I quit drinking."

There was a choking sound at the other end of the phone.

"You did what?"

"I quit drinking," Horace said. "It's not that big a deal." He knew that was probably the biggest lie he'd ever told, and he'd told a few whoppers in his day.

"Crap, man. That's insane. Have you gone all, like, AA on me or what?"

Horace sucked in a deep breath. Maybe he *should* be doing AA or rehab or something instead of torturing himself trying to impress the world—or just himself—with his willpower. "Nothing like that," he said. "I'm just drinking too much, man. I don't know if you heard, but it's not good for you."

"Lots of things aren't good for you, buddy. That don't mean they aren't a hell of a lot of fun."

Horace smiled a little. "Yeah, I know. I'll pick you up tomorrow at seven."

32

IRIS

Staying here in this lousy trailer with Jennifer and little Seth is a lot more rewarding than I ever would have expected it to be. I drove into town the other night and used a really disgusting phone booth to make a collect call home to my mom. I figured it was time I gave everybody an update, let them know where I am and what I'm doing. I've been checking in as little as possible, for a couple of reasons. For one thing, Mom and Nora and Mrs. Cairo aren't all that supportive. They think I'm crazy to be doing this, and that I should just come home and let the police handle everything. And then there's the other thing—I'm worried that Seth will call or show up back there and one of them will let it slip where I am. He's already seen me once. I don't need to go through that again.

I was sitting in the front room of the trailer this afternoon. The TV was on, tuned to *Sesame Street* even though the baby is way too young to understand any of that stuff yet. I was just feeding the little guy and waiting for Jennifer to come home from work. She'd gone back to waitressing a few days after I got here, and you've never seen anybody happier. She comes home singing or whistling some twangy country and western tune every day, even when she has to work a late shift and doesn't get in until well past midnight. It's like having me here has lifted the weight of the world off her shoulders. I kind of feel the same way about being here. Just knowing Oscar is probably close by has made me more relaxed then I've felt over this whole last year, since everything happened.

Of course, I'm not exactly making much progress finding out where Oscar's body is buried. To tell you the truth, I'm really kind of falling in love with this baby. He may look a lot like his father, but that just means he looks a lot like Oscar, too. When I look into his face, I see all the hopes and dreams Oscar and I had for starting our own family. Sometimes I think I see Oscar himself in the baby's eyes, looking out at me and smiling, like he's happy that we're together again. I probably sound like a lunatic. Thank God nobody will ever see these journals but me.

I slung baby Seth over my shoulder and burped him. Outside, I could hear the light crunch of dirt and gravel as Jennifer pulled up, driving my car. She has a pickup truck—a real old-fashioned-looking thing, with those rounded-off bumpers, you know?—but she says it hasn't run in months. I'm not going anywhere at this point, so now I let her take my car to work every day. The first time she drove it, she couldn't stop talking about how luxurious it is. I don't think the poor woman had ever seen real leather seats before she met me. I guess Seth never took her for a spin in his car. That Porsche of his would have wowed the pants off her. Actually, maybe it did . . .

"Hey, y'all!" Jennifer called as she came through the door. It's always nice to see her at the end of the day. Happy people are just so pleasant to look at. Seeing her in such a good mood almost makes me forget why I'm really here and how horrible my life is. Almost.

"Good day?" I asked, handing her the baby.

"It's always a good day, thanks to you," she said, beaming.

"Well, this little guy had a very good day, too. He ate everything I gave him and he actually slept four hours straight without a peep. I think the worst of that colic he had is over. Knock on wood."

Jennifer sat down on the sofa and bounced the baby on her lap. I sat in the armchair and watched them. Little Seth always lights up when she's around. That's not to say that he doesn't like me, though. In fact, I've never been around a baby who likes me as much as he does. I think I'm kind of awkward around kids in general. Usually, babies cry when I hold them. I get tense, and I guess they can sense that. As much as I wanted to have a kid with Oscar, there was always a part of me that worried I wouldn't be a very good mother. Now I know I'm perfectly capable of handling a child—at least one like Seth, Jr. He's the polar opposite of his father—a little angel. Maybe the evil skips a generation.

"So whatta you two been up to today?" Jennifer asked.

Several thoughts ran through my mind: trying to figure out how to bring up the fact that your baby's father is my murderous brother-in-law, the fact that I think my dead husband's body is buried somewhere on your farm, or maybe the fact that part of me wishes I could keep your baby for myself.

"Not much," I finally answered. "I tried to tidy up a bit, but as you can see, I didn't get far."

"Well, that's not your job. You're not my cleaning lady. You're my—whajja call it?"

"Au pair."

Jennifer giggled. "I just love the way that sounds. What is that, French?"

"Yeah. You can just say I'm a nanny, though, if you like that better."

"Shoot, no. I like the ring of . . . What was it again?"

"Au pair."

"Oh pear. I like that a lot better."

Jennifer is a sweetheart, but she's not always the sharpest tool in the shed. Not that I can talk. I've been here for weeks now and I still haven't asked a single question about Seth and how she met him. I'm thinking I'm going to have to get drunk. Actually, I think I'm going to have to get both of us drunk.

That gave me an idea.

"Hey, Jen," I said. "I've been here a while now and I haven't even really seen the town. I was thinking—do you know somebody who might be able to babysit tomorrow night? Maybe you and I could go out, get something to eat, maybe have a drink, have some girl talk. I'm getting a little touch of cabin fever, I think."

Jennifer grinned. "I bet you ain't spent much time cooped up in a trailer, being from New York City. I'll ask Marjorie at the restaurant if she could watch Seth, Jr., and we can hit the town. You up for some dancin'?"

I raised my eyebrows. "There's a night club here?"

"Not sure you'd call it a night club. More of a cowboy bar, but they got a guy, plays records on weekends, and he ain't half bad. You know any line dances?"

"Not a chance," I said.

"Well, we can fix that."

33

HORACE

The bar's parking lot was almost empty when Horace and Andrew pulled in. There were only three cars other than Horace's—two of them rusted-out shitboxes parked close to the building, most likely belonging to members of the kitchen staff. The other was Richard Riley's metallic gray BMW.

"Great," Horace said. "The asshole's already here."

"That his car?" Andrew asked.

"Yeah, the BMW. Wish I could say one of those crappers over there was his. That's about all the dickhead deserves."

"He may be a dickhead, but he's got good taste in motor vehicles, my friend. How fast you think that thing goes?"

"Who cares? Let's get this over with."

"Yeah, I need a drink," Andrew said.

Horace slid out of the car and slammed the door. "Do I have to remind you again not to get drunk tonight?"

"Fuck, man, I don't know if I can deal with Riley sober. I need a few shots of something hard to take the edge off. Don't you?"

Horace clenched his fists at his sides. "Didn't I tell you last night that I quit drinking?"

Andrew threw his arm around Horace's shoulders. "I didn't think you were serious about that, cuz. Come on. You and me. Drinking's our thing. It's the way we bond."

"Yeah, well, maybe we'll have to take up golf."

"Huh?"

"Let's just go."

The bar was so dark, Horace could hardly see. He felt a rush of panic as he scanned the barstools and then the tables for Riley. Finally, he was able to spot the self-proclaimed award-winning biographer sitting at a small booth in the back, with a drink in his hand.

The bartender called out to Horace and Andrew before the door had shut behind them. "What can I getcha?"

Andrew brightened and rushed over to the bar. "Shot of Jack and a Sam Adams on draft."

"What about you, buddy?" the bartender asked.

Horace felt his throat go dry. He coughed. "You got bottled water? I'll take one of those."

The bartender moved away to get the drinks. Horace sidled up beside Andrew and pulled out his wallet, as it became clear that Andrew wasn't going to make a move to pay.

"So where is he?" Andrew asked, not looking up from the twenty-dollar bill Horace had placed on the bar.

"Over there, in the back. I don't know if he's seen us yet, but I doubt he could have missed us. This place is dead."

"Eh, well. Tuesday. Not really a party night. At least not for the amateurs. You and I have seen our share of wild Tuesdays, though, haven't we?"

"Don't remind me," Horace said.

The bartender set the drinks in front of them and took the twenty, moving toward the cash register to get change.

"Keep it," Horace said. "Come on, Andrew. It's show time."

Andrew threw back his shot and slammed the empty shot glass back down on the bar with more emphasis than necessary. The bartender sent a dirty look his way, but only Horace noticed. He shrugged in apology for his cousin, then grabbed Andrew's elbow and yanked him in the direction of the booth where Riley was sitting with a grin on his smug face.

"Well, well, well," Riley said, not rising to shake Horace and Andrew's hands. "To what do I owe the pleasure of your company tonight, Horace? I was only expecting your dear cousin here."

Andrew sucked down a sip of his beer and cast a desperate look toward Horace.

"Sit down," Horace said. Andrew plopped obediently into the booth, facing Riley, and Horace slid in beside his cousin.

"So?" Riley said. "What are you doing here, Cairo?"

"Me or him?" Andrew asked.

"I knew you were coming, douchebag," Riley said. "I mean your cousin. What the fuck are you doing here?"

Horace shrugged. "Just thought I'd come along for the ride. See how you are. All that good stuff."

He twisted the cap off his water bottle and took a long sip.

"What's that you're drinking? Water?" Riley asked. "What's going on? You having surgery tomorrow or something? Liver transplant maybe?"

"Don't get your hopes up, asswipe," Horace said. "Can't a guy just drink some water now and then? It's a Tuesday night, for Christ's sake."

"That never stopped you before."

"People change."

Riley smiled. "Do they?"

Horace screwed the top back on his water and let out a satisfied "ahh!" before setting the bottle down on the table.

"Cute," Riley said. "So, Andrew, what do you have to say for yourself?"

Andrew's eyes looked wild. "What—what do you mean?"

"Are we gonna talk now or what?"

Andrew glanced at Horace and took another swig from his beer. "Um—well, that's kind of what I came here to say."

"What?" Riley asked.

"I'm not gonna give you the interview you wanted." Andrew spoke fast, then sighed, as if proud of himself for getting the words out.

"What the hell are you talking about? Did this asshole"—he pointed at Horace—"tell you not to talk to me?"

Andrew looked down. "No, man, no. Nothing like that. I just think—I don't know. I just don't want to help with your book."

"Why not? Are you saying you don't need the money anymore?" Riley asked.

Horace frowned and looked at Andrew. "Money? What money?"

Andrew leaned over and whispered to Horace, as if Riley didn't already know what he was talking about. "He offered me some cash to do the interview."

Horace shook his head, a disdainful smile tugging at his lips. "Classy, Riley. So now you're paying for interviews? That's the mark of a distinguished journalist."

Riley raised his shoulders. "Hey, you do what you gotta do, right? There's nothing wrong with that."

"How much?" Horace asked.

Riley picked up his drink and took a slow sip, looking away. Andrew lowered his head and picked at one of his fingernails.

"How much?" Horace repeated.

"Half a million," Andrew said.

"Holy shit!" Horace whispered. He stared at Riley. "Your publisher agreed to pay half a million dollars to get an interview with Andrew?"

Riley tilted his head to one side. "Not exactly."

"Then what?"

"The official policy of the publishing house is not to pay for interviews."

"So you were going to pay Andrew out of your own bank account?" Horace asked.

Riley reached for his drink, but Horace grabbed it before he could pick up the glass. "Just answer the question, Riley."

"Sure," Riley said. "I would have paid him with my own money."

Horace let the glass loose and leaned back against the booth. He folded his arms across his chest. "I get it. You never intended to pay him, did you? You were just going to get the interview and then conveniently forget about the money. Does that sound about right?"

Riley sipped from his glass.

Andrew's mouth was hanging open. He looked back and forth from Horace to Riley in shock. "Riley, you better not be fucking with me. Is that true? You were going to screw me out of the cash? After I agreed to rat out my own family?"

"Hey, buddy," Riley said. "What can I say? It was only business."

Andrew elbowed Horace, nudging him out of the booth so he could get up himself. He turned to reach back for his beer, then stopped, as if reconsidering. His eyes met Horace's for a moment, then he swung around and slammed his fist into Riley's face.

"That's for screwing with my family," Andrew said. As Riley pressed his palms to his bleeding nose, Andrew leaned down and picked up his beer, taking a sip as he walked away.

Horace burst out laughing. "Nice to see you again, Riley," he said, then turned and followed Andrew out of the bar.

34

IRIS

Wow, did Jennifer and I have a time tonight! If the sadness weren't always wrapped around my shoulders like a shawl made of lead, I would almost have forgotten why I'm really here. For a few hours, I felt like I used to back before Oscar died, when the world was still turning and I was allowed to have some fun.

Jennifer took me to a bar called O'Reilly's. From the name, I expected kind of a low-end Irish pub, a place with dark beams and a lot of neon shamrocks on the walls. I was dead wrong. O'Reilly's is, in reality, a wild country and western dance hall kind of thing. It looks like a tiny building from the outside, but inside there's a dull wood dance floor that looks about as big as a football field. And even that isn't big enough—the whole floor is packed with people—mostly couples, dancing the quickstep or some kind of country waltz, spinning round and round without ever disturbing the massive hats on their heads. It was something to see. I felt like I was in a country movie.

We sat at the bar, which was littered with crumbled peanut shells. At first, the shells strewn everywhere just seemed dirty, but they serve a valuable purpose: absorbing some of the beer suds that the quick-moving bartender lets fly all over the place as he races around, hurling customers their drinks. Just like the dancers on the floor, that bartender seemed larger than life, too much of a stereotype to exist in the real world.

"What'll y'all have?" he called to us, never glancing away from the two mugs of beer he was filling at the same time.

"Whatever you got there on tap, Orville," Jennifer shouted back, above the reverberating twang of a guitar coming from an enormous speaker hanging above the bar, looking too heavy to be safely suspended over an area mobbed with people.

The bartender shot a quick look in our direction and grinned. "Thought that was you, Jenny. Where ya been, girl?"

"You ain't heard?"

The bartender shook his head as he slid two foamy mugs of beer in front of us.

"I had a baby," Jennifer said, flipping out a sleeve full of photos of Seth, Jr.

"Well, damn, girl," the bartender said. "You been busy. What's the little man's name? He's a boy, yeah? You got 'im wearin' a sailor suit."

"Yes, he's a boy. His name's Seth."

The bartender smiled and leaned over to press a kiss on Jennifer's cheek. "Well, I'm just tickled. Congratulations. You best bring that little fella round here one day soon—but I'd come on a weeknight. We been gettin' mighty busy round here on the weekends, as y'all can see."

"I'll do that."

"Drinks are on me, sugar," he said, throwing a wink over his shoulder as he strolled away to take care of another customer.

Jennifer took a sip of beer and let out a satisfied sigh. "Damn, that's good. Ain't had a beer since the baby came. Don't think I've had much to drink 'cept Windmill Punch in ages."

"Windmill Punch? Is that some kind of mixed drink?"

She smiled. "Windmill Punch is plain ole water, ya ignorant Yankee."

I laughed. "I like that. Kind of poetic. So, what shall we drink to?"

She was silent for a long moment, then she said, "Nurture."

I frowned. "What's that?"

"Nurture," she repeated. "As 'posed to nature. Let's drink to the idea that the way I raise my little boy will make him a good man, despite the fact that he gets half his genes from his son-of-a-bitch daddy."

She raised her glass and sucked down almost half of the beer in one gulp. Now we were getting somewhere.

I took a sip of my own beer to steady my nerves and then I dove in.

"Tell me about this guy," I said. "What happened with that?"

She made a face and poured some more beer down her throat before she answered.

"Same old story," she said. "Boy meets girl, boys gets girl drunk, boy screws girl, boy tears up girl's land looking for buried treasure, boy screws girl again, so to speak."

I swallowed hard. "Buried treasure?"

She shook her head. "The asshole told me he heard from a friend that some bank robber had buried a stash of cash here a few years back, so he dug a big ole hole in my yard looking for it."

I almost smiled—this was pretty much all the proof I needed. If Seth had been digging here, it wasn't to look for buried treasure; it was to bury some treasure of his own—my treasure.

"So," I said, clearing my throat to bring myself out of my dreamy daze. "Did he find the money?"

Jennifer laughed. "Course not. No treasure to be found round these parts. Never trust a tip you get from a jailbird."

"Excuse me?"

"The 'friend' Seth had—the one who told him 'bout the money? He heard about it firsthand."

"From the bank robber?"

"Yup. That's what Seth said."

"Nice. And how exactly did Seth know this guy?"

Jennifer shrugged. "Dunno," she said. "Never got that far. Day after he tore up my yard, he was gone. And I was pregnant."

I bit my lip, not sure where to steer the conversation next.

"How did you meet him?" I finally asked.

She took a sip of beer, finishing it off, and pushed the mug toward the back of the bar, signaling the bartender for a refill.

"Funny you ask," she said. "I met him right here, 'smatter of fact. Week after New Year's. I was here, having a drink by myself, after work, you know? It was a quiet night—a Wednesday, I think it was. Kind of a lonely night. And then he walked in."

It was such a romantic picture, I almost forgot she was talking about Seth.

"What did he look like?" I asked, wanting to hear the way someone else—someone who'd slept with Seth and never knew how truly ugly he was, inside—would describe him.

The bartender slid a fresh mug of beer in front of each of us and sashayed away without a word.

Jennifer leaned back against the bar, propped on her elbows, staring at the floor full of dancers. She let out something that sounded like a cross between a sigh and a moan.

"Soooo gorgeous," she said. "Like no one I've ever seen before. Dark hair, blue eyes, great body. . . . Beyond words. Just look at Seth, Jr. and ya can see his daddy was beautiful. He sure as hell don't get his looks from me—thank the Lord."

I smiled. "Seth, Jr. is a beautiful baby, no doubt about that. But I think you're selling yourself short."

She waved a hand. "Don't matter to me one bit that I ain't the prettiest gal in the world. But sometimes I wish little Seth didn't look so much like his daddy. It makes me . . . ache. Ya know?"

"Yeah," I whispered. "I know."

35

HORACE

| PRESENT DAY |

Horace put the key in the ignition but didn't start the car right away. First, he had to lean his head back against the headrest and howl in laughter.

Andrew was grinning. "What, man? Why are you still laughing?"

Horace shook his head. "Did you see Riley's face? He never saw that punch coming."

"Nope," Andrew said. "You'd think he'd be more ready for a beating. I doubt I'm the first dude who ever took a shot at him."

"I would've thought Riley gets smacked a couple times a week, but he sure as hell was surprised."

"So where we goin' next?" Andrew asked.

"Nowhere, bud," Horace said. "I'm just gonna drop you home and head back myself."

"Aw, come on, cuz. I thought we'd go out for a drink."

Horace narrowed his eyes in reprimand. Andrew threw up his hands. "Right, right. Not a drink. I forgot! I meant—dinner. Yeah. Let's get some dinner."

Horace rolled his eyes. "I don't know. I've got a lot to do."

"Sure you do. But Angela can wait until after we eat for you to fuck her."

"Andrea," Horace said. "And that's not what I meant. I have a ton of reading to do."

Andrew grimaced. "Since when are you a bookworm?"

"It's my mother's journals, retard. If I'm going to publish them, I need to go through them first."

"Yeah, yeah. But wouldn't it be smarter just to let a professional . . . book person . . . do that shit?"

168

"If you mean an editor, then yeah, maybe. But I want to do it myself. It's a personal thing, man. I don't want some stranger going through my parents' life—at least not until I've made sure there's nothing that might be . . . bad."

"Like what?" Andrew's eyes widened. He looked like he was salivating. "Sex stuff?"

Horace sighed. "Ugh. I don't need to read about my parents and their sex life. Don't remind me about that. I just meant there could be something that might embarrass the family, and I don't want anybody talking shit about us."

"I know about that, man," Andrew said.

Horace smiled. "And Riley knows it, too, now. Come on. Let me take you home. We can have dinner tomorrow. My treat."

"Well, then. I'll pick a nice expensive place."

"Whatever you want," Horace said. "After what you did tonight, I owe you one."

Andrea was in the kitchen, stirring something that smelled like garlic sizzling in olive oil on the stove. Horace grinned as he came in and dropped his keys on the counter.

"I'm glad I didn't let Andrew talk me into taking him out for dinner," he said. "It smells like an Italian restaurant in here."

He moved behind her and circled his arms around her waist, kissing her neck.

"I take it your meeting went well," Andrea said, leaning back so he could kiss her on the lips.

"Better than I could have imagined," he said, patting her on the behind and going over to sit at the table. "Andrew punched Riley in the face. It was a beautiful thing."

Andrea smiled over her shoulder. "You'd better hope Riley doesn't sue Andrew's ass for assault. He sounds like just the kind of prick who would do it."

"True," Horace said. "But I think he's going to let it slide this time. He looked pretty humiliated. I don't know if he'd want to stand up in court and tell a jury how easy a target his nose made for Andrew's fist."

"A valid point. Do you want to crack open a bottle of wine for dinner?"

Horace felt his teeth clench. When he didn't respond, Andrea turned to look at him.

"What's wrong?"

"Nothing," he said. "It's just—I'm trying to stop drinking so much."

Her face lit up. "Really? You haven't had a drink today?"

"I haven't had a drink in a week," he said.

She dropped the wooden spoon she was using to stir the garlic on the stovetop and ran over to hug him.

"I'm so proud of you! What made you decide to do that?"

He shrugged. "It's like I keep reading all these journals of my mom's and I feel like I owe them my full attention. My full sober attention, I mean."

"I think it's great," she said. "Are you feeling okay?"

"You mean, like withdrawal?" he asked. "Not too bad, actually. I didn't puke or anything which kind of surprised me. I woulda thought I was a pretty big drunk. I've barely even had a headache."

Andrea squeezed the back of his neck. "Maybe the universe wants to make it easy on you, since you're doing the right thing."

"Yeah, sure, that's it," he said. "Or maybe it's my mom, watching over me like a guardian angel, making sure my tummy doesn't get sick."

She rolled her eyes, then jumped to get back to the stove. She thrust the wooden spoon back into the pan, then said, "Don't laugh. There's a lot about the world that we don't know."

"Ah, yes, but my mom is no longer *in* the world."

She spun around to glare at him. Waving the spoon at him, she said, "Go ahead and be all sarcastic. But trust me, your mom can see plenty."

"Okay, okay," Horace said, laughing. "I'm sorry, Andrea. And I'm sorry, Mom."

She smiled. "I'll bet your mom's waited a long time to hear that."

"Yeah," he said. "She sure has."

36

IRIS

| DECEMBER 15, 1980 |

I just put the baby to bed and now I'm curled up on this rickety cot I've been sleeping on for weeks, crying while I write this. Jennifer's working late tonight, so I have the trailer to myself. I've had the whole place—and the baby—to myself the entire day, and for some reason, it's tearing me apart inside. I don't know what's different about today. I mean, I'm alone with Seth, Jr. every day. Why is it suddenly so hard to be with him and know he isn't mine?

Maybe it's because the holiday season is in full swing, and that means Christmas is coming—and so is the first anniversary of Oscar's death. All this time, I've been so driven to achieve this mission I've set for myself—to find Oscar's body and bring Seth to justice—it's kind of distracted me from the normal kind of grief I would probably be experiencing if I were home, living my regular life. It's not that I'm not in mourning. I don't think a minute goes by that I don't think of Oscar for at least part of it. But still, this time of year is bringing it all back to me even harder. It's all I can do to hold it together and not turn hysterical missing Oscar and thinking about everything I've lost—my marriage, my husband, my would-have-been babies. God, when I look at it that way, it's amazing I haven't grabbed little Seth and run off with him. I've been through enough to make a little crazy behavior—like kidnapping—almost seem logical.

Wow, I need to get it together. And I need to knock off this charade and tell Jennifer why I'm really here. I should have done it weeks ago. But it's come to a point where the thought of losing Seth, Jr. is almost as devastating as losing Oscar was. I don't know if I'll be able to survive another loss like that. I could end up in a loony bin somewhere, confined to a rubber room for the rest of my life.

But maybe I don't have to lose Seth, Jr. I think I have an idea. This might be the best idea I've had in a really long time. I just have to talk to Jennifer.

DECEMBER 16, 1980

I don't even know if I have the strength or the words to describe what happened today. I guess I have to, though. If I try to skip it or stop writing, I know I'll start up my journal again someday and then there'll be a gaping hole in the story of my life. So here goes.

When I got up this morning, I was surprised to find Jennifer already awake and working away in the kitchen, shoving stuffing into a turkey, her hand glistening with butter or maybe just turkey slime. She turned to look at me and smiled

"Hey, you're up. I made coffee."

"Thanks," I said, moving to the counter to pour myself a mug. "You're up early."

"Yeah," she said, giving the turkey's rump a final pat and rinsing her hand off under the faucet. "Never really went to bed last night. I was in too good a mood."

I sat down at the table and took a sip of coffee. "Really? Why's that?"

She wiped her hands on a dishtowel and came over to sit across from me. "Got me a job."

I chuckled. "I thought you already had a job."

She rolled her eyes. "I do. This is somethin' else. Guy who comes in the restaurant all the time is lookin' for a secretary and he asked if I'd be interested."

"Wow," I said. "I didn't know you wanted to work in an office."

"Well, I don't want to wait tables my whole life. Touchin' all that nasty half-eaten food, the sticky pools of ketchup. Yuck. Sometimes I'm just proud when I make it through the day without barfin'."

"So you're going to quit waitressing?"

"Not right away," she said. "New job's just part-time for now—see if it works out. But if it does, I'll be out of the restaurant lickety-split."

"That's great," I said. "Congratulations."

She made an excited face. "I'm so nervous. I never worked in an office before. And this is a doctor's office. Lots to learn."

"You'll do great. I assume you know how to use the telephone. Can you type?"

"Yeah," she said. "Thank God. I always thought my granddaddy was a senile old fart, but makin' me take that typin' class in high school was one of the best things he ever did. Next to hirin' you, of course."

I coughed. "Well, then," I said. "You're all set. You're going to do great." I held up my coffee mug. "Here's to your new career."

Jennifer clinked her mug against mine and took a sip. "Thanks. And thanks for being here. I wouldna been able to take this job without you. I mean, I love Sethie to pieces, but bein' a single mom is tough when you don't have a whole lot of money."

I sucked in a breath and set my coffee down. She had thrown an opportunity in my face. Now I just had to drum up the courage to seize it.

"Jennifer, I've been wanting to talk to you about something," I said, looking down at my fingers on the tabletop. They looked strangely pale and fat, like they belonged to someone else.

"Sure, anything."

I bit my lip and looked up, but still kept my eyes away from Jennifer's. "I don't really know how to bring this up."

"Hey," she said, patting the odd fat white fingers that were somehow attached to my hands. "You can say anything to me. You know that."

I felt my eyes fill with tears. "I hope so," I whispered.

"What is it?"

I blew a long stream of breath through pursed lips and watched my hair rustle a little in the miniature breeze. "Okay," I finally said. "It's about Seth, Jr."

"Sure. What about him?"

"This is probably going to sound totally crazy, but I'm completely serious. I'd like to adopt him."

Jennifer burst out laughing. She pushed herself away from the table and moved over to the oven, leaning over to check the temperature.

"Not quite hot enough yet," she said. She turned back to me, leaning against the counter. "You got a wacky sense of humor, Iris—ya know that?"

I closed my eyes. "I'm not joking."

"What are you talkin' about?"

"I'm not who you think I am," I said. "Your grandfather didn't hire me to help with the baby. I've never even met your grandfather."

Jennifer's eyes widened. "Stop it. You're startin' to scare me."

I held up my hands. "Please!" I said. "I'm not trying to scare you. I would never do anything to hurt you or Seth, Jr. But I came here for a different reason."

"What? Whaddya mean? Why did ya come here?"

"My name is _ris Cairo. I'm a writer, and I'm president of a publishing company back in New York."

"Okay . . ."

"But I'm also a widow. My husband's name was Oscar, and he was murdered by his brother."

"That's horrible."

I smiled a little. "That's not the worst part. Oscar's brother was Seth."

"Seth?" It seemed to take a few seconds before she realized what I was saying. "You mean Seth—the rat bastard who got me pregnant and run off?"

"Yes, that Seth. The same Seth who dug up your yard."

"Lookin' for buried treasure."

"No," I said. "Burying my husband."

"Are you sayin' there's a dead body buried on my farm?"

"Yes. That's exactly what I'm saying."

She shook her head slowly and came back over to the table, sitting down.

"I'm so sorry, Iris," she said. "I had no idea. . . . Why didn't ya just tell me all this right from the get-go?"

"I don't know, really. I guess I just wanted to be sure this was the right place before I told you everything."

She was quiet for a long moment. Then she said, "But I still don't understand what any of this has to do with Seth, Jr."

I leaned onto my elbows and held my temples between my palms. "It's . . . well, that part wasn't planned. I just fell in love with the little guy, and I keep thinking about all the things I could give him, all the things he could have if he were mine. I'm . . . I have a lot of money."

Jennifer let out a sarcastic laugh. "So?"

I put my hands down. "So, you were just saying how hard it is to take care of a baby without money—I'm telling you it wouldn't be a problem for me."

"But he's my child."

"I know, I know," I said, feeling a bizarre sense of panic rising up through my body. "But I could give him things—not just material things, but opportunities and education—things he'd never be able to get here. Don't you want what's best for him?"

She stared at me. "What's best for him is to be with his mama."

"Are you sure about that?"

"Very."

I leapt up from the table and started pacing the length of the tiny kitchen. I could feel the chance I thought I'd had slipping away and I was ready to try anything—no matter how irrational it might seem—to hold onto it.

"You're not really hearing me," I said. "If you were, you'd be jumping at the chance I'm offering you. I can give Seth, Jr. everything that a mother dreams of for her child. And you can't. You know it's true."

"You've gone crazy, girl."

"Jennifer, be reasonable."

"No, *you* be reasonable. What kind of person asks somebody to give away a baby?"

"The kind of person who wants to give that baby a perfect life."

"There's more to life than money," she said.

"Of course there is," I said. "But money's important. With me, he'd have a big house with a yard, vacation homes at the beach and in the mountains, a pony, whatever he might want."

"What if he just wants to be happy?"

"You think he wouldn't be happy going to the best summer camps, the best schools, in the world?"

She shut her eyes. "He's mine."

I felt a flash of rage pound through my veins, and I realized I was panting like an animal.

"Seriously? You're really going to refuse to give him to me?" My voice sounded screechy. I was almost afraid of myself.

"Course I won't give him to ya. He's my baby."

"Fine!" I threw one hand up in the air, as if dismissing her from my presence. "It's your mistake. You'll be sorry. Someday, when that little boy is working his ass off, sweating in the sun on the seat of a plow, you'll wish you had taken this chance when I gave it to you. With me, he could have grown up to be educated, cultured, a man of influence. All he'll ever be now is a pathetic white trash bastard who lives in a trailer."

I couldn't believe the words that were coming out of my own mouth. I may write mean things about people here in my journal now and then, but I've never been the kind of person who actually says cruel things to someone's face.

I stood there, breathing hard and feeling beads of sweat trickle down the back of my neck.

Jennifer kept her eyes down on the table, never glancing up at me. She said quietly, "I think ya should go."

I laughed, a scary evil cackle. "Oh, I'm going. Don't worry about that. You'll never see me again. And neither will your little bastard child. I really hope you'll be very happy here in your squalor, if you even know what that word means."

She stood up and hurried past me, out of the room. But she paused at the doorway and said, keeping her back to me, "You can tell the police to come here and I'll show them where . . . where the body is."

With that, she walked away.

I felt a pang of guilt punch me in the gut. Even after all the awful things I'd said to her, she still had the decency to remember my loss and do what she could to help. I owed her better than I had given her, but now it was too late to undo what I'd done.

I ran into the front room and grabbed my purse. Without even bothering to pack my suitcase, I walked out of the trailer and hopped in my car, with nothing besides my pocketbook and this journal.

I found a hotel in town and I called home to New Jersey. I told my mother that I knew where Oscar's body was and asked her to get in touch with the local police who had been handling the case. I figured it would be better to let them work out the details with the officers here in Texas. I doubted it would help for me to get any more directly involved.

For now, my work is done.

37

HORACE

| Present Day |

"This one? You're sure?" Horace asked. He pinched the diamond ring between his fingers and twisted it back and forth to watch it flash in the light.

"Sweetie, I'm sure."

He sighed and placed the ring in the jeweler's palm. "Okay, I'll take it."

As the jeweler wrapped her fist around the ring and scurried off to write up the sale whose commission would probably pay her rent for the next six months, Horace turned his back to the counter and crossed his arms.

"Honey, what's wrong?"

"Are you absolutely sure about the ring, Aunt Nora? I want to get Andrea the best ring in the world."

Nora smiled and laid her hand on his arm. "It's wonderful to see you this way."

"What? Wracked with anxiety?"

"No," she said. "In love."

"Nora . . ."

"She'll love it," Nora said, giving his arm a reassuring pat. "Any woman would love it. But she loves you, so that makes it even more special."

"I guess."

"Is something else wrong?"

Horace shrugged. "No, not really. I don't know why this stupid ring thing has me all flustered. It's not like I don't buy expensive things all the time."

"Then what?"

"I have no idea. Maybe I'm having second thoughts about getting married."

"I don't think that's it," Nora said. "I've seen you and Andrea together. It's easy to see you belong together. I think it's something else."

"What?"

"Your mother."

Horace chortled. "What about her?"

"This is the first big event in your life that your mother won't be here for."

Horace looked down. "Don't take this the wrong way, Aunt Nora, but it never mattered to me much whether Mom was around or not. To tell you the truth, there've been plenty of times when I wished she *hadn't* been there."

Nora shook her head. "All kids feel that way. But when the parent is out of the picture completely—and forever—you feel very different. I did, when my parents died."

"Yeah, but you got along with your parents," he said. "Right? It's not like Mom and I had a real close relationship."

"You think that," Nora said. "But there's no one closer to you. Never has been, never will be. Not even Andrea."

"I doubt that. Andrea—she's everything to me."

"Of course she is," Nora said. "But there's a bond between a mother and a child that can't be broken, not even by death."

"I don't think even Mom would agree with that one. Didn't she spend her whole life trying to stay close to a man who died ages before? I think Mom would argue that the bond between husband and wife is the one that lasts. It sure as hell lasted after my dad died."

Nora frowned. "I suppose," she said.

The jeweler returned with the freshly cleaned ring in a black velvet box. Horace handed over his credit card and turned back to Nora.

"Thanks for doing this with me," he said, leaning down to kiss her cheek.

"My pleasure, sweetheart. But I'm sure you could have asked anybody to come along."

Horace laughed. "Yeah? Like who? Andrew? He doesn't exactly have that delicate touch. I'm not sure I trust his eye for jewelry."

"Well, I'm happy I could help. So when is this wedding going to be?"

"We haven't really talked about the details yet," he said. "I thought buying the ring might get the plans rolling."

"Do it soon," Nora said. "Don't waste time with a long engagement."

"Right. Grab her before she changes her mind."

"It's not that. It's just—when you know it's right, you should jump in and start your life as soon as you can. You never know how much time you're going to get to spend together."

"Like Mom and Dad?" he asked.

"You never know. All I'm saying, really, is to seize hold of your happiness with both hands. Not everybody gets a second chance if they blow the first one. Some of us don't even get the first one."

Horace took her hand and squeezed it. "Love you, Nora."

She grinned. "I think that's the first time you've ever said that to me."

"Oops, sorry. Didn't mean to break precedent."

"I like this."

"What?"

"This effect Andrea's had on you," Nora said. "In a couple of months she's done what your mother couldn't do in thirty years."

"Don't tell Mom."

"I won't."

38

IRIS

| DECEMBER 17, 1980 |

After my outburst yesterday, I had kind of hoped I'd be able to get out of here and back home to my normal life without ever having to face Jennifer again. I know I behaved like a spoiled brat, and I have no right to be forgiven. I'm so humiliated. I just have no idea what came over me. Plus, the thought of seeing the baby again just broke my heart. Unfortunately, it seems I don't have a whole lot of luck.

I had finally fallen asleep in my uncomfortable hotel bed sometime after four A.M. Between the rock-hard mattress, the sheets that were tucked in too tight for me to move under them, and the insanely loud rattling sound of the air conditioner, which I couldn't turn off even though the temperature in the room must have been around 43 degrees, sleep just wasn't an option. It was still pitch black outside the window when the phone rang and woke me up from my dozing, giving me an instant headache. The clock said 6:04 A.M.

"Hello?"

"Iris Cairo?"

"Um—yes?"

"This is Detective Charles Sumner from the Glenn police department."

I dragged myself up in bed. My brain was still half asleep, but I found myself wondering if this cop's parents knew they were naming him after the senator who got beaten with a cane right on the floor of Congress during the Civil War era. I think sometimes there's too much useless trivia crammed into my head.

"Yes?" I finally said.

"Mrs. Cairo, I got a call from the police in New Jersey, in regard to your husband's whereabouts."

Whereabouts, he said. Like Oscar was just hiding from me, not like he was brutally murdered and toted halfway across the country before being dumped in what I assume was a shallow grave. Seth was a lot of things, but hard-working wasn't one of them; he would only have dug as deep as absolutely necessary to get the job done.

"Mrs. Cairo? Are you there?"

I shook my head hard to bring myself back to the present. "Yes," I said. "I'm sorry. I'm here."

"We'll be conducting an investigation this morning at the site you mentioned in your tip to the New Jersey police. You'll need to come along in order to provide your testimony."

Crap, I thought. Why hadn't it occurred to me that I couldn't just drop a bomb like this and be done with it? Of course they'd make me be there and force me to make an official statement. For a second, I had a twinge of panic—what if I'd been wrong and Seth really had been digging for some kind of buried treasure? I pushed the thought away. This time, I knew in my bones that I had found Oscar.

"Yes," I said. "Of course. What time should I be there?"

"We'll send a squad car to pick you up at your hotel. Seven A.M."

Right—they would want to drive me. There was always the chance that I might be the murderer, not the grieving widow who'd spent nearly a year trying to do what the cops were too lazy to do themselves: find Oscar's body so the "other" murderer could be brought to justice. I felt sick to my stomach, like I was being accused of something I didn't do.

"Certainly. Of course. I'll be ready and waiting outside."

"Thank you, Mrs. Cairo. Good-bye."

I let the phone drop back into its cradle and fell back against the cold faux-wood headboard. That's when something else occurred to me—they might make me identify the body when they got it out of the ground. I'd come all this way, driven by an almost maniacal desire to bring Oscar home, and I had never even considered the notion that I might have to see him the way he must look now, ravaged by death and time and the elements. I had to leap out of bed and run to the bathroom to throw up. And I had thought seeing Jennifer and little Seth again would be the worst thing imaginable. Now all I wanted to do was jump into my car and point it northeast, to get the hell out of here and on the road back home.

But at the same time, I knew I couldn't do that. I owed it to Oscar—to his memory and to the unbreakable bond that still linked us—to see this through to the end, no matter how bitter that end might be. So I got up off the bathroom floor, took off my clothes, and hopped into the shower. Even if I couldn't face Jennifer and this whole situation with a clean conscience, I could at least do it with a clean body.

A black-and-white patrol car pulled up in front of the hotel precisely at 7:00. The officer who was driving got out and greeted me with a curt nod, then gestured toward the back door of the car. Great, I thought. I get to sit in the back like a criminal—which they probably thought I was. The cop opened the door and did that thing where they guide your head in so you don't whack it on the edge of the door. I don't know why he thought I needed help—it's not like I was wearing handcuffs, which tend to limit your mobility. Maybe it's just habit.

I sat in the back seat and waited for the cop to get in the car. That's when I noticed that there was another cop already sitting in the front seat. That made me feel a tiny bit better, since his presence meant the back seat was the only place for me to sit, not necessarily that I was suspected of murder. The cop in the passenger seat never said a word, never even glanced back at me. I wondered if that was habit, too—not fraternizing with the law-breaking rabble. Then I started to worry again about what they thought I might have done. Fortunately, the driving cop got in and we took off, so at least I had the passing scenery to pay attention to instead of just dwelling on my paranoia.

It felt like a long ride over to Jennifer's, but I knew from making the trip myself that it only took around ten minutes. I don't think of myself as a particularly chatty person, but the complete, stony silence of the two cops was making me even more nervous than I'd been to start with. I started worrying again that they really didn't believe my story, that they thought I was in league with Seth or something. I kept having visions of being thrown in some dusty, rural Texas jail with only one cell and—even creepier—more than one prisoner. In my mind, the Texas penal system was somewhere along the lines of a Mexican or Turkish prison—you went in but you never got out.

We pulled up to Jennifer's trailer and parked behind three other squad cars. A hundred feet or so past the trailer, I could see yellow caution tape stretched around the perimeter of a small area, and beside the marked-off section sat some kind of construction vehicle—I don't know if you call it a bulldozer or a backhoe or what.

The driving cop got out and rushed around the back of the car, opening the door for me. I thought he was just being gentlemanly, but then I noticed that there were no door handles on the inside of the car. So that's how they keep the bad boys from escaping at stoplights. You really do learn something new every day.

As I was stepping out of the car, I saw Jennifer coming out of the trailer, with baby Seth in her arms. She sent a sad, pursed-lip look in my direction. I felt my cheeks flush. Should I wave? Go over and try to apologize? Grab the baby and run for the hills? There didn't seem to be any reasonable option, so I just inclined my head a little, hoping Jennifer would take it as I intended it—as a woefully inadequate expression of regret.

"Mrs. Cairo?"

The sound of the cop's voice startled me, especially since it was the first time he had spoken to me at all.

"Yes," I said.

"This way."

I followed him over the rugged, grassless earth toward the spot with the caution tape border. My stomach lurched. Had they already dug Oscar up? Was I about to come face-to-face with my dead husband?

A man in a cheap-looking navy blue suit and ugly black shoes that looked chunky and orthopedic was standing beside the bulldozer thing. He had a manila file folder, a tiny spiral-bound pad, and a ballpoint pen in his hands. He nodded at me as I approached and shoved his pad and folder under his arm so he could extend his hand for me to shake.

"Mrs. Cairo? I'm Detective Sumner. We spoke on the phone?" I wondered why his last sentence sounded like a question.

"Of course," I said. "Thank you for calling me."

"We've been waiting for you to get here before we get started."

"Oh. Thanks."

He placed a gentle hand on my shoulder and steered me away from the other policemen, leaning down to speak softly in my ear.

"Obviously," he said. "I understand if you don't want to watch the . . . uh . . . excavation. But I'll need you to make an official statement detailing your involvement in the case from the time of Mr. Cairo's disappearance through the present."

"Absolutely," I said. "So you won't need me to . . . identify the body?"

He looked down and fiddled with his pad and folder. "No," he said, clearing this throat. "We—um—well, we assume that the—uh—state of decomposition will be far enough advanced to require identification through—um—dental records."

I felt myself flinch. Although I had known I didn't want to see how Oscar looked now, it had never occurred to me that I wouldn't even be able to recognize him. He was so much a part of me, I found it hard to believe there was anything about him I couldn't recognize—even his skull, covered by a decaying flap of maggot-eaten flesh.

"Of course," I finally said. "That makes sense. And it's a relief."

The detective gave me a kind smile. "Why don't we go inside and sit down so you can be comfortable while we talk?"

My eyes widened in alarm. Sitting down for a chat with a cop at the very table where I went crazy on Jennifer just yesterday was the last thing I wanted to do. In fact, getting any closer to that trailer than I already was would make me anything but comfortable, but there was no way I could tell Sumner that. I mean, where the hell else could we go? He'd think I was nuts if I suggested sitting in a car, and I needed to come off as sane as possible if I wanted my statement to be taken seriously and act as a launching pad for a real manhunt for Seth.

"Sure," I said. "That sounds good."

I felt my shoulders cringing the whole way to the trailer and inside. I was kind of hoping Jennifer would be in the back bedroom with the baby, so I could get through this interrogation without the added pain of seeing her. But, of course, as luck would have it, Jennifer was sitting smack dab in the middle of the sofa in the front room, with Seth, Jr. gurgling on her lap.

I froze. Jennifer shot me a look, but just a short one. Mercifully, Detective Sumner got her attention and gave her an excuse not to look at me.

"Mrs. Monroe?" he said.

"Miss," she muttered. She stood up and set the baby on her hip.

"All right if I interview Mrs. Cairo in here?"

I saw a tiny smile cross Jennifer's face. "Fine," she said. "Use the kitchen. I'll be in the back room if ya need anything."

She said she was leaving, but she didn't actually move. She just stood there, holding Seth, Jr., and waited for me and Detective Sumner to pass. My shoulders felt all rounded and hunched as I slinked past her, practically hanging on to Sumner's suit jacket. As I went by, though, Jennifer whispered, "I'm real sorry 'bout your husband."

My eyes flew up to her face. She closed her eyes and nodded solemnly.

"Thank you," I said. "And I'm sorry—about—everything."

She patted my shoulder, then brushed past me and disappeared into the bedroom. I'm pretty sure that'll be the last time I'll ever see her—or the baby.

"Mrs. Cairo?"

Somehow, Detective Sumner had made it into the kitchen without me.

"Coming," I said.

It took a good hour and a half to go through my "testimony," as Sumner insisted on calling it. It probably should have been emotionally devastating to be forced to relive all the tragic events of the past year, but I had kept Oscar so close to me that whole time that I'd never stopped thinking about my grief and pain even for a moment. Really, the hardest part about telling Sumner my story was my fear—irrational as it might have been—that he wouldn't believe me. But he seemed perfectly satisfied with everything I said, and just as he was finishing up with the interview, shuffling through some papers he wanted me to sign, one of the other officers came into the trailer, leaned over beside Sumner, and whispered something in his ear. Sumner nodded and the other cop hurried back outside.

"They found him, didn't they?" I asked.

"Apparently. Yes."

"So what now?"

He coughed. "Well, uh, the remains will be transported to the—uh—coroner's office, and an autopsy will be performed. And we'll obtain dental records to confirm identity."

I let out a long sigh. It was over. It's finally over.

Well, almost. There's one other thing that I need to do. There's only one way to keep Oscar alive, and that's to have his child. Back in the autumn of last year, when we were going through all those humiliating fertility tests, my doctor mentioned the possibility of trying artificial insemination. She thought my cervix might be a bit misshapen and that "going in" with a syringe might allow the sperm to get to the egg. She also mentioned the possibility of trying some other procedure—the one where they're making the "test-tube babies"—if the artificial insemination didn't work. She thought it would be a great thing for us to try. If she thought it was a good idea when Oscar was right there with me, then she'll certainly think it's a good idea now that he's dead.

39

HORACE

The engagement ring felt hot in the chest pocket of Horace's jacket as he drove home after dropping off Nora. He'd spent the entire trip back from the jewelry store searching the depths of his creative impulses, trying to come up with the perfect way to give Andrea the ring.

It was silly, he knew. After all, she'd already said yes—they were engaged. It wasn't like he had to worry about being turned down while poised on one knee in a candlelit restaurant somewhere while everyone at the other tables stared and the waiter stuck the champagne he'd pulled out for them back in the fridge. Still, he was determined that the moment when he put the ring on her finger would be one they'd both remember forever, in all its detail. The fact that he still hadn't thought of anything—at least, nothing that wasn't either clichéd or corny—by the time he pulled into his driveway left his mind racing. If he couldn't figure out something so simple, how would he be able to handle the complexities of marriage? He had no experience with long-term commitment himself, and he had never even seen a long-term relationship up close—unless you counted the one his mother had had with his dead father. Maybe he was in over his head.

He grunted in anger as he climbed out of the car. He should probably just put the ring aside for now. When the time was right, he'd know what to do. That—he assumed—was what his mother would have said. For some reason, knowing what his mother would have advised had become a lot more important to him lately.

As he walked up the driveway toward the house, he glanced into the blue plastic container that held the recyclables. Although it had always embarrassed him, for years, it had generally been overflowing with liquor bottles every week when he put it out for pickup. Today, it was filled once again to the brim with empty bottles of gin and other booze. But he hadn't actually consumed all that alcohol. A couple of nights ago, he and Andrea had made a party out of dumping all the liquor in the house. Horace had surprised himself by bringing out even the secret stash he kept in the not-so-obvious places, like his underwear drawer and the bottom of the hamper. He would have thought it would have hurt, at least a little, to watch all that booze gurgle away down the drain, leaving only the biting stink of alcohol floating on the air. But it wasn't. Tossing all the empty bottles away and knowing this would be the last time he'd feel the need to duck away and hide from the garbage men was the most fun he'd had—outside of the bedroom, anyway—in more years than he could count.

He nudged the recycling can with his foot and smiled as the bottles tinkled against each other. For the first time in his life, he was actually able and willing to say that things were good.

He was standing at the island in the kitchen thumbing through his mail when he heard Andrea's car roll up the driveway. He hadn't even had a chance to take off his jacket, and his hand flew to his pocket, pressing against the ring box tucked inside.

He ran to the front door and watched as Andrea got out of her car. Christ, she was beautiful. Nora had been right—he was crazy to ever have doubted that he wanted to marry her. In fact . . .

He sank to his knees right there on the cold marble floor of the foyer and tugged the ring box from his pocket. He held it forward on his palm and held his breath, waiting for his bride to come inside and officially allow their life together to begin.

The door creaked as it opened. Andrea poked her head around. She didn't see him right away—she had her eyes focused too high, since she clearly didn't expect to find him on the floor. Her head spun—a classic double-take—when she noticed him.

"What are you doing down there . . . ?" she began. Then she saw it. Her eyes immediately welled up with tears and her hands went to her mouth.

Horace laughed. "Why does every woman in the world have exactly the same reaction when they see a little velvet box?"

She choked out a laugh but didn't lower her hands or move any closer to him.

"Well, if you're not gonna come to me, I'll have to come to you," he said. He paused for a moment, then shrugged and lurched forward, shuffling on his knees. After a few inches, he stopped.

"You know, crawling on marble is a little rough on the knees. I'm not as young as I used to be. Do you think maybe you could close the door and come on inside?"

Andrea dropped her hands and used them to press the door closed. She rushed to him and dropped to the floor, throwing her arms around him. Caught off balance, he dropped the ring box. It popped open and the ring landed with a tinny clatter on the floor.

He squeezed her, then pulled back gently. "Great," he said. "I dropped the damn ring. Now that's romantic."

"I've never seen anything more romantic," she said.

"You," he said, kissing her, "are crazy. But that's why I love you. Now hold still while I grope around and find the stupid thing."

She grinned. He slid down onto all fours and crept over to where the ring had landed, a few feet away. He caught it between his thumb and forefinger and crawled back to Andrea. A little voice in his head told him that a normal person would just stand up and walk—but that would have ruined the purity of the moment, or something like that.

He took her hand and slipped the ring onto her finger. "Well, that could have been worse. It might not have fit. Or it might have fallen down into the heating vent. Then I'd have to spend another . . . oops. That is something you'll never know."

Tears streamed down her cheeks as she stared at the ring. "I don't care about money," she said. "You know that, right?"

He smiled and wrapped his hand around her finger, pretending to pull off the ring. "In that case, I guess I'll just return this."

She jerked her hand away. "Not a chance, buddy!"

He cupped the back of her head with his palm and pulled her to him and kissed her.

"I've never loved anyone else," he said.

She laid her hands on his shoulders, pressed her forehead against his, and looked hard into his eyes.

"Neither have I," she said.

40

IRIS

I'm lying in bed while I write this, and I keep having to put the pen down and shake it because it won't write upside down. I'd go and sit at my desk, like a normal person, but I'm supposed to be resting. The more I lie down, the more gravity helps me out. See, I had my baby implanted today.

Okay, so maybe it's not exactly a baby, not yet. It's an embryo. Or a test-tube baby—that's what people are calling it these days, since they put the sperm and egg together in a lab and then stick it in after it's already been fertilized. The doctor thought this would be my best chance to get pregnant. She didn't want to waste time and sperm on artificial insemination, since we only have one chance, maybe two, to get it right. Now that Oscar's gone, there's no more sperm coming.

I don't care what all the technical stuff is about. I just know that I am—at least for now, at this very moment—pregnant with Oscar's baby. After all the months and months we tried, and all the awful medical tests we went through, it feels surreal to finally be here—especially without Oscar by my side. Actually, the stuff Oscar had to go through wasn't all that bad. He pretty much only had to jack off into a cup. I'm the one who got poked and prodded, had all kinds of weird devices shoved inside me, and had to take a cocktail of hormones that left me alternating between tears and rage for the last two months. Please, God, just let this work. I don't know if I have it in me to go through it all again. Besides, if this doesn't work, Oscar will be lost to me forever. And after what happened with Seth and the police, I just don't think I can take any more disappointment.

Yesterday, I got a call from the local detective, the one who's been in charge of Oscar's murder investigation from the start. He heard from the coroner in Texas, and the dental records confirmed that the body buried on Jennifer's property was Oscar. Not that I had any doubts, but having it stamped and made official means there's really no hope left. Despite my determination to find Oscar's body, there was a secret part inside me that truly didn't believe Oscar was dead. Maybe that seems silly, but let's face it. It would be all too easy for Seth to say he killed Oscar when really he had just nabbed him and stashed him away in some dungeon somewhere. Okay, so maybe there are no dungeons anymore. A well, maybe. Or a mine shaft. Either of those would work. But now I don't even have that ridiculous thread of hope to hold onto—which means I finally have to face my grief head-on and figure out what the hell to do with the rest of my life. This baby is my last chance. If I don't get pregnant, if Oscar is really gone from this world entirely, then there's nothing left here for me. I might as well take matters into my own hands and speed things along so I can join him. I don't even know if I believe in an afterlife, some kind of fluffy-cloud heaven where you get reunited with all the people you loved while you were alive. But right now, even the prospect of nothingness—of never waking up, never existing again for all eternity—seems more attractive to me than the idea of living another year without Oscar. I never would have thought I was the kind of woman who would base her whole life on a man. I guess it's true that you can't pick who you love—or how intensely you love them.

I don't want to get my hopes up, but I have a strange feeling that this test-tube baby thing is going to work. When I lay my hand on my belly, I can feel a tingling, a kind of magic—and I'm sure it's the blossoming life of my child inside me. So I'm going to stay here, in bed, for as long as it takes to be certain. I won't get up for water or food or even to pee—not until I know without a doubt that Oscar's legacy had grabbed hold and is growing inside of me. Until then, I can't be safe. I can't even think about rejoining the world. Without this life that's half mine and half Oscar's, I have no life left to live.

MARCH 4, 1981

I just got the call from my doctor with the results of my blood test. It worked—I'm pregnant! I know it's crazy, since I've literally only been pregnant for like a week, but I keep thinking I can feel the baby moving inside me. I already know he's a feisty one. And I'm already sure he's a boy. He has to be. Oscar tried to pretend like he wouldn't care one way or the other, but I know he was dying to have a son. Oh, God. I can't believe I just said that. It's like sometimes, despite everything that's happened to me over the past year, I forget that Oscar's dead. No matter how much time goes by, I still keep expecting him to come through the door, like he's just been away on business. I wonder if that feeling will ever go away, or if I'll spend the rest of my life staring at the door, waiting for Oscar to walk back in and come home to me.

Maybe having this baby will change things. If I can—well, I guess the word is *replace*—my feelings for Oscar with love for another person, a perfect little baby who'll be just like his father, then maybe I'll be able to move on with my life.

8:55 P.M.

I don't even know what to say. I was in the middle of my dreamy thoughts about the baby when the phone rang. I almost didn't answer it—I was caught up in the pleasant fantasy, picturing myself cradling a newborn with a tiny, flawless replica of Oscar's face, but then it occurred to me that it could be the doctor calling back with more information for me, or maybe my mom, calling to find out if I got the test results. So I picked up the phone.

"Hello?"

"Why, hello there."

The sinister sound of Seth's voice made the phone frost over in my hand. Okay, so that's hyperbole. The point is, I was scared.

"Seth, is that you?" My voice was hoarse with fear.

"Happy to hear my voice?"

"Where are you?" I managed to choke out.

"Oh, nice try," he said. "You think I don't know you've got the police hunting me down? I've been running around for two fucking months, thanks to you."

"Seth," I pleaded. "Please just turn yourself in. All this can be over."

He laughed. "Yeah, permanently. Don't think so. I've got a whole lotta living to do. Hey, is that a song or something?"

"I . . . I don't know," I whispered.

"Iris? You still there?"

"Yeah . . ."

"I called because I have a proposition for you."

I shuddered.

"Iris?"

"Yeah."

"Okay, here goes. I know all about the little procedure you just had done."

I gasped. "How . . . who told you?"

"I have eyes and ears in all kinds of places, my love. You should have figured that out, staying with Jennifer and my kid as long as you did."

"You know about Seth, Jr.?"

"Of course I know. And I know about the little bundle of joy you've got in the oven, too. And I'm willing to do something for you that I was never willing to do for Jennifer and Seth, Jr."

I was crying now, and it was hard to force my squeaky voice to come out loud enough to be heard over what I guessed—what I hoped—was a long-distance phone line.

"What's that?" I finally said.

"Marry you and raise that baby," he said.

I gagged. I actually gagged. But he didn't hear it.

"I'm not hearing any reply," he said. "Need to think about it?"

"Seth, you're . . . you're like my brother," I said. I figured that was less likely to piss him off than reminding him that he killed my husband.

"Not even close," he said. "You were with my brother for a very brief time. Now you have your whole life ahead of you, and you're on your own."

"Thanks to you." That one just slipped out.

"What was that?"

"Nothing." I was grateful he hadn't heard me. I knew it was a bad idea to get him mad. He hadn't even had a problem with Oscar, not really, and he killed him. I didn't even want to think about what he'd do to me—or my baby—if I made him angry.

"So?" he asked. "What do you say?"

"Seth. I—why are you doing this to me? And Nora. You're married to Nora." Despite my advice, she had never bothered to file for a divorce.

"Doing what to you? You should be thanking me. Without me, you wouldn't be where you are today." He completely ignored my mention of his wife.

A tear streaked down my cheek and into my mouth. "You can say that again," I muttered.

"Iris!" His voice was sing-songy.

"What?"

"I didn't want to have to do this, but I guess I'm going to have to sweeten the deal."

"Okay . . ."

"Okay. Here's the thing—you get a choice: You can either marry me and come away with me, someplace where the cops you sent after me can't find us, or . . ."

I swallowed. "Or what?"

"Or I'll have to kill you. And that baby of yours."

A painful sob tore through my chest. "Seth, please. Can't you just leave me alone? You ruined my life. All I want now is to live here with my baby and try to forget everything."

"I *created* your life," he said. "You have no idea how much you owe me. Without me . . ."

"Without you, I'd still have the love of my life, a father for my baby, everything I ever wanted."

"I told you, I'm willing to be a father to your baby," he said.

I felt my spine stiffen with rage. "Over my dead body," I said through clenched teeth.

"Fine," he said. "Have it your way."

The phone went dead.

41

HORACE

"Do you know anything about how you were conceived?" Horace asked as Andrea lay in the bed with her head on his chest.

She laughed. "Well, I don't know what you learned in school, but I'm pretty sure it has something to do with the sperm meeting the egg."

He flicked a finger against her head. "That's not what I meant," he said. "I mean, did your parents ever tell you where they were when you got started? Anything like that?"

She scoffed. "Course not. It would've been creepy if they did. No one wants to picture their parents doing it."

"Yeah, well, I don't have that problem," he said.

"Your mom doesn't talk about sex in all those journals?"

"Some, yeah, but I meant specifically about how I was conceived. My father was already dead."

Andrea lifted her head and looked at him. "Then, how . . . ?"

"In vitro," he said. "I guess you're sleeping with one of the earliest test-tube babies."

Andrea sat up and leaned against him. "Wow," she said. "I didn't realize that. Your mom must have been kinda brave to have a baby all on her own like that. Even thirty years ago, things weren't the way they are now, you know? It couldn't have been easy."

He shrugged. "I guess I never really thought about it until I started reading her life. Actually, I didn't even know I was an IVF baby until Nora told me a few months ago."

"But you grew up without a father. Did you think he died when you were still a baby?"

"I think my mom told me he died while she was pregnant—not a whole year before she even got pregnant. It's just weird, having the whole timeline of your existence switched up on you."

"I can't even imagine."

"The weirdest thing?" he said. "It took until after my mother died for me to even remotely have any respect for her. The more I read her journals, the more I kind of like her."

"What was it that made you dislike her so much while she was still alive?"

He sighed. "I don't know, exactly. It's like she was always so sad and lonely and pathetic—always pining away for my dad. And since I never got to meet him, I couldn't get what could have been so great about him. I don't think I could even have imagined feeling so strongly about anybody—at least not until now."

She smiled and tilted her head to kiss him. "It's nice to see you turning into such a softie."

He squeezed her shoulders. "It's all because of you."

She shook her head and patted him on the hand. "You think that, but it's not true. I had nothing to do with this change you're going through."

"Of course you did."

"Nope," she said. "It's your mom. It's the journals. And if they're having this kind of effect on a hard ass like you, they're going to leave the average reader weeping."

"I don't know about that," he said. "But they'll sure as hell make an interesting book."

"I think you'd better get back to work then, mister. I'm going to sleep." She started to roll over.

"Wait," he said. "I had another question to ask you."

She turned back to look at him.

"Do you ever think about children?" he asked.

"What about them? I'm a teacher. Of course I think about children."

He frowned. Her eyes widened. "Oh," she said. "You mean . . . children."

He took her hand. "Do you?"

She smiled. "Yeah. I do. You?"

He nodded.

"When do you want to start?" she asked.

"The sooner, the better," he said, smiling.

"Hey, if I don't take my pill in the morning, we may already have started."

He put his hand on her cheek and turned her face so he could look into her eyes. "So don't take it."

"Now, I know I'm not the most traditional girl in the world, but aren't you supposed to be married before you start cranking out babies?"

Horace grabbed her left hand and ran his finger over the diamond on her engagement ring. "I'm ready whenever you are," he said.

"I thought you'd want to wait until you were done with your mom's memoirs."

He felt a shock of panic run through him as he remembered what Nora had told him at the jewelry store—seize your happiness, don't wait.

"Not a chance," he said. "I would marry you tomorrow if you'd agree to it."

She smiled. "I may be wrong, but I believe you need some things—like a license and someone to perform the ceremony—before they let you get married."

"We could go to Vegas."

She nodded, but she looked down, and he could tell immediately that the idea of a quickie wedding at a cheesy drive-through chapel didn't appeal to her. If he really thought about it, the notion didn't do much for him, either.

"I'm kidding," he said. "I want a real wedding. I want to see you come down the aisle in a puffy white dress. I want to do a really stiff and awkward first dance in front of two hundred of our closest friends. I want it all."

She peered at him from beneath her eyelashes, which made her look like a timid schoolgirl. "Really?"

"Definitely. Don't you?"

She nodded. "Yeah, I do."

"So when do you want to do it?"

"The sooner, the better."

"That's exactly what I was thinking," he said. "Is a month enough time to get it all organized?"

"Um—well, usually it takes like a year to plan a wedding . . ."

"Yeah, but things go a little faster when you have money," Horace said. "For once, I'll be able to put my mother's money toward a good cause."

"I can't let you pay for everything," Andrea said. "Aren't the bride's parents supposed to pay, anyway?"

Horace wrinkled his brow. "Aren't your parents dead?"

"I didn't say it would be easy to get them to pay, just that they're supposed to."

"I'm paying," he said. "It's what my mother would have wanted."

She smiled a little. "I wish I could have met her."

"Me, too. But, hey—aren't you the one who told me she's watching over me? She already knows all about you. And I'm sure she's thrilled. You've almost turned me into a human being."

She pecked a kiss on his lips. "I'm working on it."

"So, a month?"

Her eyes glistened with tears. "Yeah. That sounds perfect."

42

IRIS

After I hung up the phone with Seth last night, I immediately called the police. I asked for the same detective who'd been in charge of the case, but it was late and, of course, he wasn't there. They transferred me to some other cop who sounded about twelve years old and completely uninterested in listening to me. I thought I could hear some kind of sporting event on a TV in the background. Instead of paying attention to the woman whose life had just been threatened, I thought, this kid is watching football. No, wait—it's March. Can't be football. Hockey, maybe? Basketball? Anyway, I would have thought the threat of murder would be slightly more intriguing to a cop than some random game. Guess not.

"Did you want to file a report?" he asked. In my mind, I could picture him staring intently at the TV screen and reaching for some popcorn.

"For starters," I said. "I also want someone to come over here and stake out my house."

"Ma'am, be reasonable. Threats like these are almost never serious."

"I'd rather not base my life on 'almost.' Besides, don't you think the fact that this man has already killed once makes it pretty damn likely he'll do it again?"

The cop sighed. It sounded like he was changing position—maybe pulling his legs down off the top of his desk and hunching over. There must be a commercial on TV, I thought.

"I can send an officer over to take your statement," he said. "Other than that, there's not much we can do, at least not without a viable threat."

"What the hell do you mean, viable? What's more viable than a murderer choosing his next victim? This is insane."

"Should I send over the officer or not?"

"Yes, yes," I said, practically spitting the words out of my mouth. "I guess I have to take what I can get."

"Have a good night." That's what he actually said as he was hanging up the phone. This guy was like a human Mad Libs—plugging in pieces of conversation whether they were appropriate or not.

I hung up the phone and sat there, shaking in my chair while I waited for the cop to arrive to take my statement. The officer who showed up was quite nice, and, unlike the kid who dispatched him, at least twenty years old. He sat dutifully on the sofa and wrote down everything I told him, but when he was done, he really had no answers for me, either. Unless there was a specific, time-based threat, they couldn't offer me protection. Why not stay with family, he suggested. I smiled at that. When the person you're hiding from *is* family, it's hard to escape by hanging out with other relatives.

I thanked the cop and walked him out so I could deadbolt the door the moment he left. I leaned against the front door and wrapped my arms around myself. I was having constant chills, ever since I heard Seth's voice. He had always scared me, but now I was more than scared—I was frozen, petrified, sick with terror. It suddenly occurred to me that it was because of the baby. For the first time in my life, I had someone other than just myself to worry about. There was an unborn child inside me who needed to be protected from everything—birth defects, German measles, miscarriage, and—most dangerous of all—his evil uncle Seth.

I went to the kitchen and called Nora. She listened in silence as I explained what had happened. When I was done, she didn't say anything.

"Nora? You there?"

"Yeah."

"What should I do?"

She said only one word: "Run."

MARCH 6, 1981

My mother came by this morning to try to talk me out of leaving, but I've already made up my mind. I have to do what's best for my own safety—and for my baby. So I'm getting out of here. Tonight.

"Iris," Mom said, taking a handful of socks out of my suitcase and stuffing them back in the dresser. "Be sensible. Seth won't really come here. He knows the police are looking for him. He may be crazy, but he's smart enough to avoid getting caught."

"I think he's more interested in finishing things with me than he is worried about getting caught," I said, pulling the socks back out of the drawer. "And he's just crazy enough not to care about the cops. I get the feeling his itch to kill is a lot stronger than his fear of punishment."

"Sweetie, you're overreacting. Come and stay with me. I have a burglar alarm. You'll be perfectly safe."

I shook my head. "I'll never be safe as long as Seth is still out there."

"Let the police handle this, honey," Mom said. "You've been through enough."

"Yeah, I have. But I'd like to keep going through things, and if Seth gets to me, that won't be an option."

Mom sighed. "I don't think it's a good idea. Where are you going to go? You're pregnant, Iris. You can't be living out of motels and a suitcase. Think of your health. Think of the baby."

"He's all I'm thinking of, Mom," I whispered.

She put her arms around my shoulders. "Then let me come with you. At least I'll be able to make sure you eat right and get enough sleep."

I kissed her cheek and ducked away, going over to the bed and snapping the suitcase shut. "Thanks, Mom, but I can't put you at risk, too. This is something I have to do myself."

"Where have I heard that before?" she muttered.

I smiled. "I'll be okay. Just do one thing for me—keep after the cops. Don't let them blow this off. If they find Seth, I can come home."

"I'll do everything I can," she said. "Maybe I'll hire a private investigator to try to find him. Anything extra we can do, right?"

I nodded. "That's a good idea. And I'll pay for it."

"From the road? How are you going to work that?"

I patted her arm. "Don't worry about it. I transferred a chunk of cash into your bank account last night."

"Honey, why?"

"To keep it for me. I took the rest and put it in a new account—a few accounts, actually—under fake names. It'll make it a little harder for Seth to track my movements. He's found me before. I know he can do it again if he really wants to."

"Be careful, sweetie. And take care of that baby."

"I will."

I let her help me load my suitcases in the car, hugged her tight, and then I watched her drive away, wondering if I'd ever see her again.

43

HORACE

"Do you know how to tie one of these?" Horace asked, tugging at the ends of the bowtie that hung limp around his neck.

Andrew chuckled. "Yeah, right, man. I'm all about the class."

"Believe me, cuz, I don't think you have class. I just thought maybe somebody had taught you how to tie a bowtie somewhere along the way."

"Like who? My dad?" Andrew asked. "I think we're both in that boat. It's fucking amazing we learned how to shave without slicing our throats."

"I guess we're going to have to stick with the pre-fab bowties. I don't want to look like a moron."

"Yeah, man," Andrew said. "Angela'll castrate you if you fuck up your tuxedo."

"Andrea."

"What?"

"For the love of God, why can't you remember her name?"

"Who, Angela?"

"ANDREA!"

"Are you sure?"

"Andrew, Christ. It's *your* name, with a different letter on the end. Switch the *w* for an *a* and you're done. How can you not remember that?"

"She doesn't *look* like an Andrea," Andrew said suspiciously.

"Apparently she looks like an Angela," Horace said.

Andrew shook his head. "Nah. She looks like a Michelle, but I never wanted to say anything."

Horace couldn't hold back a laugh. "You're an idiot and you're completely nuts, but you have style, buddy."

Andrew grinned and tucked his thumbs under the lapels of his tuxedo. "So how do I look?"

"Gorgeous. But your cummerbund is on upside down."

"How can you tell?"

Horace shook his head. "It doesn't matter. We'll order vests instead. That way, I don't have to worry about you showing up at the wedding with parts of your tux on wrong. I assume you can figure out how to put on a vest and a pre-tied bowtie."

"Course I can. Like you said, I got style."

"You sure do."

"So what time should I pick you up for the bachelor party?"

Horace grimaced. He'd been hoping for the past few weeks that Andrew would forget about the bachelor party he'd been threatening to throw.

"I don't want to hang out in some cheesy strip club drinking water and watching you stuff dollar bills into G-strings. Besides, me and you and some stale peanuts isn't much of a party."

Andrew slapped him on the back. "Don't worry," he said. "There'll be plenty of guys there."

"Like who?"

"Haven't you got any friends?"

Horace chuckled. "How long have you known me?"

"Isn't there anybody you knew from, like, school? Or what about the army? Don't you know any guys from when you were in the army?"

"Nobody who's still alive," Horace muttered.

Andrew patted him on the shoulder. "You've got me, man."

"I know," Horace said. "You're actually a pretty damn good best man."

"You sound surprised."

"Nothing you do should surprise me anymore—but it still does."

"That's me. I'm a mystery."

"Not the word I would've used, but let's go with that," Horace said. "Let's take these things off so the tailor can get working on them. The wedding's in less than a week, and Andrea will freak if you and I are standing at the altar naked."

"Trust me, man," Andrew said. "She wouldn't be disappointed at all if she saw *me* naked."

Horace shuddered. "Let's not experiment with that, okay? Come on. Let's get out of here."

The next night, the two of them sat together at the counter of a '50s-themed diner with milkshakes in front of them. Andrew made a face as he sucked a mouthful of chocolate shake through a straw. He put down the glass and pushed it away.

"This is *so* boring, dude," he said. "What kind of bachelor party can we have here? There's no booze, and the only women are sixty-year-old waitresses with platinum blond wigs and poodle skirts—the same ones they were probably wearing in high school. This blows."

Horace stirred his shake with his straw, trying to melt the ice cream enough so he could drink it without giving himself a headache. "I told you, I don't want to go to a strip club."

"But it's supposed to be a *bachelor* party. You'll only have—what? Two, three of these your whole life?"

"Smart ass."

"I don't even need a titty bar. Just a *bar*—one with actual liquor, not chocolate malteds."

"You know I'm not drinking anymore, man," Horace said. "Are you trying to piss me off? I thought it was supposed to be what *I* want to do. It's *my* bachelor party."

"Whatever, cuz. Fuck tradition. You're right. We'll drink milkshakes and eat cheeseburgers and it'll be great."

"You're a shitty liar—which is surprising," Horace said. "But you're being a good sport, so thanks for that."

The waiter, dressed like early Elvis in the black leather look, slid two plates of cheeseburgers and fries in front of them, then slammed a bottle of ketchup on the counter between them before storming off as if he were angry about their order for some reason.

"Dibs on your pickle," Andrew said, reaching over to Horace's plate without waiting for permission.

"Then I get your red onion," Horace said.

"Fine. I don't want my breath to stink."

"What do you care?"

Andrew shrugged. "You never know—I could meet somebody and end up . . . bow chicka bow bow . . ."

Horace had to press his fingers against his good eyelid to keep from crying as he laughed.

"Aww, isn't this sweet? They're cousins, but you'd think they were brothers." The voice came from behind them.

Horace spun around on his stool. "Christ," he moaned. "Riley."

"Hello, boys," Riley said, laying a hand on each of the cousins' shoulders. "How've you been?"

Andrew shook off the hand and hunched over the counter, clutching his burger with both hands. "Get out of here, asshole," he mumbled, his mouth full.

"It's a public place, dickhead," Riley said, putting his free hand on Horace's other shoulder.

Horace scowled and nudged him away. "What do you want, Riley? Or do you need another beat-down? I'm sure Andrew here would be happy to do that for you as soon as he's done with his burger."

Andrew nodded enthusiastically while he chewed.

"Thanks, no," Riley said. "I was just walking by and saw you guys in here, so I thought I'd come in and say hey."

"Fabulous. Wonderful catching up with you. And now I'm done," Horace said, starting to turn back toward the counter.

"Also . . ."

Horace stopped and glanced back at Riley.

"My book is coming out in a couple of weeks," Riley said. "Thought you'd want to know so you could order a few advance copies. Let me know if you want me to sign one for you."

"Thanks so much," Horace said, turning his back to Riley and picking up his cheeseburger.

"Tell you what," Riley continued, ignoring the fact that Horace was trying to ignore him. "I'll send you a signed copy myself. And one for Andrew, and one for your aunt Nora. And, of course, I'll have to send one to Rahway . . ."

Horace dropped the burger and jumped off the stool, shoving his face right into Riley's space. "Get . . . out . . . of . . . here . . . before . . . I . . ."

Riley smirked. "Go ahead. Hit me. This time, I *will* press charges. You guys got off easy last time."

Andrew turned to watch the confrontation. "Not worth it, cuz," he warned.

Horace stepped back and sat down. "You're right."

"That's so charming," Riley said.

"What?" Horace said.

"'Cuz.'"

"He's my cousin, genius," Andrew said.

Riley smiled. "Hmm. Yes. I guess he is." He started toward the door, but stopped and turned back. "Don't forget—I'll be sending you each a copy of the book. I'll look forward to hearing what you think."

He grinned, then pushed open the door and stepped out into the night.

44

IRIS

I didn't tell Mom yesterday when I was leaving that I know exactly where I'm going. It's safer for both of us if she really has no idea where I am.

So after I drove for a few hours and checked into a nondescript motel room—the kind I've become all too accustomed to over the last year or so—I pulled out my wallet, sat on the bed, and picked up the phone. From its hiding spot, tucked behind my driver's license, I slid out the small piece of paper where Shondra Cantwell had jotted down her phone number last year when I breezed into her house, brought up the painful memory of her date rape at Seth's hands, then breezed back out again. Looking back, it occurred to me that I was probably the last person she'd want to see again—my visit hadn't exactly been pleasant for either of us. But she *had* given me her contact information, so maybe she'd play along and humor me, at least for a little while.

I dialed the phone and twisted the cord around my finger as I waited for Shondra to answer.

"Hello?"

"Uh—hi. Shondra? This is . . ."

"Iris Cairo."

I blinked. "Wow, you're good."

"Not really," she said. "It's just that I read in the newspaper about how they found your husband's body out in Texas, and how Seth has been managing to avoid the cops. I figured you'd be back on the road sooner or later—hunting the bastard down."

I sighed. "To tell you the truth, he's kind of hunting me down."

"Jesus. What happened?"

"It's kind of a long story," I said.

"How soon can you be here?"

"Day after tomorrow?"

"I'll be waiting."

MARCH 9, 1981

I pulled up beside Shondra's greenhouse just after ten in the morning. As I walked up to the door, I caught myself looking over to the spot where the mound of dirt—the place I thought Oscar was buried—had been the last time I was here. Over the past year, the dirt had been smoothed down and grass had grown over the bare spot. If I hadn't seen it with my own eyes, I wouldn't have believed I could ever have thought Oscar had been stashed here.

The front door opened before I even made it up onto the porch, and Shondra was standing there, with one hand on her hip and the other holding open the screen door, beckoning me in. I trotted up the steps and stopped to smile at her in gratitude. She wrapped her arms around my neck and pulled me into a quick hug.

"I'm glad you called," she said.

"Really?"

"Yeah. I've been worried, wondering all this time if you found . . . what you were looking for. Until I read the papers, that is. Then I knew you'd done it."

I followed her inside and we sat down in the living room. "I'm not sure *what* I did," I said. "All those months running around the country, and nothing's really changed. Oscar's just in a different grave. Other than that, it's like I never left at all."

"I'll bet our friend Seth would disagree," Shondra said.

I nodded. "I guess."

She watched me in silence for a while. Then she said, "Okay. Tell me."

I took a deep breath. "He's after me."

"Seth?"

"Yeah."

"Why?"

"Well, that's the other thing. I'm pregnant."

Her head jerked backward a little; she clearly hadn't been expecting that bit of news. A slow smile spread over her face. "So, you met someone while you were . . . on the road?"

"No. No chance of that. It's Oscar's baby."

She frowned. "Maybe I'm a moron, but . . . how?"

"You've heard about test-tube babies, right? I've got one cooking right in here." I pointed at my belly.

"Wow, Iris. That's . . . that's amazing. You are about the gutsiest woman I've ever met."

I snorted. "What's so gutsy about lying on a surgical table and having an embryo stuck inside you?"

Shondra laughed. "I assume you didn't hear your own question, because if you did, you'd know what's gutsy about it."

I shrugged. "I don't know. I just felt like I had to do it. It's my only chance to hold on to Oscar."

"God," she said. "I hope someday I'll love someone as much as that."

"Trust me. You don't. I keep thinking how much easier my life would have been if I'd never fallen in love with Oscar."

"Different, maybe. But full? Complete? Maybe not." She peered at me. "Right?"

I wagged my head from side to side. "You're probably right." I couldn't believe it—I'd only been with Shondra for five minutes and already I felt better, safer.

"So," she said. "What can I do for you?"

I sat up and leaned forward. "I don't know, really. I'm . . . basically, I'm on the run. Seth gave me an ultimatum: Marry him or he'll kill me and the baby."

"Jesus."

"Yeah."

She shook her head. "So what are you going to do?"

"I don't know. Find someplace to lay low? At least until the baby comes. Or until the cops catch Seth. I don't really have a plan."

"Well, now you do. You'll stay here," she said.

"I didn't come here for that," I said. "Honest. I just thought I'd come by to see you while I try to figure out where to go next."

"Well, this is where you're going. Unpack your bags."

"I can't—it's too dangerous—for you. If Seth comes here . . ."

"I can take care of myself. And you. And that baby you've got brewing. Besides, he won't come here. I don't think a man would willingly walk into the path of two very angry women."

I shook my head. "I think I'm more sad than angry."

"It's time to *get* angry, sister," she said. "I'm pissed off on your behalf. And on my own. That guy will be lucky if he survives with his balls intact if he comes within a hundred yards of either of us. I'm quite adept with the garden shears, you know."

I smiled. "I think maybe I *will* stay—at least for a couple of days. *If* it's not too much of an imposition."

She patted my knee and stood up. "Don't be silly. Now, come on. I'll show you your room. I changed the sheets and cleaned out the closet. I had a strange feeling I'd be getting a houseguest. . . ."

"Shondra?"

She looked back with a smile.

"Thanks."

45

HORACE

| PRESENT DAY |

He woke up before dawn on the day of the wedding. He lay in bed, listening to the silence in the house and wishing Andrea were next to him. He was afraid.

It wasn't the wedding. He was surprising himself with how much he'd been looking forward to that. It was something else—something he couldn't quite identify. He just knew that Andrea would be able to make him feel better.

He thought about throwing off the covers and traipsing down the hallway. Although he and Andrea had agreed not to see each other before the wedding, she hadn't actually left the house. She had moved into one of the spare bedrooms a few nights before, declaring herself "re-virginized" and off-limits until they were married. Horace didn't understand why it was so important to her not to have sex the week before the wedding—it seemed silly to pretend like the past few months had never happened, but he was willing to survive with just his hand for company for a few nights. No big deal. As for the superstitious bit—the idea that it's bad luck for the bride and groom to see each other before they meet at the altar—Horace was supportive of that. With the crazy life he and his family had led, he wasn't about to take any chances. A man with only one eye doesn't tempt fate.

He sighed and slid out of bed. He turned on the lamp on the nightstand and sat there, staring at the closed door and wishing Andrea would hear his desperate call for her telepathically and come running to comfort him. He shook his head at the thought.

The latest volume of his mother's journal was lying on the nightstand. He started to reach for it, then remembered something else that had occurred to him as he was drifting off to sleep last night.

He jumped up and hurried to the closet. Inside were piled the set of plastic bins that stored all his mother's things. And in one of them—although he'd be damned if he knew which one—was the thing he needed to find: his mother's wedding ring.

Horace had stumbled across the ring—a pretty platinum band with antique-looking engraving and a few dots of sparkling diamond chips—a couple of weeks ago. In fact, it had been the same day that he and Andrea had picked out their own wedding rings at the jewelry store. Even as she had smiled and nodded at the overeager saleswoman, Andrea hadn't seemed happy with the choice they'd made for her—a plain platinum band. It was fine, she'd insisted—she didn't want anything that would compete with her magnificent engagement ring. He had shrugged off the uneasy feeling that felt like a cold rubber glove gripping the base of his spine, but when he had found his mother's ring later that night, tucked inside a yellowed paper envelope—not even a ring box—he had wondered if Andrea would like it better. Of course, life had intervened over the next few weeks—Andrew and his "bachelor party," Riley and the announcement that his book was coming out, Horace's continued work on reading the journals—all of it had made him forget all about the ring, until late last night.

He had to dig through three bins before he found the right one and pulled out the envelope that held the ring that had been on his mother's finger every time he'd ever seen her—or, at least, every time he'd ever seen her alive. He shook the ring out of the envelope and held it flat on his palm. It was shining clean and he wondered if someone had washed it after his mother had died. Then he caught himself wondering whether his mother had still been wearing it when she died. It was the kind of trivial detail that he might have known if he'd actually seen his mother in the six months before her death. The guilt came rushing over him and he slumped to the floor. Jesus, he needed Andrea right now.

He closed his fist over the ring and dragged himself to his feet. Taking a deep breath, he burst through the door and marched down the hallway. He reached for the doorknob to Andrea's room, then stopped. She'd cry—she would literally break down and sob if he ignored their agreement not to see each other and went into her room. He let his hand slide off the knob and stood there, panting, deciding.

Then he heard her voice, small but strong, from inside. "You can't sleep either?"

He smiled and laid his hand flat against the door. "Nope," he called back. "Cold feet?"

"Not a chance," he said. "I just missed you."

"Me too. It's just a few more hours."

"I know. I'm sure I'll survive. I just wanted to hear your voice."

She was quiet for a moment. "Did you want to come in?"

He closed his eyes. There was nothing he wanted more. He sighed. "No," he said. "I wouldn't even think about jinxing us. I'll see you in a couple of hours."

"I love you," she said.

"I love you, too."

He backed away from the door and returned to his room.

Opening the drawer in the nightstand, he took out the blue velvet box in which the plain band Andrea had picked out was nestled. He plucked it out of the slit in the velvet and tossed it into the drawer, loose among a pile of change and stray buttons. In its place in the velvet box, he tucked his mother's ring. That's when he realized what had been making him feel so small and afraid, what had left him wide awake when he should have been getting rest on the night before his wedding: His mother wasn't going to be there to see it happen. He touched her ring once more and felt the warmth of reassurance flow through him. He'd been wrong—and Andrea was right. His mother was going to see everything.

He snapped the ring box shut, put it in his pocket, and headed toward the bathroom to take a shower and start the day—his wedding day. He smiled to himself when he realized he was whistling "Here Comes the Bride."

46

IRIS

I've only been here a few days, but being with Shondra has been like being at summer camp or something. Nothing against Nora, but Shondra is like an instant sister. I feel more comfortable talking to her after knowing her less than a week than I do talking to Nora, whom I've known my whole life. I don't know what it is—we just connect for some reason. The first night I was here, we stayed up most of the night drinking wine and talking like old friends, like two girls who went to school together and have been reunited after years apart. I think I'm babbling, not making a lot of sense. But I feel so good—almost safe, almost like I'm not a fugitive, almost like I'm just some normal woman spending time with a friend. I wish my life really was the way it feels right now.

This afternoon, I was curled up on Shondra's couch watching some soap opera—they all run together to me, but they're mindless and they're so melodramatic that they make me feel like my own life isn't as crazy as it seems. At least I don't have an evil twin—not that I know of, anyway.

Shondra came in from working in the greenhouse and scowled at the TV screen.

"Are you still watching this shit?" she asked. When all I did was shrug, she reached over and slapped the power button on the television.

I knotted my fingers together and stretched my arms, relieved that I was no longer trapped in the TV world of marriages and affairs and remarriages. "Thanks," I said. "I needed that."

Shondra tapped my knee. "Get up and take a shower."

"What for?"

"We're going out for dinner."

I bit my lip. "I don't know . . ."

"It's perfectly safe. I'm sure Seth hasn't staked out the local rib joint. I think we could both use a night out."

I smiled. "Okay. You're right. Let's do it."

It felt good to take a shower, wash my hair, and put on a dress and some heels. Nothing fancy, really, but I've pretty much been living in sweatpants and T-shirts—with jeans being "dressed up"—for this whole time, since Oscar's been gone. Not having anyone to look at you, to care what you look like, makes it easy to just give up. I was never a fashion plate or anything, and my idea of heavy makeup is some mascara and Chapstick, but while Oscar was alive, I at least made an effort to wear "real" clothes—not pajamas or sweats—because I knew he liked the way I looked in dresses and skirts and pretty little suits. For some reason, I feel like I care whether Shondra thinks I look nice or not. That's stupid, isn't it?

Shondra drove us to a little place—a rib joint, just like she said. It was basically a hole in the wall, but the food was cheap and I've never had such amazing ribs or French fries in my life.

"Have a beer," Shondra said as we sat down at the table—a small round table in the corner with one of those vinyl tablecloths with the red and white checks, like a picnic blanket. "You *need* a beer."

The waitress didn't bother to hide a smirk. "Two beers? Need any shots with that?" She laughed and started to turn away. I laid a hand on her arm.

"Actually, yeah," I said. "I'll take a shot of Jack. Shondra?"

Shondra grinned. "Make it two," she said. "And make those doubles."

The waitress tucked her pencil behind her ear and smiled. "My kind of table," she said.

Shondra leaned back in her chair. "So when's the last time you got out and had some fun?"

My mind flashed back to that night a few months back in Texas, when Jennifer and I had gone out for drinks and talked about Seth—the night I learned about how Seth had dug up her yard looking for "buried treasure." That was the last time I'd been out and had fun, if you can call finding out where your dead husband is buried "fun."

"It's been a while," I said as the waitress set our drinks down on the table.

Shondra raised her shot glass. "Then here's to fun. Let's have some."

I clinked my glass against hers. "We sure as hell deserve it."

Our eyes met over the rims of the glasses and together we tossed back the liquor. The burning of the alcohol in my throat made me shudder, but it was a good kind of shudder—the kind that makes you aware that you're alive and out and about and ready to be wild. I hadn't felt that way in a long, long time.

I reached for my beer. "I wonder if it's a bad idea to drink this much while you're pregnant."

Shondra shrugged. "I'm sure a doctor would say so. But doctors think everything's bad for you, whether you're pregnant or not. You can't do anything anymore—smoking, drinking. It's all crap. What's life if you can't live it?"

"Well argued," I said, and took a sip of beer. At the same time, I made an agreement with myself that I'd drink tonight, but I'd be careful to monitor everything I ate or drank from here on out. I couldn't risk losing this baby—my last link to Oscar.

Shondra and I munched on ribs, sucked down beers, and laughed and laughed. I was my old self again—cracking jokes, telling stories, and not dwelling on all the heartbreak and fear that had been dominating my life for so long.

We rolled back home sometime around midnight. We were both dabbing at our eyes, wiping away tears of laughter, as we slumped on the couch in Shondra's living room.

"Hey," Shondra said, grabbing my wrist. "I've got an idea."

"What's that?" I could tell I was slurring my words a little, and I felt all warm and toasty inside—I was pleasantly drunk.

"Okay. Remember the first time we met?"

"Course."

"I told you about what I grow here, in the greenhouse, right?"

I closed my eyes and leaned my head back against the sofa, smiling. "Poinsettias. So pretty. So Christmas-y."

"Yeah, very," she said. "But I also grow something else."

I dragged my head up and squinted at her. "Yeah?"

"Yup. Yeah. It's the other thing—what you *thought* I was growing." She winked.

I shook my head. My brain was fuzzy and I was having trouble focusing, but it felt good—like freedom.

"Pot," she said. "Marijuana. Cannabis. Weed. Whatever you want to call it."

I nodded slowly, still not really getting what she was telling me. "Good for you, Shondra. That's excellent."

She nudged me. "Come on, dopey. Let's smoke."

I had never smoked pot before, and I probably never will again—at least not while I'm still pregnant. That's probably hard to believe. I mean, I did grow up in the hippie generation, a child of the Sixties. But I don't know—maybe I was sheltered. Or maybe I was a goody-goody. I guess I just never got around to trying out the mood-altering drugs all the other kids my age were taking. It never occurred to me that I'd give in to the pressure to do drugs later in life, after I was already a widow—not exactly a high school girl trying to rebel against her straitlaced parents and their World War II values. *I* was always the one with the World War II values. So I was kind of surprised at how much fun I had getting high with Shondra.

I don't remember all the details. I know we watched TV for a while, but I have no idea what was on that late at night. I also know that we ate a *ton*—all the leftovers from the rib restaurant and two bags of chips from Shondra's kitchen. The whole time, we just laughed and laughed. I was giddy, and I felt lighter in both my body and my soul than I have in forever. I think I was able to talk Shondra into letting me give her some money for "rent," but even so, there's no way I can ever repay her for what she's doing for me. She has managed—in just a few days—to pull me up out of the abyss where I've been living for well over a year and to help me feel *human* again, like I might actually come out of this experience with my life and my sanity—and my baby—all intact. If I could be a little more like Shondra, the world would be a much brighter place. We should *all* be a little more like Shondra.

47

HORACE

"So," Andrea asked, twirling the edge of her veil—which was the only piece of clothing she was still wearing—around her finger. "Was it worth the wait?"

Horace lifted his eye patch and rubbed the sweat off his forehead. "I would never have believed it could get better than it already was, but crap. Wow. There are no words."

"Why, thank you, husband."

"No, no, thank *you*, wife," Horace said. He popped the eye patch back in place. "The veil's a nice touch, I've got to say."

"Thought you'd like that. Speaking of nice touches . . ." She held up her left hand. "This ring. My God, Horace. It's so beautiful."

He grinned. "Thought you'd like that."

"But what happened to the other one?"

He frowned. "Did you—I mean, do you like the other one better? Because we can switch them . . ."

"God, no! I wouldn't trade this one for anything. I was just curious where you got it, that's all."

"It was my mom's," he said.

A strange look fell over her face and Horace felt a pang of worry. "You don't like it anymore, do you?" he asked. "It's okay. We'll pick out a new one."

She leaned over and quieted him with a gentle kiss. "I love it," she whispered. "I love it even more now that I know. I'm touched—no, I'm honored—that you would want me to wear her ring."

"*She* would have wanted you to wear it," he said. "Why else would she have left it behind? I always figured she'd be buried with the damn thing."

"Maybe I will be," Andrea said.

He kissed her. "It's yours now. Whatever you want. But, hey? Can we not talk about our impending mortality? It *is* our wedding night, after all."

"Mmm. That sounds reasonable to me. In fact, I have something else I'd like to discuss with you, Mr. Cairo." She fluffed the veil around her hair, which was hanging in tendrils from what was left of the up-do she'd worn throughout the day, and crawled toward him.

"I am open to that line of discussion, Mrs. Cairo. Now get your hot little ass over here."

They spent the next two weeks popping from one Caribbean island to another, lying on the beach for part of each morning and eating a huge lunch before going back to their suite and not leaving the bed until it was time to head back to the beach the next day. It was a clichéd kind of honeymoon, but that might have been what Horace liked most about it. With the exception of the waiters who took their orders at lunch, they didn't interact with a single human being—other than each other. Horace thought he could go on that way for the rest of his life. Sure, he'd miss Nora and maybe even Andrew—a little—but if he could spend all his time with Andrea, he'd handle it. There was something freeing about being far away from the people you see every day. It was strangely pleasant to know that no one even knew where you were.

Or so he thought.

The morning before Horace and Andrea were scheduled to fly home, the phone rang in their hotel room, waking them up and leaving them blinking in confusion, not having heard a phone ring for over two weeks.

Horace reached for the phone. "Yeah?"

"Cuz, how's married life treatin' ya?"

Horace groaned. "Jesus. What the hell do *you* want? How did you even get this number?"

"Wasn't easy. I had to call like ten hotels on each of ten different islands before I finally got the right one. Where's your fucking cell phone, dude?"

"I don't know. I turned it off two weeks ago and stuffed it in my suitcase, I think. I didn't think I needed it."

"Welcome to the modern world. Way to go."

"What do you *want*? I'm busy here."

Andrew snorted. "I'll *bet* you are, horndog."

"I'm getting pissed off now. Somebody had better be dead or you're going to be," Horace said, rubbing his face with his hand as he threw his legs over the side of the bed and sat up. Andrea shot him a worried look, but when he mouthed the word *Andrew*, she smiled and rolled over to go back to sleep.

"Okay, man, don't be pissed. You'll be thanking me in a minute," Andrew said.

"Then let's get to that part, could we?"

"Okay. Get this. UPS delivered a package here last night."

Horace waited, and when Andrew didn't continue, he said, "Your blow-up doll, I assume? That's great, Andrew. You've been waiting so long."

"Cute. But that's not what I mean. It was that book."

"What book?"

"The *book*. Riley's book."

"Oh, shit," Horace said. He stood up and started pacing within the three feet or so that the length of the old-fashioned hotel phone cord would let him move. "I forgot all about that."

"Want me to send it to you? I could FedEx it or something, get it there tomorrow."

Horace sat back down on the bed, too hard, and Andrea bounced before sitting up and peering at him with a frown on her face. He put up a hand in apology and turned back to the phone.

"No, man, we're leaving tonight. I guess I won't see it until we get home tomorrow morning."

"Buy a copy at the airport," Andrew suggested.

Horace felt himself brighten. "Sometimes you're not as big a moron as you seem. That's a great idea. I'll read that piece of shit on the plane."

"Okay, well. Just thought you'd want to know."

"Thanks, Andrew. I appreciate it."

"So," Andrew said. "You been doing a lot of . . . bow chicka bow bow . . . ?"

"I'm hanging up now," Horace said. "I'll call you tomorrow."

48

IRIS

Shondra's been out in the greenhouse all day, loading poinsettias to ship all over the place. She says she makes enough money in these two months to last her the whole year. Everything else she grows—especially that stuff we smoked that one night when I first got here—is just for fun.

So I spent the whole day inside—just me and my belly, which looks about ready to burst. I can't believe it's almost time for the baby to come. I've been away from home for almost nine months and Seth hasn't found me—but then, the cops haven't found him yet, either. I don't know what's going to happen after I have the baby. I can't stay here forever. Shondra's great, and I feel like she's family now, but I have other family waiting at home for me, and they're probably worried half to death. I've sent a few postcards and called once or twice, but I never told anybody where I am—and I had Shondra send the postcards from Indiana and Pennsylvania when she went away to go to some garden shows, so nobody would be able to tell where I am from the postmark. They don't know where I am, but they know I'm safe. That's got to be good enough for right now.

I'll kind of miss this belly after the baby comes—for the past couple of months, I've been using it like a lap desk. I'll have to go back to sitting at a real desk to write again pretty soon.

Oh, shit. I think pretty soon just became right now.

December 6, 1981

The nurse just came and took the baby away, so I have a little time to myself, with no visitors and no one squalling, so I can finally write a bit.

Obviously, I had the baby. It's a boy. Although it almost made me throw up to do it, I named him "Horace"—it says it right there on his birth certificate. It's a ridiculous name—so old-fashioned. It makes me picture a skinny old guy with glasses, like the man in that painting *American Gothic*, maybe. But I had to do it. I promised Oscar, back when we were torturing ourselves trying to get me pregnant, that he could pick the name for a boy and I'd pick it for a girl. Horace. Ugh. Poor kid is going to get beat up on the playground every day if I don't take some heavy-duty precautions. I had really hoped for a girl—not that I care one way or the other in terms of raising the child. It was all about the name. I would have named a daughter something simple and sweet—maybe Jane, after my grandmother. Or Andrea. I've always liked that name.

49

HORACE

| PRESENT DAY |

"Fucking bastard!" Horace slammed the book down on the bed and threw himself back against the pillows with his arms crossed on his chest.

"Good book?" Andrea teased.

"It's just—bullshit. A big pile of bullshit."

Andrea picked up the book, gingerly, as if she hoped Horace wouldn't notice she was touching the offending object. She opened it on her lap and flipped through a few pages. "Is it not true?" she asked.

Horace scowled and grabbed the book away from her. He shuffled the pages as if he were looking for something specific, then sighed and tossed the book to the floor. "Some of it," he said. "Some's not true, exactly—or, at least, not that I know of. Riley gives details about conversations between my mother and father—things he couldn't possibly verify. And the fact that none of it's mentioned in my mom's journals makes me doubt if any of it's even true at all. Mom wrote down *everything*. So where's Riley getting this crap?"

Andrea hesitated.

"What?" Horace said.

"Did Andrew decide to talk to him after all?"

Horace shook his head. "No way," he said. "Besides, even if he did, he wouldn't know about this stuff."

"Nora?" Andrea asked.

"Not a chance. She'd never do anything to hurt my mom—or me. Couldn't be Nora."

Andrea held her breath for a moment before saying softly, "Well, there's only one other possibility."

Horace clenched his teeth. "Seth."

Andrea nodded. "I mean, right? Is there anybody else?"

"No."

Andrea took his hand and squeezed it. He forced a smile. "Or Riley could have just made it all up," he said.

"Very possible," she agreed. "If he did, you could probably sue."

"I don't know if that moron is worth the effort."

The phone rang. "Let it go to voicemail," Andrea said.

"Shit. I forgot to call Andrew when we got back. It's probably him." He stabbed the talk button with his forefinger.

"Yeah?"

"Dude! Where the fuck have you been?"

"Sorry, Andrew. I forgot to call you. I've been here—reading this piece of crap."

"Did you get there yet?" Andrew asked.

"Where?"

"Guess not," Andrew said. "Go to page 439, beginning of the last chapter. When you're done reading it, call me back." He hung up before Horace could respond.

Horace put down the phone. "That was weird," he said.

"What?"

"Andrew told me to read the last chapter now," he said, leaning out of the bed to grab the book off the floor. He thumbed through to the page Andrew had mentioned and started to read.

Chapter 56
Who's Your Daddy?

Many would say that Iris Cairo was a modern-day heroine, maybe even a saint. Devoted to the memory of the husband she lost before she could even be considered old enough to be a full-fledged adult by today's standards, she spent the rest of her life in pursuit of justice, indefatigably hunting down the man she believed was responsible for the death of her husband. But was Seth Cairo responsible for more than just his brother Oscar's murder? As this writer has discovered, there is evidence to suggest that Seth Cairo was, in fact, Iris Cairo's lover. Not only that, but confidential sources reveal that Seth Cairo, and not his dead brother, is the biological father of Iris's son—and Seth Cairo's own nemesis. Additional investigation is currently under way, and the results of that work will appear in this writer's next book: an unauthorized biography of the man who represents Iris and Seth Cairo's complex and twisted legacy: the love child of the widow and the murderer—Horace Cairo.

The book slid out of Horace's hands.

"You okay?" Andrea asked.

Horace was staring blindly. He shook his head.

"Horace? You're freaking me out."

"I think I'm gonna puke," he said.

"What's going on? What does the book say?" Andrea picked up the book and fanned the pages. "Tell me. What page?"

Horace shook his head. "You don't need to read it. We don't both need to get sick. I'll just tell you. Fucking Riley . . ." He clenched and unclenched his fists. "Riley says Seth's my real father."

A choking sound came out of Andrea's throat. "What page?"

"439."

She ran her finger down the right margin as she scanned the text. While she read, Horace pressed his palms to his stomach, feeling his insides churn with fury or terror or some other emotion he couldn't quite identify.

Andrea slammed the book shut and tossed it to the foot of the bed. "Well," she said. "It's nonsense. And it's libel."

Horace looked down and nodded slowly. "Yeah," he said. Then he turned and met her eyes. "But what if it isn't?"

50

IRIS

Some days, I find it hard to believe that this is really my life—or that this is real life at all. It's no wonder I did pretty well as a novelist—I barely have to fictionalize my own life at all to tell stories that seem impossible to believe. But this one's true, whether you believe it or not.

The baby and I were discharged from the hospital today. Shondra told me last night before visiting hours were over that she'd be there to pick me and Horace up by 10:00 A.M. So, needless to say, I was a little—no, a lot—worried when 10:00 came and went but Shondra didn't. I tried calling the house but no one answered. Naturally, I started jumping to conclusions: She must have gotten into an accident on the way to the hospital, and now she and the car were upside down somewhere in a ravine, or maybe she just decided she's had enough of me and my newborn brat and ditched us so she wouldn't have to take care of us. Can you really blame me for having some abandonment issues and a tendency to be melodramatic? Look at my life. And it's only getting worse.

Around 12:30, I was starting to feel like a fool, with all the nurses staring at me with such obvious pity—me, the poor pathetic loser who has no one to pick her up from the hospital. So I called for a cab and asked the nurse to wheel me out front so I could wait where nobody would stare at me and my lonely little baby.

By the time the taxi dropped us off in front of Shondra's house, my stomach was doing flips, I was so worried. When I saw that Shondra's truck *wasn't* in a ravine—it was parked right in the driveway like normal—my whole body started to shake. Something was really wrong—and I have enough experience with catastrophe to know it when I see it.

The baby must have felt the tension in my arms as I held him and got out of the cab because he started shrieking and wouldn't quiet down no matter how much I bounced him or made kissy noises in his ear. The taxi pulled away and left me standing there, staring at the silent, menacing house and holding my inconsolable baby. I felt my face twist into that awful expression you make right before you cry, but I ignored it and took a deep breath, then forced myself to march toward the door.

Maybe she just overslept, I thought. Maybe there was an emergency with her dad in Indiana and she had to rush to the airport and forgot to call me. About a million of these wishful thoughts rushed through my mind as I went up to the front door and twisted the knob.

When I walked into the house, it was like walking into a movie—and it was a horror movie.

Shondra was tied up with clothesline rope to one of the kitchen chairs, and there was a piece of duct tape over her mouth. Propped up right in front of the door so she'd be the first thing I saw when I came in, her eyes were wild, but not with fear—it was fury. I had hardly processed what I was seeing before the door clicked shut behind me and I realized that Shondra and I weren't alone—although I guess that really should have been the first thing I realized when I saw Shondra.

"Hello, Iris. So nice to see you."

I don't know why I was surprised to hear Seth's voice, but I was. It was like the safety I'd enjoyed over the past few months had made me forget why I'd ever come here in the first place. I suddenly had the thought that I should never have assumed Shondra had been in an accident when she didn't show up at the hospital; Seth was always the most obvious danger.

I closed my arms tighter around the baby, foolishly thinking maybe Seth wouldn't see him if I held him close enough. I felt Seth's breath on the back of my neck and I knew without looking at him that he was smiling.

"Why don't you put that . . . down?" Seth moved around in front of me and gestured toward the baby—pointing at little Horace with a butcher's knife that glinted just like a movie prop. I caught myself hoping it *was* just a plastic prop, but logic told me that wasn't very likely.

My voice came out weak and cracked a little. "Okay," I said. "I'll put him in the bedroom."

"Hurry back," Seth said as he settled down all casual on the sofa and spread his arms, knife in hand, behind him.

I covered the baby's face with my fingers and ran on unsteady feet to my bedroom, where Shondra and I had set up a crib in the corner. As I set the baby in the crib, I choked up a little—it was the very first time I was putting my child to bed, and I was doing it under duress, with the baby's insane, knife-wielding uncle waiting for me in the other room. I pressed my palm to my lips, then laid my hand on the baby's forehead. He gave me a gassy smile and I felt a sob shake me. I swallowed hard and was about to leave when I saw the phone on the night table and ran for it. I had already started to dial the police when I heard Seth behind me: "Ever resourceful. That's my girl. But I cut the phone line hours ago. You don't give me enough credit."

The receiver fell from my hand and bounced on the rug. I turned to face him.

"Seth. What do you want?"

He smiled. "Haven't we already had this conversation? You know what I want."

"Seth, I . . ."

"I want to hold the baby," he said. He went over to the crib and peered down at little Horace. "Can I pick him up?"

All I could see was the knife in his hand. "You have to put down the knife first," I said, hoping he wouldn't put it down by plunging it into my heart or the baby's. He looked at the knife as if he didn't remember that he was holding it, and now he didn't know what to do with it.

"I'll hold it," I said.

"Nice try," he said. He put the knife on the floor and pressed his foot on top of it. He glanced at me, like he was asking permission, then leaned into the crib and picked up the baby.

I have to admit, he looked strangely comfortable holding a newborn. I realized I had forgotten that he already had a child—Andrew—not just the illegitimate one in Texas he'd never met.

"Weren't you surprised?" he asked, his voice hardly more than a whisper.

"Surprised by what?"

"Surprised by how much you love him, even though he's really just a stranger," Seth said. He smiled at the baby, and Horace made a cheerful, gurgly sound. Stupidly, I wondered for a moment if Horace was thinking this was his daddy.

"He's amazing," Seth said, not taking his eyes off the baby.

I don't know what came over me, but I felt myself being drawn to his side, like he—or maybe the baby—was a magnet. I leaned over his shoulder and stared down at my son.

"He is," I said. "The most amazing thing in the world."

"Technology is a great thing, huh?"

His mention of the test-tube baby aspect pulled me out of my strange trance. I took the baby out of Seth's arms, brushed a finger against his rose-petal-soft chin, kissed his forehead, and laid him back down in the crib. I gripped the edge of the crib with both hands, not wanting to turn around and face the next step in Seth's insane plan.

"Iris."

I closed my eyes, tensed my arms, and spun around. Before I could open my eyes, I found myself being crushed in Seth's arms, and his lips were on mine. I don't know what happened. Maybe it was the fact that I haven't had sex or even a kiss in like two years. Maybe it was my post-pregnancy hormones playing with my emotions. Maybe it was just that he smelled and felt and tasted so much like Oscar. Or maybe—and I hope this isn't it—I'm actually attracted to the son of a bitch. All I know is that I was kissing him back, and my hands were twisted in his hair and running across the muscles of his back, his shoulders. And then we were on the bed and his fingers were on my throat and under my blouse, and that's when I remembered two things: that I had just given birth a couple of days ago and that the man I was getting ready to make love to was the one who had killed the love of my life.

I tore myself away from him and sat up on the bed, struggling to smooth my hair and clothes back into place.

"What's wrong?" he asked.

"Are you kidding?" I asked. My eyes were darting everywhere, trying to reestablish some sense of normalcy in a world that had apparently stopped turning. That's when I saw the knife, still lying on the floor beside the crib.

"Come on, Iris," Seth said. "I've waited forever for this to happen. Don't back out on me now."

I couldn't stop staring at the knife. It was hard to concentrate enough to keep talking to him without making a run for the knife. But I did my best.

"I . . . Seth, I can't," I said.

"Fucking Oscar."

"No," I said. "I mean, I just had a baby. I . . . well, I can't . . . *physically.*"

He let out a long breath—not a sigh, exactly. It sounded more like . . . compassion. He crawled across the bed and wrapped his arms around me, kissing my neck.

"Iris, I'm sorry," he whispered. "I wasn't thinking. I'm just so . . . happy."

I was just sitting there, trying not to cringe at his touch, with my eyes still glued to the impossible-to-reach knife, when I felt the impact. I never heard a thing, but one minute, Seth's arms were tight around me and the next he was slumped on the floor at my feet. I turned.

"Shondra?"

She was holding a few shards of terracotta—the remains of the pot-ted poinsettia she had smashed against Seth's skull. The duct tape was still stuck to her mouth and she had a shredded piece of rope dangling from one of her wrists. She shook her head, looking irritated, and dropped the pieces of terracotta before tearing the tape off her lips.

"Shit, that hurt!" She bent over to look at Seth's immobile body before looking at me. "Are you okay?"

I stood up and ran to the crib, picking up the baby, who had remained as quiet as a mouse throughout the whole ordeal. What more could you ask of a child who might have to spend his entire life on the run from his blood-crazed uncle? It suddenly occurred to me that he had been wailing as we walked up to the house from the cab—he had only stopped crying when he saw Seth. Strange.

"I'm fine," I said. "Let's get the hell out of here and call the police."

Shondra reached over and picked up the knife off the floor. She turned it over in her hands as she stared at Seth with a scowl on her face.

"You go," she said.

I felt my eyes widen. "What are you going to do?"

"Nothing," she said. "You should just get out of here, take the baby, and get the police. I'll stay here and make sure he doesn't wake up and get away."

It sounded reasonable enough, but the way she was fondling the knife made me worry that she had crossed over to Seth's side of the road—the bad side.

"Are you sure?" I asked. As much as I wanted to help her, to stay here and protect her—even if it was just from her own dark impulses—I wanted to get away and make sure my baby was safe even more.

She turned and smiled at me. "I'm okay," she said. "I'm not going to kill him. I promise. Now go and get the police. And hurry up."

I gathered up a few things—a carrier for Horace, some diapers, that sort of stuff—and rushed out to my car. Shondra still had the knife in her hand as she waved me off. I really thought she was going to go back into the little bedroom and slice Seth's throat.

Now I just hope he didn't do it to *her*.

Half an hour later, when I rode back to Shondra's in the back of a police cruiser with the baby beside me, the house was empty. Other than the broken bits of terracotta and a few poinsettia leaves on the bedroom floor, there was no sign that either Seth or Shondra had ever been there.

51

HORACE

"Is it true?" Horace asked as soon as Nora opened the door to let him in. He pushed past her and started pacing.

Nora pressed the door closed and leaned back against it. "Of course not," she said. "Your mother absolutely did *not* have an affair with Seth." She took his elbow and led him over to the couch. "You're letting this get to you," she said.

"Wouldn't you?" he said. "How can you be *sure* it's not true?"

"Sweetie, come on. Your mother hated Seth." She made a sour face. "We all do."

"Yeah, but . . ."

"But nothing. It's nonsense."

"Then why did Riley put it in his book?"

"Why does that man do anything? To make money. Don't let it upset you."

"I have to talk to Riley."

Nora patted his hand. "If it'll make you feel better."

"The only thing that's going to make me feel better is to kill Riley. Or hear it from Seth. Or maybe take a DNA test."

"Honey, you're making this into something it's not," Nora said. "Just . . . let it go."

"Is that what *you* would do?" he asked.

She smiled sadly. "That's what I *did* do. My entire life."

"Nora . . ."

"No," she said. "It's fine. We're not all fighters, like you. Or your mother. Some of us just let things happen to us."

"I think you've been very brave, just to survive everything you've been through."

She shook her head. "I'm not brave. I'm the biggest coward there is. But that doesn't mean I'm unhappy. Once you get used to it, it's not so bad being a nobody."

"Aunt Nora, you're not a nobody."

"Okay, okay. Maybe 'nobody' is harsh—but I'm mediocre. Average. Nothing special." She put up her hands to stop his protests. "Don't argue. It's true, and I'm fine with it. I just wish I'd realized it sooner, that's all."

"Sooner than when?"

She shrugged. "Before I married Seth. I thought being with him, having him propose to me, all that, would make me more than I was. All it did was destroy our entire family. In a way, it's all my fault—everything that happened to your father, your mother, you . . ." She pointed to his eye patch. "It's my fault."

"That's crazy," Horace said. "You had no way of knowing Seth would go nuts, start killing people, all that stuff. You were just trying to live your life."

"Yes, well." She rubbed his knee and stood up. "Want some coffee? Water?"

"No, thanks," he said. "I just wanted to talk about this a little. I've got to go." He stood up, kissed her on the cheek, and started toward the door.

"What are you going to do now?" Nora asked.

Horace looked over his shoulder at her. "Go see Riley. Or a lawyer. Maybe just the lawyer. I'm afraid of what I'll do to Riley if I see him outside of a courtroom."

She nodded. "Don't do anything stupid. Promise me?"

"Of course. Thanks, Aunt Nora."

That night, over dinner, Andrea said, "I just don't know if it's worth the hassle and the publicity to sue Riley. Why dignify his b.s. with a response? That's what he wants. The madder you get, the more books he sells."

Horace considered this while he chewed. "You're probably right. If I ignore it, it'll drive him crazy."

"He's basically obsessed with your family," she said. "You guys have been his meal ticket for years. Not getting a reaction out of you could kill him."

"Wouldn't that be nice?" Horace said. "Okay. You're right. I'm going to let it go."

"Forgive and forget?"

"Not quite," he said. "But indifference. That's what I'll give him. It's worse to be ignored than to be hated."

"Exactly. When you hate someone, they're affecting you. You're wasting time and energy and passion thinking about them and wishing bad things for them. Indifference is a killer. It's like when the ancient Egyptians destroyed all carvings of a pharaoh's name when they didn't want him to be remembered—it erased him from existence."

Horace grinned. "I love that nerdy side of you. It's really hot."

She made a face at him. "If you didn't want nerdy, you shouldn't have married a teacher."

"I'm glad I did."

"Me too."

He pushed himself up on his elbows and leaned over to kiss her, but the phone rang and interrupted him. He sighed.

"Should I be indifferent to the phone?" he asked.

"I don't think it'll care if you hate it or love it or whatever," she said. "Just answer it."

He got up and grabbed the phone. "Hello?"

"Hey, man, it's me."

"What's up, Andrew?"

"I just wanted to ask what you wanted to do about this whole Riley thing."

"I'm not going to do anything," Horace said, sitting back down at the table and taking Andrea's hand.

"Nothing?" Andrew said. "Are you crazy? We've got to sue the bastard."

"It's not worth it."

"What? The hundred million we could get? I think it's fucking worth it."

"It's not your problem," Horace said. "And I just want to ignore it."

"Fuck, man. I'm going to a lawyer myself. It's my family, too. I'll sue him with or without you."

"Andrew, just let it go. He *wants* us to get pissed off and make a public spectacle so he'll sell more books. I'm not gonna help him get rich."

"Why not help *me* get rich, dude?"

"You're rich enough," Horace said.

"Easy for you to say."

"You got something you want to say to me?"

Andrew was quiet for a long time. "No. I'm done talking." He hung up the phone.

52

IRIS

| December 13, 1981 |

I'm back home in New Jersey, staying at Mom's house while the Ohio police try to figure out what happened to Shondra and Seth. I won't hold my breath. It's been almost two years, and the Jersey *and* Texas police haven't been able to find Seth. Somehow I doubt Ohio will have a lot more luck.

At first, when we found Shondra's place empty, I don't think the cops believed my story. They looked at me a little suspiciously, like they thought I was just some crazy lady who wanted attention. It wasn't until I called the New Jersey police myself to report this latest development in the Seth saga that the Ohio cops started to come around—and then they were just plain stunned. I don't think they get all that many kidnappings or—God forbid—murders out in these parts. Once they realized they had an actual crime on their hands, they had every employee from the local p.d.—a good twelve or so people—swarming through Shondra's house, poking at things and dusting for fingerprints. I caught a few of the younger officers beaming, like they couldn't believe they were finally getting to do some real cop work, besides pulling people over for driving forty in a thirty-five-mile-an-hour zone.

They questioned me for hours, and when they finally decided I was telling the truth about not knowing what the hell was going on, they let me go. I immediately threw a few things in my suitcase, packed the baby's stuff, and called the airport. By midnight, I was on a plane back to New Jersey, with my newborn baby in my arms. All I can say is, I hope little Horace's life improves a *lot* and *fast*. In less than a week of life, he's been abandoned at the hospital, held hostage by his crazy uncle, and torn away from the place that might have been his home under more normal circumstances. What else could go wrong for this poor kid?

DECEMBER 25, 1983

I just put Horace to bed with his new stuffed bear in his arms and the red plastic fire truck he insisted on keeping with him beside his pillow. Everybody has gone home, so I'm left here alone with my journal and the remnants of wrapping paper that are still littered around the base of the Christmas tree.

Mom just came in to say good night before she went to bed. It's odd—I've been living with her for two years now, and half the time I forget she's here. Half the time I forget *I'm* here. Despite the fact that I grew up in this house, I barely remember it as my home. In some strange way, I've come to think of Shondra's place in Ohio as my "home," the place I really belonged. But two years and no progress at all from the police, and I've got to start to admit to myself that Shondra isn't coming back and I'll never be her houseguest or friend or whatever I was again.

I just have to hope Seth isn't coming back, either. All day today, I jumped every time the phone rang. For some reason, I was sure Seth would be in touch before Christmas is over. Call it ESP or women's intuition, whatever you want, but I felt like he wouldn't let the holiday pass without making me aware that he's still out there, waiting for the right moment to pounce. True, he didn't call last Christmas, but it had only been a year since the whole episode at Shondra's. He was probably worried that the cops would have my phone tapped or whatever they do to figure out where someone's calling from—I never *was* a crime novelist, so I'm not up on the lingo. But now that another year has gone by, it seems like the time is ripe for Seth to make one of his intrusions into my life, disrupting what little peace I've been able to establish.

DECEMBER 26, 1983

I stayed up until midnight last night, sitting right next to the phone, waiting for Seth to call. When I finally breathed a sigh of relief and slid into bed at 12:15, the phone rang. I lunged for it, hoping it wouldn't wake up Mom or Horace and because, in some perverse way, I was much too curious about what Seth would say.

I didn't even say hello. I let him speak first.

"Merry Christmas, Iris."

"You're fifteen minutes late for that," I said.

"Really? I guess I lost track of the time. It's hard to remember, with the time difference."

I felt myself breathe a little easier, knowing he wasn't nearby. But— and I hate myself for thinking it—I was simultaneously just a tiny bit disappointed, almost like I *wanted* to see him. I know, I know. I'm sick.

"So you're in a different time zone?" I asked.

He chuckled. "Such a clever girl," he said. "Always trying to figure things out. I think we've talked enough about *me*. How are you? And how's my . . . nephew?"

"We're fine. As long as you're nowhere near us, we're fine."

"Iris, come on. Don't be like that. We've shared one of the most intimate things two people can share."

I felt my face contort into a scowl, and I was glad. It meant I still hated him. "I hate to disappoint you, Seth, but I've kissed lots of guys." Okay, so that was a lie—and I knew he knew it.

He was quiet for a long time. Then he said, "Sure. Right."

"Seth?" I wasn't sure it was a good idea to bring up the next topic, but it seemed like the right thing to do. "Where's Shondra?"

He sighed. "You're always the little worrier, aren't you?" He started imitating me. "'Oh, is Oscar okay? Is Shondra okay?' Could you ever just focus on *me*?"

Tears filled my eyes and I was afraid my voice would crack if I tried to speak.

"Oh, great," he said. "Now she's crying. That's just great."

"If you can't stand me, if I annoy you so much, why don't you just leave me alone?" My voice was even more whiny than I'd feared. And that made him laugh.

"You don't annoy me," he said, chuckling. "All your quirky little traits are endearing."

A fat tear rolled down my cheek. It felt like something was breaking apart inside me. I realized in that moment that he was never going to let me go. We're going to be locked in this—struggle, relationship, whatever the hell it is—until at least one of us is dead.

"Iris," he said. He sounded really far away because his voice had to penetrate the many layers of fear and understanding that had just built up around me. "Are you still there?"

"Yeah." My voice wasn't squeaky anymore; it was just breathy with exhaustion.

"What are you doing New Year's?"

A shot of terror ripped through me. He started to laugh, hard and uncontrolled. Then he was gone and the phone line was silent.

53

HORACE

| PRESENT DAY |

"Andrew? It's me. We need to talk."

"Man, I got nothing to say to you."

"Come on, cuz," Horace said. "Let me take you to dinner. It's important."

"Is it about Riley?"

"Yeah, kind of. I really need to talk to you."

Andrew was quiet for a few seconds, then said, "Okay. Pick me up and we'll eat. But not at that fucking '50s place. Someplace with booze—even if you're being a goddamn choir boy."

"Fine. I'll be there in half an hour."

As soon as the waiter brought their drinks, Andrew gulped down his beer and asked for another. The waiter flashed a look of desperation at Horace, who just smiled and took a sip of his ice water.

"So," Andrew said. "Lay it on me."

Horace put down his glass and shoved it forward with his finger. "I've been reading these journals of my mom's, right?"

"They're like diaries?"

"Yeah, journals, diaries. Whatever. The point is, I'm starting to wonder about some things."

"Like what?"

"Like what Riley said in the book."

The waiter put Andrew's second beer down on the table and darted away before Andrew could demand yet another one. Andrew reached for the beer but stopped himself and looked at Horace.

"Are you saying your mom fucked my dad?" he asked.

236

Horace shook his head. "I don't know," he said. "Not in what I've read so far. But there was this part I read the other day, about right after I was born, and my mom was making out with Seth."

"Shit," Andrew said, taking a long drink of beer. "Does my mom know about that? She swore to me that it wasn't true about Dad and Aunt Iris."

"I doubt it. I don't think anybody would have known. Mom just wrote *everything* down, good or bad."

"Can I read it?" Andrew asked.

"I don't have it with me," Horace said. "I've been afraid to read much more. I mean, what if I keep going and find out they really *were* together?"

Andrew knit his brow. "Wait a sec," he said. "You said your mom wrote everything down, right?"

"Right."

"But she didn't mention sleeping with my dad before you were born, did she?"

"Well, no . . ."

"Then Riley's wrong. My dad isn't your dad. If you're right about your mom writing it all down in her diary, she woulda written about it. Why would she admit that she made out with him and not mention fucking him?"

"Maybe you're right," Horace said. "I never thought of that." He grinned. "Hey, wait a minute. What's with you? How did you get so smart?"

"I've always been smart, bro. I just don't like to show off my big brains."

"Well, you seem to be in a better mood than the last time we talked. What changed?"

"Nothing. I don't know. I guess I'd rather be mad at Riley than you."

"I'm pissed as hell at Riley, but I just don't think we should get into it with him."

"Cuz, doesn't it seem like we're pussies if we don't stand up to him?"

Horace shook his head. "We'll stand up to him plenty when we put out my mom's book. It'll knock his piece of crap out of print and make us millions." Horace leaned over and looked Andrew in the eye. "And, by the way, we're gonna split the profits evenly, three ways—you, me, and your mom."

Andrew's face lit up. "Seriously, man? I thought you wanted the money to go to charity or some shit."

"Yeah, well," Horace said. "I'll give my share to one of Mom's charities, but you'll get the rest. I wouldn't have done the book at all without you and your mom. Besides, you introduced me to Andrea. So I owe you a few million, I'd say."

"You mean Angela," Andrew said. Horace started to protest, but Andrew cracked a smile and pointed at his cousin's disgusted face. "Gotcha."

"You are one crazy SOB."

"Yeah, well. I gotta be me," Andrew said. "So, when is this book of ours coming out?"

"I have a meeting with the editor-in-chief at the publishing house tomorrow. I'd like to get it done by Christmas. It's only a few months, but if we can do it fast enough, we can really crush Riley—and that would be worth whatever work it might take to get the thing done."

Andrew raised his glass and waited for Horace to clink his own against it. "Here's to your mom and her crazy diaries."

"And to your mom and her crazy husband."

"Amen, brother."

54

IRIS

I wasn't going to tell my mother about Seth calling, but she walked in on me when I was on the phone with the police, trying to make them see why they need to post someone here all the time to protect us and to tap my phone (if that's what they call it) so they'll be able to trace the call the next time Seth contacts me—and I feel like that'll be soon. I didn't even hear Mom come into the kitchen—I guess I was sighing too loudly in my frustration with these Keystone cops.

"Who are you talking to this early?" she asked as she reached for the empty coffeepot, glaring at me because I hadn't made any coffee yet.

I put up a finger to keep her quiet while I finished talking. When I hung up, I bit my lip as I tried to decide as fast as possible whether to make something up or tell her the truth. Like always in real life—as opposed to one of my books—my imagination failed me and I ended up just blurting out the truth.

"That was the police," I said. "Seth called here last night."

Mom dropped the coffeepot and it shattered on the floor. I leaped up to sweep up the glass, hoping the crash hadn't woken up the baby.

"My God, Iris, is this starting again?" Mom said. She bent down to try to help me clean up the mess, but I pushed her aside gently.

"I've got this. Go sit down. Or make some tea, maybe. We're obviously not having coffee today."

"Iris."

"It's not starting again, Ma," I said, brushing the glass into the garbage can. "It never ended in the first place."

DECEMBER 31, 1983

I just put Horace to bed in his ugly little room in our new rental house—
it's a tiny townhouse inside a ski resort in the Pocono Mountains. Horace
was thrilled because he gets to sleep in a "big boy bed," since that's all
the place, which came furnished, had. I'll probably go buy him a small
bed or at least something with rails later this week—assuming he doesn't
fall out of bed tonight and kill himself. I shouldn't joke about accidental
death, not when I'm constantly being stalked by the nonaccidental kind.

Mom was devastated when I packed up and left again, but I couldn't
stay with her any longer, not with Seth knowing I was there. It was too
dangerous for all of us. I wouldn't tell her where I was going, just that it
would be someplace Seth would never think to look for me. A hatred
of cold weather and winter sports—it's pretty much the only thing Seth
and I ever had in common. He'd never expect me to be living inside a
ski resort. Besides, when I left, I bought four sets of airline tickets in my
name and Horace's—to the Bahamas, to Paris, to San Francisco, and to
Mexico—just to lead Seth on a wild goose chase and give us as much time
as possible to settle down under our fake names in our dull new life in this
very snowy place.

Now it's New Year's Eve and while other people—probably even
Seth—are out drinking champagne and blowing noisemakers and kissing,
I'm here sitting on a scratchy brown plaid sofa watching Dick Clark on a
black-and-white TV whose picture keeps jumping randomly and giving
me a headache. I miss being one of those normal people who get to do
everyday things like go to work and to parties and pay bills and go to the
park with their kids. I keep thinking that if this goes on much longer, I'll
end up leading most of my life in hiding. Why can't these cops find Seth?
He's *one* guy—and it's not like he's some kind of Lex Luthor/evil genius.
He's just evil. How hard can it be to track him down? He seems to have no
trouble tracking *me* down. I just hope I've really lost him this time.

55

HORACE

| Present Day |

"Lynn, it's great to finally meet you," Horace said. He shook the editor's hand, trying to look at her face but finding himself casting sneaky glances not at her cleavage like most men would have been doing but at her office—because it was the same one his mother had used when she still worked here. Despite the years she had been on the run, they had left her office intact—at least until she died. It was strange to look at these walls and not see all the huge framed pictures of his father and mother that used to hang there.

"Mr. Cairo, thanks for coming in."

"Please, call me Horace."

She started toward the desk, which *was* the same one Iris had used, and then stopped, turned, and settled onto the couch, patting the cushion beside her so Horace would sit down.

"Now," she said. "Tell me what I can do for you."

He slapped his palms on his knees. "Well, it's about my mother's journals. I want to publish them."

She looked startled. "I didn't realize Mrs. Cairo had kept journals. Did she . . . um . . . how do I put this? Are they something she would have *wanted* the public to see?"

Horace laughed. "You must think I'm trying to make an easy buck off my poor dead mother. No, nothing like that. She actually requested that I have them published after she died."

Lynn sat back, clearly relieved. "Oh, that's great. I was just—well, I wouldn't want to do anything that would ever have hurt Mrs. Cairo. She was . . . really, she was more than a mentor to me. She was like a mother."

A tear dropped from her eye and she flushed red. She turned and fanned her fingers in front of her face. "I'm sorry," she said. "I didn't mean to get all emotional."

Horace smiled. "It's okay. Sis."

She looked at him quizzically.

He shook his head. "Sorry. That was stupid. You just said my mom was like a mother to you, so . . . since she'd be *your* mother *and* my mother . . ."

Lynn chuckled. "You're so different from how I imagined you."

He leaned in and smiled. "How did you imagine me?"

Her mouth gaped open. "I don't . . . well, I mean, I didn't really . . . I don't know what I'm saying."

Horace sat back and laughed. "I can't believe I'm embarrassing you this much. I apologize. You expected me to be an asshole, right?"

Her eyes widened and he could tell she was trying to decide whether or not to tell the truth. She finally smiled. "I guess you could say that, yeah," she said.

"Don't worry about it," he said. "I *am* an asshole."

"That seems hard to believe."

"Okay, well, I *was* an asshole—before I met my wife."

"That's right! I heard about your marriage. Congratulations. Your mother would have been so happy."

Horace nodded. "Yeah," he said. "I think she would."

"So," Lynn said, picking up a legal pad and pen off the coffee table. "Tell me about these memoirs."

"There are a ton of journals, actually. I've been reading through them myself, picking out the best entries—the ones that seem most relevant to telling the story of Mom's life."

"You don't want to publish the entire set of volumes?"

He frowned. "I don't know," he said. "Maybe eventually. But for now, I just want to put out a sort of 'best of' collection, if that makes any sense."

Lynn was scribbling on the pad. "That sounds ideal. We'll be able to judge by the sales whether future expanded volumes would do well. So, how soon were you hoping to get this book out?"

"That's probably the tough part," he said. "I want it out for Christmas."

Lynn sucked in her breath through her teeth. "Ouch, that's a tight schedule."

"I realize that, but with Richard Riley's book about Mom being out, I just thought . . ."

Lynn stabbed the air with her pen. "You're right! We can use Riley's sales to help launch our own book."

Horace grinned. "It would probably be the first time that sleazebag will ever be helpful to anybody."

She giggled. "Not many people talk trash about a successful writer like Riley, but . . ." She leaned in toward him and whispered, "I couldn't agree more."

He held up his fist and she bumped hers against it. Horace felt like they were on the same football team and had just scored a touchdown.

"So, that's less than six months," Lynn said, writing something else on the pad. "But if the journal entries don't require a lot of editing . . ."

"I want them published exactly the way I give them to you. I'll do the editing myself."

"Oh," she said, and stopped writing.

"I realize I'm not an editor," he said. "But I'm looking at this as sort of a family project. In fact, I want to pay for all the costs out of my own pocket, not through the company."

"Well," she said. "It's unusual. But I think we can do it."

"That's what I wanted to hear," Horace said. "I'll have everything for you by the end of next week."

56

IRIS

| DECEMBER 6, 1991 |

Today was Horace's tenth birthday. I just tucked him into bed, which wasn't fun because he's been crying and shouting at me most of the day. He was angry because I didn't let him have a big party with all his little friends from school, with a magician and a big cake and all the balloons and everything. It killed me to have to say no to him, but the thought of getting too close to people, letting ourselves get too exposed, terrifies me. The longer we go, the more time that passes without the police catching Seth, the more I'm convinced that he's lurking around every corner. I know I'm defying logic. I realize we've kept ourselves hidden well—moving every two or three years to a new ski town, changing our names, and—especially—keeping Horace home as much as possible and not letting him make any real friends. But still. I know Seth is capable of anything and he seems to have a supernatural talent for doing evil. In all this time, a full decade, the police have not only *not* found Seth, but they haven't found Shondra—or her body—either. There are days when I spend hours sobbing, thinking about the fact that I have probably been responsible for the deaths of two of the people I cared about most in the world. I might as well have killed them myself; I'm just as guilty. The only way I can make myself feel better at all is to remind myself that I'm protecting my son, doing everything I can to make sure nothing will ever happen to him. If Seth ever got to him—if anything . . . I can't even think about it or I'll start to get hysterical—I'd literally die. I couldn't live with the guilt of knowing yet another person had suffered just because of me.

Every year on Horace's birthday, I can't help but look back and be thankful that we've made it through another year. But at the same time, I wonder what kind of damage this crazy nomadic lifestyle is having on him.

I know he may never forgive me for all this—not letting him make friends, never letting him see our family or our "real" home, and—maybe most of all—just bringing him into this world knowing full well that he'd never get the chance to have a father. I just hope someday—even if it's long after I'm gone—he'll realize that I did it all with the best of intentions; I did it all out of a love so strong, I can't even describe it. I thought what I had with Oscar was more powerful than gravity or the expansion of the universe, but what I feel for Horace—my God! It permeates every one of my cells, every pore, every snippet of DNA. Knowing how much he hates me right now—even if it *is* in his petty, little boy way—is killing me. Seeing the hurt and disappointment in his eyes breaks my heart. Maybe next year . . . maybe I'll break down and let him have the stupid party.

If it weren't for the karate class I let him take this year, which Horace loves, I think he would probably have tried to run away from home. And that thought terrifies me. I think the karate is a great thing for him. Besides the friendships—however superficial—he gets to make, he's also learning to protect himself physically, which is of absolute necessity in our life. I just hope it'll be enough if Seth ever manages to track us down.

December 6, 1996

Horace turned fifteen today—or should I say Henry? That's what we're calling him these days. Me? I'm Lily. I try to stay in the realm of flowers when choosing my aliases. So far, I've been Daisy, Rose, and Flora. I also called myself "Mari" for a while—short for "Marigold," but nobody else had to know that.

All this name and flower nonsense—I'm just distracting myself from what I don't want to think about: the fact that Horace stormed into my room tonight and demanded that I let him go to a military school about fifty miles from here. My immediate reaction was to tell him no, outright. I couldn't even process the thought that I might be separated from the person who's been with me every single day since he was born, the one I've devoted my whole existence to trying to protect.

He didn't take it well. He marched out and slammed the front door behind him. I assume he went to hang out with his friends. They're all probably drinking stolen beers in somebody's basement and listening to Led Zeppelin right now. Wait. Do kids even listen to Led Zeppelin anymore? God. I can't think straight.

Now that I've had a little time to consider the situation, I'm thinking maybe it's best if I do let him go. Where would he be safer than at a military school? Besides, if I say no, he's getting to that rebellious age where he might shun me or even run off on his own—and then I'd lose him forever. Boarding school is just a few years—and then he'll be back. Okay. I'll tell him tomorrow.

57

HORACE
| PRESENT DAY |

He was surprised to find there were tears in his eyes as he clipped together the last set of photocopies of the pages he wanted to publish from the journals. Reading through all these little books, especially the ones that covered the years during which he'd been alive, had shown him sides of his mother he had never known existed. She had always seemed weak and overprotective, annoying and cloying in most ways. But what she hadn't let him see was the ferocity and strength of her character—what enabled her to raise a difficult child under impossible circumstances and, despite the fact that she could almost never physically be in the office, the way she continued to build her company into one of the most respected in the industry. He wanted to slap himself for having been too stupid and stubborn to notice what must have been obvious to everyone else—that his mother was possibly one of the world's most extraordinary women.

It made him sick to think of Richard Riley writing about his mother. Someone like that shouldn't be allowed anywhere near the memory of a woman as amazing as Iris Cairo had been.

He felt Andrea's fingers on the back of his neck. "Hey, you," she said. "You okay?"

He snuffled, not bothering to try to hide the fact that he'd been crying just a little. "I'm good. It's just weird, how different I feel about her now."

"Respect?"

"Yeah. But more than that. It's like—I don't know. I finally see a reason to love her."

Andrea wrapped her arms around his neck and hugged him from behind. "You're a good guy, you know that?"

He shook his head. "I wish I had been better. For her, I mean. If I knew then . . ."

"Don't torture yourself. Everybody feels that way and it never helps."

"Maybe not. But she deserved better than I gave her."

Andrea kissed his cheek. "She knows," she whispered in his ear.

"Yeah," he said. "Sure she does." He still wasn't sure he believed it.

Horace had just kissed Andrea good-bye and watched her leave for work when the phone rang. It was unusual for anyone to call him before 7:30 in the morning, so he peered at the caller ID screen, which only gave him the all-too-common and intensely disappointing "Unknown Name." He frowned, considering whether to let the call go to voicemail, then, more out of boredom than curiosity, decided to pick up.

"Hello?"

"Cairo! I'm surprised I haven't heard from you before now."

"Fucking Riley," Horace muttered. "You're not hearing from me now, asswipe. *You* called *me*."

"Only because I've been dying to know what you think of the book."

Horace took and released a long breath, tensing his body to try to keep himself from letting the insults fly like he wanted. Finally, he said, "I'm sure you already know what I think of the book."

"Come on. Give me more than that. I expected more of a reaction."

"I'm sure you did. And that's why you're not getting one."

"So how soon should I expect the lawsuit to start?"

"What lawsuit?" Horace wished he could pat himself on the back for the incredible tone of patience in his own voice. He could almost hear Riley's rising panic right through the phone line.

"Don't be cute, Cairo. I know you're pissed."

"I'm always pissed at you, Riley. But I leave it at that."

"I—I don't understand . . ."

"I know what you're trying to do. You wrote all that stuff to try to get me to sue you, since that would be a huge public scandal and people would rush out to buy your piece of shit book to see what all the fuss is about. I'm not going to help you sell books. Sorry, Riley."

Riley was silent. "It wasn't just to sell books, though," he eventually said.

"What?"

"I didn't just write that stuff about your mother and your uncle to try to get you to sue me."

"Then why did you?"

"Because your uncle told me it was true."

Horace felt a coldness seep through his chest, but he tried to ignore it and remain logical. "You can't believe a word my uncle tells you," he said. "Maybe you're forgetting the fact that he's a liar and a murderer, among other things."

"Seth and I have a pretty good relationship, after all the interviews I did with him for the last book. Why would he lie to me?"

Horace laughed. "Why would he kill his own brother? Why would he spend twenty years stalking me and my mother? He's insane."

"I don't know," Riley said. "He's always seemed pretty lucid to me."

"Whatever, Riley. Believe what you want. The point is, I don't care what you do."

"I doubt that's true, but have it your way. I'm sure I'll be hearing from you soon enough. After all, I'd love to get an interview for my next book."

A choking guffaw came out of Horace's mouth. "That's right! I almost forgot. My unauthorized biography. Maybe they didn't teach you what the word *unauthorized* meant in college, but it means without my help. Got it?"

"Yeah . . ."

"This is over. I have a life of my own to lead."

"Right, right," Riley said. "How's married life? Finding it hard to turn over that leaf?"

"What do you mean?"

Riley chuckled. "Come on, man. You've got to know you have a bit of a reputation for screwing a lot of women. That's not a habit that just fades away."

"People change. Maybe not assholes like you, but some people."

"Sure they do. You're changing all the time. When's your book coming out, by the way? Playboy turned editor. It's a nice story. I'm actually looking forward to writing it."

"I'm done here, Riley. I'm hanging up."

"Wait, wait! How's Andrew? I really thought he'd have some strong feelings about the book, even if you were able to suck it all up."

"Andrew is fine with it. He's my cousin. He supports my decision."

"Don't you mean he's your brother?"

"Fuck off, Riley."

"Seriously, man. You're not wondering at all? Not even a little?"

Horace's throat was dry with the effort of lying both to Riley and to himself. "Not even a little. Good-bye, Riley."

58

IRIS

Horace just dropped me off at my hotel and headed back out to go to a party with his friends to celebrate their graduation. I would have liked to spend the whole evening with him, but I guess I should be grateful that he stooped to go out to dinner with me. It was obvious enough the whole time we were at the restaurant that he couldn't wait to get out of there—or, more precisely, that he couldn't wait to get away from *me*. Part of me thought, or hoped at least, that all his hatred toward me was just a phase—teenage rebellion. But he's seventeen now, practically an adult, and I don't see any signs that he hates me any less. God, I thought losing my husband was the hardest thing I'd ever have to go through, but this is worse. Having the person you love most hate you with such bitter intensity has got to be more painful than any type of grief—because it *is* a kind of grief; you lose the person but you never get to move on with your life. You just keep waiting for them to start loving you again, even when it seems pretty clear that's never going to happen. And I'm running out of time. Despite all my arguments and pleas, he joined the army. No college, just the army. And as if that's not bad enough, he won't even have two weeks to enjoy his post–high school days before he gets dragged away to boot camp. It's crazy, I know—he's basically been strapped to a cradle-board on my back for seventeen years and I feel like I don't know him at all. I just know he has no interest in knowing *me*. What can I do to make him think I'm a decent mother—not great, just decent?

DECEMBER 25, 2000
I took a chance this year and came home to New Jersey to be with the family for Christmas. I even managed to swing by the office yesterday,

surprising everybody while they were knee-deep in eggnog and tinsel, getting just a little drunk before heading home to be with their loved ones for Christmas Eve. It's funny; a lot of the younger people working at the publishing house now—the editorial assistants and fresh-out-of-college marketing kids—have never even seen me before. To a lot of them, I'm just some kind of mythical figure—like Remus or Romulus, coming in to found the place and then disappearing into the mist of history. Their faces were so charming, so scared and excited and awestruck. I threw back a paper cup full of eggnog with them, toasting the holiday, and then I helped the editor-in-chief, Bill Reynolds—a friend of Oscar's and mine from college—hand out the Christmas bonus checks. I had forgotten how much fun it can be to just watch other people and listen to them talk about their lives—even the ordinary things, *especially* the ordinary things, like picking up dry cleaning and driving kids to Cub Scouts. I wonder if that's how God feels, if that's why he made the world—to have something interesting to watch. Like TV. Wow. I'm losing it. The point is, it makes me sad when I think about all the things I've missed. And now it's way too late for me to even dream about having a normal life.

Speaking of which—just when I had started to enjoy the normalcy of everything around here, settling in as if it might actually last, Seth called tonight. Somehow, despite the fact that my mother has changed her phone number at least five times over the years and hasn't had it listed since the mid-'70s, he always manages to get hold of it and track me down. He would have made a brilliant cop or PI. Hell, he's been able to evade trained detectives in three states for going on two decades. He could have done almost anything with his life. But all he's ever done is follow me.

"Merry Christmas, Iris," he said. "It's been too long."

"That's a matter of opinion," I said, and a nervous giggle tickled my throat.

"Aw, don't be like that," he said. "I've missed you."

I cleared my throat. "So, where are you these days, Seth?"

He laughed. "You're getting bolder over time, Iris. Not as timid and subtle as you used to be."

"I like to get right to the point. I've wasted enough time on you."

"Now, that's just rude."

"Well . . ."

"So," he said brightly, changing the subject. "Home for the holidays?"

"Obviously you know I am," I said. "Why ask?"

"Just making conversation. When are you heading back to . . . ?"

"Nice try," I said. "You're getting less subtle, too."

"I guess people change."

"Really? Have you?"

"Nope," he said. "Nothing can change the way I feel about you."

I squinched my eyes shut and pinched the bridge of my nose between my fingers, trying to ward off the tension headache I could feel building. "Seth, when is this going to be over?"

"You know when," he said. "When you say yes."

"God, Seth, we're *middle-aged*. I have a grown son in the *army*. We're not kids anymore, and this isn't some romantic movie. This is real life, and we're both missing out on it."

"You look just as good now as you did when we were teenagers," he said. I swung around toward the windows with a gasp, suddenly certain that he was watching me. My skin started to crawl and I felt myself shrinking down toward the floor, trying to hide.

He started to laugh. "Relax," he said. "I can't actually see you. This is a long-distance call. So get up off the floor."

Despite the fact that I knew he could be lying, my body unclenched and I stood back up and leaned against the kitchen counter.

"If you can't see me, how did you know I was on the floor?" I asked.

"I just know *you*. I don't have to see you to know what you're doing."

This will probably sound insane, but something about that statement was kind of touching in a bizarre sort of way. Maybe because I had to admit he was right. He really *does* know me better than anyone else does, maybe even better than Oscar did.

"Seth . . ." I started, but I had no idea what I wanted to say.

"How *is* our boy, by the way? Enjoying working for Uncle Sam?"

"Don't call him that."

"What?"

"*Our* boy. He's nothing to you. I only regret the fact that he shares even a little bit of your DNA." I was relieved that my anger at him had returned. It always scares the hell out of me when I start to feel as if I might *like* him.

"Don't be like that," he said.

"Seth, I'm getting angry."

"I love it when you get angry. Your eyes get so green, it's like they're made of kryptonite."

"I'm done now."

"All right, then," he said. "Merry Christmas. Give everyone my love."

"Go to hell."

He chuckled. "Eventually. Maybe I'll see you there." He hung up.

It had been five years since his last Christmas call, his last contact—the call that had made me move to a rented room on a cattle ranch in Wyoming, for a while at least. I guess after all this time, I thought he had finally decided to move on and let me go. I guess I was wrong. I guess that's never going to happen.

59

HORACE

| PRESENT DAY |

"If it worries you that much, just have a DNA test," Andrea said.

"Oh, Riley would love that. He's probably bribed the staff at every nearby hospital to tip him off if I show up."

"So use an independent lab," she said. "There're places you can just send the samples and they'll tell you if you're related. You don't even have to give your real name."

Horace shrugged. "I don't know. Where would I even get a sample they could compare to mine? I'm sure as hell not going over to the prison to see Seth."

"Can't you just send them a sample from you and from Andrew? That should be able to tell if you're cousins or brothers?"

"I don't know," Horace said. "I'm no expert on DNA or anything, but I wonder if the fact that Andrew and I are the kids of women who were sisters and men who were brothers would screw things up. We're not exactly regular cousins."

"Huh. That's an interesting point. I have no idea. We don't exactly teach advanced genetics in third grade. But I would think they'd be able to tell the difference."

"I think there's a part of me that doesn't really want to know either way," he said.

"If you want my opinion, I think you should just let it go. It's not worth opening a big ole can of worms."

"That's what I'm thinking, actually. Okay. That settles it." He got up and kissed her. "Thank you. I'm just going to check my email and then head up to bed. See you there?"

"Definitely. Don't take too long."

Grabbing a bottle of water from the refrigerator, he went to the room he liked to call the "den," though it was little more than a simple office with a desk, a chair, and his computer. He had never even bothered to buy a lamp for the room, so he always had to sit in the dark, with only the glow of the monitor lighting his way, whenever he used the computer at night.

He scanned over the list of emails, most of them spam, but stopped when he saw one from Lynn, the editor-in-chief of Cairo Books. Excited to read the first report on the progress of his mother's journals, he clicked the email open.

Dear Mr. Cairo:

Oh, crap, he thought. Not a good start. Something bad is coming.

> *I just wanted to keep you informed about the status of your publishing project. The pages have been typeset and proofread, and will be going to the production department for layout at the end of the week.*
>
> *In the meantime, our director of marketing requested that I contact you about two matters: First, we need to choose a title for the book and would like your input in the process. We'll be holding a meeting next Tuesday at 10:00 A.M. to discuss potential titles, if you'd like to attend, either in person or via conference call.*
>
> *Second, in light of the controversy that has arisen as a result of certain charges regarding your parentage brought up in the recent biography of Iris Cairo by Richard Riley, our marketing department is interested in getting your thoughts on the best ways to use the publicity to increase sales of your book. We can discuss this topic at next week's meeting as well.*
>
> *Please let me know if you will be able to join us next Tuesday. If another day or time would better suit your schedule, we can arrange something else.*
>
> *Best,*
> *Lynn*

Horace coughed. He should have known it was coming. Lynn had as much as said they would use Riley's book to boost their own sales. He just hadn't really expected it to happen. Maybe the fact that he had begun to develop so much respect for his mother made it hard for him to believe that the business she had loved and excelled at could be so sleazy and manipulative. Using Riley to help himself wasn't the problem; he had no qualms about screwing over the libelous son of a bitch. What bothered him was the thought that using the scandal to sell his own book would necessarily help sell more of Riley's books, too. That just seemed wrong and unfair. Horace had seen this project partly as a way to crush Riley in retaliation for hurting the Cairo family, but in reality, Riley would be absolutely thrilled with everything. Horace's attempt to stop Riley would most likely end up making the hack rich enough to retire without ever having to write another one of his crappy books.

But it would also give Horace's mother the legacy she had wanted—and that she deserved.

He clicked "Reply" and typed:

Lynn,

I'll see you Tuesday at 10:00. And don't call me "Mr. Cairo." I told you before—I'm just Horace.

60

IRIS

| MARCH 13, 2003 |

My God, this day has been a nightmare. Whenever the thought floats through my brain that my life has gotten as bad as it can get, I should remember that line from *King Lear*: "The worst is not so long as we can say this is the worst." It can *always* get worse. And today it did.

Horace has been here, at Mom's, visiting me and the rest of the family before he has to report back to Fort Bragg. I know I should be glad I got to see him at all. It's not like he visits much. But this time, I'm worried. He's been in the army for a long time now—too long for my taste. But now—now that they're talking about going to war in Iraq—I'm scared out of my mind.

He never tells me much, but I assumed this army thing was all just temporary, that after he served his time, he'd come rushing back home to me and be my son again—with shorter hair and better posture, maybe, but the same kid, except maybe he'd also be a little more respectful. I almost had myself convinced that the military was ultimately going to be a good thing for both of us. Until today.

Horace came home too late for dinner, mumbling something about having eaten something while he was out with his friends. He started up the stairs, looking like he was going to lock himself in the guest room and avoid me like he's been doing the whole three days he's been here. I stopped him.

"Horace, could you come sit down for a while?"

"What for?"

"I . . . I don't know. We just really haven't had much of a chance to talk since you got home."

He shuffled back into the kitchen and slumped into one of the chairs, not even glancing at me. I tried to ignore his coldness and sat down across from him at the table, sitting there all excited and perky, like an idiot, actually thinking we might have a meaningful conversation.

"So," I began. "How are things?"

"What things?"

"You know. The army. The guys you've been meeting. The place you're living. All that."

"It's fine."

I forced a smile, but he wasn't looking at me, so it was pretty much useless. "Fine? That's it? Can't you give me any more detail than that?"

He leaned back, letting his head hang back over the top of his chair, with his arms hanging slack at his sides. "I'm not into details, Ma. You're the writer, not me."

"I'm not asking for pages of prose, just a little information."

He sighed and thrust his body forward, hunching over the table and playing with his fingers, studying them so he wouldn't have to look at me.

"Horace . . ." I stopped because I had absolutely no clue what to say. To my surprise, when I went silent, he actually looked over at me, but his eyes flew back down the instant they met mine. I frowned. I could feel that burning feeling in my throat—the feeling you get right before you're about to start crying when you *really* don't want to start crying. Just when I thought a sob was getting ready to burst out of my mouth, Horace spoke.

"There *was* something I wanted to tell you."

The burning feeling and the potential sob went away instantly. "Really?" I said, my voice much too eager. "What's that?"

"I'm getting sent overseas."

I almost choked on my own saliva. "What do you mean?"

He shrugged. "I don't know much, and what I do know I'm not supposed to tell anybody."

"Oh my God. Jesus. You're not—I mean, you're not going over *there*, are you? To Iraq?" Having a son in the army these past few years, since 9/11, has been a real test of my nerves. But somehow it never occurred to me that Horace might really have to *fight*. I tend to think that the army these days is mostly just for teaching kids discipline and preparing them for college or trade school. They don't fight *wars* anymore. Do they?

"Mom, I don't know. I can't really talk about it. But I have to leave tomorrow night."

"God, honey. You just got here."

"It's just a quick trip. To say good-bye before I have to leave."

"Sweetie, we can get you out of this," I said, not even believing myself as I was saying it. "We can find a way to make them let you stay here."

He shook his head and chuckled a little. "Don't be stupid. What do you want, for me to go AWOL? Come on. It'll be fine."

"I don't know. I have a bad feeling. . . ."

"Ma, don't take this the wrong way, but you *always* have a bad feeling."

"That's because bad things are always happening!"

"That's life, right?"

I slapped my hand down on the table as the tears started to flow. "No," I said. "It shouldn't be. Most people—*normal* people—don't have lives like this."

"Well," he said. "We've never been normal." He actually smiled as he stood up. He started to turn toward the stairs, but he stopped, leaned over, and kissed the top of my head. It was the first time in years I could remember him making physical contact with me voluntarily—and it made me want to throw my arms around him and snuggle him like a baby. But I restrained myself.

"Good night, Mom."

What I heard was "Good-bye"—although I guess I should admit that he already told me that years ago.

61

HORACE

| PRESENT DAY |

"Thanks so much for coming in, Mr. Cairo. I know you must have a busy schedule." Alan Pierson, director of marketing for Cairo Books, held out his hand for Horace to shake.

"Yeah, not working and having no hobbies really fills up my day," Horace said.

Pierson stared, his face too serious, clearly trying to figure out whether or not to laugh. Finally, he managed a stiff smile and sat down at the conference table, gesturing for Horace to do the same.

Lynn strode in carrying an unruly pile of papers and manila folders that had been labeled, crossed out, and relabeled multiple times. She beamed at Horace and shoved the door closed with her hip before shuffling to the table and dropping the pile of paperwork with a huff. She reached over to shake his hand.

"Nice to see you again," she said. "Can we get you anything? Coffee? Tea? Bottled water?"

"I'm fine, thanks. Curious to see how all this publishing stuff works," Horace said.

"I'm surprised you didn't learn all about it growing up with a mom like yours," Lynn said. Pierson cleared his throat loudly, obviously trying to get her to shut up. Horace smiled to himself, wondering what kinds of conversations went on when he wasn't here.

Lynn frowned. "I'm sorry . . ."

Horace held up a hand. "Not at all. It's fine. I'm sure my mom would have loved for me to follow in her footsteps and work here, but . . . well, I guess it's just not for me. I can't spell worth a damn anyway, so you should probably be glad I'm not around."

Lynn glanced at Pierson and they exchanged a tense, flat-lipped smile. "Should we get started?" Pierson asked.

Lynn dug through the pile of papers and passed a stapled bundle to each of them. Horace scanned the first page, which was covered with measurements and specifications and publishing terms he didn't know—trim size, binding, 4C, 2C. He shook his head lightly and looked up at Pierson with a smile.

"Most of this stuff is inside jargon—info for the production department and the printer," Pierson said. "If you turn to the third page, that's where it gets into some of our title ideas. Please, jump in anytime if you have questions or comments."

Horace nodded. Most of the titles were the things you'd expect: *Iris Cairo: The Journals*, *Iris Cairo: Her Life in Her Own Words*, that sort of thing. The one that caught his eye was the last one on the list: *Life on the Run: The Journals of Iris Cairo*.

He pointed at that last line with his finger and said, "I think that about sums it up."

Pierson shifted in his seat. This guy had to be the most socially uncomfortable man Horace had ever met. You had to wonder how he got into marketing. Suddenly, Horace had a thought that his mother might well have played some role in elevating Pierson to his current job. If so, there must be some talent buried beneath the stiff exterior.

"Yes, well," Pierson said. "We try to provide a range of choices."

"I like it. And I think Mom would have liked it."

Pierson brightened and his body visibly relaxed. He shot a smile at Lynn and pulled himself up closer to the table. "Great, great, then we've got a title," he said. "That was easy."

"Is it usually this quick?" Horace asked.

Lynn laughed. "Not a chance. We usually end up in a three-way brawl, with the editor against the marketing department against the author. This is a nice change of pace."

"Glad to be of help, then," Horace said. "So, what's next?"

Pierson's face went dark again and he looked down at the table. He coughed into his fist. "Well, there's . . . the—uh—matter of Richard Riley's book."

Horace sighed. "I almost forgot about that. So, what's the plan?"

Pierson was careful not to make eye contact as he spoke. "Well, in light of the controversy Riley's stirred up about the question of your biological father . . ."

"Wait one second," Horace interrupted. "There's no controversy. It isn't true." Horace was irritated to note that Pierson's face fell, disappointed.

"Oh," Pierson said. "Then, well . . ."

Lynn jumped in. "Then it's libel."

"It is!" Pierson was much too excited for Horace's taste. "Why don't you sue him? That would get us a lot of press. It would be like a—like a battle to the death, our book against his."

"Truth versus fiction," Horace muttered.

"Exactly!" Pierson said.

Horace shook his head. "No chance. I've already thought about a lawsuit. I'm not going to let Riley have the satisfaction."

"Mr. Cairo . . ." Lynn began.

"Horace."

She smiled in apology. "Horace," she said. "I'm sorry. It's just—well, what about your *own* success? Why spite your own book just to get back at Richard Riley?"

"I see what you're saying," Horace said. "I do. But I'm really pretty set against suing."

"Then you probably won't like our other idea," Pierson said.

"What's that?"

"To take a DNA test."

Horace sneered. "You're right. I don't like it. I thought about that, too. But it's an insult to my mother's memory to doubt her word. Oscar Cairo was my father, not Seth. I don't need to prove that to anybody."

"You don't *need* to, no," Pierson said. "But if you want to sell books, it would sure help."

Horace rubbed his thumb over the closed lid of his good eye. "I'm getting a massive headache," he said.

Pierson patted Horace's hand in that manly, superficial way. "Hey, we don't have to decide anything now. Give it a little thought, all right?"

Horace just nodded.

"Okay, then," Pierson said, popping up from his chair with enthusiasm as if none of the tension had ever existed. "Lynn will be in touch to set up another meeting in a few weeks. You take care of yourself, Mr. Cairo." He thrust his hand out.

Too exhausted to protest, Horace shook Pierson's hand. "Fine. Good."

He dragged himself up from the table as Pierson left the room so fast it looked like he was fleeing. Lynn stepped in front of Horace and said softly, "May I say something?"

"Sure," he said.

"I know how you feel about Riley, and I couldn't agree more. And I know how you feel about your mom—and again, couldn't agree more. But here's the thing." She paused and leaned over to catch his eye. "What better way to stick it to Riley than to discredit his whole book and maybe destroy his career?"

Horace felt the logic of her statement like a slap across the face. She squeezed his arm.

"Just think about it," she said. "I'll be in touch soon."

"Okay," he said. "Okay."

62

IRIS

God, help me. They're invading Iraq. It's all over the news. Please, please, please don't let Horace be there. I can't even take the thought of it. He's lived his whole life running away from danger; why is he running so hard *toward* it now? Is this all just to punish me? If it is, it's working. I didn't know I could feel this terrified. Maybe time has taken the edge off the harshness of the memory, but I don't even remember being this scared in those awful days when Oscar was first missing. How did mothers get through all those years of war—World War II, Korea, Vietnam? I've never had much of an opinion either way about politics, but picturing my baby somewhere in the desert with a machine gun or something strapped on his back has quickly turned me into an antiwar dove. Please, let this all be over soon, and let Horace be okay. I can't take any more loss. I think it was Mother Teresa who said that God only gives you as much as you can handle, but she wished he didn't trust her so much. I can relate. Why is this my life? Did I do something so horrible that I deserve to be slapped down over and over again? Is my karma all messed up? Am I going to come back as a dung beetle in my next life?

Don't get me wrong—I know I have blessings in my life. I have talent, I suppose; I've had more success than anyone could ask for; I have money and financial security (if no other kind); and I have a strong, supportive family—one that has been able to make it through some of the most difficult things people can go through. But still. It seems like all those good things are balanced, if not outweighed entirely, by negatives. I don't know. Maybe I'm just selfish and ungrateful. It's true that I never pray except when I want something. I don't think I've ever said a prayer just to say thank you to God or the universe or whatever. Maybe I'm just getting what I deserve.

Well, that's fine. Punish me, God, I don't mind. You can do whatever you want to me—make my life into something that would make Job look like he was living at Club Med. Just protect Horace. Please. That's all I ask.

AUGUST 15, 2004

I guess it's actually August 16, but this is supposed to be my birthday entry, so I'm keeping that date. It's not my fault I didn't get home until well past midnight. I'm just happy I got back at all.

Horace came home yesterday for my birthday. He's on a two-week leave or whatever they call it. I'm kind of surprised he decided to come here, to come home to me, when he could have gone somewhere with his friends.

By "home," of course, I mean my mother's house. I guess I've pretty much come to accept that I'll probably never have an actual house of my own again, at least not anytime soon. So I keep bouncing from rented place to rented place and coming back here for holidays. It's silly, really. I'm supposed to be hiding from Seth, but he has obviously figured out that I come back here for every major occasion—it's not exactly a great way to stay incognito, being this predictable. So I suppose everything that happened today is my own fault—just like everything else that's happened before now.

I got up this morning and came downstairs. Mom was sitting at the kitchen table grinning at me. At my place at the table, there was a cup of coffee and a blueberry muffin with a candle stuck in it.

"Happy birthday!" Mom said, clapping her hands like a child as I slid into my chair, pretended to make a wish, and blew out the candle. I haven't bothered making birthday wishes or wishes on stars or any of that nonsense since Oscar died. They never come true anyway, so why put any thought into them? You're just setting yourself up for disappointment. Huh. It's funny. Up until I just wrote that, I never thought of myself as a pessimist.

"Thanks, Mom," I said, pulling out the candle and laying it next to my plate. "But I think it's getting to about that time when I'm gonna want to stop counting birthdays. After forty, it's just not fun anymore."

"You don't look a day over twenty-five, sweetie!"

"Yeah, right. Then why do I *feel* like I'm about eighty?"

Mom frowned a little. "You've been through a lot, Iris. We all know that. But the best thing about you is the way you've been able to keep your chin up. Don't change now, honey. You've come too far to give up now."

There was a shuffling from the hallway and Horace stumbled in, wearing a wife-beater undershirt, boxer shorts, and dog tags. He looked like he should be starring in some kind of bad mob movie.

"Coffee?" he muttered.

"In the coffeepot," I said, struggling not to sound sarcastic. It's so very strange to see my son all grown up and realize he's nothing at all like I thought he would be.

He slopped some coffee into a mug and stirred in some sugar and cream. By the time he picked up the cup and took a sip, it looked like there was more coffee on the counter than in his cup. Part of me wanted to scold him, like he was still a little boy, but these days, I don't risk making him angry. He's angry enough all the time anyway, without any provocation from me. I wish I knew what the hell he's been doing over there in Iraq. He doesn't talk about it—not that he's ever really talked to me much.

He sat down next to me at the table and hunched over, drinking his coffee silently.

Mom cleared her throat loudly, but Horace didn't even glance up. She tried again and I flashed her a warning look. Ignoring me, she went for a less subtle approach.

"Don't you have something to say to your mother?" she asked Horace.

He glanced over at me with sleepy, half-closed eyes, then turned back to his coffee without answering. Mom leaned over, trying to get a look at his face. I rolled my eyes, but she had given up paying attention to me. All of her focus was on trying to make Horace remember to wish me a happy birthday, which, frankly, kind of defeats the whole purpose.

"Horace?" Mom said.

"What?"

"Don't you have something to tell your mother?"

He sighed and set the coffee mug down, too hard, on the table. He leaned back in his chair and took a good, long look at me. Finally, he sneered a little—with the corner of his lip raised, like that classic Elvis expression. He picked up his coffee again. Before taking a sip, he said, without looking at me, "Oh, yeah. Happy birthday."

I didn't know whether to be thrilled that he remembered or angry that he needed so much prodding to say it.

"Thanks, honey," I said.

"I got you a present, but it's up in my suitcase," he said. I don't think his voice could have held less enthusiasm, but I couldn't help smiling.

"That's so sweet, hon," I said.

"I'll go get it," he said, starting to push away from the table.

"No!" Mom shouted. "No presents yet! That's for after dinner."

Without a word or even an expression crossing his face, Horace sat back down and picked up his coffee again.

"It's dinner, then cake, *then* presents," Mom said. "That's just the way it's done."

I tried to shoot Horace a look so he'd know I thought his grandmother's formal birthday ritual was just as ridiculous as he did, but he refused to look at me.

Mom stood up, brushed nonexistent lint off the front of her pastel blue slacks and matching T-shirt with patchwork hearts on it, and put her coffee cup in the sink. "Well," she said. "I'll see you both later."

"Where are you going?" I asked. "I thought the whole family had to be together on a birthday." I winked at Horace, but again, he ignored me.

"Don't be smart, miss," Mom said. "I have a few errands to run *for* your birthday. But if you keep making fun of me, you won't be getting a cake."

"Okay, okay, I'm sorry. Please make me a cake."

She narrowed her eyes at me, but like always, it was easy to see she wasn't really mad. "I'll be back later."

"Bye, Mom." I waited for the door to click shut behind her before I turned to Horace. "So, what do you want to do today?"

He slurped up the last of his coffee and got up. "I'm supposed to meet up with Andrew," he said.

"Oh," I said. "Okay."

He stopped at the door. "What? Did you want me to stay here?"

Yes! I was thinking. Of course I do! You should *want* to be with me on my birthday. But what I said was, "Of course not. Go see Andrew. Have fun. Just be back for dinner or Grandma'll have a coronary." I smiled, but he didn't smile back before he turned and shuffled upstairs, leaving me alone with my coffee and my sudden knowledge that I was now too old for my son to ever think I was cool.

At least, I *thought* I was alone.

But then I heard it—*his* voice—from behind me, at the back door to the house.

"Happy birthday, Iris."

I stiffened. I don't know why I didn't expect this, that he'd show up in person again someday, but I didn't. All these years running and hiding, you'd think I'd be in constant fear. But it hasn't been like that. I suppose you get used to it and you start to think that's just the way life is. But everything can change in an instant.

I heard myself whisper, "Seth," and I felt a tear slide down my cheek, but none of it seemed real. It was like watching myself in a movie.

He came up behind me and wrapped his arms around my shoulders, leaning down to kiss my neck. If I hadn't spent all these years trying to be honest and record everything that happens, I'd never admit this, but hell—you already know about that other time, so why not? I felt a pulse of—I don't know—sexual energy, I guess—shoot through me when his lips touched my skin. He smelled the same way he did twenty years ago—warm, kind of musky, with an oddly pleasant hint of orange or some other kind of citrus. He smelled just like Oscar—whose scent is still part of me, even after all this time. I almost swung around in my chair and grabbed him. I probably would have thrown him down on the floor and torn his clothes off right there, but I remembered three things all at once: I'm twenty years older now, and my body shows it in every wrinkle, every flap of loose skin, every paunchy roll of fat; Horace was right upstairs; and—most important—this was *Seth.*

I wiggled my shoulders out from under his grasp and stood up, spinning around so I could face him. For a moment, I half expected him to have that knife in his hand—the one he had used to hold us captive that day at Shondra's—but his hands were empty. I almost relaxed, thinking the fact that he wasn't armed meant he wasn't dangerous.

I squeezed the back of the chair between my fingers to keep my hands from shaking. "What are you doing here?" I asked.

"It's been too long," he said. "Too many years. I never thought things would end up like this."

"Me neither," I whispered.

"The first time I saw you, when I got to ride the bus to school with you guys for the first time, you were wearing a gray skirt—the nubby kind—tweed, is it? And a fuzzy pink sweater. And you had your hair down, but there was a pink plaid headband in it. You looked so pure and sweet—not at all like someone who'd end up sleeping with my brother a few years later."

"Seth . . ."

He held up his hand to stop me. "I'm not finished," he said. "There are things you don't know—about Oscar, I mean. He wasn't such a nice guy like everybody thought."

"Seth, please. Can't this all be over?"

He ignored me and kept talking. "The first time you slept with him, Oscar came home and told me everything. He told me what you looked like, the kind of noises you made, all the details. And then he picked up the phone and called all his friends and told them, too."

I didn't know whether to slap him in outrage for lying about his dead brother or to cry because I knew it could very well be true. I mean, Oscar was perfect for *me*, but he wasn't perfect. Nobody is.

"Seth, come on."

"You don't believe me?"

I hesitated because I didn't know whether I believed him or not. "It doesn't matter," I said. "It's all done. It's in the past."

"Not for me," he said. "It was then—the night that Oscar decided to spit on you, on your reputation and all your love for him, that I realized what a fraud he was. And I realized that *I* was in love with you and that you and I belonged together." He moved toward me and touched my hand. "He didn't deserve you. He didn't deserve to live."

I tore my hand away and backed up until I was pressed against the counter. "Seth, I'm begging you. Just leave me alone."

There were actually tears in his eyes, and I almost felt sorry for him. "It doesn't have to be this way," he whispered. "There's still time for us, if you'll just give me a chance to make it all up to you. You can't even imagine how much I love you. Everything I've ever done has been for you."

I shook my head slowly. "That's the problem. Everything you've ever done has caused me pain. That's not love, Seth."

"It *is* love," he said. "It's the only love I've ever known."

"Sometimes my heart breaks for you," I said. "And then I remember that it's already broken—and that it's your fault."

"Iris . . ."

I closed my eyes and pressed my fingers over my eyelids, trying to hold back the tears.

"What the fuck are *you* doing here?"

My eyes flew open at the sound of the voice, and I turned, in horror, to stare at Horace, who was standing in the doorway, still dressed only in his underwear and holding a small wrapped box in his hand.

Seth smiled. "We finally get to meet," he said. "I'm so happy." The sarcasm was like syrup dripping out the side of his mouth.

"You won't be happy when I tear your fucking throat out," Horace said. He slammed the present down on the table, straightened his boxer shorts, and lunged at Seth.

All I heard was a long, witch-like cackle come out of Seth before the two of them became a blur of fists and rage. I stood there, paralyzed, pressed up against the counter, not knowing what to do. I'd never really witnessed a fight before—not a real one, a fight that wasn't just for show, a fight that could easily end up being to the death. What are you supposed to do? Do you scream? Step in and try to stop it? Call the police? Shoot somebody—if you have a gun, that is? I still have no idea. So I did nothing. I just stared in stupefied terror as blood splattered on the walls and the floor. I heard something plink against the floor and saw that it was a tooth. I thought that was the worst of it, until that . . . that *sound* roared out of Horace. It was partly a scream and partly a growl, and it was the most terrifying thing I've ever heard because I knew it meant my son was in some kind of unbearable agony. And that's when I saw it—a strange, bloody gob on the floor, something I couldn't identify, until I saw Horace pressing his hands over his left eye and blood gushing down his face.

Seth was laughing again, his mouth open and bloody, with a gap in front where he had lost his tooth. As Horace writhed in pain, bringing the fight to a stop—at least for a few seconds—Seth crawled over to the gob—I mean, the eyeball—and smashed it into a pulp with his fists.

That's when I started to scream, but only for a moment before Seth leaped to his feet and slapped his hand—all covered in blood and vitreous fluid—over my mouth to shut me up. I thought about trying to bite him, but I didn't get a chance because suddenly Horace's arms were wound around Seth's neck and I was alone again. I think I blanked out there, for a few seconds, maybe even a few minutes—I have no idea. The next thing I remember, Horace had Seth pinned down on the floor and his fingers were pressed against Seth's throat.

"Mom," Horace said.

I didn't hear him at first.

"Mom!" His shout pulled me out of my trance and I blinked hard as I looked over at him.

"Horace?" I whispered.

"Mom, get me a knife," he said.

"What?"

"Get me a knife off the counter so I can finish this right now."

In a daze, I started to move toward the butcher's block that held all of my mother's cooking knives. I had my fingers on the handle of a huge cleaver before I realized what I was doing. I shoved the knife back into the block and ran to the phone.

"Mom!" Horace yelled. "What the fuck are you doing? Give me a fucking knife!"

Seth was laughing, as much as he could beneath the pressure of Horace's military-trained hands on his windpipe.

I dialed 911 and, through tears, begged the dispatcher to send a policeman over to the house.

"Mom! Goddamn it! Don't do this!" Horace sounded hysterical and I saw his fingers tighten around Seth's throat.

The dispatcher told me to stay on the line, but I dropped the phone on the floor and fell to my knees beside Horace.

"Don't," I said. "Don't kill him. Don't let things end like this."

"This is the only way we *can* end it," Horace said.

"No, it's not. The police are on the way. It's over now. We're finally going to get justice."

Horace shook his head. "Death is the only justice for this son of a bitch."

"No," I said. "Death is too easy. He deserves to suffer. And he'll suffer more locked up in prison than he will if you kill him right now. He *wants* you to kill him. Don't give him the satisfaction."

Seth made a gurgling sound.

"Shut up," I said. "Just shut up."

There was a pounding at the front door and the police burst in.

"In the kitchen!" I yelled.

Two bulky cops appeared, wrestled Horace off of Seth, and handcuffed both of them.

"Jesus," one of the cops said. "Where's your fucking *eye?*"

The other cop used his radio to call for an ambulance, while his partner gently pushed Horace into a chair before dragging Seth out to the police car.

It took hours—hours upon hours of interviews at the police station and the hospital—before everything was straightened out. The doctors kept Horace in the hospital, but I went home with Mom, not saying a word.

Now Horace won't talk to me. All these years, I've protected him, and today he protected me. You'd think going through all this would have bonded us together, but instead, he's so angry—angry that I stopped him from getting the vengeance he wanted—that I don't even know if he'll ever talk to me again. I thought this was all going to be over, but it seems like nothing ever ends around here.

I just went downstairs to the kitchen to try to find something to drink—scotch or tequila would have been nice, but all Mom had in her liquor cabinet was a dusty old bottle of port, so I poured myself a juice glass full of it and stood there, sucking it down and looking around at the kitchen, thinking it looked odd *not* covered in blood and bodily fluids. I guess Mom must have cleaned up while I was hosing off in the shower after we got home from the hospital. Then I noticed it—the present Horace had brought me—sitting all lonely on the kitchen table, looking bizarre—so out of place and festive—after the events of this morning.

I went over and picked it up, turning it over in my hands. Should I open it? I couldn't decide which was more inappropriate—to leave the gift sitting there as a terrible reminder of the fight or to open it, even though Horace was lying in a hospital bed with one eye missing at this very moment. Curiosity got the better of me and I slid my fingers under the wrapping paper, pulling out a small black lacquer box. I let the wrapping fall to the floor and pried open the box. Lying on a bed of black velvet was a sparkling silver pendant. It took me a second to figure out what the symbol was—I knew it was familiar, but I hadn't seen one in years, not since I had studied ancient Egypt in school. It was an ankh—the ancient Egyptian symbol for eternal life.

I tugged gently on the silver chain and held the necklace up to the light. Through the years, Horace had given me birthday gifts, but they had always seemed obligatory—handmade ashtrays he made in school (despite the fact that I've never smoked), boxes of chocolate, flowers—pretty much the kind of things men come up with to give to women when they have no idea what women really want. This was the first gift Horace had ever given me that looked like it had taken some thought.

I turned over the pendant and saw "Made in Egypt" inscribed on the base of the weighty ankh. That explained it—at least in part. He must have found it somewhere in the Middle East while he was serving in Iraq. I caught myself thinking that it was just another of his typical thought-less gifts, a trinket he picked up in transit, but something deeper made me think I was wrong—that there was more meaning to this gift than I would probably ever be able to comprehend. And for the first time since everything that happened today, I smiled. I clasped the necklace around my neck and went back up to my bedroom. It's possible—just a little tiny bit possible—that my son really does love me.

63

HORACE

"I think Riley knows something's up with the publishing company," Horace said as he sat down across the restaurant table from his aunt Nora. "He's been driving by the house, just staring at the front window. And when he sees that I see him, he guns it and zips away, like I won't realize he was there. I almost feel bad for the poor schmuck."

Nora smiled. "So what *is* going on with the publishing company?"

"I don't know," he said. "I'm trying to decide. That's why I wanted to have lunch with you. I could use your advice."

"Ask away."

He blew out his breath through pursed lips. "Well, they want me to take a DNA test. You know, to publicly disprove Riley's claims in his book."

Nora frowned and started picking at the piece of sticky paper holding her napkin and silverware together in a roll.

"What's the matter?" Horace asked. "Do you think I shouldn't do it?"

"I don't want to tell you what to do," she said. "But . . ."

"But what?"

"But I don't think it's a good idea."

"Why not?"

She shrugged. "I don't know exactly. I just worry that something could go wrong."

"Like what?"

"A mistake at the lab? A crooked lab technician who alters the results for money? What if the results don't come back the way you want them to?"

"Aunt Nora, I know we've all led some pretty screwed-up lives, but I think you've got an overactive imagination. How likely is any of that? I think it'll be fine."

She pursed her lips. "It's your decision. I'm just giving you my opinion."

"I know," he said. "I appreciate it. You're one of the only people I can trust to be honest with me."

A strange airy laugh came out of her nose.

"What?" Horace asked.

She shook her head. "Nothing. I—I just feel bad for you. The way you've had to live your life. It's not fair."

He smiled. "Nobody ever said life was fair, right?"

"I don't think anybody has had to put up with the kinds of unfairness you have."

"It doesn't matter now," he said. "That's all in the past. Things are good now. Great."

She touched his hand. "I'm glad, sweetie. You deserve to be happy."

"So do you, Aunt Nora."

"Well."

He handed her a menu and picked up his own. "So what are we going to eat?"

"Horace? What about the DNA test?"

He lowered his menu. "I don't know," he said. "I've got to think about it some more."

"Think about it a lot, honey, okay? I don't want you to get hurt. Got it?"

"Got it. Thanks, Nora."

He went home and found Andrea out in the front yard, digging a line of dirt along the edges of the sidewalk that wound from the street to the front porch.

He got out of the car and called over to her. "What are you doing? Don't you know it's November? Isn't it a little cold for gardening?"

She looked up, her face streaked with dirt. "Don't you know anything? I'm planting bulbs. You do it in the fall so the flowers come up in the spring."

He stepped over the exposed earth where she was digging and stood behind her on the sidewalk. "You're always teaching me something new," he said. "Jesus, that's a lot of digging. How long have you been out here?"

She squinted up at the pale sun, which was already low in the gray sky. "A while, I guess. I don't know."

He leaned down and kissed her, then brushed a trace of dirt off her cheek. "Well, come in soon, okay? It's gonna be dark soon, and I'll want my dinner, woman."

She smiled. "Didn't you *just* get back from lunch?"

"What can I say? I have a big appetite." He kissed her again, lingering longer and letting his tongue trill over her lips.

She wrinkled her nose. "You sure do," she said. "Go on. I'll be in soon."

He stood up and wiped his fingers on his pants, feeling like they were dirty merely because he was around so much dirt. "Okay. Want some coffee or anything?"

"Sure, that sounds good. And you can turn the oven on—350—and when it's warm, pop the baked ziti in. I put it all together it this morning, so all you have to do is take it out of the fridge. By the time I finish up here and take a shower, it should be ready to eat."

"Got it. And let me know when you're going to take that shower—you might need some company."

"Yeah, yeah," she said. "We'll see. Now get out of here and let me finish or I'll be doing this with a flashlight later on tonight."

He ran his palm over the top of her head and went inside. He dropped his keys on the kitchen counter and stood there, trying to remember what he was supposed to be doing. Ziti, ziti. It finally came to him, and he trotted over to the oven, turned it on, then went to the refrigerator to get the tray of noodles and cheese. He was about to put the pan into the oven when the phone rang, so he set the ziti on the counter and answered.

"Yeah?"

"Mr. Cairo? I mean, Horace?"

"Hi, Lynn," he said. "What's up?"

"You recognized my voice?"

"I recognized your reluctance to call me by my first name."

"Well, I guess that's still something. So how are you?"

"You tell me," he said. "What's going on?"

"I just wanted to call and see if you've had a chance to think about what we talked about."

He sighed. "The DNA test."

"Yeah, well. Have you decided what you want to do?"

"Not really," he said. He turned around and looked out the window above the sink. It was getting dark fast now. He stood on his toes, but he couldn't see Andrea on the sidewalk anymore. She must have gone around to the backyard. But the view wasn't empty—Horace had glanced out just in time to see Richard Riley pull up in front of the house in a black SUV. Horace noticed that he'd stopped driving his usual BMW lately—maybe he was trying to make it look like he *wasn't* staking out Horace's house. Idiot.

"Mr. Cairo? I mean, Horace? You still there?"

He turned back around, away from the window. "Yeah," he said. "Sorry, Lynn. I just a got a little distracted."

"So . . . what are you thinking about doing?"

He turned once more to look out the window, and Riley must have seen him because there was a sudden squeal of tires as the SUV tore away. Instead of the rumble of the engine he was used to hearing as Riley took off, though, there was a sickening crunch. Horace thrust his head forward, squinting to see in the blue-gray dimness of the dusk. All he could see was the SUV, stopped, and then a blur of light-colored clothing—Riley— leaping out and dashing around to the front of the car. A scream came out of Riley's chest and suddenly the whole world was moving in slow motion. Even through the windowpane, Horace could hear Riley shouting: "Cairo! Call 911! Cairo! Jesus Christ! Cairo, I'm so sorry!"

Lynn's voice was small on the other end of the phone. "Mr. Cairo? Horace? Is everything okay?"

"I'll call you back," he said. He pressed the off button on the phone, then hit the talk button and dialed 911.

"911. What is your emergency?"

Horace heard his own voice, calm and automatic. "My wife's been hit by a car. Please hurry."

64

IRIS

| JUNE 23, 2004 |

The jury came back today. They convicted Seth of first-degree murder, not to mention assault charges against Horace. The sentencing isn't until next week, but he'll get life, at least. I really doubt it'll be the death penalty—New Jersey never fries anybody anymore. I don't even know if we have the death penalty here. There's a part of me that wishes we had been living in Texas when Seth killed Oscar—but then I remember that if I really wanted Seth dead, I would have let Horace do it last summer. I'm still (mostly) convinced that I was right. Seth will suffer more in prison than he would dead.

The thing is, I've waited over twenty years for this day—for justice to finally be done—and I feel strangely hollow, empty. It's almost like I'm not going to have anything left to live for now that I don't have to spend all my time and energy hiding from Seth. Maybe I'd actually be happy, ready to celebrate the freedom that I've waited decades to enjoy, but it's hard to be happy when Horace won't talk to me. It was bad enough all these months while we waited for Seth's trial to start; I knew Horace was angry at me then, but I figured we'd come together again at the trial, when we were thrown together as Seth's witnesses and victims. For three months we sat next to each other on a rock-hard wooden bench outside the courtroom, waiting for our turns on the stand, but he hardly spoke a word to me. And then today, when the jury foreman said "Guilty," Horace looked at me from the back of the room with his good eye—he wears a patch over the other one now—and then he pursed his lips and gave me a tight little nod. He turned around and slipped out of the courtroom as everyone else erupted in the chaos of approval and—for a select few of those creepy women who fall in love with killers like Seth—indignation at the verdict. Something about the way Horace walked out, the look in his eyes—I mean, eye—when he nodded at me, told me that he may never speak to me again. At least, he'll never speak to me of his own choice. Maybe he'll be civil if I grovel and approach him. But I've lost him. After all these years trying to save what little was left of my life, I've lost it all.

DECEMBER 6, 2005

Horace turns twenty-four today. Not that I've seen him—or even heard from him. No, I've only heard from his lawyer. Some shyster called me up yesterday to remind me that as of nine this morning, Horace's trust fund opens up and he has access to all that money. I don't even know how much is in there these days, but I know it's a lot. So much that he'll never have to work a day in his life. He would have gotten the money in another year, at twenty-five, but I stupidly changed the date after the— um—accident. I thought he could use the money sooner, especially since his injury made him leave the army. So now he doesn't have to work. Of course, other than his time in the army, which isn't exactly a regular job, he *hasn't* worked a day in his life. That's my fault, I know. It's not like I let him have a normal life, working the drive-through at McDonald's or something. But I had no idea that things would turn out like this. I guess I figured he'd grow up watching me write and run the publishing company, even from the road, and want to be just like me. I thought we'd come back here someday, after the cops finally caught Seth, and we'd run the publishing house together. I guess it's silly to have dreams like that. Those kinds of fantasies never come true—especially not in my life.

DECEMBER 6, 2006

I just got off the phone with Horace's . . . I don't know *what* the guy is—a butler, maybe? Assistant? I don't know what they call him. All I know is that his name is Pete and he's a human barrier, preventing me from getting to my son. Of course, I'm not so naïve as to think Horace isn't behind it, but I still have to believe that if I could just talk to him directly, I'd be able to get through to him.

I called to say happy birthday. Horace is twenty-five today. I didn't even bother trying the phone at Horace's big new house—he's always got someone, whether it's Pete or somebody else—answering that one. I went right for his cell phone, figuring there's a better chance that he'd answer that. Instead, I got Pete.

"Horace Cairo's line. Pete speaking. How may I help you?"

"Uh—hi, may I speak to Horace, please?"

"May I ask who's calling?"

I love the politeness of these exchanges, especially considering we both knew very well who was whom and what was really going on.

"This is his mother," I said, trying not to sound irritated.

Pete cleared his throat. "Well, Horace is tied up at the moment . . ."

I could swear I heard people laughing in the background, and I wondered if Horace was standing there, making fun of his poor pathetic mother while carousing with one of those cheap women he's been hanging around with (according to the magazines, anyway—I haven't actually seen him, but I do notice the tabloid headlines when I stand in line at the grocery store).

"Oh," I said. "When would be a better time for me to call?"

There was a long pause. "Ma'am, what's this in reference to?"

That did it. I began to seethe with fury. "In *reference* to? I'm his *mother*, you little weasel. Now why don't you put Horace on the goddamn phone?"

"Ma'am, I apologize. I can't do that."

"Fine," I said. "Just tell him I called to wish him a happy birthday, okay? Did you get that reference?"

"Ma'am . . ."

"Another thing," I said. "Ask your 'boss' why he even bothered to send me his phone numbers and address if he didn't want me to contact him. Okay? Nice talking to you."

I slammed the phone down. Then I sat there and waited, thinking (stupidly, I know) that Horace might call me right back to say he was sorry, that there had been a misunderstanding and that Pete was supposed to have put me through to him. I don't know how long I sat there and waited, but it was long enough to make me start crying. I know it's silly of me to keep reaching out to him when all he does is slap me back down, but he's my son—I have no other choice but to love him whether he loves me back or not.

65

HORACE

| PRESENT DAY |

"Cairo, Jesus, I'm so sorry," Riley kept saying as Horace paced in front of him in the waiting room of the emergency room.

"Riley, just shut up, man. I can't deal with you right now, okay?"

Riley held up his hands and slumped back into his seat, watching with a timid, guilty look on his face as Horace moved back and forth, pausing at each end of the path to glare in Riley's general direction.

Horace had no idea how much time had passed since the EMTs had wheeled Andrea on a gurney out of the ambulance and into the emergency room, breezing through swinging doors and shouting orders as nurses and doctors buzzed around and Horace jogged to try to keep up with them. When the doctors pushed the gurney through the final set of doors and the EMTs stopped and turned to leave, their part of the work done, a broad-shouldered nurse in pastel scrubs with teddy bears printed on them stepped in front of Horace.

"You'll need to wait out here, sir. They're taking her into surgery now."

The nurses tried to keep his mind off his terror by occupying him with paperwork and insurance cards, but he followed all their instructions in a daze. Most of him—his heart and soul—was somewhere back beyond those swinging doors, lying on a surgery table with Andrea.

He glanced down at the tiled floor, suddenly realizing that he had been pacing for a long time and surprised that there was no visible wear pattern to show for it. He sighed and sank down onto the orange-padded sofa beside Riley.

"Cairo?" Riley said.

Horace held up one hand and covered his face with the other.

"Cairo, it's the doctor," Riley said.

Horace dropped his hands into his lap and looked up, exhausted, at the white-coated figure standing there with a stethoscope around his neck, all clean and normal, like this was any other day and nothing at all out of the ordinary was happening.

"Mr. Cairo, I'm Dr. Greenwald."

Horace nodded. Why wouldn't this guy just spit it out?

"Your wife," the doctor said. He stopped and cleared his throat. "Your wife sustained massive internal injuries in the—um—accident."

Riley shifted in his seat, pressing his body as far away from Horace as possible.

"Mr. Cairo, I'm very sorry," the doctor said.

Horace frowned and shook his head. "Sorry about what?"

"Jesus," Riley muttered.

The doctor knitted his brow. "Mr. Cairo, I'm—well, I'm afraid your wife didn't survive the surgery."

Horace sat there, staring at a balled-up piece of cellophane—a candy bar wrapper, maybe—under a chair across the room. Even as the doctor stood there waiting for some response, Horace couldn't stop looking at that piece of trash.

"Mr. Cairo?"

Horace felt a little smile tug at his lips as he continued to stare at the candy bar wrapper.

"Cairo, Christ," Riley said, his voice high and whiny, desperate. "Say something."

Horace squeezed his eyes shut and shook his head before forcing himself to glance up at the doctor.

"She's dead?" Horace said.

"I'm sorry," the doctor said. He stood there for a long, awkward moment, obviously trying to decide whether his task was done and he could safely escape back to his office or the OR or wherever he came from and get away from the irrational, numb husband of the dead patient.

"Okay," Horace said. "Okay."

The doctor shrugged at Riley, then backed away and disappeared through the double doors.

"Cairo?" Riley said. "You okay?"

Horace was looking at the candy bar wrapper again. Something about that piece of trash felt symbolic to him. He wanted to go over and pick it up, put it in his jacket pocket, bring it home. If he had a scrapbook or a journal like his mother, he would have pasted it in.

"Cairo?" Riley said. "I don't know what to say."

"Just go," Horace said, burying his face in his hands, just to make himself stop looking at that candy bar wrapper. "I'm okay. Just go."

Riley leaped up from his chair, but hedged, doing an uneasy dance in front of Horace.

"Riley, for Christ's sake, go."

"Cairo, I'm so sorry."

"Please. Just go."

Riley sighed hard and started to walk away, but stopped and turned back. "But, Cairo—I need to know—are you going to have me arrested?"

Horace looked over at him. "I don't give a shit whether the cops arrest you or give you the fucking chair. Don't you get it? Nothing matters now."

"But, Cairo . . ."

"Get . . . the . . . fuck . . . out . . . of . . . here."

Riley clenched his teeth and his fists, then turned and fled, leaving Horace alone in the waiting room with only his grief and the candy bar wrapper.

66

IRIS

If I had any sense, I'd stop recognizing this date as special, as my only child's birthday. Every year, I mark it on my calendar, watch anxiously as the weeks go by, and then make that humiliating phone call, where Horace either refuses to talk to me at all or takes the phone for maybe fifteen seconds, long enough to grunt his "thanks" for my birthday wishes. And he never acknowledges the gifts I send him. I know the things I pick out are probably silly to someone like him—a young man living the fast life, out at the clubs and surrounded by all those models and actresses who show up with him in pictures on the cover of tabloids. I mean, I imagine a man like my son doesn't really want a hand-knitted argyle sweater or a leather-bound journal for recording his thoughts. But it's been so long since Horace and I had a real relationship—if we ever did—that it's impossible for me to know what kind of gifts he'd appreciate. Part of me thinks he wouldn't appreciate *anything* I got him, even if it were something he had dreamed of having his whole life. I should just stop trying, and sometimes I think I will, but then I reach up and touch the silver ankh that I still wear around my neck at all times—the one he gave me on the last birthday of mine that I recognized—and I just can't let him go.

December 4, 2008

Something strange is going on. I just set aside all my pride and made my annual birthday call to Horace. He picked up the phone, which surprised me, since he usually does his best to dodge me.

"Horace! It's so good to hear your voice!" I said.

"Mom?" He sounded a little confused. "What's going on?"

"I'm just making my regular birthday call. Happy birthday, sweetie."

"But my birthday isn't for two days," he said.

"Don't be silly," I said. "Your birthday is December 6, and today is December 6. So, by the transitive property, today is your birthday."

"Except that today is December 4."

"Honey, I know you've been partying a lot, but you might want to take it down a notch—and also buy yourself a calendar."

"I'm looking at the calendar on my computer right now, and all I can tell you is that it's December 4," he said. "Maybe you're the one who should lay off the booze."

I frowned and pulled out my datebook. I flipped through the pages. He was right. I had mixed up my dates.

"Huh," I said. "You're right. I got the date wrong." I paused, feeling my head swim a little, trying to figure out what could have made me so confused. It was unusual for me. I've always been great with dates, and my memory is one of those metaphorical cage traps. Wait—that's not right, is it? Wow, I'm losing it.

"Well, okay," Horace said.

"I guess I'll talk to you in a couple of days then," I said.

"Can we just skip it? Let this be the birthday call? I'm really busy these days, Ma."

It felt like a kick in the chest. "Um—yeah, I guess so," I finally said. "Happy birthday, Horace."

"Thanks." And he hung up without so much as a good-bye.

FEBRUARY 12, 2009

What a horrible day! I went in to work in the office, planning to stay there for a few hours and then come home around lunchtime to pick up my mom and take her shopping and out for an early dinner to celebrate her birthday. I was packing up my briefcase around 11:30, but I couldn't find my keys anywhere. No exaggeration, I spent over half an hour tearing apart my office, my purse, my coat pockets, and my desk trying to find the damn keys before I finally called in Lynn, one of the senior editors, to help me look. She stood in the threshold of the door for all of two seconds before she said, "Wait—didn't you park in the garage downstairs?"

"Yeah . . ." I said slowly, trying to figure out why that would matter.

"Well, then, doesn't Pat the parking attendant have your keys? I always leave mine with him."

I rolled my eyes. "Oh my God, I can't believe I forgot that. I must be an idiot."

Lynn smiled. "Nah," she said. "It happens to all of us sometimes. Have a great afternoon!"

I drove home, thinking the whole way about whether what she had said was true. *Does* it happen to everybody, or am I just unusually forgetful lately? I feel like I'm a little young to be having "senior moments," but maybe I'm just kidding myself. I'm not exactly the twenty-one-year-old girl I picture myself to be in my mind. Maybe time is finally catching up with me.

MAY 14, 2009

I just got off the phone with my doctor. I had to make an appointment for a checkup. There is something seriously wrong with me. My memory is shot. I completely forgot that I was supposed to pick up my mom and take her to her podiatrist and then out to lunch. It's really kind of pathetic when your seventy-eight-year-old mother has a better memory than you do, right? So I made an appointment for next week, but now I'm starting to get a little worried. I've been a real mess the past few months—losing things, forgetting where I'm supposed to be going. All I can think is— what if it's a brain tumor? I mean, that would explain everything—but it would also mean I'm going to die. Okay, I have to calm down. It won't be anything that bad. It never is. I've always been a little bit of a hypochondriac, I think. I'm sure everything will be fine.

MAY 19, 2009

I think I'm still in shock. I got home from the doctor hours ago, but I've been sitting here on the couch, staring at the TV even though it's not on, and trying to figure out if all this is really happening or if maybe tomorrow morning I'll wake up and this will all have been a terrible dream. Who ever would have thought I should have been rooting for a brain tumor? At least that would have a tiny chance of being fixed with surgery or chemo or something. But no. The doctor is pretty sure I have Alzheimer's—early-onset Alzheimer's, and very aggressive. He's going to do some more tests and he says there are drugs we can try, but he had that look—that grim, hopeless look—on his face when he was telling me everything, and I knew what he was really saying. I should accept the fact that my life is pretty much over and take care of arranging things so my family won't have to do it after I turn into a drooling vegetable. I'm almost laughing when I picture myself propped up in a wheelchair in some nursing home, completely unaware of what's going on around me. But deep down, it's not funny at all. It's gut-wrenchingly, world-shatteringly terrifying. And there's no way I can stop it.

67

HORACE

| PRESENT DAY |

He sat on a metal folding chair at the front of the room, staring at the open coffin but not seeing the still, waxy form of his wife lying there.

"Sweetie, you okay?" Nora asked, sitting down beside him and rubbing her palm on his back.

"Yeah."

Nora frowned and waved Andrew over. He sat down on Horace's other side. "Hey, bro," he said. "How you holding up?"

"Fine."

"Hey, I guess one-word answers beat no answers at all, right, dude?"

Horace said nothing. He was hardly hearing the voices around him. His mind was trapped in a spinning wheel of confusion and compassion for his mother—something he'd never felt during her life, but that he understood only too well now that he knew firsthand the kind of pain she had suffered when she lost her husband. He wanted to go back in time and beg her forgiveness, then embrace her so the two of them could sob together, commiserate, figure out a way to face the world as a team of widowed warriors.

"Cuz?" Andrew said. "You're freaking me out here. You gotta snap out of this."

Horace smiled a little. "Did my mom snap out of it after my dad died?"

Nora leaned her head on his shoulder. "No, sweetie," she said. "She didn't. But you know better than anybody that it wasn't a good thing, the way she lived. If Iris could have moved on with her life . . ."

"Then what? We wouldn't have had to run from your crazy husband? She wouldn't have missed my dad? Come on, Nora, don't be stupid. You have no idea what this is like. There *is* no way to move on."

"Cuz, I promise you," Andrew said. "I can help you move on. We can go out tonight, pick up some chicks."

"Andrew!" Nora said. "What is wrong with you? Just get out of here. Go out front and greet people when they start showing up."

"Just trying to help," Andrew said as he slinked away.

"Horace," Nora said.

"Don't bother," Horace said. "It's not worth it. I know you love me and you want to help me, but I'm not ready to be helped, okay? I need some time to deal with this." He pointed at the coffin and felt himself choke as he saw Andrea lying there, as if it were the first time he'd actually admitted that she was dead. He crumpled against Nora and let himself cry.

He didn't know how he got through those hours of the viewing, as friends and family members, people who had known him and Andrea, all the little kids from Andrea's class, sobbing and snuffling, came up and hugged him and murmured awkward words of condolence in his ear. He saw them all and accepted their embraces and kept saying "Thank you" over and over, but he felt like he was watching it all on some old newsreel, the kind where the film speed is all erratic—too fast, too slow, stuttering and stalling, with Babe Ruth running haltingly around the bases. None of it was real at all.

"Just another half hour, honey, and then we're all done," Nora whispered at some point.

"Until tomorrow," he said. "There's still the funeral."

Nora sighed. "Yes, well. We'll get through it together, okay?"

He nodded, though he didn't agree. Sure, she was there and she was working hard to make him feel better, but he was in this alone. Nobody could help him deal with this—except maybe his mother, and it was too late for that now.

"Cairo?"

Horace flinched but didn't look up. Nora stood and smiled. "Hi," she said. "I'm Horace's aunt Nora. Thanks for coming."

Horace felt himself smile. Without looking up, he said, "Aunt Nora, you're thanking the guy who killed my wife for showing up to admire his handiwork."

"Cairo," Riley said. "I came to say I'm sorry. Again. I felt like I *had* to come. I—I don't even know what to say."

Horace looked up at him. "That's never stopped you before, Riley. Just make something up."

"Cairo, can't you give me a break? I'm trying to do the right thing here."

"Ah, yes. New territory for you."

"Mr. Riley, maybe you should go . . ." Nora said.

"No, no, it's fine. I don't mind having him here." Horace stood up and moved over to the coffin. The two old women who had been standing there, paying their respects, saw the wild look on his face and scattered.

"Come here, Riley," Horace said. "Check it out. You did a hell of a job. Killed her but left her looking perfect. What, did you practice on squirrels, cats? Work on hitting somebody at just the right angle . . ." He ran his palm down the length of Andrea's motionless torso.

Nora leapt up and grabbed him by the shoulders. "That's enough," she said. "I think it's time to go home now."

"I'm so sorry," Riley whispered. He started to back up toward the exit, staring at Horace, who was still gaping down at his dead wife.

"I can't believe you still get to walk the streets and spread your bullshit misery," Horace said without turning around. "It's not right. *You* should be the one lying in this fucking coffin, Riley."

"You're right," Riley said. "I kinda wish I were, to tell you the truth."

"Sure. Sure you do, asshole. Just get the fuck out."

Riley sighed. "They're going to try me for murder. Second degree, they're saying. My lawyer wants me to take a plea down to manslaughter."

Horace smiled and turned to look at Riley. "That's the best news I've heard in days. Too bad you won't get the chair."

Riley nodded. "You think I'm bullshitting and I don't blame you. I've bullshitted plenty in my time. But you should know this is the truth. I agree with you. That's why I'm not taking the plea. I'm turning myself in this afternoon and I'm going to plead guilty to the second-degree charge."

"So now you're a martyr, right?" Horace said. "What? Are you gonna go to prison and use the experience as material? That's pretty pathetic, Riley, even for you."

"I'm done," Riley said. "I'm done writing. I'm—well, I guess I'm done with everything. I just wanted to come here and tell you that."

He bowed his head in the direction of the coffin and a tear gleamed in the corner of his eye. He smiled sadly at Nora. "Nice to meet you, ma'am," Riley said. "And, Cairo—I'm sorry. I don't know what else to say."

He ducked his head down and scurried out of the funeral home.

68

IRIS
| MAY 31, 2009 |

Well, there's good news and bad news today. The bad news is that my mom died this morning. I got a call from Nora around eight A.M. that Mom had a heart attack and was in the hospital. By the time I got there, she was gone—but, of course, the doctors didn't actually come out and *tell* us she was dead until like one in the afternoon. I know I should be more upset about Mom dying, but the good news kind of outweighs my grief: The good news is that now I don't have to tell her about the Alzheimer's. She doesn't have to watch me suffer—again—like she's had to watch me suffer so many times over the years. It's kind of a blessing. She went the way she wanted to go—fast, relatively painless, and believing that things were finally all right with her loved ones. It's true that ignorance is bliss, so I'm glad I never got up the nerve to break the news to her about what's happening with me. Maybe I had help in this one from God—I'm thinking God took Mom now to spare her what's coming. And if I'm right, then what's coming is bad—really, really bad.

JUNE 2, 2009
We buried Mom today. That really should have been the low point of my day, but in typical Iris Cairo fashion, it all got worse after the funeral, just when things were supposed to be looking up.

Horace actually showed up at the funeral. I had left him three messages, but I didn't hear back from him, so I had no idea whether to expect him or not. Nora kept telling me he'd be there, not to worry, but she always sees the best in people, so I figured she was just being naïve. But she was right. He wandered into the church just as the last notes of "Amazing Grace" were fading away from the pipes of the organ. He sat in the back, not up with me and Nora, but just knowing that he was there made me feel better—until I remembered that Mom's death isn't the only tragedy going on in my life right now. If Horace stayed, I was going to have to tell him that I'm sick—and I *really* dreaded his reaction to that. With Mom, I'd been too worried that she'd be devastated to tell her; with Horace, I was terrified that he just wouldn't care.

He refused to ride to the cemetery in the limo with Nora and me. At first, I thought he was going to leave, but I felt my whole body unclench when I saw his sporty silver car—a Porsche, maybe; I'm not much of a car aficionado—pull into the line of vehicles with their headlights on, following the bulky, depressing hearse in slow formation toward the graveyard.

"Are you okay, Iris?" Nora asked, trying to get me to stop peering out the small rear window of the limo.

"You mean other than Mom being dead?" I said. She frowned.

"I'm sorry," I said. "I'm just worried about Horace."

"Is that all? You've seemed—off—the last few days," Nora said.

"Not to be rude, but duh. Mom just died, remember?"

"Well, I don't mean to be rude, either, but you've been acting weird since before Mom died."

I realized I was caught, and I rushed through an inner argument with myself over whether this was an appropriate time and place to tell Nora about my diagnosis. I decided it wasn't—telling your sister about your terminal illness in the car on the way to bury your mother is about the meanest thing you can do—but I also decided that I needed her to know—*now*.

"You're right," I said. "I *have* been acting weird. There's something I've got to tell you, but I've been—I don't know—waiting for the right time. And I know this isn't it—this is about the opposite of the right time—but I've got to tell you anyway."

"Okay . . ."

I sucked in a long breath as I got myself ready to spit it out and be done with it. I let the breath go and said, faster than I've ever said anything before: "I have early-onset Alzheimer's disease." Then I sat back, somehow feeling *happy*, or at least relieved, that somebody else was finally in this little boat full of misery with me.

Nora just stared at me without saying anything. She kept moving her head back and forth, like she was trying to catch a glimpse of me from a different angle, like that might help her figure out if I was telling the truth or just making some kind of really tasteless joke.

"You're not kidding?" she whispered.

"Even I don't have that bad a sense of humor."

"Oh, God, Iris."

"It's okay," I said. And for the first time in weeks, since I first found out that Alzheimer's might be a possibility, I actually believed that it *would* be okay.

"It's not," she said. "It's not okay at all. Did you . . . I mean, like . . . did you get a second opinion?"

I smiled. "I've been to specialists and everything. There's no getting around it. It is what it is."

"Jesus, why do people say that? I hate that. It's giving up."

I had to laugh. "It's funny to hear you talk like that."

"I know. I've never been a fighter or a survivor or special, like you, but I've also never given up."

I leaned over and kissed her on the cheek. "You're plenty special. And you've survived more on your own than most families—hell, most *nations*— have to survive all together. Don't ever forget that—even when *I* do."

She didn't laugh at my lame attempt at a joke. "You can't just give up."

"I'm not giving up," I said. "I'm going to take all the drugs, do whatever experimental therapies they come up with. Don't worry about me— I'll end up outliving all of you."

Nora turned to stare out the window. "*That* I can believe," she said.

"Yeah, right," I said. The limo was slowing to a stop on one of the narrow lanes of the cemetery. I could see the mound of freshly dug earth beside the little white tent set up next to the hole that would become my mother's grave. "Let's go. We're here."

"Iris . . ."

I squeezed her hand. "I know," I said. "I love you, too. Now let's get through this. And I thought the funeral was going to be the worst part of my day."

"Yeah, me, too."

"But there's a lot of torture still ahead. I'm going to have to tell Horace, too."

"Oh, God."

"I'd wait, but who knows when he'll condescend to let me see him again? This might be my only chance—and time is the one thing I don't have a whole lot of anymore."

"Don't talk like that," Nora said.

"Why not? There's no reason to hide from the truth. Not now. Come on. Let's go."

I didn't pay a lot of attention to all the "The Lord is my shepherd" stuff during the service at the grave. I was too busy trying to plan how to tell Horace about my illness. I was so out of it, Nora had to nudge me when it was my turn to toss a flower onto the coffin. She probably thought I was having one of my senile episodes. When the minister was finished, people started drifting away toward their cars, eager to get to the restaurant we'd rented for the post-funeral reception. I guess everyone assumes (probably rightly) that people with money put on a good funeral.

Nora was standing off to one side of the grave, chatting with some little old lady—one of Mom's friends, I guess. It occurred to me that I would probably never get to be one of those little old biddies—I'd die much earlier, or, if I did get to grow old, I probably wouldn't know about it. Something about that made me want to cry. It devastated me so much that I almost didn't see Horace slinking away, apparently hoping to escape without having to speak to me. He was only a few feet from a clean get-away when I called out his name. He stopped dead, with his keys in his frozen hand. Slowly, he turned to look back at me.

"You're coming to lunch, aren't you?" I asked, walking as fast as I could toward him so we wouldn't have to hold our conversation by shouting across the tombstones.

He shrugged. "Wasn't going to."

I felt panic rise up inside me. "Aw, come on, you have to. Everybody'll be there."

He scowled. "Like who?"

"Um . . . well, me, your aunt Nora, Andrew . . ."

"Fabulous."

"Just come, okay? I have to talk to you," I said.

He let out a disgusted-sounding sigh. "Whatever. There booze there?"

I was suddenly grateful that I had paid extra to have an open bar at the luncheon. "Of course," I said. "Anything you want. So you'll be there?"

He just grunted and got into his car. I knew that was a yes.

I waited for him next to the bar, sipping a watered-down white wine and wondering how long it had been since the goofiness I'd felt after drinking liquor had been because of the alcohol and not just my messed-up brain.

He spoke to the bartender before he talked to me, ordering himself a gin and tonic. He waited until the drink was in his hand and he had taken a long sip before he finally said, "So what's up?" He never looked directly at me.

"Not here," I said, tugging him away from the bar by the cuff of his sleeve. He made some sighing sounds of protest as I dragged him into a small alcove near the restrooms where we could have a little privacy, but at least he came with me. When I stopped walking, he jerked his arm away from my grasp and sucked another long swig out of his drink. I heard the ice cubes clink against his teeth.

"What?" he asked, his voice almost a hiss.

I felt my face squish up, like I was going to cry, but I took a deep breath. "Just let me get it out, okay?" I said. "This isn't easy."

"Sure," he said. "Nothing's never easy with you."

"Horace . . ." I started, then realized scolding him wasn't worth the effort. These days, I think a lot about what's worth doing in the limited time I have left.

"Okay, here goes," I finally said. "I just found out that I have Alzheimer's disease."

He rolled his eyes. "I know you're a fiction writer, but that's a stretch, even for you. You're not *that* old. I would've gone with Parkinson's or something. Better believability factor."

It was the most he had said to me in about a decade, and he was making fun of me.

"I wish I were kidding, but I'm not," I said. "It's early-onset Alzheimer's."

He peered at me through squinty eyes over the rim of his glass. "I don't know where you're going with this," he said.

"I'm not going anywhere. It's the truth." I got choked up and had to look away.

"Huh," he said. "So you're serious?"

I just nodded.

He frowned. "Well . . . uh . . . I'm sorry?" The question mark he put at the end of his sentence was a little irritating, but at least he had said the sensitive thing. I raised my eyes and blinked at him, forcing a smile.

"Thank you," I said.

"So," he said. "I guess you'll be turning the company over to me?"

I wrinkled my nose. "What do you mean?"

"Well, you can't run things if you're senile," he said. Whatever sensitivity I thought he had in him was gone.

"I'm not senile," I said, adding the word *yet*, but only in my mind. "Besides, what would you want the company for? You're not interested in publishing."

"No, of course not. But I *am* interested in money. I'll just sell it."

"Sell it? But it's everything your father and I worked for . . ."

He smiled. "That's what makes it so valuable."

I shook my head. "I can't believe I'm hearing this. I tell you something serious, and you . . . instead of *caring*, you're . . . you're like a vulture waiting to pick the flesh off my bones."

"I'm asking you to surrender the flesh to me now, so I don't have to work as hard to get it off the bones later," he said.

I stared at him for a long moment. I think I heard the sound of my hand slapping his face before I even realized I had moved. He didn't flinch. He just glared at me with his one good eye and panted a little, like an animal, waiting to see if I would fight or flee.

"I'm done," I said, setting my drink down on a ledge. "I'm done with this. I don't need this today of all days." I turned and started to walk away.

From behind me, he called, "Then I guess you'll be hearing from my lawyer." I pretended I didn't hear him and kept walking.

69

HORACE

| PRESENT DAY |

When Andrew walked in through the unlocked door, Horace was sitting at the kitchen table in the dark with a glass in front of him. Andrew flicked on the lights and went over. He picked up Horace's drink and said, "Getcha a refill? Gin, is it?"

"Water."

Andrew sniffed at the liquid. "Damn, it really *is* water. Don't you know you're supposed to get drunk when your wife dies tragically?"

"It's always about getting drunk for you, isn't it, Andrew?"

Andrew shrugged. "That's me. I'm the Lord of the Underworld."

Horace smiled, surprising himself. Andrew was always good for levity. That was worth something.

"So what are you doing here?" Horace asked.

"Just came to see how you're doing," Andrew said. "Mom was worried."

"Of course she was. Tell her I'm fine."

"Are you?"

Horace shrugged. "Hard to say. I'm not sure I remember what fine is supposed to feel like."

Andrew sat down. He pointed at Horace's face. "I don't think it looks like that. Just my opinion."

"I'm doing well enough," Horace said. "I'm not drinking, I'm not snorting coke, and I'm not looking for a razor to off myself. I guess I can't expect to be any better than that at this point."

"Guess not," Andrew said. "Heard about Riley?"

Horace shook his head. "Haven't been watching TV. What about him?"

296

"They took him into custody yesterday. He's supposed to be sentenced next week."

Horace sighed and took a sip of water. "I don't even know how I feel about that."

"You should feel—I don't know—stoked. Vindicated. The SOB who killed your wife is going to jail. For a couple of years, at least. It's not the chair, like he deserves, but it's something."

"I don't know," Horace said. "Was it really his fault? It was an accident. He's an asshole, but he didn't mean to kill her. And I did hear one thing about him. He retracted his statement about your dad being my dad, too, so that whole DNA mess is over with."

"I can't believe you're sticking up for him, dude. That's bullshit."

"Maybe I'm mellowing in my old age," Horace said. "Like my mom. She wouldn't let me kill your father, even though he sure as hell deserved it. Sorry about that, man. Maybe you have to lose everything to get some perspective."

"Perspective on what?"

"I don't know. Life. Justice. Eternity. I don't know. All I know is that I can't blame Riley for Andrea, as much as I'd like to. Things just . . . happen."

"I think you *really* need a drink," Andrew said.

Horace smiled. "No, I'm good. Tell your mom I'm doing okay, will you? She shouldn't be worrying about me. She's got plenty to worry about with you."

"Me? I'm a perfect angel of a son," Andrew said.

"Oh, yeah? I thought you were the Lord of the Underworld."

Andrew grinned. "I'm complicated. You sure you're okay, man?"

"Yeah," Horace said. "I will be."

70

IRIS

| JUNE 10, 2009 |

Despite Horace's threats at the funeral, I haven't actually heard anything more about his wanting to take the company away from me. But I can't stop thinking about it. Maybe he's right—maybe it's only a matter of time before I won't be able to handle things for myself anymore. Maybe I *should* turn things over to him—or to somebody else, somebody who would actually give a damn about whether the company survives or not. I would have loved for Horace to be the one, but he has no interest in books; he only wants the money. And that's maybe the saddest part of this whole thing. I'm realizing more and more that I don't know my son at all, and he doesn't know the first thing about me.

AUGUST 2, 2009
Well, I did it. I talked to my lawyer today and we came up with a deal to offer Horace. He gets ten million dollars in exchange for relinquishing control over the publishing company. Ten million is a lot of money—but I wonder if it'll be enough to satisfy his greed. Who *is* this person? He's not the boy I raised. *My* son was sensitive and sweet and loved his family more than money. But then again, maybe that's the Alzheimer's talking. Maybe the things I think are memories are nothing more than dreams or wishes.

AUGUST 5, 2009
Horace's lawyer got back to my lawyer today. My greedy son wants not only the cash but also a controlling interest in the company. I almost threw a fit when I heard that. Why would he care what goes on at my company? He's ignored it his entire life—what's different now? Just the money. He knows he can keep getting profits without working if he

owns the company, and God forbid he ever has to lift a finger. I want to cry—where did I mess up raising him? Am *I* as greedy as he is? Somehow *I* must have made him this way, but I don't know how.

So I told my lawyer that Horace can retain ownership if he agrees not to have any say in how the company is run, who works there, or what it publishes. He'll need to be the most silent silent partner in history if he wants this to work. I'll immediately put some people in place, people who'll do things like *I* want, or would have wanted, if I had the choice of staying. But I think my work is done. It's too depressing to be there, knowing what my success has done, and the monster I've made out of my own son. I would have been better off if I had just survived by waiting on tables or something. Maybe Horace would have turned out to be a better person.

August 15, 2009

Nora took me shopping for my birthday. She wanted to buy me a bunch of new clothes and I joked, "What's the point? Pretty soon I won't be able to remember what's in my closet, so I'll be surprised each day when I get dressed, even if it's the same old stuff. Why do I need new things?"

"Stop kidding around about this," Nora said. "It's not funny."

"If I can't laugh about it, I'll have to cry all the time, and nobody needs that."

"What did the doctor say?"

I shrugged. "I'm taking a bunch of meds, and he's got me coming in to take all kinds of cognitive tests every week, to see how I'm responding. But we have to be realistic, Nora. I'm running out of time."

"Don't say that," she said. "There's all kinds of things that could happen. They could find a cure . . ."

I laughed. "You don't believe that any more than I do. Maybe in ten, twenty years, but not anytime soon, when it might do me some good. It's okay. I'm going to be okay."

Nora sighed. "How can you be so brave?"

"Bravery has nothing to do with it," I said. "What choice do I have?"

"I don't know. Rage?"

"Rage against what? Life? My brain? God? It seems silly to get all riled up over something that can't be changed."

She shook her head. "I wouldn't be able to handle it. I'd go crazy."

"Um—yeah. That's kind of how it works."

Nora glared at me. "Stop joking around. You're pissing me off."

"Good," I said. "Be pissed at me. Don't be pissed about the Alzheimer's. There's no point in that."

She closed her eyes and nodded. "Let's go have lunch."

"Lunch?" I asked, making my eyes go crossed. "What's lunch?"

Nora slapped me on the arm. "Knock it off!"

I put my arm around her. "I love you. You know that, right?"

Her eyes welled up as she nodded. "I should've been a better sister to you."

I smiled. "That would have been impossible."

"Mom and Dad were right," Nora said. "You really *are* the better daughter."

"They never thought that."

"Of course they did," she said. "I'm just saying they had good reason."

"Nora . . ."

"I love you, too, Iris. That's all I'm saying. Will you remember that?"

I crossed my eyes again and made a goofy face, but then I let my face go back to normal. "*That* is something I'll always remember," I said. But even as I said it, I wondered whether it was true.

AUGUST 15, 2010

I can tell things are going downhill. It takes too long to write. I can't always think of words. Not the words I really want. It's so hard. Some days are better than the next. Wait—that's not right. Today is bad. From now on, I'm only writing when I feel good. I am fifty-four years old today. Or is it fifty-five?

DECEMBER 6, 2010

Today is Horace's birthday—I know that much—but I can't for the life of me remember what year he was born. The drugs keep me focused, I think, but sometimes I think they might be mixing up my brains even more than my disease. It's getting hard to tell anymore. And it's getting harder and harder to manage around the house. I keep losing things, and I haven't been able to drive in months. Nora said I should come live with her, but I can't put that burden on her—or anybody, at least not without paying for it. So tomorrow I'm going to start looking for a place where I can stay until the end comes, whenever that might be.

DECEMBER 24, 2010

Well, this is my first (and—you never know—maybe my last) Christmas in my new "home." I moved into the assisted living place yesterday. I'm the youngest person here by a good fifteen years, if not more, but that just makes the place even more depressing. Nora was here earlier, with a fake smile plastered on her face and a stack of presents in her arms. She tried to be cheerful, but I told her not to bother.

"I know where I am and I know what it means," I said. "You don't have to pretend it's anything different."

"You can still come stay with me," she said.

"No. It's too much to ask. Trust me. You don't see the worst of it. And I don't want you to. This is for the best."

"If you ever change your mind . . ."

"I know," I said. "And I'm grateful."

She wanted me to come over for Christmas dinner with her and Andrew tomorrow, but something about that idea seemed even sadder than being here, alone among the wheelchair-bound statues and mumbling zombies. God, how soon before I'm one of them? Yeah—it's a very merry Christmas.

June 5, 2012

I don't even know if I can write about this. I don't know if I'll ever be able to write again. I got a letter from Seth—I'm going to put it in this journal for safekeeping, but I don't know if I can bring myself to describe it. I'm—I don't know what to do. The whole world is changed. I need to talk to Horace.

June 6, 2012

I've left Horace six messages and he won't call me back. One of his assistants picked up once when I called and told me Horace said I should contact him through the offices of So-and-So Esquire, and that he had nothing else to say to me. This is insane. He can have the fucking company if he wants it. This is *much* more important.

June 7, 2012

He won't talk to me. I can't get him to listen. What am I going to do? I've lost everything—my husband, my freedom, my child, my business, and my ability to live alone. I'm slowly but surely losing my mind. This journal seems like the only thing keeping me in this world, and I feel like I'm slipping away. Some days, it's hard to get up the energy to write.

71

HORACE

| PRESENT DAY |

He had been doing his best to ignore the phone and not checking his email for weeks after Andrea's funeral, but for some reason, when he saw "Cairo Books" on the caller ID screen that morning, he decided to break his self-imposed isolation and pick up.

"Hello?"

"Mr. Cairo? This is Lynn, from Cairo Books."

"Of course," he said. "How are you, Lynn?"

She coughed. "I'm fine, just fine. I—uh—I'm so sorry for your loss."

"Thank you," he said. "I got your flowers. I appreciate how thoughtful you and everybody at the company has been. So, what can I do for you today?"

"I just called to let you know that the galleys for your book are ready for you to look at," she said.

"Okay, call me stupid. What are galleys?"

"Printouts of the pages," she said. "Basically, an unbound copy of the book. The last chance to look everything over before it goes to the printer."

"Oh, great," he said. "I guess I would've known that if I'd listened to my mom more."

"Yes, well . . ." Lynn sounded nervous.

"Relax," Horace said. "I'm not looking back in sadness or anything like that. Just an observation. So when should I expect the . . . uh . . . galleys? Was that what they're called?"

"Yes," she said. "They'll be there tomorrow. By FedEx."

"And what? I just read them?"

"Right. Read them through and mark any changes you think are necessary."

"I'm sure they'll be fine."

"Well, you let me know," she said.

"Thanks, Lynn."

After he hung up, he felt a tingle in his stomach—a sense of pleasant anticipation, something to look forward to. He had almost forgotten that there could be anything pleasant in life. Knowing that he still cared about his mother's book was reassuring. There had been moments—more than he cared to admit—over the past few weeks when he had considered—with more seriousness than he cared to admit—the possibility of taking matters into his own hands and ending the seemingly never-ending grief he was feeling. He didn't know why he hadn't done it. Maybe he was just a coward. It wasn't like he hadn't been up close and personal with death before, during his stint in the army and, of course, with Seth, but there was something about the notion of bringing death upon yourself, deliberately, that sent a cold shock through him. He was afraid not of death itself, necessarily, but of the awesome power of his own personality if he found the guts within him to do something so irrevocable. Now, thanks to the prospect of reading a handful of computer printouts, he suddenly realized that he no longer had to wrestle with his own psyche, trying to figure out whether the Horace he knew or the darker, maybe stronger, Horace would ultimately win out.

He hardly slept that night; he was too excited about seeing those galleys the next day. All morning, he sat staring out the window, waiting for the FedEx truck like a little kid waiting for the ice cream truck to roll into the neighborhood on a summer afternoon. When FedEx finally arrived, he had to will himself to sit still and not leap up to meet the delivery guy at the door. He waited for the doorbell to ring, then forced himself to walk at a normal pace to the door. He signed for the package, closed the door, and then took off running for the den with the box hugged to his chest. He tore the package open and tossed the box aside, not bothering to clean up the mess before settling into his recliner and starting to read.

He had always thought of himself as a slow reader, but he flew through the galleys as if he were rushing to read a homework assignment before class started. Having already read all these journal entries before, he didn't expect to find anything new. But in one of the last passages, he noticed something he had missed the first time through. His mother had written, in what proved to be the last entry before her death:

I can't talk about any of this anymore. It's too hard. But I want my son to know—he needs to know the truth, so I'm leaving that in the letter, which I'm tucking inside this last journal—the last journal of Iris Cairo.

How the hell had he missed that? She talked about writing him a letter to tell him "the truth," but he had never found any letter. Was all that just a figment of his mother's imagination? A false memory created by her Alzheimer's? Or was there actually a letter somewhere, among the chaos of her belongings—still upstairs in Horace's closet—that contained her last communication to him, and to the world?

He dropped the manuscript and ran up the stairs.

He had to dump out and sort through the contents of four bins before he found a loose envelope with his name on it. It must have been stuck in the last of his mother's journals and fallen out while he was trying to organize the notebooks and photographs that would be included in the new book.

His hands were shaking as he held the envelope in his fingers and moved over to sit on the rumpled bed, which he hadn't bothered to make even once since Andrea died. Taking a deep breath, he opened the envelope, pulled out the letter inside, and began to read:

Dear Horace,

I would have liked to be able to tell you this in person, but it's obvious that's not going to happen anytime soon, and I don't know how much time I have left before I won't be able to talk to you at all anymore, so I thought I should get this down while I'm having a good day and everything is still clear in my mind. I'm writing to you—not to Nora or anybody else—and I'm not putting this in my journal, since I know those might be published someday. I want you to have the choice about whether this information becomes public or not—it's your life and your choice, now that my life is pretty much over.

Last week, I got a letter that turned my whole world inside out. I can only hope this letter of mine won't do the same to you.

The letter I got was from your uncle Seth. I almost threw it away when I saw that it said "East Jersey State Prison" on the envelope, but the fact that he decided to reach out after so many years made me—well, curious, I guess. I wish now that I had gone with my first instinct and tossed out the letter without ever reading it. But there's no going back now, so here it is.

Seth told me that he is your real father. Before I had the procedure that made me pregnant, he says he paid a nurse at the hospital to switch the semen samples—swapping his own in place of your father's—I mean, well, Oscar's. It was Seth's sperm that got me pregnant. It was Seth's child—you—that I carried and gave birth to and raised.

When I first read Seth's letter, I wanted to believe he was lying, but I know deep down inside me, on the same level as basic survival instincts, that it's the truth. Maybe, in a way, it helps explain why things between us have always been so hard. I don't blame you in any way, and I promise, I don't resent you. I still love you as much as I ever did before I found out what Seth did. Really.

You may not want to accept this information, just like I wanted to deny it all at first. You can get DNA tests, whatever you need to do. But I know that you know, just like I do, that it has to be true.

I wish I could have lived out what little time I have left without ever having to face this or—worse—forcing you to face it with me. But I've always thought truth was important—no matter how much it hurts. And I'm sorry—so sorry, more than you can ever know—for everything I've ever done to cause you pain and for anything that may cause you pain in the future. You have been my life—my reason for existing in this world. You are the greatest gift I could ever offer the world. Please, let the world see the wonderful treasure you really are. I love you, Horace.

—Mom

He let the letter drop beside him on the bed and stared at the wall in front of him. Suddenly, it all made perfect sense.

72

IRIS

I don't know what the date is. I'm not even sure anymore what year it is. But it doesn't matter. It's all done. The letter is written and tucked safely away in this journal. Now it's time to dig deep and try to find the courage to finish this once and for all.

73

HORACE

| PRESENT DAY |

With the letter still lying on the bed beside him, Horace reached for the phone and dialed 411.

"I need the number for East Jersey State Prison," he told the computerized operator.

It took a while to connect to the right office, but he finally found out when he could go to the prison and visit Seth.

When he pulled into the parking lot, he couldn't stop staring at the big, ugly, hulking gray dome on top of the prison. He'd never seen it up this close before—he had only stolen glances at it from a distance, while driving on the highway, then looked away, satisfied, knowing that Seth was tucked safely inside and out of his life. Now he was about to invite the bastard back in—at least, that's the way Seth was sure to see it. And that made Horace want to puke.

It took over half an hour of rigmarole with guards and pat-downs and going into and out of locked and gated rooms before a burly guy in a beige and brown uniform with a nightstick strapped to his side led Horace into the kind of visiting room that's always on TV—the kind with a long line of cubbyholes with phones, and a prisoner seated on the opposite side of a pane of glass, with a cubbyhole and phone of his own. Seth was there, sitting with his hand on the phone and a massive grin on his face.

Horace sat down and picked up the phone, trying to keep his face even, expressionless. He wanted to sneer but didn't want to give Seth the satisfaction.

"So good to see you, Horace," Seth said into the phone, his voice almost a purr. "It's been too long."

"Not for me," Horace said.

"Then why come see me? Don't be like that. We're family," Seth said. He winked. "By the way, you're looking good. New eye patch?"

Horace sucked in his breath through his teeth, willing himself not to take the bait and lash out.

"Yes," he finally said. "Ordered it online. Like it?"

Seth's brow furrowed. Horace smiled. It was fun to watch Seth deal with his confusion when he didn't get the reaction he expected.

Seth cleared his throat. "So, to what do I owe the honor of this visit?"

"I think you know why I'm here."

Seth raised one eyebrow. "Do I?"

"Don't be an ass," Horace said. "I'm here to find out if it's true."

The corner of Seth's lip twitched—it looked like a suppressed smile. "If what's true?" he asked.

Horace sighed. "This is going to take all day. Just say it. Yes or no."

Seth held his eyes level and stared straight at Horace. Without blinking, he said, "Yes."

Horace looked down. Knowing it was true before getting here somehow didn't make it any easier to hear now. He felt something well up in the back of his throat and he wanted to gag or weep. He swallowed as hard as he could.

"Why?" he said. "Why did you do it?"

Seth shrugged. "For her. For Iris. Because I loved her."

Horace shook his head. "You obviously have never had any clue what love is."

"And you do?"

"Yeah," Horace said. "I do. I do now."

"Well, good for you, son."

"Don't call me that."

"Why not? It's what you are."

Horace clenched his teeth. "Then you wouldn't object to a DNA test to prove that?"

"Course not," Seth said. He put up one finger, put down the phone, then reached up and tore a tuft of hair out of his scalp. He picked the phone back up. "Here," he said. "I'll give this to the guard and you can take it with you."

But Horace knew he didn't need Seth's hair; the mere fact that he was so willing to give it up meant a DNA test was unnecessary.

"Forget it," Horace muttered.

Seth held the hair on his palm and shoved it toward the glass partition. "What? It's good. It'll work."

"I know. It's not worth it."

Seth smiled. "Come on, it'll be fun. I pulled out some hair, you'll pull out some hair. It'll be like a bonding experience—a father and son . . ."

"Don't even say it," Horace said.

"Why not? It's true."

"The truth is an ugly thing."

"That's not what your mother would have said," Seth said.

"Yeah, well, I didn't always agree with my mother."

"It's too bad. She was a smart lady—up until . . ."

"Shut up. I think I'll go now."

Seth waved his hand. "No, no! Stay. We have plenty of time left to talk."

"Did it ever occur to you that I don't *want* to talk to you?"

"Then why did you come?"

"I don't know. . . . I don't know. I guess I just needed to see for myself . . ."

"You just wanted to see your father."

"Shut up. You're not my father."

Seth made a "*tsk*" noise. "Now, now. Don't be like that. We both know I am, so you might as well get used to it."

"I don't *want* to get used to that," Horace said. "I'm leaving." He started to hang up the phone but Seth's voice, hollow and tinny over the line, stopped him.

"Horace."

Horace sighed and pressed the phone back to his ear. Grinding his teeth, he glared at Seth from beneath his brows.

"You've spent your whole life looking for something, and not finding it," Seth said. "Haven't you? You hated your mother because she smothered you, loved you too much. What you needed was a father."

"You're not . . ."

"Hear me out," Seth said. "Just let me finish, and then you can leave and never see me again. If that's what you really want. Okay?"

Horace rolled his eye and shrugged with just one shoulder, irritated, but at the same time, more intrigued than he wanted to be about what Seth was about to say. He suddenly understood why his mother had been so torn in her feelings toward Seth at times. The son of a bitch was somehow . . . charming.

"You hated your mother for bringing you into this world without a father," Seth said.

"That's ridiculous," Horace said. "I didn't even know my father—I mean, Oscar—was dead before she got pregnant with me until a few months ago. How could I resent someone for something I didn't even know?"

"Believe me," Seth said. "We all know a lot more than we realize."

Horace made a rolling motion with his hand. "Just get on with it."

Seth smiled. "Whether you knew it or not, you knew you had a messed-up life, and you knew it was because you had no father."

"No," Horace said. "It was because you were chasing us, you nut job."

"Tomato, tomahto. The point is, you missed out on having a father figure in your life. And now you have one."

Horace cackled. "You? Oh, sure. Great role model. You realize we're in a *prison*, right?"

"Things happen," Seth said with a shrug.

"We *make* things happen," Horace said.

"Oh, really? I hear Richard Riley made some things happen with your wife."

"Fuck you, Seth."

"No profanity!" a guard called out from the corner. Seth grinned.

"See?" Seth said. "Maybe if you'd had a father, you'd know better than to swear in public."

"I'm leaving," Horace said.

"No, wait. I'm almost done."

"Hurry up. I've had enough."

Seth inclined his head, as if trying to show respect. "All I'm saying," he said, "is that I'm here for you. Always will be." He brightened and chuckled as he glanced around him. "Literally."

"I don't want or need you," Horace said. "So just piss off."

Seth shot a look at the guard, as if trying to determine whether the word *piss* qualified as profanity. The guard narrowed his eyes and shifted his weight but said nothing.

"Well," Seth finally said. "It is what it is."

Horace snorted. "I hate when people say that. What does that even mean?"

"It means I've put it out there, and you can do what you want with it," Seth said. "I'm your father—whether you like it or not. I'm here if you want me. If you don't, well . . . I'm still here."

Horace peered at Seth through the glass. He seemed sincere, and that was disarming. Not that he knew Seth well. In fact, the first time they met in person had been the day they fought and Horace lost his eye—unless you counted the time Seth came to terrorize his mother a few days after Horace had been born. That made Horace think of something.

"What ever happened to that woman my mom was living with when I was born? Shondra?" he asked.

Seth smiled. "What difference does that make?"

"You're already in prison for life," Horace said. "What do you care? Just tell me. You killed her, didn't you?"

Seth laughed. "No," he said. "I'm not some cold-blooded murderer."

"Of course not," Horace said. "You only kill the ones you love."

"I like that," Seth said.

"So—what about Shondra?"

"She's fine. Lives in California, I think."

"I don't get it. What happened?"

Seth shrugged. "Nothing. I took her with me when I left. We stayed together a while—couple of years, I guess. Then we moved on. You know how it goes."

"Not really," Horace said. "If she's alive, why didn't she ever get in touch with my mother? Or the police? Why didn't she ever report you?"

"For what? I didn't do anything to her."

"You tied her up, threatened her with a knife, kidnapped her . . ."

Seth shook his head. "You've been misinformed. Shondra and I . . . we were together for a long time. We were together. I mean, when your mother was pregnant and living out there, Shondra and I were together."

Horace felt a chill. "She was in on it?"

"In on what? I didn't do anything. I just wanted to be there when my son was born. What's wrong with that?"

"Jesus. . . . But Mom said in her journals that Shondra attacked you, knocked you out."

Seth smiled. "Yeah. I didn't see that one coming, either. What can I say? The girl's a hell of a good actress. Really got into the role. But whatever. It's not a big deal," Seth said.

"My mom would have disagreed." He stopped, lost in thought. "Now it makes sense. It was weird. In Mom's journal, it said Shondra only met you once, but her name was already in your address book. And Mom had that before you were supposed to have met Shondra. God. How did Mom not see that? I guess she was too focused on the craziness. *Your* craziness."

"Your mom was always a little dramatic," Seth said. "She was a writer. They're all drama queens."

Horace swallowed. "And what about your other kid? My half-brother, I guess? The boy in Texas? And his mother? Was she in on it, too?"

Seth shook his head. "No," he said. "Jennifer was just a dumb, sweet little slut. Your mom took care of them. Sent them a shit ton of cash. But the kid—he wasn't as smart as me."

"What the fuck does that mean?"

"Profanity!" the guard yelled.

Seth smiled. "Potty mouth. Anyway, the kid got himself killed in a motorcycle accident a few years back. Great way to go, if you ask me. Better than the electric chair."

"I have to go."

"Horace? Just think about it, okay?"

"About what?"

"I don't know," Seth said. "Me, I guess."

Horace stared into Seth's eyes. God, he was so hard to read. Even with a lifetime of experience telling him Seth was evil and shouldn't be trusted, Horace found himself wanting to reach out and grab hold of the only father he would ever have a chance to know. He sighed.

"I've got to go," he said.

"Bye," Seth said. "And, Horace? For what it's worth, I'm sorry."

"For what?"

Seth shrugged. "All of it, I guess."

Horace stared at him again, then nodded slowly. He hung up the phone and, forcing himself to look away, turned and followed a guard out of the room and through the labyrinth of hallways and gates until he was back in the parking lot.

He got into his car and sat behind the wheel, lost in a haze of confusion and ambivalence and memory. His mind trailed back to the day he had found out his mother was dead.

He had been hung over, still in bed tossing and turning, waiting for that merciful burst of sleep that would finally come over him, sweeping him out of consciousness and at the same time whisking away the headache and nausea, leaving behind only an intense hunger for fried food and, of course, more booze. He didn't answer his house phone when it rang. He had only groaned at the shrillness of the ring tone and pressed his head deeper into the pillow. But when his cell phone rang right after the house phone stopped ringing, he reluctantly reached over and flipped it open.

"Yeah." His voice was little more than a hoarse groan.

"Mr. Cairo?"

"Yeah."

"Mr. Cairo, this is Peggy at Meadow Ridge—your mother's assisted living facility?"

"Yeah." He got impatient. It seemed like he'd never get off the phone and back to the pursuit of sleep.

"Um—well, Mr. Cairo, I'm very sorry to tell you . . . your mother . . . she's passed away."

He dragged himself onto one elbow and opened his eyes. "She's dead?"

"Yes, sir. I'm so sorry for your loss."

His mouth was so dry, he could hardly speak. "Was she—I mean, besides the Alzheimer's—was she sick? I—well, I haven't talked to her in a long time."

There was a long pause. "Mr. Cairo, um . . . no, sir. She wasn't sick."

"Then what did she die of?"

Another long pause. "Well, sir, um . . . well, she committed suicide."

He shot up and suddenly found himself standing beside the bed, his headache gone and his mind crystal clear.

"What the fuck are you talking about?" he asked.

Peggy coughed. "Maybe you should come in and speak to our director, Dr. Schwartz."

"No, just tell me. How did she kill herself? Why?"

"Sir, um . . . well, she took an overdose of sleeping pills. If it's any comfort, she went as peacefully as you could hope for."

"But *why*?"

"I—I have no idea, Mr. Cairo. I'm very sorry."

She had droned on after that about funeral arrangements and collecting his mother's belongings. Horace had barely registered any of it. All he could do was wonder what the hell would have driven his mother, who, despite her owns claims of pessimism, had been an eternal optimist, to commit suicide. It had to be the Alzheimer's, he had thought. It was the only thing that made sense.

Until now. Horace realized with sudden clarity that his mother had killed herself just days after she got the letter from Seth telling her about Horace's conception. And after she had tried—and failed—to contact him.

Now it all fit together. Iris had been able to live through the loss of her husband, years of being a refugee, estrangement from her only child, and even a diagnosis of Alzheimer's disease. But learning that Seth was the real father of her son—that had been too much for her to bear.

And Horace wanted Seth to suffer for it.

How hard would it be to have Seth killed in prison? he wondered. It wasn't unheard of, and money made even difficult things pretty damn easy. And getting rid of Seth would be . . . liberating. It would be justice. Wouldn't it?

Iris hadn't thought so. She had begged Horace not to kill Seth when he had the chance. But that was before she knew that Seth had switched the semen samples and forced her to bear his child without realizing it. If finding out the truth had been enough to drive her to suicide, then murder certainly didn't seem out of the question.

But then again—Iris had had money and connections, too. She could easily have knocked off Seth herself, but she chose instead to end her own life. Had she been right, all those years ago, when she told Horace that Seth would suffer more in prison than in death?

Wow, he thought. He was even more confused now than he'd been when he first left the prison.

What about Andrea? he thought. *What would she have thought of all this?*

Andrea always wanted to minimize tension and make life less complicated. Let it go, she would have said. Just move on with your life—move past Seth. Move past your mother's death. And move past me.

Horace sucked in a breath that was more like a sob. He was picturing Andrea's limp body lying there on the road in front of their house, with Riley's SUV hulking over it. Riley was an opportunistic bastard who had done his best to profit from Horace and his family's troubles, and then he had killed Andrea—even if it was an accident. As much as Horace hated Riley—had always hated him—he had never even considered seeking vengeance. He had done what Andrea—and what Iris—would have done: let it go, move on.

And there was the answer. If he could leave Riley alone despite killing the love of his life—someone he had valued much, much more than himself—then how could he even consider attacking Seth? It was illogical. It was senseless.

He suddenly laughed. All those years, Iris had tried to instill some sense of character and justice in her son, and it was only after her death that he was finally catching on. *Well*, he thought, *at least she was having an influence.* She would have liked that. He could almost hear Andrea's playful voice echoing in his head. Andrea would have liked it, too. But no. He was wrong to use the conditional tense. Andrea and his mother *did* like it—now. They both would have said that they hadn't gone anywhere. They were still right here, with him, same as always.

He smiled. Maybe it was true. Maybe they really were there. Maybe they were just waiting for resurrection or reincarnation or redemption. Or maybe just for him.

AUTHOR'S NOTE

The story of the Cairo family is based loosely on an ancient Egyptian myth. Here's how the myth goes:

The Egyptian goddess Isis and her husband-brother, Osiris, fell in love while they were still in the womb of the sky goddess, their mother. On Earth, they cherished one another, even though they were often forced to be apart while they jointly ruled the mighty land of Egypt in its earliest days. Theirs was a charmed existence, but, like all life on Earth, it was tragic as well.

Fiercely jealous of their power and passion, their brother, Set, murdered Osiris, sealing him in an anthropoid casket and covering it with molten lead before throwing it into the Nile. The casket was carried out to sea, and landed in the fork of a growing cedar, where it was hidden deep within the trunk of the massive tree. Although she searched and wept long and hard for her lost lover, Isis could not find Osiris.

In time, the tree in which his body rested was harvested and put to use as a column in the palace of the king of Byblos. Eventually, the goddess's travels brought her to Byblos, to the very palace in which her husband's body had been accidentally imprisoned. Knowing that only she could come up with a plan to retrieve the corpse of Osiris, Isis disguised herself as a serving woman and offered her services as a nurse for the newborn son of the queen of Byblos. The queen, though great in power, had not been blessed with sons who could take over their father's throne upon his death, and this new child was her last hope for an heir. Eagerly, she accepted the offer of the strangely beautiful foreign woman, hoping the extra attention to the household would help this child survive, unlike his dead siblings before him.

316

As the days passed, Isis came to love her tiny charge, aching inside over the knowledge that she would not be able to bear her own child with her beloved Osiris. To make the queen's baby seem more like her own, Isis began to cast a spell—one that would make the child immortal, even stronger in his resistance to death than any god, since the gods, like Osiris, could be killed. Each night, before singing the baby to sleep, Isis passed his tiny body through the flame of the hearth, whispering the magical words that would shield him from the immediate threat of the fire and the future approach of death. On the seventh and final night of the ritual, just as Isis lowered the baby into the blazing fire, the queen of Byblos burst into the room and screamed in horror at the sight of her only living son seemingly being burned alive. Furious at the interruption, Isis lifted the child from the flames and hurled it carelessly at its mother's feet.

"You have cost your son immortal life, and worse, life itself. I would have made of him a god, but now, he shall die like those before him, and the throne of Byblos will pass to your foes," Isis cried, tearing her hair in anger over the loss of another beloved companion.

Trembling in fear, the queen of Byblos asked, "Who are you?"

Breaking into bitter tears, Isis fell into her chair and muttered through choking sobs, "I am Isis, Queen of the Universe. I have come here seeking the body of my dead husband, whose coffin is trapped within one of the columns that hold up this great palace."

The queen, who knew well the pain of grief, gave orders for the column that held Osiris's casket to be cut down and the body restored to the dead god's wife so that she could bring it home to Egypt for burial. Like any Egyptian, Osiris could only hope to be resurrected if he was buried in his homeland.

With her husband returned to her, Isis sailed back toward Egypt. Along the way, her evil brother Set again attacked Osiris, stealing the coffin and tearing the corpse it held into a dozen pieces, which Set scattered into the river Nile. Frantic to retrieve what she had only so recently found after such a lengthy search, Isis and her waiting women combed the shores and were able to collect all the pieces of Osiris's mutilated body but one: the phallus.

Determined to outwit the wicked Set, Isis fashioned a phallus of shining gold and reassembled her broken Osiris. With the help of Thoth, the god of writing and magic, Isis transformed herself into a swallow, and, as she hovered above the still body of her husband, breathed enough life into his form to allow him to come alive briefly and plant within her womb the seed that would grow to become the great god Horus—king of Egypt and of the gods themselves.

Once Isis had conceived the god-to-be, she bade farewell to Osiris and watched in solemn resignation as he crossed the Nile west into the setting sun—to the land of the dead, where he would rule for all eternity, judging the deeds of those who passed on from this world and determining whether they would be worthy of resurrection into the everlasting paradise of the next world.

For her part, Isis nurtured the growing life within her, hiding in remote villages and caves to protect her unborn son from his terrible uncle Set, who was bent on the destruction of anything that bore any relation to the departed Osiris. Isis gave birth to a strapping child, who grew up as fearless and bold, yet as honest and fair, as his father had been before him. Horus ruled Egypt wisely and left behind a legacy for the pharaohs—who were known to be Horus incarnate on the Earth—to follow.

Against his mother's wishes, Horus even attempted to avenge his father's death by doing battle with his uncle Set. In one brutal encounter, Set tore out one of Horus's eyes, but, in the end, he was left defenseless before his powerful nephew. Just as Horus moved to strike the death blow, however, Isis stepped in to plead for her brother's life. Horus angrily agreed, knowing that evil is a necessary, if terrible, part of the world his ancestors had created.

ABOUT THE AUTHOR

Addison L. Jones is a freelance writer and editor living in southeastern Pennsylvania. She has published several nonfiction books for young adults and has edited hundreds of books and teaching materials. *Eye of Horace* is her first novel.